PRAISE FOR

"Filled with love, death, and fear, this riveting and dramatic portrayal will emotionally move the hearts and minds of every reader." —Chris Matthews, host of NBC's *The Chris Matthews Show* and MSNBC's *Hardball with Chris Matthews*

"*Season of Betrayal* is a rollicking, and at times, intense read. It follows a group of journalists covering the civil war in Beirut during the 1980s. As the tragedy of the Lebanese war unravels, so too do the lives of the journalists covering it who encounter both love and loss in Margaret Lowrie Robertson's affecting book." —Peter L. Bergen, author of *Holy War, Inc.*

"Robertson's story provides the perfect backdrop for those with little knowledge of the region's complicated struggle.... Her presentation of fact and fiction in the novel is well-balanced and thoroughly detailed." —*The Jerusalem Post*

"There are no heroes in this wrenching novel; no one behaves well and everyone's motives are suspect. With years of experience in news broadcasting, including a year in Beirut as a stringer for CBS radio, Robertson writes with authenticity about a city and a people destroyed by civil war. The contrast she draws between the grand scale of the Lebanese civil war and the small scale of Lara's battle to win back Mac is quite effective. An exceptional first novel, gripping and real. Enthusiastically recommended for general collections."

—*Library Journal* (starred review)

"Debut novelist Robertson draws a powerful story out of Lara's first-person narration. The author solidly dramatizes the ironies and ambiguities, moral and otherwise, of Lara's desperate encounters."

—*Publishers Weekly*

"Amidst the chaos of the characters' lives, which parallels that of the outside world, Robertson deftly weaves in descriptions of the conflict that has brought them all together.... *Season of Betrayal* is no 'feel good' tale but an engrossing one where 'the Marine's disastrous mission parallels Lara's own countdown to disaster.'"

—*ForeWord*

"Robertson's singular accomplishment is weaving fact with fiction. The novel manages to be entertaining as well as enlightening, and helps the reader hack through the web of cultures and beliefs that make up the complex tapestry of the Middle East." —*BookPage*

"Vividly populated by hacks, idealists, shady translators and brutes on the make, *Season of Betrayal* is a harrowing tale of how war lays siege to innocence and morality."

—Dan Fesperman, author of *The Amateur Spy*

"*Season of Betrayal* is a vivid, engrossing and finely drawn story that plunges the reader into the maelstrom of a city torn apart by violence while also involving one in the individual destinies of the principal characters—and of love in a 'pink and gold memory.'"

—Jonathan Fenby, author of *Generalissimo: Chiang Kai-Shek and the China He Lost*

"A deft and engrossing debut. In *Season of Betrayal*, Margaret Lowrie Robertson brings to bear her impressive journalistic expertise, taking us behind the scenes in Beirut to places we've never been before. But more important, she uses those insights into politics and terrorism to lead the reader to a deeper understanding of the human heart."

—Michael Mewshaw, author of *If You Could See Me Now*

"Margaret Lowrie Robertson's novel movingly explores betrayal in friendship, love and war. Layer by layer, it reveals Beirut, its journalists, and a marriage. It is a page-turner in the best sense of the phrase." —Masha Hamilton, author of *The Camel Bookmobile*

SEASON OF
BETRAYAL

SEASON OF BETRAYAL

MARGARET LOWRIE ROBERTSON

A HARVEST BOOK

HARCOURT, INC.

Orlando   Austin   New York   San Diego   London

www.HarcourtBooks.com

First U.S. edition published by Tatra Press, 2006.

Library of Congress Cataloging-in-Publication Data
Robertson, Margaret Lowrie.
Season of betrayal / Margaret Lowrie Robertson.—1st Harvest ed.
p.   cm.
"A Harvest book."
1. Lebanon—History—Civil War, 1975–1990—Fiction.   2. Beirut
(Lebanon)—Fiction.   3. United States Marine Compound Bombing,
Beirut, Lebanon, 1983—Fiction.   4. Americans—Lebanon—Fiction.
5. Journalists' spouses—Fiction.   6. Marriage—Fiction.   I. Title.
PS3618.O3172S43   2007
813'.6—dc22   2007024600
ISBN 978-0-15-603395-4 (pbk.)

Text set in Adobe Caslon Pro
Designed by Stephanie Bart-Horvath

Printed in the United States of America
First Harvest edition 2007
A C E G   I K J H   F D B

To my husband and my children,
and to my parents

ONE

THOMAS'S DEATH IS SO inextricably linked with my own story that I never could have imagined forgetting a single freeze-frame moment of that awful day, when we watched him die, over and over again, in painful slow motion.

One moment he is alive, standing on a wooden crate, blindfolded, a rope knotted around his neck. His time is running out, and he knows it. His hands are clenched, and his body twitches with fear. A foot kicks the box out from under him. His neck snaps, and his dangling body jerks and sways. And he is gone.

I remember it was stifling that June afternoon, in the makeshift office we'd set up in that Damascus hotel room. I remember the framed Syrian Air poster, in lurid hues, on the wall next to the door, the fraying teal carpet, the view of the swimming pool with its cracked tiles. I remember Predrag, sweating, working the controls of the editing machine, muttering "holy shit" under his breath, again and again, and Richard, stunned, silent, taking notes. But, somewhere along the way, I lost a central piece of this tableau and no matter how hard I try, I can't recall how I reacted. Surely, I wept. Surely. Didn't I? I remember heavy breathing—perhaps it was my own?

Does it matter?

I once considered that the longest hour of my life.

Now I know there are others equally long, if not as painful, others filled with fear or anxiety or incapacitating sadness. None, however, dealt such blunt shock. Not in Beirut, when the Lebanese shopkeeper died in front of me, nor in Iraq, where, after reluctantly intimate study, I realized the charred object in front of me was a Kurdish child, incinerated by Iraqi Army artillery. Not in Cyprus, when police finally let us close enough to see the bodies of the Israeli couple, shot by Palestinian terrorists on the deck of their yacht, the wife, middle-aged and plump, in a stained, white nylon nightgown that made her real in a way the stench of her decomposing body did not. I wasn't sick that day, though I wished I were.

There is no catharsis for these things. You carry them with you forever, each adding another notch on the yardstick by which humanity measures such horrors.

But I was utterly unequipped to measure the enormity of Thomas's death and who was responsible for it. I've tried to collect every detail, every scrap of information still available so many years later to put together this account, but I can only tell this story my own way—how Mac and I came to meet Thomas, and the effect it would have on our lives. You already know the ending. Or, think you do.

A quick peek then at my twenty-ninth birthday in Cyprus, the night before Mac and I left for Beirut. In the morning, we would join the ranks of other uneasy travelers and a bootleg cargo of champagne, cigarettes, and Coca-Cola to be ferried across the Mediterranean, God and circumstance willing, in an old container ship.

Mac had booked a table at a nearby fish restaurant to celebrate, and I was ready to go when he announced a change in plans.

"You'll have to go to dinner alone with those guys, Lara. I need to call the magazine, make some fixes in my story," Mac insisted, picking up the telephone on the bedside table.

"This'll take a while. Sorry," he added, avoiding my stare.

I hesitated in the doorway, hating to go alone. They weren't really my friends. They were his colleagues—a married couple we'd known slightly in Rome, Mac's last posting, staying by chance in the same hotel, along with a couple of other Beirut-based journalists we'd undoubtedly come to know better in the months ahead.

"Please," I said, drawing out the syllables. "They're waiting in the lobby. It'll be fun."

"No. Go on. Shoo."

"Come on, Mac. It's my birthday."

But this birthday already was proving as ungratifying as the last, when Mac, covering the imposition of martial law in Poland, couldn't shout even an apology down a crackling phone line until several days after it no longer mattered.

"Hello?" Mac said into the receiver on this night. "Operator?"

I couldn't see his face, only the top of his head, and the thatch of graying, brown hair.

"Barrett McCauley, room 305. I want to place a call to New York, please."

"Mac?" I tried again.

He waved me away.

"Sorry, this is going to take a while, Lu."

The pet name gave me hope. I waited, smiling expectantly, in the doorway. Mac finally looked up.

"Okay, okay, I'll try to join you later," he said at last, his voice softening a little.

But we both knew he wouldn't.

I returned a few hours later to find he'd left a chunky, antique silver Palestinian bracelet, perhaps chosen by someone else, on the pillow on my side of the bed. There was no card with the desultory offering. It wasn't even wrapped.

Mac was asleep, evidently aided by the half-empty scotch bottle and the remains of a room service dinner. Sadly, the wine I'd drunk at dinner wasn't enough for a similarly quick transit to sleep. Instead, I fidgeted quietly on my side of the room into the small hours of the night, a natural worrier sleepwalking through the anxiety-strewn terrain of the Middle East in 1983.

The next morning, Mac gulped the coffee and juice that served as breakfast. There wasn't time for more before we left for the boat, with our mound of belongings, the suitcases and duffel bags and knapsacks and plastic carrier bags, crammed with last-minute panic purchases from shops near the hotel.

"Sorry I didn't make it down last night, I was on the phone for freaking hours. Like the bracelet?"

"Very nice, thanks." I held out my wrist for him to examine and hugged him—the hug half-heartedly returned.

This wasn't the morning to pick a fight, but the truth was I hardly wore jewelry, just my wedding ring and the Tissot watch Mac paid a lot of money for in the Vienna duty-free during the layover on his way back from Poland. Gold, not silver. As Mac noted when he gave me the watch, it better suited a pale complexion.

As we crossed to Beirut that day, I slid the bracelet off my wrist, a small silver shackle cast into the glinting waters of the Mediterranean. I was prepared to lie, but Mac never noticed it was gone.

I choose this starting point of January 1983, so you'll understand that, although I was still young, I was no longer naïve. Though I was still hopeful, the illusions were wearing thin and I feared what might lie on the other side of a failed marriage.

Although I worked part-time and was going to grad school when we met, my own vague career prospects dissipated in the churn of Mac's ambitions and his string of assignments around the globe. He acclimated and thrived, happy to have someone look after him when he was home and miss him when he was not. But marriage only intensified the sense of isolation I'd felt since childhood, when my parents' very closeness as a couple excluded me, the late-in-life child. A perennial outsider. That was how I felt again, in the first year of my own marriage, as Mac spent much of his time in a succession of foreign capitals, while I stayed behind in New York.

Then, too, things were still good between us, and we both hoped the next posting, to Rome, would give us more time together. Within months, however, the pattern resumed: Mac off somewhere interesting and dangerous, with me at home, only this time in a city where I hardly knew a soul.

In many ways, it was a privileged life. The magazine paid for our huge, light-dappled apartment on Via Terme di Tito—named for the thermal baths of Emperor Titus—just a block from the Colosseum and the Forum, and Mac's frequent absences meant time to become familiar with these mighty ruins, and begin a Renaissance romance with Florence and Lucca and Siena, only as far away as a timetable and my imagination. Accountable to no one for my days, I became an unashamedly knapsack-toting perpetual tourist, with a hardcover diary of sorts to capture stray bits of information, occasional musings or clumsy attempts to render the beauty surrounding me.

I took Italian lessons twice a week, at a language school in a seventeenth-century palazzo a few minutes' walk from the Spanish Steps, and duly attended cookery workshops on regional cuisines and wines, though I never used our own kitchen unless Mac was home. I picked up the flute again for the first time since childhood, and found an elderly Polish gentleman, who, for a weekly fee of 10,000 lire—about five dollars—came to Via Terme di Tito and listened in gloomy silence to my amateur fumbling, perhaps daydreaming of the time when he proudly served as first chair flutist at the Warsaw Conservatory, in the years before the Nazis stopped the music.

No, I won't complain. But these pursuits were largely solitary, and by the time Mac announced our move to Beirut the sense of disconnect was nearly complete. America had become a void for me. My parents were dead, a traffic accident just before we moved overseas, and any remaining link to my North Carolina hometown disappeared with them. There were a couple of Kershaws, cousins on my father's side, and only one Wedgeworth left, my mother Florence's much older sister, Parthenope, a retired school teacher, who lived in Meridian, Mississippi, in the low-built house where they grew up with their little brother Henry, a picture page out of America's past. A long, white railing girded the veranda, and upon it sat an oak rocking chair and a rusting, squeaky glider bench that hadn't been oiled since Henry failed to return home from the Korean War.

Friends and acquaintances dotted the map, here and there, of course, from grad school or the New York years, before and during my marriage to Mac. Living in Rome, however, did nothing to foster ties, and it's fair to say that over time Mac came to mean everything to me: home, family, and, as unforgivably old-fashioned as it now sounds, for all intents and purposes, my career.

This was enough for me, for both of us—or so I hoped. But by the time we left for Beirut, the first cracks appeared and, as cracks generally do, started to spread.

"*Passeports.*"

The customs official nodded indifferently at us; the overhead fluorescent lighting did his complexion no favors.

We'd arrived at the port of Jounieh after sunset, some twenty kilometers up the coast from Beirut, which meant crossing the Green Line in the dark, if we were to keep to our plan to reach West Beirut that night. But now we were actually here, on this cusp of a war zone, and what had seemed a fine plan in Cyprus now appeared alarming. How much safer—more sensible, I put it to Mac—to stay overnight in Jounieh and brave the Green Line by daylight the next day.

But Mac was determined to spend our first night in this new post at the Commodore Hotel, the unofficial headquarters of the Beirut press corps. He'd even telexed ahead to his old friend Martin Sawyer before we left Cyprus, to expect us in time for happy hour. I tried pointing out that if there really were such a thing at the Commodore, it surely would've come and gone while we waited to go through customs.

Our queue moved with the haste of a watched pot, much to Mac's exasperation. To my own embarrassment, he fidgeted and sighed heavily, each noisy puff of air expelled in the hope of pushing things forward. Instead, we only drew stares from fellow passengers, mostly Lebanese, who, having stoically borne the rough sea crossing, were unperturbed by a lengthy wait on land.

"*Passeports, s'il vous plait,*" the sallow customs man repeated, when, finally, we reached the barrier.

I handed mine to Mac, and he presented them both with a flourish, and indeed, the sight of our covers seemed to animate the official's impassive features. Foreigners were hardly flooding into Lebanon.

"American, I see, Mister..." He rifled through the pages of Mac's passport.

"McCauley," Mac supplied. "Barrett McCauley."

"Barrett *George* McCauley," the official corrected, peering closely at the colorful array of exotic visa stamps and entry permits that served as effectively as any travelogue in summing up the past few years of Mac's life. "You have many countries here. This is first time in Lebanon?"

His manner was chatty, informal, a host welcoming guests at a party.

"That's right." Mac's tone was equally affable, though I sensed him tensing up at a potential conversational delay.

"Hello, lady."

My turn. He looked curiously from me to my passport picture and back again, trying to reconcile the tired, anxious face before him with the untroubled one affixed to the page.

"This photograph from long ago, yes?"

"Not really. Last year."

"You much more old looking now."

"Thank you."

But we both smiled.

"You have good journey?"

"It took longer than I expected."

"I think weather is not so very fine," he apologized sincerely, as if failing in his social obligation.

"Is it always so cold?" I shivered, despite a fleecy sweater and woolen peacoat. Beside me, Mac shifted his weight from one leg to the other as though in agreement, but frustration rather than cold prompted it, for he also leaned over and groaned softly, near my ear, "Shut *up*, Lara."

"Yes, always, in winter, lady." For a moment, the official looked downcast, then brightened as he added, "But is possible to make skiing on Mount Lebanon, if you like." He gestured expansively, as if the mountain were his to give.

"Hear that, Mac? You can ski here."

"Of course I heard, I'm standing right here, listening to you waste another hour."

The official looked at Mac in surprise.

"What's your hurry, Mister? You a spy?" He smiled, a big, wide smile this time, revealing teeth surprisingly white.

"I'm a journalist." The smile Mac returned was artificial, a thin, disapproving line, his lips remaining closed so that only his annoyance showed.

"Same thing, no?" The man laughed.

"Not at all. That's insulting."

"Why, you don't like CIA? All Americans are CIA." He laughed again.

"That's not funny." Mac looked around angrily to see if anyone was listening. "You could get us killed."

"Calm down, Mister, just having fun." He flipped open Mac's passport again. "Okay. *Journaliste.* Same word in French. In Arabic . . . *sahafi.* You know this word?"

"I do now." Mac glared at him.

"Mac," I said warningly. But his patience had expired.

"No offense," he said in a way guaranteed to convey it, "but could we skip the language lesson and move this process along? We still have to cross the Green Line tonight."

The atmosphere changed in an instant. No longer guests. Gate-crashers.

By way of reply, the official summoned a nearby guard, with an M16 strapped across his chest, who appraised us coldly while the customs official spoke rapidly in Arabic.

With the barrel of his rifle, the guard pointed at a table against the wall, about twenty feet away, and motioned us to follow. Mac mumbled "shit" under his breath as he picked up his portable type-writer and nudged me forward with his shoulder bag. I needed no prodding to do as instructed.

The guard smacked the table with the open palm of his hand to indicate where to put our belongings. Without a word, he strolled off, around the corner, out of sight.

We looked at each other helplessly. No one came to take his place, and no one came to tell us what to do. Back at the barrier, the customs official, busy with other arrivals, ignored us.

Mac was spitting with indignation. "This is a total mind-fuck. Who do they think they are? I'm an American journalist. They can't do this to me."

I tried to calm him, but I was pretty sure they could. Ten minutes passed, then twenty, ticking uselessly by, while the sky darkened. The room emptied. The last of the passengers from our boat completed passport and customs checks. We watched the customs man lock up his stamp and inkpad and disappear behind a partition.

"What do you think they'll do?" I asked Mac.

"They can't do anything. We're fucking *Americans*. I'm going to call the embassy and the Foreign Ministry about this crap. They'll be sorry they tried to jerk me around."

Mac raged on, and I stopped listening. Eventually he fell silent. Really, there was nothing else to do.

The guard with the M16 finally returned, accompanied by a tall, slender man, who, judging from his demeanor, the stripes on his sleeve, and the high gloss of his shoes, was a commander.

"I demand to speak to the U.S. embassy," Mac insisted, as they approached.

The commander ignored him. He eyed our possessions on the table with suspicion, his gaze falling upon Mac's hard-shell Olivetti on the table. He picked up the typewriter, gingerly, by the handle, and held it out toward Mac.

"What is this?" he growled.

I flinched; Mac stood firm.

"It's a typewriter."

The commander stared hard at Mac, while his fingers slowly opened. The typewriter hit the floor with a crash and the hard-shell cover broke off, bouncing on the floor a few feet away.

"Oops," the commander said flatly.

"Why'd you do that?" Mac demanded angrily.

The commander was already walking away. We scrambled to collect the broken plastic pieces, while the guard watched. Then, he nodded curtly toward the exit door. Apparently, we were free to go.

As we left the building, the customs official, the first man we'd talked to, poked his head out the door after us, a host bidding farewell.

"Good-bye, lady."

I started to turn around but Mac grabbed my arm and propelled me toward the waiting taxi his friend Martin had sent for us.

"Oh, and mister," the man called out, "be very careful in Lebanon."

"Stupid son of a bitch," Mac muttered, as we climbed in. But his head was turned, so only I heard him.

TWO

THE DRIVE FROM Jounieh to East Beirut along the coastal high-way was surprisingly quick, hardly time to assimilate the jumble of images of this city, its alien architecture and people, glimpsed at shutter speed through the smoke-tinted windows of our taxi.

We had to stop twice, at checkpoints manned by Phalangists, the Christian militiamen, unnerving in their severe haircuts and uniforms, but the driver assured Mac it was routine. The first time there was just a quick exchange of words with the driver—and barely a look at us—before waving the taxi through.

We were not so lucky the second time. Five or six cars in front of us slowed down and came to a halt near the Green Line. We were too far back to see much except the taillights of our predecessors.

"What's happening?" Mac asked.

The driver seemed less certain this time. He rolled down his window to decipher the chaotic sounds that rushed in with the bitter, cold air—people talking loudly in Arabic, some shouting, car doors opening and slamming shut.

"Maybe look for Moslems," he said, eventually.

"And if they find some?" I couldn't help but ask.

The driver looked at me.

"Maybe nothing."

"Or maybe . . . ?"

"Maybe kidnap. Exchange for Christian prisoners on West Side."
He let it sink in.

"Or maybe . . ." His voice trailed off meaningfully, as he drew
his finger across his throat.

Up ahead, a couple of cars started their engines and drove off.
At the same time, a group of men in military fatigues appeared in
our headlights and surrounded the car directly in front of us, about
ten feet away. One of the men broke away and came toward us,
waving his arms and yelling at the driver to switch off the car
lights, and roll up the window, or at least I assume that's what he
said, for that's what the driver quickly did.

The frightening scene unfolding before us seemed unreal, even at
the time, akin to watching a grainy, crackling, old-fashioned news-
reel, with a muted soundtrack and only a Spielbergian touch of color
here and there, flickering in the half-light of the moon, as we huddled together in the taxi, literally a captive audience. The soldiers
yanked a man from the driver's seat, and he struggled frantically,
before one of the soldiers whacked him to the ground with a rifle
butt. From the passenger side, a woman emerged, a child in her
arms, and I started to cry out, in horror, but Mac put his hand across
my mouth and whispered fiercely, "Be quiet," and wouldn't take his
hand away until it was clear I would. The soldiers closed in on them
then, blocking our view, one gestured back at us to move on.

"*Yalla*," the driver breathed, almost to himself. Let's go.

As we passed by, I glimpsed the woman through the soldiers.
An instant only, long enough to see her back was to us, with the
bewildered oval of the little boy's face perched atop her shoulder,
a black-and-white snapshot of fear.

"Can't we do something? Can't we help them?" I leaned forward to plead, though I already knew the answer.

"Just go!" Mac ordered the driver, pushing me back against the seat.

As he spoke, we heard shots. Maybe they came from a different direction altogether. I didn't ask.

Mac broke the silence after a few minutes, his voice shaky and defensive.

"There's nothing we can do about it. Surely you realize that."

I looked away first and tried not to cry. My second lesson in as many hours. Trouble could erupt at any moment here, a dormant volcano awaiting a cue. When it did, just hope to hell you weren't in its path.

Shortly, we reached the Green Line, where we would cross to the west side of the city, our taxi gliding swiftly, silently, a barge on the River Styx, into the dark, deserted cavern of Beirut's ruined port. The journey was tense; the driver uncommunicative now. Mac hoarded his thoughts, as I did my own, afraid and queasy. It seemed to take forever. It was all I could do to keep the cheese sandwich I'd eaten on the boat at lunchtime from making an unauthorized reappearance.

Finally, we spilled out onto the other side, racing through the streets of West Beirut, where the night shadows were alive with men and guns. Eternity abruptly ended as we pulled up in front of the Commodore Hotel.

It was unimpressive at first sight—a boxy, nondescript building. It was just another second-tier hotel until the international press corps gradually took it over after Lebanon's civil war broke out in earnest, in the mid-1970s.

We entered its dimly lit bar that night tentatively, unsure whether Mac's friend would still be there, when a voice called out of the crowd.

"Hey Mac, buddy, over here." Martin Sawyer. Stocky, outgoing, American as Budweiser. Mac knew him well from Vietnam, where his work for a wire service won several prestigious national awards and a promotion to Beirut bureau chief.

"Guys, this is Barrett McCauley—Mac." Martin stood up and scraped his barstool aside so Mac could get a better look around.

A thin, weary-looking middle-aged man seated at the curved bar offered a bony hand, "*Ahlan wah sahlan*. Welcome. Ian Fretwell, *London Telegram*."

"Nice to meet you, Ian."

"And this is Victor de Lara, from EFFE, you know, the Spanish news agency, and that, of course, is the famous Coco," Martin said, pointing at a round, mustached man poking pretzels through the bars of a bird cage in a corner near the door. Inside, the large, gloomy-looking parrot nibbled more out of boredom than hunger.

"Hey, Coco, incoming!" Martin called. The mustached man gave a friendly little wave but the bird ignored everyone. "Sorry, Mac, guess he's not in the mood. He also does the first few bars of Beethoven's Fifth. Never mind. You know Boz Whitfield from the Beeb, don't you?"

They shook hands, as Martin continued the introductions. Mac took up a position, leaning against the bar, his back to me, as I seated myself on a stool next to him. The overall effect, though unintended, obscured my presence.

"You remember Nils Erik Engelstoft and behind you over there is Doug from CBS and Kifner from the *Times*." Mac nodded reciprocal acknowledgments.

"Mac's replacing Roger Schuster, you know," Martin announced to the assemblage. There was a general murmur of sympathy.

"Poor Roger." Fretwell shook his head morosely. "So ironic..."

"Yeah, yeah, poor old Shu," Martin concurred hurriedly, moving the conversation along lest it shipwreck on this depressing, clearly much-reviewed topic. "So. Barrett McCauley in the Lebanon."

"Couldn't dodge the bullet this time," Mac grinned.

"Well sonny boy, what a fiefdom you've inherited... Schuster's flat on the Corniche... Nadia and Abdel Farid... and, of course, Thomas here, Beirut's finest fixer."

Martin pronounced Thomas's name with a heavy, fake Eastern European accent—Tow-*maas*—and mimed theatrically in his direction.

From his seat, Thomas started to protest, but Martin overrode him, clapping him on the back and whispering, in a jokey voice, "Next round on you, Warkowski," before turning back to Mac.

"In addition to your own august publication, Thomas here also works for that Polish rag you need five shots of vodka to pronounce. But he's good, Mac... want to interview the Russian ambassador?"

"What?" Boz Whitfield put in. "He doesn't talk to anyone."

"True, except the other Commies," Martin considered. "Yep, not even Thomas and he's half Polski. But he can get you just about anyone else."

"Martin," Thomas tried again. Too politely, lost in the swell of Martin's exuberance.

"Plus—and this is key, Mac—an exchange rate you haven't seen since the fall of Saigon, my friend. Hello, expense account heaven! For two Linda Ronstadt tapes and twenty bucks, he'll get your accountant knocked off if he questions it." Martin aimed his fingers and pulled an imaginary trigger.

Mac was silent throughout. Now, he raised an eyebrow at Thomas. "Really?" He asked, coolly.

"Of course not. Martin's insane," Thomas said, with a smile. "Nobody listens to Linda Ronstadt anymore. It's Emmy Lou Harris now."

Everyone laughed, except Mac, who lit a cigarette instead.

"I didn't mean Linda Ronstadt, I meant you." Mac exhaled slowly. "No offense, pal, but I never heard of you."

He spoke mildly enough, but the challenge hung in the air. In Mac's defense, you should understand Abdel Farid, the driver, and Nadia, the translator, came with the territory. They were the backbone of the magazine's Beirut bureau. That, we knew. But this, astonishingly, was the first we'd heard of Thomas.

Tow-*maas*. On the magazine payroll?

"It wasn't a formal arrangement with Roger," Thomas spoke with a slight accent that didn't sound Polish. He was a bit of a mess, really—his hair too long, his trousers inexpertly pressed, cheap brown shoes that had seen better days. But his features were drawn with patrician grace and, when he smiled at Mac, his dark eyes were shiny and eager to please.

"So your 'arrangement' is with New York then?" A frown flickered across Mac's face.

"Oh, no," Thomas explained hastily. "I had no retainer, nothing like that. I billed Roger for the stories as we went along. That's all.

No, no obligation. Martin is too kind, he overstates my importance."

Thomas made what can only be described as a formal, little bow. "Of course, if you need help, Barrett, I am at your service."

"Yeah, sure, I'll keep it in mind," Mac said noncommittally, before turning away to ask Fretwell about a mutual friend at the *Telegram.*

Mac didn't like surprises and Thomas undeniably was one, pressed upon him before he'd even had a chance to get his bearings. Whether that explained his instantaneous dislike, or whether Thomas simply rubbed him the wrong way, I knew Mac well enough to know this hard, first impression would likely stick.

As for me, not a word had come my way. My presence simply hadn't registered, half-hidden as I was behind Mac. Thomas was first to notice.

"And you are . . . ?"

"That's my wife." Mac answered before I could.

"Ah," Thomas said, in a slightly mocking tone I'd soon learn was out of character for him, "She doesn't speak?"

"Lara," I announced, louder than intended, and at once everyone seemed to be tuning me in, like a fiddly new channel on a shortwave radio that required extra effort to hear properly. I cleared my throat. "Well, Larissa, actually. But most people call me Lara."

This was what I hated about going someplace new with Mac. Establishing credentials. Reserved by nature, I found this excruciatingly awkward, like a blind date or a job interview. It was all about comparing résumés and information about previous postings, discovering mutual acquaintances, exchanging war stories— the journalistic equivalence of a dog marking territory. Mac rose

with vigor to each fresh challenge, part of the necessary and familiar journalistic mating ritual he had performed in countless bars
and press clubs since he first went to Vietnam in the late '60s as a
young magazine writer.

"Larissa—from the Greek, yes?" Thomas eyed me critically for
another moment, but before I could reply, was questioning Mac
again. "And where are you coming from?"

With exaggerated patience, Mac explained we'd come from
Rome, New York before that, and that he, of course, had been in
Southeast Asia, in Hong Kong after Vietnam, that he knew not
only Martin but several of the other journalists based here.

"And what will you do here, Larissa?" Thomas looked at me.

"Lara," Mac said pointedly.

"Lara." Thomas agreed. Then, to my embarrassment, he picked
up my hand and peered at my fingers. "You are perhaps an artist?"

Mac snorted in disbelief and Thomas dropped my hand.

"She's my wife."

This was more than two decades ago, remember, and although
Mac was visibly annoyed with Thomas, his remark wasn't meant as
dismissively as it sounds in the retelling. For that was how I, too,
thought of myself in 1983. Mac's wife. Still, I felt foolishly flat-
tered by Thomas's attention.

"Thank you. Sadly, I have no talent."

"That is difficult to believe," Thomas countered gallantly.

"Believe." A smile, unbidden, escaped.

Could I have stopped there? Looking back, it seems impossible;
the almost Darwinian progression of events that would spring and
mutate from this swamp of mindless barroom chitchat was already
underway.

So even as Mac looked on disapprovingly, I added, "I'm not sure yet what I'll do here. Who knows, maybe I'll get a job."

I was qualified for nothing, certainly nothing in a war zone, nothing in *Beirut*.

You see it? The loosening of another shackle. Already, I was responding to Thomas's knack of divining a virtue in me where Mac did not, or indeed, where none existed. I found myself ignoring all the danger signs—Mac's raised eyebrow, my own thumping heart—in my wish not to disappoint him.

❁

That first night, drinks segued into a lengthy dinner with Martin and several of the others, and then dinner into more drinks back at the bar. When Mac volunteered what we'd seen at the checkpoint in East Beirut, Martin said, "Welcome to Lebanon, folks," and everyone nodded in agreement and offered up similar stories, incidents they'd witnessed or heard about, on both sides of the Green Line. Conversation paused once or twice to gauge the occasional spit of distant gunfire, though all agreed it was a quiet evening by Beirut standards.

The volcano's rim, however, makes an anxious perch, and it was hard to act as nonchalant as our new friends about the turmoil that seethed just outside the oasis of the hotel. It seemed impossible this day had begun with breakfast in Cyprus. Fatigue washed over me. I finally excused myself and retreated to our room on the hotel's seventh floor, leaving Mac in the bar.

The upper floors were always popular, the pretty, young receptionist had told us—further away from the point of impact, in the event of a car bomb. Of course, it wasn't such a smart place to be if the Christians started shelling across the Green Line, she confided cheerfully. When that happened, you couldn't give away an east-facing room on the top two floors. Or a room on the top floor, period.

Our room that night was unremarkable, indistinguishable in memory from any of the countless other hotels I'd visit in years to come. What I do recall clearly, however, is a section of metal drainpipe under the bathroom sink, for that is where I crouched, clutching a dripping toothbrush and shaking with fear, wedged between the toilet and the shiny, white-tiled wall, when the volcano blew.

"Just a small disturbance nearby, nothing serious." The receptionist was reassuring when I crawled out of the bathroom to call the front desk ten minutes later. "Please not to worry."

Our waiting luggage was neatly lined up where the bellman had dropped it. Mac hadn't even called upstairs. For a while, anger and fear lent a manic energy to my unpacking efforts. But shoving the last empty suitcase into the closet, I felt perversely satisfied: I hadn't crumpled at the first sign of seismic activity, after all.

I got into bed and read *Vanity Fair* until my eyes hurt and gullible Amelia Sedley sent me into a fitful sleep, in which explosions rocked the great iron gates of Miss Pinkerton's Academy for Young Ladies on Chiswick Mall, and a small boy in tears stumbled through the clouds of smoke, looking for his mother and father, while I tried to shout to Thomas to run, run, run.

Mac woke me up when he stumbled into the room an hour later and turned on the light. Had I heard that bomb go off earlier? Probably just a few sticks of dynamite, a reminder from neighborhood militiamen to a nearby café owner, behind in his protection payments, he said. Not a big deal.

More important, he enthused, not a single drink was spilled in the Commodore bar when the bomb exploded. Mac described how everyone placed their drinks on the counter, fanning out in one graceful, fluid movement, before pitching themselves to the floor. He hadn't seen anything like it since Saigon. No, better than Saigon—drinks were spilled there.

Mac had never set foot on Lebanese soil until that morning. He knew little about the country or its history and none of its language, but, at least in the Commodore, he was back among his own tribe.

Mac was home.

In this way, I would come to learn, Thomas was Mac's mirror opposite. Fluent in the languages and cultures of other lands, yet at home in none.

Thomas's father was Polish, an engineer working first in South America and later in the United States, for a multinational oil company. His Brazilian mother was a poet who never lived up to the success of a first slender volume, published before Thomas's birth. Because his father's work took the family around the Americas throughout Thomas's early years, he never actually lived in either parent's native country. His mother took Thomas and his brother to see family in Rio every summer; nonetheless the few cousins there remained unfamiliar, unfriendly. Boarding schools in Caracas and Buenos Aires, Dallas and—as his father moved up the corporate chain—Washington, happily opened their doors to him, a paying student who excelled in academics and languages. He spoke his mother's Portuguese and although he'd only once visited Poland, then under Communist rule, was literate in his father's language, as well. American schooling polished his English, and Argentina and Venezuela bequeathed him yet another tongue. At university, he added Italian, French, and Arabic.

By the time we arrived, Beirut was as much a home as any Thomas had known in his thirty-five years. He'd lived there longer than anywhere else, arriving on Beirut's doorstep along with the civil war in 1975, innocent as a babe in a basket, fresh from graduate school at Cairo University, with an advanced degree in Arabic Studies. He also carried a bankroll from his father—nearly two thousand dollars, a relative fortune in those times, which had the unintended effect of enabling him to drift away, an ice floe from an arctic shore, further out to sea, until he disappeared entirely from family view.

By the time his funds ran out, he was finding freelance work as a journalist, first for a chain of Brazilian newspapers, and, later, Polish ones with, as Martin said, impossible names. Over time, he did come to know the Russian ambassador, and the French, the Swedish, the Libyan—all the diplomats who passed through Beirut's trenches. He knew the aid workers and the academics who came to teach at the universities, knew the Scandinavian army officers from the United Nations peacekeeping force in southern Lebanon, and the ever-changing cast of fellow journalists, the writers and photographers, the TV cameramen and correspondents—the ones who lived here and those who simply slipped in and out of the story, from safer, saner bases in Cairo or Cyprus or London. He knew the Peruvian consul's Lebanese mistress and the American nurse from an international charity, who divided her favors between a top Palestinian official and a respected journalist from New York. He knew why the Dutch businessman was in trouble back home, knew why a certain British professor drank too much, and who among the TV correspondents snorted their paychecks.

Thomas distinguished between those who approached Beirut as another notch on the career belt and those lured by a genuine love for the Levant, for the Middle East. He knew the foreign community well and equally, the Lebanese host community upon which it depended—the translators, drivers and fixers, the Lebanese journalists who covered their own war with no choice but to live it as well, and, consequently, went about their grim business with little of the fuss and fanfare that accompanied journalists in from other countries.

He knew which Beirut news seller was Armenian and which was Druze, knew Christian shopkeepers who chose to stay in the west, on the predominantly Moslem side, and Moslem merchants who defied Hezbollah to sell alcohol in their cafés. He knew landlords and warlords, sometimes one and the same; haunted the offices of government bureaucrats; drank endless cups of sweet, thick coffee with politicians and was invited inside the homes and lives of the men and women who kept the city running, even if the electric grid sprang to life for only a few hours each week.

Yes, Thomas knew a lot.

But it seems he forgot the basic law of nature articulated by Newton, that to every action there is always an opposite and equal reaction. And this would rebound on him, for Lebanon was an unforgiving place. There were no false steps, only fatal ones. Thomas would tap into forces he couldn't control, with the result that he would become part of the history of the place himself.

THREE

IMAGINE A SCENE that took place seven years before I came to Beirut: it is Friday, June 18, 1976, at 11:00 A.M. in Washington, D.C., and President Gerald R. Ford has summoned his cabinet for crisis talks at the White House. In New York, where I have yet to meet Mac, Lebanon is just an angry newspaper headline. But three thousand miles and half a world away, Thomas is witnessing its disintegration firsthand. Around him, thousands of Lebanese are dying in ferocious fighting between Christians and Palestinians and Moslems. Proportionately, it is as if two million Americans have died.

Spiking the crisis for Washington is the fact that two days earlier, radical Palestinians kidnapped and shot to death Francis Meloy, the newly appointed American ambassador, the embassy's economic officer Robert Waring, and their Lebanese driver, Mohammed Moghrabi.

The ambassador's body was dumped in a Palestinian-controlled sector of West Beirut years before we arrived, and his killers wouldn't come to justice until many years after we were gone and I no longer followed Lebanon's travails, even from afar.

This is important, because they were the first high-profile American casualties of the Lebanese conflict, killed by virtue of their passports. Another 272 Americans would die while I was there in 1983—most of them U.S. Marines sent to Lebanon as part of a Multinational Force, peacekeepers, on a self-described "mission of presence."

In the course of trying to assemble this picture, I came across an official memorandum of the Washington meeting, declassified and released many years after the event. An evacuation is planned, it reports, but the President says that essential U.S. embassy staff will stay behind and there are about 1,400 other Americans still in Lebanon. His secretary of state, Henry Kissinger, emphasizes it's not clear how many of them will opt to leave. Many have no other home.

"There is no security in Beirut," Mr. Kissinger says. I am with him so far. In that sense, little will have changed by the time we arrive seven years later. He adds, "But none of the responsible groups has any real interest in killing Americans, because if there was, it could be done quite easily at any time. But there are, of course, totally irresponsible elements."

I guess that's the way it looked in Beirut in 1976. Only totally irresponsible elements would kill Americans.

⁂

We didn't know that, didn't know quite what we were wading into. But it was about to become a lot harder to differentiate between the "responsible groups" and "totally irresponsible elements." I don't mean the general citizenry, but the warlords and militias loyal to them, an alphabet soup of warriors—PSP, PLO, DFLP, PFLP—multistrands of fighters plaited together by guns and money and the hatred inherent in longstanding rivalries.

Middle East veterans such as Thomas and Fretwell and Boz— and, by now, Martin and most of the others, for new hands quickly become seasoned in war zones—could still distinguish between those considered "responsible" and those not—and distinguish they did. To me, however, it often seemed they were one and the same.

※

"When the Christians shell the Moslems, it also sends a message to Damascus," Thomas explained patiently, as I waited for Mac one afternoon. He'd hailed me from across the Commodore lobby, and joined me with apparent pleasure on one of the leather banquettes.

I, in turn, was happy to see Thomas. He stood out in welcome, stark relief against the Commodore's crowd of hard, polished players, though he got on well with most of them. Except for Mac.

Despite that, I liked Thomas. He was surprisingly easy to talk to, and seemed gratified when asked to draw on his vast reserves of knowledge—years of observation built on a bedrock of fascination, not only with Lebanon but the Middle East as a whole. Intricacies. Intrigues. Unlike Mac, he didn't ridicule my lack of knowledge. I'd tried the monographs and political science journals lining the shelves in our living room, but found them too dry, too academic. Too hard to concentrate, anyway. I, who often went through two or three or even four books a week, was still stuck on *Vanity Fair* a month after our arrival. The big book of *New York Times* Sunday crossword puzzles proved a godsend.

It was Thomas who illuminated my dark Lebanon.

Across the way, a well-dressed Syrian businessman, waiting for his key at the front desk, looked into the eyes of his olive-skinned companion, fingering her absurdly yellow ringlets, stiff with hairspray. I touched my own loose, shoulder-length hair self-consciously and tucked it behind my ears before I realized Thomas was watching me. He smiled, as if to indicate he understood the gesture was reflexive, not coquettish, then proceeded with his take on the Israelis.

"It's a bit tricky. They support the Christians but are also arming the Druze." The Druze, he'd already explained, adhered to a secretive, mystical offshoot of Islam but didn't consider themselves Moslem, and their blood feud with Lebanon's Maronite Christians unreeled over a hundred years of confessional hatred.

The businessman now steered his lady friend toward the elevator. In teetering heels and a flamboyantly colored dress that clung to ample bosom and bottom, she wiggled all the way, a peroxide Carmen Miranda, minus the fruity headwear. A porter followed, pushing a trolley stacked with Louis Vuitton luggage.

Thomas smiled at the man. "Sorry, Lara. That's Ahmed. A friend. He owns a textile factory just over the Syrian border and sometimes comes here at the weekends."

He switched gears again. The Russians, he said, backed just about everyone, except the Christians—the Syrians, the Druze, other Palestinian factions. Even giving guns now to Hezbollah, the Shiite crazies.

"The Russians want to be on the winning team," he said. "But the Americans are sneaky, too. Great friends with the Christians and the Sunnis, yet they've got to be throwing money at Amal— the mainstream Shiite militia—so it can fight Hezbollah, do their dirty work for them."

Thomas added that Amal's leader, Nabih Berri, had relatives in Detroit, as if that explained everything.

In a way it did. It helped explain why the Shiite driver at the CBS bureau asked Mac to pick up his favorite brand of scotch on his transit through the airport duty free, his wife and daughters unashamedly attired in western dress, while his neighbor and co-religionist in the Shiite shantytowns in the southern suburbs insisted females in his family enrobe themselves in the head-to-toe black chadors, increasingly seen on the streets of Beirut, a swarm of ravens coming silently to roost.

I hardly ever cooked in our apartment overlooking the sea. That first evening in Beirut proved the prototype for the months that followed, for that was what we did in Beirut when "the situation," as it was euphemistically called, allowed: drinks in the bar at the end of the working day, dinner in the dark, Polynesian-themed restaurant at the back of the hotel, perhaps a nightcap in the bar or coffee in the lobby, before stumbling out to find Abdel Farid waiting patiently in his old yellow Mercedes outside the hotel.

Mac naturally gravitated to those we met the first night, and we came to know them well: Martin was someone with whom Mac was always happy to share a foxhole or a bar tab. Boz Whitfield was an old Middle East hand, and his wife, Jan, the daughter of a British diplomat who'd spent twenty years in the Arab world. Nils Erik Engelstoft reported for a rival newsweekly. An authority on Chaucer, he claimed descent from Danish kings, and often draped a blue blazer as regally across his shoulders as a royal ancestor might have donned a cloak. Nils once famously began a sentence, "In the reign of Gorm the Older," during an argument about the Lebanese civil war and was never allowed to forget it. Amiable, Cuban-born Victor de Lara needed little prompting after a few drinks to recount his long-ago role in the CIA's bungled invasion of the Bay of Pigs.

Along with the others, they were a hodgepodge fraternity, swapping loud tales of real time derring-do in Lebanon, and—often louder—tales about past exploits, particularly about Vietnam, the last great conflict to galvanize the international media, another war fought in barrooms and battlefields. As for myself, I rarely contributed. It was enough to sit and listen, to sip my wine, to soak it all in, as I had so many times before, until time to go home. It was a constituent part of Mac's world and therefore of mine, as well.

❉

For me, it is always 1983 in Beirut, a year frozen in time, mired in failure—that of Lebanon's political leaders, of the policies of well-meaning western governments, and, beyond all of that, of my own, deeply personal failure. Everyone lost: I among them.

I simply don't register news about Lebanon now. I ignore articles, change channels, tune out conversations. I'm not even sure which year the civil war officially ended: for me, Lebanon was over long before.

Having said that, a few years back I caught fragments of a television documentary detailing the rejuvenation of that city I once reluctantly called home and so, without wanting to, I know the Green Line is gone, long removed to the category of urban archaeology, obscured by deconstruction, reconstruction, new construction.

Yet I remember the gash on civilization it once was. The first time I went through the Museum Crossing, I wept—partly out of fear, but mostly because the devastation ripped at my heart. From the start, it seemed I lacked the capacity to see the old, vivacious Beirut beneath it all, the glitter of spirit Mac and his colleagues mined everywhere, culled from the jumbled cityscape like a Lebanese *Where's Waldo?*—the smuggled shiny red cans of Coca-

Cola for sale, despite the Arab boycott, at the smart new deli, Goody's, itself a minor marvel. Fresh caviar at Smith's, the family-run grocery that never seemed to close; the latest French fashions on Hamra Street; the swimming pool open for business at what remained of the otherwise-derelict St. Georges Hotel. All these things, touted as symbols of the defiant Lebanese spirit.

Their anecdotes were packed with dark little lumps of farce, nuggets of pathos, liberally laced with irony, a dense fruitcake of a story—the kidnap victim who demanded, and received, taxi fare home from his kidnappers; the Goody's shoppers, mostly women, who produced pistols from every conceivable hiding place—handbags, garters, waistbands, pockets, holsters—when another shopper shouted "Stop, thief!" at a pickpocket. Where Mac's crowd applauded the irony of an army of well-armed, well-heeled housewives, I felt a bizarre sense of kinship with the unwitting thief.

No, I couldn't get a purchase on the spirit the others embraced so effortlessly. I didn't see it that way at all. I saw only the vast destruction of Lebanon's surface, the shattered buildings, the defaced city. Unlike our circle of Beirut acquaintances, I wore my New York City Police–issue bulletproof vest everywhere, at least at the beginning, and then again towards the end. Mac never wore his, of course—not that I was aware of, anyway.

Because he was so rarely shaken out of a basic belief in his own invincibility, fear in Beirut for Mac was largely anecdotal, anyway: me cowering in the hallway, bulletproof vest, grabbing cigarettes and scotch at the first sound of trouble.

"I told her, it's not here . . . that gunfire's coming from over by the television station—three miles away!" Mac roared over the evening's libations in the Commodore.

When an RPG hit a nearby office building in the dead of night, catapulting me out of sleep and into near-hysteria, I tried to shake Mac awake.

"So I ask her, 'Are you hurt? Am *I* hurt—did I miss something? The cat? Did it hit our building? So why'd you wake me up?" he reported and everyone laughed. Even me, silly me, scaredy-cat me, afraid of things that went thump and thud and bang in the night. Afraid of .50-caliber machine guns and rocket-propelled grenades, silly Lara. Even I laughed, though I wanted to weep.

After regaling the bar with these tales, Mac might add, in a stagey, avuncular aside to me, something along the lines of, "Nothing wrong with being scared, Lara. It's nature's way of keeping you on your toes," and pat my hand consolingly. But we both knew he didn't believe it. Nor did the others who now populated our world, much of it newly redefined by the parameters of the Commodore bar.

I couldn't share Mac's delight in having a balcony overlooking the Mediterranean. So much glass worried me, though the French doors were covered with a sticky, transparent film to keep them from shattering in an explosion. Sure, the view was splendid—if you looked straight out to sea—framed by swaying palms on the Corniche. But a glance in either direction quickly spoiled the effect, revealing a mottled periphery where the evidence of war, old and new, belied the more rustic charms of this once-grand avenue. And when the guns of the neighborhood militias fell blessedly silent, the distant boom of dynamite used by Druze fishermen to blast their prey out of the water filled the gap.

There was no peace. There was no quiet. This was Beirut.

❀

"... And the Cairo Agreement was born out of that political stale-mate," Thomas was explaining, another evening, as I waited for Mac. "It gave all the parties in Lebanon a face-saving way out."

A dour Lebanese man sitting nearby grunted. His name, I knew, was Hamid, and he ran the Beirut operation for TV Kansai, Japanese TV.

"A suicide letter. Lebanon signed its own death warrant," Hamid said in disgust.

"How?" I no longer worried about sounding stupid.

"The Lebanese allowed the PLO to keep their guns in the refugee camps, and then turned a blind eye when they attacked Israel," Thomas replied.

"Why'd they agree to that?"

"Because they are fools," Hamid said, in a low rumble, but he quickly lost interest in our conversation and returned to eaves-dropping, quite openly, on the UN peacekeeping officers, one Turkish, one Dutch, on the other side of him.

"The Lebanese had no control over the Palestinians anyway, and the Palestinians agreed to respect Lebanon's sovereignty and its laws," Thomas said.

Fretwell, tired and dishevelled, entered the bar in time to hear the last few words.

"Evening, all. Thomas, you leave that poor girl alone. Just because she's polite doesn't mean she's interested."

"It's okay. He's on a roll," I said.

Fretwell signalled for a round of drinks.

"Just a wee one, then home. Long day." He gave a small shudder.

"So where were you in this discourse?"

"The Cairo Agreement."

"Right. The next agreement they signed gave the Palestinians virtual autonomy, legitimizing 'Fatah Land,' their mini state-within-a-state in southern Lebanon, and, by turns, the Palestinians grew bolder and started using Shiite villages in the south to launch attacks on Israel."

Fretwell's drink was placed before him.

"See where this is heading, Lara?" He sipped gingerly. "Too strong, Marwan. Spare some tonic, please?" The barman obliged.

"You know, Lara, it wasn't a total *fait accompli*," Fretwell said, waving away the bowl of nuts Marwan offered. "When the Israelis hit back at the Shiite villages, the Shiites fled—that's why there're so many Shiite refugees in Beirut now. Half the bloody country came north, creating even more instability. And, of course, giving the Pixies an excuse to visit."

"Pixies?"

"Pixies from Dixie, as the Americans say—the Israelis, from the south. You know, the Israeli invasion last summer, to get rid of the Palestinians." He removed his glasses and wiped them with a dingy handkerchief plucked from his shirt pocket, before settling them back on the bridge of his bony nose.

"Operation Peace for Galilee," Thomas supplied.

"Now there's irony. No peace since the Pixies invaded." Fretwell sighed.

"That's why we had that gloriously colorful evacuation of the PLO fighters last summer, helped along by your countrymen, the United States Marines," Fretwell concluded. "Which brings us to where we are today."

"Which, I would say, is going home time," Mac boomed.

My husband had arrived. He strode into the bar, a fine cut of man, big and broad-shouldered, his very presence visually overpowering Thomas's long, slender frame and Fretwell's stooped one. Beirut agreed with Mac, as I said. He thrived in the volcanic atmosphere, and while my own inability to rise similarly to the challenge irritated him, he was happy and it showed in our own relationship. His desire had returned, and, I have to confess, Mac still had the capacity to thrill me.

"Sorry, I'm late, Lu darling." He kissed me, and gave me a surreptitious squeeze. I squeezed back in the right places and Mac said, "Whoa, woman," and I laughed out loud at my own boldness.

"Hey, Ian." Mac shook hands with Fretwell, though not with Thomas. He did, however, nod and say "Thomas" in a neutral kind of way, which pleased me as he usually just said "Warkowski." I didn't even mind that he pronounced "Thomas" the American way, which by now sounded rude to my ears. Not that Thomas took offense. No, he gave Mac a friendly smile and said, "How are you, Barrett?"

But Mac had already turned his attention to Marwan, who, unasked, put a finger of scotch in front of him, which he quickly drained. He slapped some Lebanese pounds on the counter.

"Keep the change, Marwan."

Mac slipped his arm through mine to help lift me off the seat. "Sorry to hit and run, folks, but gotta get this princess home before our coach turns into an RC can."

As we made our way out of the bar, I heard Thomas telling Fretwell, "It's what they drink in the American south. There's also a beverage called Mountain Nectar, as I recall."

"Jeez, that guy never shuts up," Mac said to himself, while I made a mental note to tell Thomas about Mountain Dew—and Dr. Pepper—next time we met.

Perhaps it was the wine, but I only pretended to scold Mac when he slipped his hand up my skirt and we giggled together like teenagers in the backseat, wondering how much Abdel Farid could see in the rearview mirror, as he drove us home through the streets of Beirut.

Back in the flat, Mac managed to shed all his clothes between the front door and the bedroom but our anticipated pleasure was cut short by a burst of automatic weapons fire outside our building. While Mac quickly recovered, the moment was gone for me and he fell into bed alone, grumbling, while I spent most of the next hour, huddled in the windowless hallway, still fully dressed, with Mac's best bottle of single malt for company, a carton of cigarettes and Graham Greene's *The Comedians*, because I couldn't find *Vanity Fair* in the dark.

"Mac?" I whispered later. "You awake?" I shook his shoulder gently but he just groaned, mumbled, and turned over in his sleep. I crawled into bed beside him, and warmed myself against the unforgiving hump of his back. In the distance, the gun battle still raged, but the sounds were faint enough for sleep.

❊

I couldn't name for you today the councilors who represent the leafy London borough where I live, but I still remember the men who pulled the strings in Lebanon's politics in 1983, who controlled its streets and its gunmen. They formed a roll call central to my daily well-being: Gemayel, Jumblatt, Berri, Karami, Franjiyeh—and in the background, the growing sinister influence of Sheik Mohammed Fadlallah, from Hezbollah. These warlords—*zuamas*—were themselves usually dependent on masters in other capitals—in Damascus and Baghdad, in Tripoli, Tel Aviv and Teheran, in Peking, as we still called it.

But the real power lay in the hands of those who sculpted and directed policy from Washington and Moscow. Under the cover of civil war, the Cold War played out daily, by proxy, in the streets of Beirut. In capitals around the world, events were taking place, policies shaped, strategies put in place—things of which I knew little, yet would have a direct influence on our lives, in this city under siege from within.

❋

That was the big picture.

The little picture was that, no matter how many times a day we came and went, the gunmen at the end of our street never gave any sign they recognized us. Fine with me. I sought anonymity behind large, dark-lensed sunglasses, encased in a bright red plastic frame, which Mac insisted had exactly the reverse effect. He may have been right, but they were mine, and I'd paid an awful lot of money for them in New York the previous summer, when Lebanon was still a place name that hardly figured on my own geopolitical map. I suppose they were my own symbol of defiance.

I usually nodded at the gunmen on duty, too intimidated to trot out my two or three words of Arabic. Mac, however, almost always attempted a cheerful conversation.

"*Marhaba,*" he'd call out. Hello.

"*Kifak?*" How are you, he'd continue, with a charmingly rueful smile as if to apologize for his atrocious Arabic, but equally sure he'd be forgiven by grace of having tried in the first place. Congeniality through sheer dint of force.

This much-practiced tactic worked wonders with cranky wait-resses, recalcitrant store clerks, harrassed flight attendants. But Mac was never rewarded for his efforts in Beirut. The gunmen always waved us through—tensely, when things were tense; lazily, when they were not.

The day might come when that would change, of course, but for now, we were inconsequential, anonymous in the daily census of violence.

⁂

Ambassador Francis Meloy arrived in Beirut in April 1976. Killed on the way to present his credentials to the Lebanese president in June, his death achieved the kind of distinction no one seeks: the shortest time served in a post of any American chief of mission since Benjamin Franklin was appointed the first U.S. representative overseas in 1778.

His driver, Mohammed Moghrabi, was one of Lebanon's unsung heroes, all but forgotten today except to family and friends. And to the group of American and Lebanese journalists he rescued from the Hotel St. Georges, trapped by fierce fighting there early in the civil war. "Go get those guys," he was told and he did. Imagine.

It would be eighteen more years and four more presidents before two men were finally arrested for these crimes. Unusually, for Lebanon, where so many went unpunished, they were tried, found guilty, and sentenced to die.

Two years later—twenty years after the killings—a Lebanese appeals court overturned the convictions, under a 1990 amnesty for political crimes committed during Lebanon's civil war.

There is no such amnesty in my heart for Thomas's killers.

FOUR

OUR EVENINGS MAY have been dictated by the Commodore, but our days were loosely structured, at least in the beginning. God only knew when the faithful Abdel Farid arrived each morning; for all I knew, he slept out in front of our building, as even on the coldest January mornings, he was always waiting outside in the car, its exhaust visible in the icy air, waiting to take Mac to the magazine's office, two streets away from the Commodore. Nadia, the translator, came every day when it was busy and, when it wasn't, took Sundays off. She answered phones, translated local radio and TV newscasts, and clipped stories from the newspapers. She also went out with Mac on stories, smoothing the way with rackety politicians or skittish militiamen at checkpoints, her glossy beauty an obvious asset in dealing with these situations. With Mac and his colleagues, she was forceful and animated, her laugh confident, her manner flirtatious. With me, however, she was offhand, verging on rude, and had an unpleasant habit of dropping constant references to people and places of which I'd never heard, and events with which I was unfamiliar, and then evincing astonishment at all the things I didn't know.

I was out of my element in Beirut. I knew it, she knew it. Everyone at the Commodore knew it. Mercifully, she was the only one who rubbed it in. But I was careful not to tell Mac this. He'd only think I was jealous. I was. Looking back, that is clear.

❈

Despite Martin's early assertion of Thomas's indispensability to the magazine, Thomas only showed up at Mac's office once or twice; the cool reception would have put him off trying again. Once or twice, at the Commodore bar, he offered to help with stories Mac was working on, but Mac shrugged him away, barely bothering to conceal his disinterest. In fact, when we came across him at the hotel, Mac usually left me to sit with Thomas, the wall-flowers at the prom, while he sought more stimulating company.

❈

The Polish magazine Thomas worked for couldn't afford an office, and his telephone connection at home, when it worked, was good only for local calls. Instead, he depended on TV Kansai, tucked away in an annex behind the hotel. Not unusual; lots of news organizations shared resources. I don't know if his magazine paid TV Kansai or if Thomas had a private deal with Hamid. Probably the latter. That's the way it was. Everyone had their own deals going.

As for Mac, he evidently had more than enough help from Nadia and Abdel Farid. He fired off dispatches staccato style— intense, firsthand accounts of war, terse political assessments, news analysis, an occasional quirky feature—every Friday night, when the magazine "closed" the issue for the upcoming week. On those days, he sent his stories by telex from his office.

❈

We had a telex machine at home, too, a big hulking metal monster that spewed out endless rolls of paper with urgent messages from New York and other points around the world. Sometimes it surged into action late at night, keys clattering, when the electricity un-expectedly came on, urgent, loud, and frightening as gunfire.

✾

One evening, Thomas made the point that Lebanon's political sys-tem favored the Christians, because it was based on a fifty-year-old census showing them as the majority, though it was no longer believed true.

"So the President is always Christian, the Sunnis pick the Prime Minister and a Shiite is always Speaker of the Parliament," Thomas warmed to his theme.

"And Parliament is stacked in their favor—six seats for every five Moslem ones," Fretwell piped up, "it's in the 1943 National Covenant."

Mac, walking in, caught the last three words and, rolling his eyes at me, quickly made for Martin and Nils Erik, on the other side of the bar.

Out of the corner of my eye, I saw Nadia join them. She was Christian, I knew.

"It worked for a few decades," Fretwell continued, "Beirut became the hub of banking and commerce, movies, music, you name it, in the Arab world."

I half listened. Across the room, Martin and Nils Erik greeted the Whitfields, and they wandered off to the restaurant together, leaving Mac and Nadia at the bar, and while it was hard to be sure it looked as if they'd drifted closer together, their bodies now touching.

My heart sank. Warily, I watched out of the corner of my eye, while Thomas and Fretwell plowed ahead with the history lesson, unaware.

"Sorry, Ian, you were saying?" As I spoke, Mac ran a finger down Nadia's arm. My stomach knotted. I fought the urge to flee.

A French television crew bustled in, and, inserting themselves between Mac and Nadia, clamored for Marwan's attention, while simultaneously giving an excited account of a shoot-out they'd just witnessed from the canned goods aisle in Smith's grocery store.

It wasn't enough to derail my companions.

"I was saying, Moslems have a higher birthrate, but the Christians won't admit it."

"It would shift the whole balance of power," Thomas added helpfully.

I turned, to see the French crew, drinks in hand, head out the glass door to the patio. One of them bumped into Nadia on the way out and Mac put his arm around her to steady her.

I stood up abruptly.

Thomas looked alarmed at the prospect of losing his audience.

"The Christians don't want another census," he said hurriedly, anxious I not miss the final point. He would have continued, I'm sure, for he grabbed my sleeve to slow my exit. "It would be tantamount to political suicide."

I manufactured a smile as I went over to Mac and recognized Nadia's as equally false. Time to go, I told Mac, firmly. He came away without argument, looking slightly guilty.

I didn't want to bicker in front of Abdel Farid, so I said nothing on the way home, and by the time we got there I started to feel a little foolish. How petty and pointless to make a federal case out of the fact my husband had stood closer than I liked to his translator in the bar.

Or, did I instinctively hold my ammunition for a bigger battle to come?

⁂

My suspicions predated this, of course, back to our years in Rome, sown in the late, often lost, hours, on the occasions Mac wasn't away on assignment; in hang-up calls that occurred only when I answered our phone; in stray hotel receipts or matchbooks from restaurants I didn't recognize. Did I look the other way because things, otherwise, were still good between us? Mac did work long hours and Italian phones *were* notoriously tricky. Did I know every restaurant in Rome where Mac might dine his sources? Maybe he'd paid that bill at the small, expensive hotel near the central train station for a visiting colleague and claimed it back later on expenses.

I didn't really believe Mac slept with the bureau intern, fresh out of the Missouri School of Journalism, despite her crazy allegations in a crumpled letter I found, stuck in a wad of papers on the desk in the study. I refused to believe he'd slept with a prostitute, though there was no other convincing explanation for the half-empty packet of condoms in his jacket pocket when he returned from Warsaw—Mac would have used them only if he feared disease of the commercial variety.

Mostly, I overlooked these things because I still believed his love for me was far more substantive than any transient pleasure, blowing like tumbleweed across his path.

Or, maybe, it was this simple: I wanted to believe him.

Did I look the other way? A lot of marriages were built on less.

⁂

Mac surprised me by popping home at lunchtime one afternoon. It was cold but the sun was shining and his spirits were high.

"Cairo, Lu. Arab League meeting in Cairo Wednesday. Crisis talks." He picked up a round, plastic container from the counter and peered dubiously into it.

"Leftovers?" He smelled it and made a face.

I grabbed it away. "It's a face cream, thank you very much. Avocado and yoghurt; Suha made it. At least I think it's for my face."

"Yuk. Doesn't it need refrigeration?"

I pushed past to rummage in the refrigerator myself. "Don't worry, I'll find something. Sandwich okay?"

He picked up a couple of oranges from a bowl on the kitchen table and juggled them in the air.

"So, want to go?"

"Where?" With no electricity for two days running, the refrigerator proved as unyielding as a fallow field. A sad carrot, two sorry tomatoes, and a smell more pungent than the face cream.

"Cairo." One orange hit the floor, then another. "Isn't there any bread? Never mind." He ignored the oranges and pulled me to him.

"How about you come too, do the tourist thing while I cover the meeting. Things are quiet at the moment. Maybe I'll stay on in Cairo a couple extra days and do a feature. You can help and then the magazine will have to pay for your ticket."

⁂

The plane hardly taxied on the runway at Beirut International before a sharp ascent into the skies that made me wish for solid ground, even if it were back in Lebanon.

"Vertical takeoff. Harder for a sniper to hit it this way." Mac grinned at my reaction as the plane bumped and fought its way through the cloud cover. "There you go, the smoking sign's off already."

I smoked and fretted about flying projectiles and turbulence and hijackers all the way to Cairo. But weeks of Lebanon-induced stress fell away as we stepped out into the shambling Arrivals Hall at Cairo airport, as if worries and fear could be stowed in a large suitcase, for mandatory collection on departure. Over the next few days, I'd face nothing more challenging than deciding how to spend free time while Mac was wrapped up with the Arab League. I felt unburdened in a way I had not since we left Rome, and I determined to make the most of it.

While Mac pursued Arab officials the next day, I spent hours trawling the Egyptian Museum, gawking at the dusty collections along with thousands of other tourists. During a break in the meeting the next afternoon, I coaxed Mac out to the pyramids, in a hotel taxi that belied its decrepitude to make the journey to Giza in a bone-rattling twenty minutes. While the driver waited in his ancient vehicle, we hastily toured around the great stone structures, ignoring offers of would-be guides and entreaties from trinket sellers and the hordes of small ragged children who dogged our steps, begging for *baksheesh*. Mac posed for my camera in front of the Sphinx with only minor complaint, but refused to ride a camel, despite the insistence of the man leading the bedraggled beast along by a red belt that must have once belonged to a woman's dress. That night, we joined the Jessers, old friends of Mac's, and their friends, the Goldmans, for dinner at the Gezira Club on the island of Zamalek, in the middle of the Nile, and Mac was careful not to drink too much, in case there was a development in the Arab League story when we got back to the hotel. There wasn't and so we had a tender night.

The meeting broke up by the next morning, and Mac dragged

me off to the Khan al-Khalili, the sprawling bazaar, where he bought a dark leather camel seat, after haggling good-naturedly with the shopkeeper, which pleased the shopkeeper enormously, and then, because it seemed to please Mac enormously, I let him buy me a gaudy, silken caftan, plum colored with golden embroidery down the front, that I knew would hang unworn in my closet, alongside other unloved garments—an inappropriate cocktail dress, a jacket with padded shoulders—Mac had chosen for me over the years.

We took our lunch late in the afternoon at a café in the bazaar and, while the grilled fish was excellent, we didn't spot any of the Cairo glitterati our taxi driver assured us frequented the place. Afterward, I accompanied Mac on an interview for his story, featuring an elderly architect who'd designed an eco-friendly village in the Nile Delta several decades before such things were fashionable. The architect lived in the crumbling remains of an Islamic palace, though with the gnarled warren of other buildings that had sprung up around it over a couple of centuries, it was difficult to distinguish where the palace started or stopped, or, indeed, that it had ever been a place of grandeur at all.

While Mac talked with the old man, I wandered up a flight of stairs, found an opening to the roof, and stepped out to discover a breathtaking panorama of the Old City unfolding before me.

As the sun pooled in regal hues over the rooftops, a man appeared several buildings away and opened a large metal cage, releasing a flock of white homing pigeons. In splendid formation they flew until almost out of sight, then soared back, dipping and swerving in huge, graceful arcs.

I don't know how long I watched, but eventually I heard Mac

call from the doorway and signalled to him to join me and as he did, the first echoes of the *muezzin* wafted on the evening air from the minarets of the city, a thousand voices as one, calling the faithful to prayer.

I held Mac's hand, transfixed, and for a few moments, because my heart was so full, it felt like God was right there, wrapped around us in the cool of the air, and I wanted to tell Mac that.

Instead, I said, "I love you, Mac," and held my breath as I waited for his reply.

❈

Back in Beirut, life acquired a rhythm and pattern of its own. Twice, I went to the Whitfields' flat near the American University to meet Boz's wife, Jan, for coffee. Tall and blonde, she was relentlessly cheery and enthusiastic—what Fretwell called "jolly hockey sticks." Her late father's diplomatic postings had included Cairo, Damascus, and Beirut a few years before the civil war, and though Jan and her sister stayed behind at an English boarding school during term time, they'd spent holidays and summers with their parents exploring the region.

Lebanon's current state distressed but didn't faze her, not so far. Certainly, Jan said, some people left after the Israeli invasion— diplomats sent their families away and several press corps wives, in particular those with children, sought sanctuary in Cyprus or Amman. But she wouldn't go unless Boz wanted to, and he had no intention of leaving this story. No, the Whitfields and their daughter, Hanna, were in Beirut for the duration, however long that might be. In the meantime, there was still plenty to do, as long as one took sensible precautions. The Lebanese were wonderful, cultured people—Christian and Moslem alike—gracious hosts, she said, and I'd soon realize there was a great camaraderie here, a bit like London during the Blitz. It was just a question, really, of making the best of a bad situation and the Lebanese were certainly skilled at that. We could all learn from them.

To me, she was practically a parody of the British stiff upper lip. Conversely, she must have found me naïve and woefully unprepared, for although she was always friendly, it was clear she held no brief for those of us made of lesser stuff, and I resented the condescension I presumed cloaked her kindness.

Funny enough, all these years later, I was reminded of Jan recently, when reading the obituary of Britain's Queen Mother, who refused to evacuate the young princesses from London when Nazi bombs pounded the city. "The Princesses would never leave without me, and I couldn't leave without the King and the King will never leave." Why, that was Jan Whitfield, I thought with a shiver, and in my heart, sent her a silent apology for the way I had judged and found her wanting.

For at the end of my tale, who will you judge to have been the better woman? Despite my twenty-nine years, I, Larissa Helen Kershaw, known forever now to one and all as Lara McCauley, was still governed by a poverty of spirit. I was still a girl in those early months of 1983. Though I would not be for much longer.

Another time, when I met Jan at the Summerland Hotel for lunch, she brought a British friend, Emma Khadouri, a pretty, silver-haired woman who'd lived in Beirut since her marriage twenty years before to a Lebanese banker, now retired. In turn, the Whitfields and Khadouris came for a dinner I cooked myself. Nothing complicated from my Italian repertoire, just steaks from

Smith's and produce from the local greengrocer. The faithful Suha helped serve and clean up. Mac and I also went to a cocktail party given by a professor at the American University, where I met another university wife, who invited me to a tea, where, in turn, I met several other women, including a Lebanese sculptor and a woman doing a Ph.D. on the impact of war on the migratory patterns of birds, particularly storks, a subject I was sure would have interested my parents. Thousands of birds, she said, had been slaughtered so far in Lebanon. Machine-gunning flocks of birds was a favourite pastime of bored gunmen, particularly some of the younger ones. In the absence of a childhood, what else did they have to do?

But I digress. I was explaining how I tried to fit in. The truth is, the acquaintances I made didn't extend much further than an occasional return invitation. Mac preferred the boisterous atmosphere at the Commodore to entertaining other couples at home. We were all too busy anyway. Staying alive, like the Bee Gees song. Just staying alive. There was too much going on for half-hearted alliances to flourish the way they might have in a city not at war. I didn't mind. I wasn't that keen on Jan Whitfield and her friends. My world already revolved around Mac; that was the way we both preferred it.

While he was out tending to the news of the day, I did whatever necessary to fill my own. Mornings for me usually passed in the apartment, listening to the BBC world service on Mac's short-wave Sony, doing crosswords, perusing week-old issues of the *International Herald Tribune* or the *Times*—the London one, not New York. With a fragmented attention span, it was easier re-reading old favorites, and I cheated boredom this way, with Trollope, Eliot, Jane Austin. On a whim, I bought again not just *The Quiet American,* but every Graham Greene novel I could find, because I'd only brought one. The others were in storage back in Italy, along with most of our other belongings.

Often, I went out somewhere, anywhere, just to get out, to Smith's for groceries, to the dry cleaner's, the newsstand for cigarettes, the shops along Hamra Street, though I didn't buy much there. I also spent more than a few hours at the kitchen table—a book propped open in front of me, the radio or Ella Fitzgerald on our portable tape player, humming in the background—and tore huge hunks of flat, unleavened Arabic bread into tiny pieces, to make feed for the birds. The bread, soft when fresh, quickly became tough if left out any length of time, and, to Suha's bewilderment, I did this until my fingers ached and the bowl was full.

I'd spread the fruits of this obsessive labor out on the wide balcony rail, and then wait inside to see if there were any takers. Usually not. Local militiamen, probably.

More often than not, the dried crumbs, like good intentions, simply lifted off the balcony and vanished in the Mediterranean breeze.

An attempt to re-create Cairo, to inject some of the magic of that moment into a lonely life in Beirut? The explanation is simpler, I think. It was a form of escape, it helped tick off the hours until time to go to the Commodore.

That, of course, was the centerpiece of my day. In Rome, I'd helped out at the magazine office from time to time, answering phones, for example, when Mac's assistant was on holiday. Here, however, Mac discouraged me from meeting him at the bureau. Too busy, too small, too crowded already, he insisted. Better to wait at the Commodore. Of course, there were days when it was unsafe to travel even that short distance, and I'd stay home, waiting for the fighting to ease up enough for Mac to make his way back. Most evenings, however, I left our flat on foot, skittering through still-light streets, propelled by the urgency of fear. Occasionally, I called the Commodore and they sent a taxi over.

In another city, perhaps in another marriage, I'd have chosen to stay home by myself, but this was Beirut and even a smoky bar filled with the driftwood of the international press corps was preferable to an evening cowering alone in the hallway. Not just that—I was learning and the Commodore was my classroom. My time abroad hadn't yet turned me into a seasoned expatriate. I was no Jan Whitfield. I'd followed European politics when we lived in Rome and kept up with American events from afar. But, because it hadn't affected my life directly, I'd hardly ever read stories about the Middle East, except on the front page—hijackings, political assassinations, uprisings. I had read the stories about Israel's invasion of Lebanon the year before and all the horrific things that followed, of course, but I would've paid far closer attention had I known we'd shortly be living there ourselves.

But I didn't know, and consequently, it's fair to say that until I came to Lebanon, I had no Middle East world view, no grand framework in which to slot the events unfolding around us.

"The French always take a long view, not the quick fix. They're concerned with implementing policy over two or three decades. That's why they were such an effective colonial power," said Fretwell thoughtfully, as he watched Coco shred the newspapers lining his cage.

"The important thing, Fretwell, my man, is the colonial legacy—beautiful women, excellent cuisine, and beaucoup de sunshine," said Martin, raising his glass slightly in tribute.

"Copy that." Mac clinked glasses with him.

"Ah, the French. The French," growled Hamid. "They learned their lesson in Lebanon once already. They will learn it all over again, the hard way, along with everyone else."

He grumbled along those lines for a moment or two, then turned to me.

"And you, Madam McCauley." He always said "Madam" to me in quotes, as though I were a marital impostor, even when the man to whom I was lawfully wed sat only a barstool away. "You think the Americans are safe here? I can tell you, your passport won't be worth two piasters, it won't protect you when they come for the Americans. These are very bad people who are coming up now. They will not respect you because you are a woman. They will not care. They will howl your blood."

"'Howl your blood?'" Martin hooted, "Hey, that's a new one."

"Cut it out, will you, Hamid," Mac said. "You're scaring her and she can hardly get through the day without pissing herself as it is."

Unnecessarily crude, okay, but truth underlay the remark and we all knew it. Mac cut off my protest, signalling Marwan for another round. He also gestured for a refill of Hamid's glass, which Hamid accepted without thanks, while I sulked quietly until we left for home.

FIVE

ONE MORNING, I awoke before Mac, quietly slipped into my clothes, and crept out of the flat, closing the heavy wooden door gently behind me. Weeks earlier, at the Whitfields' apartment, Mac had admired their extensive collection of beautiful old Persian carpets and begged Jan to show me the shop near the Commodore where she bought them for a fraction of what they'd cost in the outside world. I'd managed to get out of it twice, to Mac's annoyance, but I could only claim to be busy so many times. Now, the day had arrived and I'd agreed, without enthusiasm, to meet her for breakfast at the Commodore first.

The sun was just skirting the horizon and our neighborhood wore an early-morning air of desertion. Closer to the Commodore, however, heavy traffic clogged the streets and above the honking and cursing rose the unmistakable dull rumble of a crowd on the move. I briefly considered turning back, but I was already late. Jan would be waiting. The thought of having to explain my cowardice spurred me onward, though I was worried about what, exactly, I was heading toward.

The sounds drew closer but before I realized what was happening, I'd turned a corner to behold a parade of grotesque pageantry, a thousand fighters strong, a frightening array of men and metal to rival anything either reality or my own overwrought imagination, thus far, had conjured up. Tough young Druze militiamen jostled Kurds with rocket-propelled grenade launchers strapped to their sweating backs; fierce Libyans with bayonets on their rifles marched stubbled cheek by bearded jowl with equally sinister Shiite and leftist gunmen, automatic weapons tight against their chests, flanked by Palestinian fighters with black and white checkered keffiyehs, the head-covering popularized in the western mind by Yasser Arafat. In the middle of it all, pickup trucks and jeeps packed with fighters hanging out the windows, sitting on top of the vehicles, crawled along like bizarre, martial floats

I pressed as far back into a doorway as possible, praying no one would see me, and trying not to hyperventilate. As the last of the crowd passed by and the street cleared, I spied Thomas and Martin on the other side, standing with a couple of Canadian journalists I knew only by sight, and rushed across on wobbly legs to join them.

"What in God's name was that all about?" It came out as a cry.

"Funeral procession," Martin called over his shoulder, already mentally preparing to file his story. "'Scuse me, got to run."

"Sheikh Hamdi Khaleed," Thomas spelled out for the Canadians, who scribbled in their notebooks, and scrambled off to catch up with the procession.

"An influential Druze mufti," he explained to me.

"Well"—I hid my trembling hands in my jacket pockets—"I certainly wasn't expecting that before breakfast."

"Yes, it was rather impressive," Thomas allowed. "Everyone was there. Normally, they'd all be trying to kill each other."

"And here I was afraid they'd try to kill *me*," I laughed unconvincingly.

Thomas pretended not to notice. He was good at that.

"Come on, I'll escort you to the Commodore."

As we walked along, Thomas explained such a rare display of unity among Beirut's fractious militias was testimony to the mufti's popularity. Hard as it was to believe, he added, only about two percent of the population was armed.

Two percent! And yet it seemed to me that just about anyone who'd ever had a bad thought in his head came to Lebanon to try it out.

❖

One thing I never understood was why so many of the foreigners who lived in Beirut stayed on the West Side, giving rise to a common perception it was somehow less dangerous than the Christian side. Not safer, mind you. Less dangerous. Despite the impressive panoply of violence—the shelling and shooting and other violence bridging both sides of the divide—the Christians were the ones exercising tight control over their turf, from what I was seeing. On the West Side, constant chaos reigned: shelling from the East, big car bombs and small dynamite bombs and clashing militias, as our local gunmen, Leftists and Moslems of all stripes, turned their weapons on each other almost as often as they did the Christians.

For Thomas, living on the West Side, the lack of a central authority—the lack of any authority—meant his killers would never be called to account.

At least, not in any certain way.

I did meet up with Jan, but the day didn't go well. I was still shaken from the funeral procession, which, irritatingly, seemed to amuse her.

"It must have been quite a shock," she chuckled, when Thomas deposited me in the Commodore lobby, where she was waiting. "Why, you're a wreck, you poor dear," she added. "We'll get you a good, strong cup of tea. Leave the carpets for another day."

It turned out she'd also seen the funeral procession, a few blocks north of where I'd stumbled across it. But she wasn't shaking like a leaf. No one pitied her.

I offered her a cigarette. I forgot she didn't smoke. I drank the tea she ordered, the whole time wanting a coffee. No wonder we didn't get on.

Fear was not the only thing that set me apart from the Commodore crowd, but it was always there, a glass wall—transparent but impermeable. The sheer thrill of daily survival that pumped adrenalin into them somehow eluded me. Each day presented a new menace, like a living video game. Survive one horror and another popped up.

I feared I'd be a casualty of this war I was only visiting, my memory consigned to bleary-eyed reminiscing in the bar: remember Mac's wife, killed in crossfire on Hamra; killed crossing the Green Line; killed when a shell hit her building; in a car bomb; by a twelve-year-old Hezbollah recruit with a Kalashnikov at a checkpoint? Or, better, killed by militiamen sniping at avian innocents?

There were too many ways to die in this, a war I hardly understood, a war that started long before we came, and would continue long after we left. Most of all, perhaps, I feared irony would underpin my death in the Commodore closing time conversation: Hey, remember Mac's wife? Afraid she would die—and look, she did!

It was such an end that greeted Mac's predecessor, Roger Schuster, the great war correspondent who'd survived Korea, Vietnam, the Congo, and was dutifully working his way through the Lebanese conflict when death and irony struck in tandem: a skiing accident on holiday in the French Alps.

As if the single fact of his death weren't enough, it was the irony of how he died that was bemoaned.

This was how it flowed most evenings, the gossip and the guessing. Like Wall Street brokers gathered at the end of the day to exchange stock tips in a volatile market, the Commodore bred its own style of insider trading: careful, snipers at the Port Crossing today; the Belgian political attaché's wife is back and doesn't know about the translator from German Radio; new flying checkpoint overnight on the airport road; heard Engelstoft's in trouble over expenses; masked gunmen smashed up Ali's café, robbed diners at gunpoint, oh shit.

For most of the foreign press corps, many of the foreigners, and quite a few Beirutis themselves, the Commodore stood at the confluence of it all, information, fact, rumor, and lies, cascading in a ceaseless roar.

Against this setting loomed Hamid, large and gloomy, with the hooded, sunken eyes of a lizard. He usually took his drink in a quiet corner of the bar, with hard-looking men Mac speculated were Syrian intelligence, or with Thomas, Fretwell or Victor, or one of the other European journalists. He scorned his Lebanese colleagues, along with the Americans, and most of all he kept to himself, contributing an occasional cynical comment or doom-laden observation to whichever conversation he homed in on. Hamid regarded most of the foreign press corps with contempt. The only journalists of whom he approved were those who'd been in Beirut at the start of the civil war. Most of them were, by now, gone. But their bravery and talent, according to Hamid, were of legendary proportions, dwarfing any efforts by this current crop of second-rate correspondents, these has-beens and won't-ever-bes.

Everyone knew Hamid was corrupt, that he skimmed hundreds—thousands—of dollars off the office accounts every month. Who could say whether it was one hundred or five hundred dollars he'd paid in bribes or protection money to keep local gunmen from blowing up the office or kidnapping the correspondent for ransom? You had to stay on the good side of the militias, no argument there. And who knew exactly what arrangements were made with the drivers hanging around outside the office? Most spoke little English and, in any case, depended on Hamid for their livelihood. If he charged the company one hundred U.S. dollars a day, who could say what portion they got and what percentage he kept for himself? Who, indeed, was brave or foolhardy enough to challenge Beirut bookkeeping? For accountants, in Tokyo, New York or London or Paris, this was an accepted part of the cost of doing business in a war zone.

Perversely, I felt more of a bond with Hamid than almost anyone else I'd met so far in Beirut, though it was hardly mutual. The bond, as I saw it, was fear, although ours were different, and expressed in different ways. I feared the unknown. Hamid's had a more tangible core—an awful miscellany of casual Lebanese violence, readily recounted by the others. A young son, his only child, killed riding his bicycle at the start of the civil war; a favorite aunt and uncle killed in shelling; legions of friends and acquaintances killed or kidnapped and never seen again; his home near the National Museum destroyed, his half-Syrian wife long removed to relatives in Damascus, distant, disengaged. He could have followed, but chose to stay, money and power believed his anchors. The money helped pay the large mortgage he took on a fancy villa on the outskirts of Paris, chosen by his wife. His power, at least its illusion, derived from the fact everyone believed he also worked for Syrian intelligence, or at the very least Lebanese.

Did we really need to know more? Wasn't it obvious it might be safer not to, especially if he did have connections in high places?

❖

Hamid never seemed to go home, even on the weekends, and no one seemed to know where he lived now. He was usually lurking in the vicinity of the Commodore—in the lobby, the coffee shop, the bar, the restaurant, in the TV Kansai office, or in the office above it, which housed German TV. I wondered if he slept in his office, but as he wore a different crisp Egyptian-cotton shirt every day, it seemed unlikely. Possibly he had his own arrangement with the Commodore, I never knew for sure. Like I said, everyone had something private going on. Hamid discouraged intimacy, and, as most people were a little afraid of him, few inquired too closely. Even when I came to know him better, I never attempted a trespass into his confidence.

I could have asked Thomas. But forthcoming as he was about most things, I felt he'd keep his own counsel on this matter, and had I asked, it's likely I would've learned little.

Instead, I asked Thomas about jobs. Mac might've forgotten what

I said that first night, but I hadn't. Nor, apparently, had Thomas, for he didn't seem at all surprised one evening when I asked him about finding a job. He immediately suggested talking to Gifford, the hearty Australian tape editor in the TV Kansai office, to see if he'd let me observe him at work, to learn about putting television news stories together.

By the next day, Thomas had started the ball rolling, though I don't suppose it was ever Gifford's intention I'd turn up nearly every day. Nor was it mine, at first. But soon enough, I found myself regularly heading for the backroom at TV Kansai, where the editing suite was set up. Gifford was generous with his expertise and an undemanding companion. Rendered taciturn most mornings by a habitual hangover, he usually reached sociability by midday and I timed my visits accordingly. He didn't seem to mind and I gratefully listened to him expound upon the finer points of his craft. Eventually, he began letting me experiment with the edit machines, the high point of any session for me.

This was the early '80s, before the endless cycle of corporate mergers, cost cutting, and layoffs now routine in the television news industry, and the money still flowed in a big way. The U.S. networks, in particular, manned by the last generation of giants, were prepared to spend whatever it took to stay on top of breaking news. That meant a bureau in a place like Beirut had the proverbial cast of thousands: reporters, producers, cameramen, sound technicians, fixers, translators, videotape editors. Even the drivers played a vital role, shepherding crews and reporters from one terrible incident to the next, along dangerous routes, through shelling or shooting, running the gauntlet of gunmen along the Beirut-

Damascus highway to get the videotape safely over the Syrian bor-der. It was impossible to feed videotape from Beirut, as Lebanese TV's feed point had been destroyed during earlier fighting, which meant all edited stories and pictures had to be put up onto the satellite from Damascus in order to be relayed on to Tokyo, London, New York, and points beyond.

Yoshi Takemura, TV Kansai's correspondent, was a bit of a loner himself. I rarely saw him; he was either out in the field or sequestered in his office in the bureau. He was elaborately polite but hardly ever spoke to me, perhaps having learned through expe-rience with Hamid not to inquire too closely, no matter how odd the arrangement. Beirut was full of anomalies. He knew I was Mac's wife; perhaps he thought I was also Gifford's girlfriend.

Hamid, of course, knew better.

I didn't realize it at the time, but, at least initially, I'd never have been allowed to spend so much time there if Hamid hadn't given his tacit approval. I'm not sure why he did; he certainly didn't care much for Mac and it was clear he thought I was useless.

I became Gifford's protégé and unpaid assistant by default, run-ning small errands for him or making phone calls. I also helped Hamid, when he deigned to let me. Sometimes, he had me run messages to other offices, or pick up newspapers from across the street—the sort of things the drivers usually did.

But I didn't mind. It was fine with me. I needed something to do. It wasn't so much that I needed a job as a place to *be*.

SIX

THE ISRAELI INVASION of Lebanon a year earlier and the subsequent exodus of the PLO left Beirut a crazy quilt of vengeful violence, where the control of neighborhoods changed overnight. Bushy-bearded Hezbollah fighters, loyal to the ayatollahs of Iran, might suddenly appear where the gunmen from mainstream Sunni Moslem militias were just a day before. In other parts of town, Druze warriors turned their guns on the Shiite Amal militia positions, and, all the while, kept up the ever-present cacophonic artillery exchanges with Christians across the Green Line.

Beirut police weren't particularly bold. With good reason. The militias had bigger guns and far less hesitation about using them. Which explains why the police often remained barricaded in their stations, perimeters reinforced with mountains of sandbags.

Even the police were scared.

The Israelis still occupied a slice of Lebanon that ran up into the Chouf Mountains, and several times since we'd been here, Israeli soldiers made preliminary probes of the U.S. Marine lines, as if to test their determination and ability to keep them from going further. So far, the Americans had, without major incident. But as these attempts intensified, in a manner more and more hostile, these ostensible allies found themselves pointing weapons at each other. Mac reported in the magazine that a special meeting was called between U.S. and Israeli officers in Beirut, to try to agree on precise boundaries beyond which the Israelis would not go. An emergency communications network was set up between them.

A few days later, on February 2, three Israeli tanks attempted to pass through a Marine checkpoint commanded by a Captain Charles B. Johnson.

"He told them to halt and, when they didn't, drew his pistol, jumped on the lead Israeli tank, and told them to back the hell up," Mac recounted with relish. He loved these stories.

The incident was still being discussed in our living room, a few nights later, when several dozen people came for a belated house-warming.

I moved around with a tray of Lebanese delicacies Suha had prepared.

Fretwell was deep in conversation with Brigette Steiner, a French photographer whose graphic black-and-white images of the first days of the civil war can still be found in smaller, arty shops around Europe.

"Bloody Israelis, poking around for trouble, as if there isn't enough already," Fretwell was saying.

"Provoking the Americans," Brigette agreed. She turned to include me into the conversation.

"Aren't they allies?"

"They're not supposed to be—mission of presence and all that, you know. The U.S. is here as a neutral force," Fretwell said.

Brigette nodded vigorously.

I was baffled. Why provoke an ally? Why pretend not to be allies?

"You're doing some work now for the Japanese, I hear?" Fahti, from the Reuters news agency asked me, as he accepted another miniskewer of minted lamb off the platter.

"Heavens, no," I said. "Bruce Gifford lets me watch him edit videotape. That's all."

"You have a good teacher. Bruce has been around and seen a lot."

"Yes, wonderful," I said, momentarily distracted as I spied Nadia, talking to Nils Erik and Doug Allen across the way. She glistened and shimmered, like malevolent heat off a summer sidewalk, hair swept up in a tortoise shell clip, lips and eyelids coated with glittery goo. Her dress was laced with metallic thread, a clichéd glimpse of black lace in the confident cleavage. Even across the room, she looked over-perfumed, as proximity soon proved.

"Hello, Lara."

"Would you like one?" I offered the tray, an exemplary hostess.

She shook her head, casting a critical eye about the room. "You haven't done much, have you? It looks as bad as when Roger was here."

It wasn't what she said, but how, and though I was wary of Nadia her caustic tone caught me off guard.

"Barrett is an important man here in the Lebanon. His home should refract his position."

"You mean, reflect."

"Yes, of course. Reflect," she said quickly. She seemed as taken aback by her error as my correction of it. Still, she persisted.

"What do you do all day long, anyway?"

"Excuse me?"

"What do you *do* all day? Suha cleans your flat. She shops. Washes your laundry, cooks."

I should have said, so what, this is her job, we pay her for these things. But I didn't. I knew Nadia saw me as a spoiled American housewife, frittering away my days, making no useful contribution whatsoever.

"I do cook." I tried not to sound too defensive.

She looked at Suha's handiwork, on the tray I held, with raised eyebrows.

"Well, not all of it. I also help Mac."

"Yeah, someone's got to pry the scotch glass from his sorry ass at night." Martin laughed, as he sidled up to us. He winked at me and said, "Hello, doll face." Then he put out a hand to stroke Nadia's hair and said, in teasing admiration, "Look at you, sweet cheeks, good enough to eat."

He pulled her close, as if to make good on the threat; she drew back with a slight grimace. From his breath, it wasn't his first drink of the evening. Martin tried to keep his arm around her, but she cast it off.

"Excuse me," I said, hurriedly. "Must go check on Suha."

I headed for the kitchen, but was waylaid by our landlord, a white-haired Dutchman in his sixties, who'd lived with his Lebanese wife in this quarter of the city for the better part of the last forty years. He offered me a cigarette and took one himself.

As he talked about his daughters, his grandchildren and their accomplishments, I saw Mac, an odd look on his face, step out onto the balcony. I stubbed out my cigarette, made a hasty excuse to Mr. Van de Voort, and threaded my way through the crowd.

I stopped in the doorway. I could see Nadia out there, in the shadows, standing in the corner of the railing against the wall, look-ing out at the sea. She wouldn't be visible to those inside the living room; only at this angle, this close, was her outline apparent. Mac must have known she was there, for he went straight up behind her and to my horror, reached out and furtively caressed her buttocks.

She turned, smiling, to face him—and, in that instant, me, as well. Or so I thought, for I was certain she looked straight at me and, for at least a heartbeat, was just as shocked. I can't say for certain. But then she chuckled, low in her throat, and, murmuring something I could not hear, held her arms open to Mac and pressed up against him.

I turned and stumbled through the living room. I stayed in the bathroom off our bedroom, waiting until most everyone left, before emerging. Among the few remaining, no one had noticed my absence. Nadia was gone, although I didn't know under what circumstances. Very quickly now, the last of the guests trickled out, several of them determined to brave the Green Line, to continue the revelry at a jazz club in East Beirut, even at this hour. Suha, who stayed to helped tidy the apartment, left in fairly short order, and soon I was alone with Mac.

He was in the bedroom, taking his clothes off, and to my amazement laughed out loud when I confronted him.

"God, Lu, you are so silly sometimes. Nadia works for me. So she had too much to drink and got a little carried away. Hey, I have that effect on women. Doesn't mean a thing." He flung his shirt on the bed and started to remove his trousers.

"Mac, I saw you."

"I'm telling you, it was nothing."

He stepped out of his boxer shorts.

"Listen, Lara Lu, Nadia does have a certain kind of sex appeal, maybe, for some guys, but she's not my type."

I glared at him.

"Besides, she's got a boyfriend."

He lunged at me, trying to tickle me. "And I've got a wife"

"I saw you, Mac," I cried, brushing away his fingers. "You promised me, last year in Rome, you promised you wouldn't."

"What? Don't be such a goose."

He stuck his lower lip out in exaggerated pleading, picked up the boxer shorts and put them over his head, the elastic waistband framing his face like a picture frame, and, with arms extended, called, "Come on, Lu. Please. Don't be mad."

Angry as I was, he looked so comical, I couldn't help laughing, first a little, then helplessly, as his fingers found their target and plucked my ribs like a guitar.

I never met Colonel Johnson, but Martin and Fahti and Doug did, and, for a while anyway, he was something of a folk hero in Lebanon. The American who stood up to the Israelis. Afterward, the Israelis tried to make light of the incident, accusing the Beirut press corps of exaggerating a routine event. The ranking Israeli officer at the scene claimed at one point that Johnson was drinking. The attempt to vilify him backfired. Here was splendid irony: apparently, the man was a teetotaller.

Despite the frantic pace, the TV Kansai edit room felt a safe spot in a sea of insanity. Nothing seemed to crack Gifford's composure. His large, loud, Australian presence was reassuring, especially on days when the city foamed with violence. No matter what the distraction outside, he kept going, invulnerable in this self-contained world, working his TV magic, constructing video tales by marrying bits of tape and sound with Yoshi's recorded narrative.

It was more than a refuge. Little by little, I was picking up a valuable skill, which might one day enable me to find gainful employment—as indeed, it did, and does to this day.

But that was yet to come, you understand, and, at the time, I was under no illusion that learning to edit suddenly made me a journalist. Gifford was, without a doubt, a fine one—for all his bluff and good humor, he had a sharp, insightful editorial eye. But while he could teach the technical aspect of editing, there are some things others simply cannot impart to you, and the truth is I didn't have the requisite self-tools to be a journalist. By then, I knew enough to know that I didn't share their passion or soul, that, unlike these hardy men and women, I had no sense of mission, felt no calling.

Unlike Mac, unlike Thomas, Fretwell, or Martin, unlike the photographers and TV crews who faced incessant danger to get their footage, I had no desire to go out and witness events for myself. Lebanon didn't need *me* to tell its story. I wasn't here by choice; I'd come as Mac's wife, nothing more.

During a brief visit to Meridian once, my aunt, Parthenope, asked Mac if he wasn't afraid to go to dangerous places, like Vietnam or Beirut, and Mac replied, very seriously, that, yes ma'am, he surely was.

Then why did he go, she wanted to know, shaking her loose grey curls, to which Mac, clutching hands to chest, replied theatrically, in a booming baritone, "Destiny overruled me . . . A spirit in my feet said go . . . and I went!"

My aunt loved it. I was impressed. Mac was so clever.

It was actually a quote from the American Civil War photographer Mathew Brady. I didn't know that until years later, when leafing through a book about the original combat photographers that had belonged to Schuster.

For all of that, it was as true for Mac as it was for the others.

❖

Why *did* they do it? It wasn't all heroics and grand ideals. Maybe there was another element—a horror of being ordinary, ending up as the night copy desk chief at the *Kalamazoo Herald,* like Mac's college friend, polishing someone else's lousy prose.

A front-page byline, a magazine cover story, footage picked up by the networks—all these things came with a kind of endorphin high, an addiction more confounding than the nightly rounds of drinks they shared at the Commodore. And all the while, deriving comfort from the knowledge that what they did mattered. They'd escaped the ordinary.

I was almost jealous. There was no spirit in my feet. I wasn't a journalist. I was hardly a reliable witness to history. Some days I felt I'd slipped through a crack in reality and ended up here. Once or twice, I woke up in the morning surprised to find myself still in Beirut, having dreamed my way out in the night.

SEVEN

FEBRUARY 1983 WAS EVEN colder than January, ushered in by one of the worst winter storms in Lebanese history. There was no central heating in those old buildings, and, had there been, no power to run it most of the time, anyway. Daytime was just about bearable, but as the moon emerged from the sun's wake, the miserly patches of heat generated by our portable gas heater quickly dissipated in the chill. I wore an old fisherman's knit sweater over a flannel nightdress from L.L. Bean and thick woollen socks with leather soles, and even Mac, who preferred to sleep nude, wore a sweatshirt and pajamas to bed every night.

In the heart of the Middle East, I was never colder.

By the third week, thick snow draped the mountains beyond Beirut, and there were reports of villages cut off, travellers stranded on rural roads.

Peacekeepers from the Multinational Force pitched in, with the Americans offering helicopters and mechanized equipment. In the tentacles of Lebanese politics, however, even a straightforward humanitarian act morphed into a political problem, and because the areas affected were behind positions held by Syrian soldiers, the Americans weren't allowed to help until Syria agreed.

Syrian president Hafez al Assad cooperated, but Mother

Nature was more willful. Treacherous, icy conditions forced an almost immediate halt to U.S. helicopter attempts to reach the area. When they tried again the next day, one helicopter suddenly found itself at the center of a radar lock, almost certainly Syrian. The American pilot decided to chance the landing and, just as suddenly, the lock disappeared.

❊

"You know how it is, enemies one minute, the next minute, they're kissing you on both cheeks like long lost brothers," Martin said at the Commodore bar later. He still had on the down coat and heavy boots he'd worn up into the mountains that day, before getting turned back at a checkpoint.

"So, these Americans land their chopper," he continued, "and the Syrian soldiers, probably the same guys who had them in the crosshairs just a couple minutes before, come out of nowhere, like, and offer them coffee."

"From what I hear, sounds like the Syrians should've offered to share their hot rations with those Lebanese civilians who were stuck in their cars," Mac said.

"Too late," Martin said, in answer to my puzzled look. "There were two dead people in the first car the Marines reached. Trapped for several days, froze to death, probably." He looked thoughtful. "But they were only about half a mile from the Syrian position. You have to wonder if they knew."

"But Mac said they airlifted out survivors." I was surprised.

"Yeah, like I told you three times, that was the second helicopter," Mac said, impatiently. "You don't frigging listen."

I fiddled with my glass. Perhaps I hadn't listened carefully. But this kind of public criticism was new. He'd scolded me recently at the bar in front of everyone, saying I needed "to keep up," when I hadn't followed a news story as closely as he thought I should have, and we'd fought about it later, at home.

I tried to smile like I didn't mind.

"You know, that second chopper had to pull off a pretty intricate maneuver to get in there," Martin said kindly, as if to make amends. "They managed to get four other people out and *they* were still alive."

"No thanks to the Syrians," Fretwell put in. He wearily slung his weight onto the stool next to Martin, spilling an untidy wad of newspapers onto the countertop, and letting his leather shoulder bag slip to the floor. Marwan expertly slid a gin and tonic across to him.

"Hey, Ian. Yeah, the Syrians sure slowed things up on the ground. Lebanese had to reroute the U.S. and the French mechanized columns, the amtracs, to keep them out of Syrian-controlled areas," Martin continued, shoving Fretwell's debris to the side.

"Guess they didn't want to take any chances—piss off the Syrians and bingo! There goes your freakin' amtrac," Mac said, swirling the ice cubes around in the amber liquid.

"Amtrac?" I ventured. A flicker of annoyance crossed Mac's face.

"Amphibious tractor," Martin explained. "Can surf waves up to thirty feet."

"In the mountains?"

Mac stared hard at me.

"Works on land too." Martin said.

Fretwell sighed. "Bloody Syrians actually stopped the Italians about six miles short of their destination." He sighed again. "Bloody politics."

"Maybe not, Ian. Perhaps they knew there was no point, that the people were already dead," Thomas contributed.

"Well, they certainly would be dead, if they didn't get any help." Mac mimed a drink request to Marwan, listening quietly, arms folded, leaning against the cash register.

"I can assure you that was not the case." Thomas spoke firmly but politely.

"Oh, can you now?"

Thomas misread Mac's sarcasm and started to explain, but Mac talked over him.

"Tell me, Warkowski, you got a direct pipeline to the Syrian military command? Or old Hafez himself? Got a Syrian connection you want to share with us, pal?" It would have been barroom banter from someone else, from Martin for example, but with Mac, it just wasn't.

Thomas looked taken aback.

Martin spoke up quickly.

"Oh shut up, Mac," Martin gestured to Marwan. "Marwan, sir, could you bring another round for these gentlemen, please? Mac here's buying."

❁

Geography, too, conspired against Lebanon, for the Bekaa Valley soon flooded with the runoff of melting mountain snows. This time, the Lebanese government borrowed small boats from the Marines for the rescue effort. As I saw it, the U.S. was working hard to preserve its image.

❁

President Reagan sent U.S. Marines to Lebanon twice in 1982. First, in August, following the Israeli invasion two months before. It involved around eight hundred men from the U.S. 32nd Marine

Amphibious Unit, or MAU as they called it and along with France, Italy, and Britain they composed a Multinational Force to oversee the evacuation of the PLO and other Palestinian fighters and Syrian soldiers from Beirut.

It was to be a limited engagement, the president insisted, "in no case . . . longer than 30 days." Washington's foreign service elite and its top military men were at odds over the deployment. Diplomats hoped it would help Israel and Syria agree to the evacuation. But the Pentagon questioned the wisdom of committing U.S. forces without a clear military objective.

The Pentagon would be hideously vindicated.

However, that particular outcome was not foreseen in September 1982, when, amid great scenes of "celebratory" firing, the PLO left, without major incident. Mission accomplished, the Marines withdrew on schedule. Imagine the collective sigh of relief from Washington to Tel Aviv to Tunis, where the PLO leadership was to be lodged.

What no one calculated were the odds of the Marines returning to Lebanon, which is, of course, exactly what happened, and with such fatal consequences.

They returned before the end of the month, on September 30, 1982.

※

For a few weeks in between, a little bud of autumnal optimism blossomed—the lights came on at night, shopkeepers returned to their premises, rubble was removed from the streets, and repairs were underway to damaged buildings. A string of American bigwigs dropped by Beirut, flush with the mission's success.

But this was Lebanon. The Americans had yet to learn that fresh calamity brutally nipped optimism wherever it dared flower.

※

The lesson wasn't long in coming.

Lebanon's new President Bashir Gemayel, himself a Christian warlord, was assassinated. Fingers pointed at Syria, as they would again two decades later when Rafik Hariri was killed. Lebanon's fragile coalition government fell apart and shortly after Sabra and Chatila became international synonyms for atrocity, when, in a frenzied few hours, Christian militiamen massacred hundreds of Palestinian civilians, vulnerable in the camps without the protection of the fighters who had been evacuated. In the ensuing tumult, Parliament picked President Gemayel's younger brother Amin to be his successor, and one of his first acts was to beg the MNF to come back to protect West Beirut, until the Lebanese Army could take over.

The U.S. agreed to return to restore order, and optimistically coined this effort a "mission of presence." Establishing a "presence," had never before been part of Marine training. It was a new vernacular. New territory. Marines were a fighting force, used to being on the move. Now they were asked to assume a static role as peacekeepers, under rules of engagement that would prohibit them from firing except in exceptional circumstances. Their weapons wouldn't be loaded. Permission would be required to put a round in the chamber.

Twelve hundred Marines went in this time. Just before returning, the 32nd MAU received a commendation for its role in the PLO evacuation, in a ceremony aboard a U.S. warship off the coast of Lebanon. Thus honored, and thus, perhaps, restored, the

Marines linked up with more than two thousand French and Italian troops already in place, and a British armoured regiment of 1st The Queen's Dragoon Guards.

Beirut was divided up into different sectors under MNF control. The Marines were barracked at Beirut International Airport, south of the city, in a poor, crowded Shiite area, a buffer between Israeli troops and the citizens of West Beirut.

❈

My aunt Parthenope mailed us a cartoon from a North Carolina newspaper, showing Marines clustered around a picture of a bottomless pit entitled "Map of Lebanon." The commander, pointing to it, tells them, "OK, Marines—we're faced with Druze and Shia Moslems being backed by the Syrians against the Christian Phalangists. The Druze and the Shias are divided among themselves, as are the Christians. The Israeli pullout is leaving a gap that the Lebanese Army probably can't fill and the PLO is creeping back in. Nobody likes us and it's all preceded by 2,000 years of bloodshed. Any questions?"

❈

The first Marine casualties came almost immediately upon their return. A corporal was killed and three others wounded when a cluster bomb exploded. The bomb was manufactured in the U.S. and left behind by the Israelis, irony underscoring the peril of the Marine's new mission.

We weren't in Lebanon yet, but I say this so you'll see how the chain of events that constituted the next stage of our lives was already unfolding.

❈

By the time we arrived in January 1983, the Multinational Force had been in place again for just over three months. It would be a couple more before the metaphorical shoe dropped. The MNF came under direct attack for the first time in March. An Italian peacekeeper was killed and nine comrades wounded. The next day, a hand grenade was lobbed at Marines as they patrolled on foot. Five soldiers were injured. A fundamentalist Islamic group claimed responsibility in a telephone call to one of the wire services.

It was starting to unravel.

Maybe we should have seen where it would lead, but I don't believe anyone could have predicted, even after the first attack, that events would unfold quite as catastrophically as they did.

⁜

That's not exactly true. Hamid's visions of the future had been increasingly direful. One chilly afternoon not far into the month, he turned down the volume on the battered Sony radio on his desk at TV Kansai and turned around to see me, a smug look on his face.

"It is a wake-up call. They are fools. They will all leave here in body bags," he said.

"They're trying to help, Hamid."

I still believed it then, you know, still believed the United States had the right idea, that it could save Lebanon from itself, from its own warring factions. If a few American servicemen were injured in the line of duty, why that was truly regrettable, and I was saddened, both as a human being and as an American myself, but it was, unquestionably, part of the price of doing what was right.

"They do not understand Lebanon or the Middle East. They barge in and say it is to keep peace, but it isn't, because there isn't any peace and hasn't been for years," Hamid snarled. "No. They are here to save Christian government, which is supporting the

Lebanese Forces, which is fighting Moslems and which you, Madam McCauley, must see yourself by now."

Gifford called me from the back room, allowing me to make a timely exit. I could easily picture Hamid's reaction if I said the U.S. was acting in what it believed was Lebanon's best interest. He'd savage me. And he'd have lots of company. Most Lebanese I met were convinced an unhappy outcome was the only possible outcome. Hardly anyone seemed to share my views, not the other ex-pats, not the journalists, my own husband included. Mac said I was naïve and uninformed. Typical American. I retorted I'd take that as a compliment. He said that just proved his point and we went to bed mad that night.

⁂

Hamid took special delight in trying to scare me.

"They will kidnap your husband and they will torture him," he might begin, carefully setting out his food on the newspapers spread over his desktop at lunchtime.

"You will never see him again," he'd continue, in a dramatic, gravelly voice.

"They will kidnap all the Americans." This, between big bites of *khubz Arabi*, Lebanese bread, seasoned with *zaatar*, and dipped into hummus.

Hamid ate greedily, noisily, his appetite proportionately enhanced by the scale of the danger he described.

"You must leave right away," he'd continue enthusiastically, scooping up *tabouleh*.

"Your passport will not save you. No, it will be your death warrant," he would say, flicking away bits of parsley intent on clinging to his moustache.

I was at once oddly thrilled and appalled at the impending catastrophe, described in almost loving detail—being dragged through the streets, the chanting of the crowds, the public execution.

At home, when I complained about Hamid to Mac, he shrugged it off.

"Ignore him, for Pete's sake. He wants all the foreigners out so nobody will question what kind of racket he's running."

"But no one questions him now. Everyone's afraid of him. So why does he want everyone to leave?"

"Witnesses."

"But if Yoshi goes, and everybody else goes, the office would close and he won't make any money."

"Hamid was here long before Yoshi and Japanese TV came in and he'll be here long after all of us are gone. If he doesn't work for the Japanese, he'll work for somebody else."

"If anyone's left."

"Look, Lara, none of the networks want to pull out first. It's a game of chicken. Even if it gets too dangerous to keep a foreigner here, they'll always need people like Hamid to keep their operations up and running until things settle down and they can send the big boys back in."

I learned not to discuss the politics of the U.S. mission with Mac, but Hamid wouldn't let me off so lightly. He continued to goad me whenever he saw me, which was nearly every day. I had to wonder if that was why he tolerated my presence.

I was his personal American to hector and bully.

EIGHT

ONE AFTERNOON, Hamid was well into a rant and I was gamely listening, when, without warning, he produced a key from a trouser pocket, and, with a great flourish, unlocked the bottom drawer of his desk and pulled out a pistol.

He placed it on the worn, green cardboard blotter on his desk and tilted his head up, looking expectantly at me. In a country awash with the heavy weaponry of war, it looked about as dangerous as a stapler. Nevertheless, it was a gun, probably loaded, and in Hamid's hands, more than enough to scare me.

Tears of fright sprang into my eyes.

"Hamid, please—put it away!"

Apparently gratified by my response, he picked it up and examined it carefully.

"This . . . this is my own protection."

"Hamid, please!"

"Ah, but you see, I have photographs," he said, confidingly, and looked up at me with a smirk. "I can prove any time I want."

"Photographs of what? Prove what?" My voice was wobbly with fear.

"Never mind. Mind your own business."

Hamid admired the pistol a bit longer, then shoved it back in the drawer, locked it, and returned the key to his pocket.

"Not a word, Madam McCauley, or you will be sorry," he concluded, sounding triumphant, a broad, nasty smile on his face.

❈

"Okay, I agree, that was stupid of him, but don't get too worked up about it," Mac said, when I relayed the incident to him over a late dinner at home that night. I was still confused; Hamid seemed to be testing me and I couldn't figure out whether I had passed or failed.

Mac thought I was overreacting. He finished his dinner and watched me push mine, mostly untouched, around on my plate.

"Oh, come on. It's not like he pulled the gun *on* you. He's showing off. That's Hamid for you. You know that. He's a power freak. He's a lunatic."

"How can I go back, knowing he's got a gun in his desk?"

"Get over it, Lara."

"Get over it?"

"It's nothing. Certainly not worth getting worked up about. He's letting you know who's in charge, that's all. Trying to scare you. Don't give him the satisfaction."

"Too late, it worked. Scared the hell out of me." The memory prompted an involuntary shudder. I pushed my plate away.

Mac speared a piece of meat from it and shoved it in his mouth, chewing furiously.

"This is Beirut, remember?" He gave a half laugh. "If you're never more than ten feet away from a rat in New York City... well, it's the same thing here, only guns. Rats, too, probably. But guns, you bet your ass."

"You know, Lara," he said, after an icy pause, "Nobody told you to go to TV Kansai in the first place. It's not like you have a real job. If you don't like it, don't go. It's that simple."

"But I enjoy it, Mac. It's just Hamid. He scares me."

"There's a lot worse could happen in Beirut than Hamid giving you a hard time. Get used to it. Go or don't go, who cares."

Mac was mad. I could see that, and I should have stopped there, but I was trying to understand.

"How can I go back after this? I wish you could have heard him."

"Don't you ever shut up?"

Mac flung down his fork; it bounced onto the floor. He stood up abruptly and shoved his chair into the table, and all the dishes clattered, as if begging his forgiveness.

"There's *real* danger here and you're worrying about some office Bozo. Understand this, Lara: you're not important enough for Hamid to give a shit about, one way or another. You don't matter. So, either shut up or stay home."

He grabbed the bottle of scotch off the sideboard and headed for the balcony. I slunk off to bed alone, wondering if he was right. If I had got it wrong. And if so, what the implications were.

Mindful of Mac's words, I moped around home the next morning, sprawled on the sofa in the living room, with a mug of coffee and a fresh pack of cigarettes, listening to the English news bulletin on Voice of Lebanon, the most reliable of the Christian stations.

The news wasn't good. Leftist forces, the Druze and Palestinians—they weren't all gone, you know—turned their heavy guns on Beirut Airport instead of each other, for a change, and two

Marines and a sailor were wounded. Even I needed no expert to see the emerging pattern of attacks against the MNF, the airport, and the Lebanese Army.

I drank another coffee, this time on the balcony, wrapped against the chill in a heavy woollen bathrobe, seeking a thread of the pleasure the sunshine and sea view always brought Mac. It proved elusive. I brought out the damaged Olivetti and tried to type a letter to friends back in New York, but found little to say. Hope all is well, we are fine, Lebanon is very interesting. I sought the casual tone I imagined Mac would take, were he the sort to write letters home. That, too, eluded me.

It was hard to argue with Mac's logic about not going to TV Kansai. But it was harder to stay away.

Hamid was shouting down the phone in Arabic, too busy to look up, when I scurried through the front room. Apparently, the crew was stopped on the way to take pictures of the attack at the airport. It wasn't clear who stopped them—militias, Lebanese Army, or Americans.

In the edit room, Gifford seemed as unconcerned as Mac when I closed the door and recounted the incident with Hamid.

"Aw, get over it, mate, it's nothing. It's an old pistol Hamid's had forever. He likes to wave it around now and again, when he's had a bit too much to drink, just so's you know who's boss. So what." He flicked the control wheel of the player unit with his forefinger and spun the pictures forward.

"He wasn't drunk, Bruce. He was eating lunch."

"Same difference."

"He said he had photographs or something weird."

Gifford punched the stop button.

"Lara. You're a new audience, yeah? You get on pretty good with him, considering how he treats most people, yeah? He hardly even speaks to me, only that kind of grunt thing he does. You don't want to go rocking the boat now, do you."

"I guess not."

"Don't give him a hard time, and he'll leave you alone." Gifford pressed play and looked at his watch. "I've only got thirty minutes to finish this piece, eh, and it's touch and go about the driver making Damascus in time. Yoshi's flipping out."

He turned his attention back to the silent images scuttling across the screen in double-time.

Hamid ignored me on my hasty exit, as well, seemingly engrossed in the torrent of words issuing from the radio.

✻

Moslem militias were not the Marines' only problem. Relations with the Israelis deteriorated rapidly after the incident with Colonel Johnson. In mid-March, the Commandant of the U.S. Marine Corps complained the Israelis deliberately carried out a campaign of systematic harassment against the Marines. It was, he said, "inconceivable . . . why Americans serving in peacekeeping roles must be harassed, endangered by an ally." These incidents, he said, were evidently orchestrated to serve "obtuse Israeli political purposes."

Mac speculated they hoped to convince the Americans of the need to coordinate actions, which, in turn, would emphasize they were partners—contrary to the U.S. position of neutrality.

✻

Mac had mixed feelings about my going to TV Kansai. Thomas's role in arranging it was only a small part of it; mainly, Mac was jealous. For the first time in our marriage, I had something separate, independent of it, something that didn't involve him, something that wasn't filtered through him. He was childish like that, you know. He pushed me to socialize, to fit in, to rise to the occasion—the situation—and hoped TV Kansai would help in that respect. At the same time, the orbit of our shared life unmistakably revolved around him and he found subtle ways to discourage me from forming close ties with other people.

So this was difficult. Used to calling the shots, he suddenly faced a perceptible shift in the marital balance of power. Perhaps a defining shift, although I was hardly aware of it then.

But understand it was neither to please nor punish Mac that I ended up going back to work with Gifford. Quite simply, I didn't want to stay home.

However, I made a tactical decision to avoid Hamid as much as possible. Discreetly, so as not to cause offense.

⁂

The sun was high overhead outside as I left the office one afternoon, the wail of Taroub, a popular Egyptian singer, trailing me down Hamra Street. On impulse, I turned and retraced my steps to buy a tape from the boy at the side of the road, his cart piled high with cassettes. *Ya Sitti Ya Khityara*. The tune has stayed with me to this day, although I never listened to the tape again once I left Lebanon.

The Armenian-Lebanese man who owns a deli in my London neighborhood recently translated the title for me and it surprised me to learn this haunting tune, the background score for my Lebanon memories, was, essentially, a jolly little ditty, called "My Old Grandmother." Only through ignorance, uninformed listening, and a subsequently over-romanticized recollection had it acquired any deeper significance. In retrospect, a metaphor for my life in Lebanon.

But at the time, it was my first such purchase from a street vendor, a small, satisfying achievement. The boy asked for twelve Lebanese pounds—about three dollars. I handed it over and tucked the tape into my shoulder bag.

"Far too much," said a quiet voice beside me. I looked up.

"Hello, Thomas. No, three dollars isn't a lot. I don't want to quibble."

"Maybe, maybe. But he expects you to negotiate. It's part of the art of the transaction."

"Surely he's just happy to have the money." I adjusted the strap on my shoulder bag and we set off down the street together.

"Lara, this is more than simple commerce," Thomas stopped and made as if to lecture me. "It is part of a social equation and you have skipped an important step. It's supposed to go this way: he asks too much, you say a lower price, this happens once or twice more, then he suggests a compromise and you agree. You save money; he saves face. You're happy; he's happy. Simple, really."

We both laughed, and walked on, in companionable silence, for another block. I wasn't sure, but it suddenly seemed we were going somewhere together and the prospect made me lighthearted.

Thomas stopped in front of a shabby shop, its sign "Gifts" in English, French, and Arabic still legible, though dulled by age and city grime.

"Try again?" He smiled and my heart gave a happy little bounce. Mac almost certainly would get mad when he learned about this impromptu shopping expedition, but it seemed a small price for the pleasure of an hour spent in Thomas's company.

I was already weighing up options, you see, and making choices. Taking risks.

Thomas held the door open. I stepped inside.

⁂

"Thomas, *ya habibi*," the shopkeeper greeted him effusively, with a hug and a flood of courtesies exchanged in Arabic.

"Salim, this is Lara McCauley."

"Ah, yes, American you are? *Ahlan wa sahlan*. Welcome, Mrs. Lara, welcome."

It was a fact of my life in those days that almost everywhere I went, people instinctively knew I was American. No one ever mistook me for Canadian or British or Australian, as if "Made in the USA" were stamped across my forehead in ink, visible to all, save myself.

"Come, we will have tea," Salim snapped his fingers and called out. A small boy poked his head out through a beaded curtain hiding a room behind the counter. I knew it couldn't be so but he looked remarkably like the boy who sold me the tape.

Within minutes, he had returned with a silver tray, balancing three glasses filled with steaming, minty tea, a mound of sugar resting on the bottom, like crystals on the seabed. I hated to disturb it with my spoon.

We sat on small stools, Salim and Thomas talking in English, for my benefit, though I didn't contribute much. Instead, I sipped tea and stared at the dusty jumble of goods. I'd never seen this shop before but, like the boy, it all looked familiar, like so many of the other touristy shops found in the sadder quarters of the

Middle East's cities: rough woven cushions, fashioned from carpet cuttings or old saddle bags, heaped in a corner, shelves filled with ornamental coffee pots, with domed tops and arced spouts, in copper, in brass, tarnished by neglect. Embroidered cotton tablecloths were piled on the counter, near pairs of solid brass candlestick holders shaped like serpents and peacocks. The glass cases held carved Koran holders and inlaid wooden boxes, a speciality of Lebanon and Syria and Egypt, covered inside with maroon felt, some designed for backgammon or chess. Ceramic plates and tiles festooned the walls, decorated with geometric designs, or with calligraphy.

Thomas followed my gaze. "Inscriptions from the Koran. You'll see them everywhere because Islam forbids using the human form as decoration."

He smiled at Salim. "Salim must show you the Jezzine ware, he has a fine collection. It is a speciality of the South, from the Christian village of Jezzine."

Salim obediently opened a thin leather box.

"The handles are made from the horns of the African buffaloes."

It was cutlery, surprisingly beautiful, and inlaid with mother-of-pearl.

"They are making them since before 1800," Salim said, pointing with a trembling, nicotine-stained finger, its nail yellowed and cracked, revealing his ancient age, like the inner rings of a redwood tree.

"See the bird, Mrs. Lara. It is the firebird. They gave them as presents to the sultans of the Ottoman empire."

He said this last bit so hopefully I felt I had no choice. I bought a set. I wasn't sure how much it cost in the end. Thomas negotiated the price and I had to borrow some of it from him. Afterward, he assured me it was excellent value for the money.

The argument with Mac wasn't as bad as anticipated. Genuine interest in my purchase outweighed his irritation about Thomas's role in it, and eventually he forgot to act angry. Jezzine was in an enclave in southern Lebanon, controlled by a Christian militia, and Mac was keen to interview its leader, a renegade former Lebanese Army major named Saad Haddad. Of particular interest to Mac's editors in New York was the fact Haddad's South Lebanon Army was armed and funded by Israel. At its peak, the SLA boasted a force of up to three thousand men. Haddad was a colorful, flamboyant fellow, but the interview was proving difficult to arrange.

That evening, Mac admired the pieces as he held them up for individual inspection, and the praise fell like water on parched flowers.

❈

The cutlery was far too grand for everyday use. I put it away in its huge, silk-lined, leather presentation case. We never used it in Beirut and the time is past now.

❈

The photographs Hamid mentioned? I never heard anything else about them, not from him nor from anyone else. Much later, I wondered if they'd involved Thomas in some way, but eventually concluded that, as with so many other things in Beirut, the episode was simply another lunatic moment at the edge of the world.

NINE

THE U.S. EMBASSY was blown up on April 18. As was too often the case in Beirut, the sun rose over a normal day, only to set over a fresh horror.

On this day it was a suicide bombing. The first time this tactic was used against American interests, anywhere. Ever. In hindsight, it was also a first toll of the bell for events leading to the World Trade Center, and a war to come in Iraq.

Mac left early that morning, without a good-bye. Our morning routine had changed. Our first few months in Beirut, bright light leaking through the heavy curtains woke me each day and I got up to make Mac's coffee. By April, however, Mac was getting his own, while I obstinately clung to sleep. That explains why, on this particular morning, as Suha left her home in East Beirut to navigate her way through the treacherous obstacle course that was the Green Line, I was still under the duvet in West Beirut, slipping in and out of a light, uncomfortable sleep and a dream that had me captive in a taxi endlessly negotiating a concrete maze of overpasses, around a city I could not identify.

Suha's key turning in the door awoke me and I emerged from the bedroom to see her carrying a brown bag of groceries for us—

fresh bread, tomatoes, and a trussed chicken from a market on her side of town. She communicated, quite effectively, with her own unique patois—a rough mixture of French, Arabic, with a sprinkling of English, a couple of German words and an impressive flurry of expansive gestures—the problems she'd had getting to our side of town that morning.

Suha was short and stout, an expression of permanent worry tattooed on her face. Her dark hair thinned along the center part and threaded with gray; her fingers were knotty, disfigured by years of hard work and, at a glance, there was little to distinguish her in a crowd of her countrymen. And, as with most of them, she commanded a daily ration of courage few outside a place like Beirut could imagine, much less summon. Though only a few miles as the crow flies, her commute was of breathtaking proportion, through some of the most dangerous territory on earth.

Suha came with the posting, like Nadia and Abdel Farid, and took her job as seriously as they did. Keeping house for the magazine's resident correspondent was a sacred duty, one she'd performed without complaint five days a week for the last ten years—well before the civil war started. She usually crossed the Green Line in a *service*, a communal minibus taxi, but even when fighting closed the crossings, Suha more often than not made the difficult passage on foot.

As Suha hung up her coat, exchanged shoes for house slippers, and prepared to restore order to our household, I poured myself a mug of tepid coffee left over from Mac's breakfast, and had an unsatisfactory wash with cold water. I checked the telex for messages from the New York office. Nothing. The electricity had been off several days. Mac left behind a fairly recent *International Herald Tribune*, which I thumbed through in the living room, listening to the female presenter on Voice of Lebanon rattle off various clashes and armed incidents around town, the way her counterparts in Boston or Chicago might give traffic or weather updates. She noted which parts of the city would have electricity that day and for how long. I made a mental note; the laundry was piling up. Our gasoline-powered generator sat on the little balcony outside our kitchen, but even with the door shut, it made a fearsome racket and because it frightened me, I used it only when Mac was home. I hated having a tank of gasoline just outside my kitchen anyway. One stray bullet and the flat was a fireball.

⁘

I planned to go into TV Kansai, so laid out lunch earlier than usual—hummus, cheese, pickles, and rich black olives to go with Suha's bread. I set a place for her, as well, and we ate together in comfortable silence in the vast kitchen.

She finished her work and had just left the apartment, and I was getting ready to leave myself, when a massive explosion shook West Beirut.

Frantic, I tried to call Mac. The line hummed with static but no dial tone. A curtain of chaos descended on the streets almost immediately: a cacophony of sirens wailing, horns honking, people shouting, bursts of automatic-weapons fire nearby. From the balcony, I could see stopped cars; Lebanese Army soldiers from the 6th Brigade and scores of gunmen had arrived quickly, blocking off the Corniche and the entire spectrum of human reaction: people gathering, milling about, frightened, unsure what to do or where to go.

That was the middle. Then, the extremes: people running toward the blast, spurred by Samaritan impulse, while others fled in the opposite direction, acting on primal instinct, self-survival. There was more of the latter, naturally. In Beirut, bombs often came in twos, sequentially, ten or fifteen minutes apart, with the second timed to kill would-be rescuers arriving on the scene. Given that, it never failed to amaze me how many Lebanese knowingly rushed headlong into the danger zone, a triumph of impulse over instinct.

Within minutes, Suha returned, sobbing hysterically and hyperventilating.

"American embassy, American embassy!" she shouted, waving her arms.

"Oh God, Suha, the embassy?"

"Boom, boom!"

That was clear enough. So, too, was the huge plume of smoke that billowed from the direction of the embassy, like a half-mast flag of gray, unfurling to the sea. Suha flung her arms around me and together we wept. Her panic was infectious and I couldn't think, couldn't decide whether to stay and wait for Mac or try to reach the Commodore. In the end, I took my cues from Suha, and we ran out together into the street, holding hands like lost children, to try to find out what, exactly, had happened.

We only gained a few hundred yards down the Corniche before soldiers stopped us. Pandemonium. By now, the men with guns had taken over the streets, shooting at anyone foolish enough to try breaching their lines. Beyond them, militiamen were firing shots into the skies above, and even in my present state I was mindful of the adage that what goes up must come down. So for a while, we stood on the fringe of the anxious crowd, catching glimpses of the frenzied scene on the other side; but it was impossible to decipher, and eventually we maneuvered through the swell of people to return home.

The radio stations carried the first accounts: Suha tried to translate, in her own fashion, the Arabic reports. Most of what she said was lost on me.

Eventually, of course, we'd all learn what had happened: how a van carrying a lethal payload of two thousand pounds of explosives had driven past a lone, sleeping Lebanese guard, crashed through barriers and into the embassy lobby, setting off a blast so powerful that the center portion of the seven-story building collapsed. We'd learn that sixty-three people died, seventeen of them American, and that many of them were in the embassy's lunchroom eating, just as Suha and I had been shortly before the bomb exploded. Most of the embassy's own security-guard detachment was inside the building when the bomb went off, and those not hurt were temporarily stunned.

French Marines from the MNF were the first on the scene. The embassy was in the sector under their control. A U.S. Marine reaction company arrived in short order. They would not have expected to come to Lebanon to have to help their own in this way.

❧

I will always remember the thick smoke and how it poured out of the ruined building. Not only could I smell it, I could taste it in the air, like bitter, charred hope, for days.

❧

Mac worked throughout the night. Everyone did.

He returned home briefly the next morning for a shower and clean clothes.

"Nightmare. More than sixty dead for sure—at least a dozen of them, maybe more, American."

I made coffee and brought it to the bedroom.

"And, get this: they got practically all the spooks," he sighed heavily.

I sat on the edge of the bed, holding socks and a shirt Suha had pressed in the pre-bomb hours the day before.

"How do you mean?" I handed him the socks and he sat down next to me to slip them on.

"The Middle East Director of the CIA was visiting from Washington," Mac said. "He was meeting with the Beirut Station Chief and his guys, up on the top floor of the embassy. They got 'em all."

"They're all dead?"

He nodded. "This isn't playtime for the boys at the end of the block, Lara. This is big stuff."

Chilling words. There was nothing to say.

"Your coffee's getting cold," I finally said.

He looked at it with distaste. "Just what I need. More caffeine. I'm already bouncing off the ceiling."

He sipped at it, grimacing.

"Mac, what does this mean?

"Who the hell knows what it means. It means whoever did this had inside info. Or they were lucky." He shook his head in disbelief. "Fucking. Lucky."

Mac was probably right. An American diplomat he interviewed some time afterward said he believed it was both and doubted the

U.S. intelligence community would ever recover from it. Ever is a long time, but I took his point.

※

We focused on the Americans, but most of the dead were Lebanese, for the inferno consumed the consular section.

Imagine the scene before the bomb exploded: anxious young men and women hoping the bureaucracy that parted them will reunite them with overseas fiancés or family; college students worried about the start of exams at UCLA or Seattle or MIT. Elderly women wanting to visit grandchildren whisked away from the war and growing up American now, in Florida or Michigan. Businessmen seeking a fresh start, or those returning briefly from new lives abroad to check on property and loved ones left behind.

Families would have queued for hours, smiling apologetically for the commotion their children made, for, bored with the long wait, they would have turned upon each other with the ferocity of lion cubs. Mothers would be tired and cross, alternately hushing them and unwrapping bits of food and producing bottles of water to buy a few minutes of peace. Careworn fathers would have clutched family passports and official forms and the crumpled documents that served to identify them as citizens worthy of U.S. visas—priceless tickets to a safer world. In a conflict riddled with irony—the sniper who unwittingly kills adherents of his own faith, the bomber who accidentally blows up a member of his own family—even in Lebanon, after all these years of war, to my mind it was harder to find irony greater or sadder.

Later that day, I heard on the radio that the Lebanese president called the American one to convey his "profound regret and sorrow" on behalf of the Lebanese people and asked the U.S. to persevere in the search for peace. President Reagan agreed, warning "this criminal attack" wouldn't deter the United States from rededicating itself to "this noble end."

"We will do what we know to be right," he said.

I knew Mac and his friends would mock the president. But I felt proud hearing those honorable words and I hadn't even voted for him. These were trying times, frightening times, but we were all only trying to do what we believed to be right, in the crucible that was Lebanon.

⁂

The dead Americans included a visiting journalist, State Department employees, AID staffers, three U.S. Army trainers, and, as Mac said, most of the CIA's Beirut station. I don't remember seeing the names of the Lebanese killed, though surely the Arabic press would've published them? Death equalizes in clichés only, and it seemed Lebanon already had suffered so many deaths, that more dead Lebanese—unless of local or international prominence—did not constitute big news the same way dead Americans did, at least not in the international media.

⁂

Comparing this with the New York attacks may seem an exaggeration, but the forces were gathering, and it's fair to say the shock of the assault and the terror it implanted in the hearts of Americans and other foreigners in Lebanon was proportionately equal, given the circumstances, in that time, in that place. And, as I now see, it was a first step on a road two decades long, that would, one day, snake around the ruins of the World Trade Center and on to Baghdad.

The world would never be quite the same. Henry Kissinger's "totally irresponsible elements" had seen to that. When protestors stormed the U.S. embassy in Teheran a few years earlier, they didn't blow themselves up. Now, people were not only interested in killing Americans. They were willing to kill themselves in order to do so.

⁂

With time, it would become apparent the bombing also marked another turning point: the first step in an ultimately successful campaign, orchestrated by Iranian-backed extremists, to force the U.S. out of Lebanon. In years to come, Hezbollah would boast it only took two men to do it, and they would be right: the suicide bomber at the embassy and his successor, six months later, at the Marine barracks.

⁂

An ominously named group claimed responsibility in a call to the French news agency, just minutes after the embassy exploded. *Al Jihad Al Islami*. Islamic Jihad. Only a few recognized the name at first. Soon, everyone would. Martin pointed out it also claimed the attacks on American, Italian, and French MNF soldiers in mid-March and seemed to be an offshoot of Hezbollah, sponsored by Iran and Syria. The caller after the embassy bombing warned it would strike against "the imperialist presence," including the Multinational Force, until western governments pulled out of Lebanon and stopped meddling in its politics.

If not articulated in precisely that fashion, everyone pretty much knew it, anyway.

"This is the beginning of the end," Hamid warned furiously from his perch in the Commodore a few days later.

"You will all have to go. No one is safe. They will not stop until you are all gone and we are all dead," he insisted, with what seemed grim relish.

"But we don't represent the U.S. government," I argued, as though logic might protect me. "We're neutral."

"Great, put that on a T-shirt and wear it," Martin said, with a laugh, " 'Neutral.' Think that'll stop them?"

"Think they'll stop to read it?" Nils Erik joined in. "In English?"

"Aw, shucks, do it in Arabic," Martin laughed again.

"I'm serious," I said, exasperated. "They need the press corps to get their story out. If you go, who will tell it?"

"Oh, Lara, they don't need us, darlin'. They'll get their story out, with or without little old you or little old me," Martin said, to general assent from the group.

Mac was sitting on the other side of Martin but, for once, not participating in the conversation. Our eyes met for a split second and as he turned away, I realized, with a start, he'd been watching me. Like a stranger. No, not watching. Judging.

With a sinking heart, I looked around to see if anyone else had caught this strange interplay. The others were still talking, but Hamid dropped out of the conversation and sat closer to me, with only an empty barstool between us.

It dawned on me that he'd been waiting for me to notice him.

"Fools," he muttered, with a little nod of his head in their direction. Then, resting one of his large, hairy arms on the empty stool, he leaned toward me.

"Listen to me, Madam McCauley," he said, urgently, his voice dropping, a magnet to draw me closer, as he waggled his finger at me. I moved in to hear him better. "Yes?" I said, voiced low to match his.

"You are ... *American,*" he pronounced, with the gravity of having diagnosed a terminal disease, along with all it implied.

In the days that followed, Hamid's prophecies were lavished upon us more and more frequently. That was his style and, as you know, it worked on me. For Mac and his friends, however, it was far less effective.

No one contradicted Hamid, not to his face. But the journalists were a largely cynical lot, and there were often unflattering remarks made out of Hamid's hearing. "Howl your blood" quickly became a favorite catchphrase around the bar, though I'm certain even some who snickered as they repeated the words had to suppress a small, internalized surge of fear.

If they coped through humor and camaraderie and alcohol, well, that was part of the job. Most of the press corps, it seemed, viewed the embassy bombing as a worrying development, but worrying developments were the norm in Lebanon. Among the journalists, maybe a few drank a bit more than usual, laughed a little too hard at some of their own lame jokes, but no one, really, talked of leaving.

❈

"I think we should leave," I told Mac a week later.

Without his knowledge, I'd called a shipping company that morning to inquire about the logistics of such a move. Most of our things were in storage. But we'd acquired new possessions in our few months here, too many to fit in the suitcases we came with. It wasn't just the eighty-eight-piece Jezzine cutlery, but the tall silver candlesticks Mac brought back from a trip to the East side; a huge Persian carpet he'd finally bought himself, from the shop near the hotel; two framed David Roberts prints I'd fallen in love with; and a large, wooden Damascus chest that Mac used to house his collection of single malt whiskeys. We also had a tric-trac table, intricately inlaid with wood and ivory, that Mac bought off a departing journalist for next to nothing; a set of antique silver serving bowls given to us by Mrs. Van de Voort, the landlord's wife, as a housewarming present; and, of course, the camel seat Mac insisted on bringing with us on the plane back from our trip to Cairo.

The woman at the shipping company wanted to know our destination and date of departure and I had no answers.

"Cut it out, Lara!" Mac barked. "You're driving me crazy. If you want to go, *go*. I can't. *I* have a job to do. This *is* my job."

He looked disgusted. "Nobody else is leaving anyway."

"It's not safe here anymore."

"Was it ever? You're out of your mind if you thought so," he said. "The embassy bomb doesn't change that."

"It does for me."

Mac motioned me over to where he sat on the sofa. I complied and he patted my knee.

"Nobody's after you personally, nobody's gunning for you. Sure, it's dangerous. But it's not any more dangerous for you, *personally*, than it was before."

It didn't feel that way.

But, of course, I didn't go. As scary as Beirut was, there wasn't much of an alternative. Besides, I had no intention of leaving Mac in Beirut with Nadia. We were drifting further apart and leaving now would be the final wrench.

I had nowhere else to go, anyway, and so we carried on, Mac and

I, yoked together like beasts of burden, harnessed to our marriage and the Beirut routine we'd fashioned for ourselves.

✷

For a time, the Americans operated out of the British embassy down the road. Eventually, the U.S. embassy would move across the Green Line to Aukar, on the Christian side, apart from a small consular staff, which remained in an otherwise vacant building on the Corniche, guarded by militiamen in a machine-gun nest, visible from the hill above.

Washington decided East Beirut was a safer place for the embassy. It was not possible to see Aukar's future, too, held a bombing, in which another sixteen people would die. That was still a year away, and by then the "mission of presence" would be over, I myself would be gone, and, I'm sorry to admit, this kind of horror would seem remote.

✷

Twenty years on, the U.S. embassy bombing of April 1983 has been reduced to a single entry in an ever-growing chronology of international terrorism—words on a page that do little justice to what happened in that particular place in that particular time.

I'll never forget my first sight of that shattered building, in the days after the bomb—the bare ugliness of the scene, the twisted rubble, the charred debris, the piles of dust coating it all. Ashes to ashes. I wanted to imprint it on my heart, to be able to remember how it touched me. Otherwise dimmed by time and distance, it would be reduced to merely another sorrowing memory, and it shouldn't. People died here and I wanted to honor them in some way more permanent than the cellophane-wrapped sympathy bouquet I added to the mound of flowers on the nearby pavement.

Perhaps if you walked by at the time you would have noticed me, eyes closed, lips moving, as I said a silent prayer for those whose names I knew and for those I'd never know. It didn't seem enough, even then, but I didn't know what else to do.

❁

"The end" Hamid was so fond of forecasting didn't come right away. But I thought of his words many times in the months that followed. Should I have left, gone without Mac? I wouldn't have changed the course of Lebanon's history by leaving then, but I do believe Thomas would still be alive, if I had.

TEN

THE EMBASSY BOMBING inked in a new, bold detail to the general backdrop of our lives in Beirut. But we were outsiders. It didn't have the same impact on the Lebanese. This was a land and a people familiar with the terrain of tragedy—not just the last seven years of civil war, but generations of bloodshed preceding it. By now, I'd skimmed enough of Schuster's library to know Lebanon's history was a checkerboard of invasion and conquest— the Romans, before Christ; the Arabs, seven centuries later. Trampled by Crusaders on their way to Jerusalem in the early twelfth century and subsumed by the Ottomans after defeating the Mamaluks in the sixteenth century. As for the savagery of its own tribes, Lebanon's Christians and Druze, still fighting in 1983, ended their first civil war in 1860, just as America's own War Between the States was heating up.

With the Lebanese nature thus honed by centuries of turmoil, you can understand how, in this circumstance, Beirutis allowed a momentary surrender to shock, an acknowledgment of the devastation and death. And then on with the business of living, as they had so often before, and would so often again. There was a return to more predictable, routine forms of violence—local gun battles, East-West artillery duels—and "the situation" regained a more familiar, even reassuring, rhythm.

Still, it curtailed my travels, already fairly restricted. I now kept to a narrow corridor between our flat and the Commodore, as if inside the protection of an ancient settlement's fortified city walls.

A few weeks later, however, I was feeling less jumpy, and a bit more settled, when Katya Karlstrom, from Swedish Radio, invited me to go to the souk, the old marketplace, in Basta. Formerly a Sunni stronghold, refugees from Shiite villages in southern Lebanon flooded into Basta, after the Israeli invasion the summer before, and the character of the neighborhood was changing. But many shops stayed open, despite being unable to sell the exotica amassed over the years for wealthy Lebanese and foreigners with hard currency—carpets, old paintings and books, inlaid furniture, china, silver, and silks. Jan Whitfield offered once, in a vague sort of way, to go there with me. But after the day of the mufti's funeral procession, when we didn't go to the carpet shop, she never brought it up again, and I didn't either. I did, however, ask Mac more than once. He was too busy.

So Katya's invitation pleased me and, as I was used to being appended to Mac's invitations, it also surprised me.

If the only picture you have of Beirut in 1983 is the one sketched by me so far, it might seem all the journalists were men. They far outnumbered women in the press corps, and as far as Mac's small circle went, predominated. But the women, too, formed a remarkable sorority, bold and brave in equal measure—whether Armenian like Katie, Lebanese like Nora, French like Francoise, or American like Jane and Robin and Cynde, or British like Julie. They wrote for newspapers that influenced foreign-policy makers from Washington to Paris to Riyadh; reported for wire services, so commuters could read about Lebanon's war from the safety of the 7:35 express to Penn Station. They wrote books explaining the rise of Shiite Islam in the Middle East, shot photographs and television footage that shocked the world and became the raw, new symbols of modern barbarity.

Like birds of a rare and sophisticated plumage, they dazzled and intimidated, and I mostly admired them from afar. The very fact they were here in their own right—not as dependents, not wives or girlfriends—required an assurance of personality I felt I'd never possess and made me aware how little I'd accomplished myself. Mac's assignment brought us to Beirut. And who was I? Mac's wife.

As I said before, Beirut presented Mac with an instant set of familiars, while my only goal was to survive this experience, with life, limbs, and marriage intact. Adjusting to this new life, keeping Mac happy, the pressure of my self-styled TV apprenticeship—all that was more than enough.

Perhaps tellingly, the woman I liked most so far wasn't a journalist or a journalist's wife, but an older woman, Lebanese, named Amina, a great friend of Thomas's. Tiny, sharp-featured, and still beautiful in her sixties, she was the widow of a well-known historian. Hostilities permitting, she hosted small, impromptu gatherings, where a Lebanese politician and a local artist might be found mixing with a French diplomat and an Australian academic. Not quite the glittering café society of pre-war Beirut, but a surprisingly robust little social salon for a war zone, especially given how many of her contemporaries had fled.

I visited several times and enjoyed her company. Friendly, not exactly friends—fine by me. Until Beirut, I never had time for other people, anyway. Until Beirut, I never had the need.

Katya was one of the few women, other than Amina, who went out of her way to try to connect with me. Thomas told me she'd married an archeology professor at Stockholm University while a graduate student herself, and that their messy divorce several years later resulted from his near-pathological jealousy over her blossoming career. Beirut offered the chance to go far, far away and the simultaneous benefit of being a clever career move, young female war reporters then being something of a novelty. She quickly found a niche in Lebanon, her calm manner earning the respect of male colleagues, not lightly bestowed in a war zone.

"Nerves of steel," Mac reported, after they'd spent several hours together stuck in a cellar off Hamra Street, with Martin and Nils Erik, during a particularly harrowing round of East-West shelling. Katya won the poker game they started to pass the time, which sent her stock even higher, and Mac could hardly contain his admiration. By contrast, I'd spent that evening in the concrete stairwell of our apartment building, with our downstairs neighbor and her eight-year-old daughter. We sat on separate steps, trapped with our own thoughts and fears. Noise from the shelling made impossible what would've been difficult with the language barrier, anyway. The little girl watched with wide, worried eyes from her seat below, as I lit one cigarette from the stub of another, and sipped directly from the bottle of scotch I'd grabbed on the way out. By the time the shelling stopped, it was all I could do to stagger back upstairs to the apartment and into bed.

At the Commodore afterward, Mac winked at Katya as he toasted her, flirtatiously. She lifted her glass, politely, in return, prompting

Mac to recount their ordeal, in even more glowing terms than before, which made Katya look rather uncomfortable. Perhaps I only imagined sympathy in her look when she glanced my way.

Not long after, Mac must have tried to know her better. He began complaining loudly whenever her name came up.

"Frigid old boot," he said once, with disgust. "She'll never get a man with that act."

Katya seemed fine to me the way she was, but I thought it wise to let it lie.

Mac vetoed the plan, when I first told him about Basta. Too dangerous. Nothing I said—including a reminder of the visits he'd made himself—swayed him. Before I had the chance to tell Katya, she approached Mac in the Commodore lobby, and, after a bit of banter, mentioned how pleased she was I was going, and of course, there was no way he could oppose it without looking ridiculous.

The night before the outing, he issued a number of caveats, as if to make up for the momentary lapse in judgment.

"Be careful not to call attention to yourself, for Christ's sake, Lara," he scolded, in a tone that implied I certainly would, if I hadn't already.

I pulled a plain white scarf out of a drawer and tentatively covered my hair with it, checking the mirror. My pale face and eyes looked alien beneath it. An Islamic imposter.

"Put that away. You look foolish. Maybe you've noticed, Western women don't cover up here, only Moslem ladies, and not all of them by any means." He pulled at some of my hair revealed below the scarf. "But don't flaunt it. Tie your hair back off your face."

"I'll be fine, Mac, stop worrying," I insisted, more bravely than I felt. But I removed the scarf.

"You really should lose those sunglasses. I told you, they're too much. Makes you stand out.

"And whatever you do, jeans are a no-no," he warned, heading for my wardrobe to rummage through the sparse collection hanging there.

"Here, wear this." He removed a long, shapeless, flowery cotton skirt and shoved it at me.

"It's too big for me, too loose around the waist."

"Ever heard of safety pins? And better wear dark tights or long socks. Cover your legs. Arms, too, unless you want to get pinched. Or worse."

He took a step back and folded his arms, looking critically at me. "If you do run into trouble, pretend you're Swedish, too. Talk gibberish, they won't know. Act like you don't understand. Do whatever the ice queen says; at least she knows how to take care of herself."

Mac left me so nervous I found it difficult to sleep that night, not much helped by the sounds of a running gun battle waged a few neighborhoods away.

I couldn't imagine Katya wasting one minute fussing about this outing or what to wear on it. A trivial event in her daily diary; in our household, it had taken on the proportions of a polar expedition.

The next day, she picked me up in a taxi from the Commodore which dropped us a couple of blocks from the souk. Despite Mac's warning—or, perhaps, because of it—I wore jeans, after all. Lack of sleep left me feeling peevish. I blamed him for that and for managing to turn my anticipation into anxiety.

Besides, he'd already left for the office and would never know.

On the walk to the souk, I tried not to look around, afraid to make eye contact with passersby, afraid to attract unwanted, potentially dangerous attention. It felt as if there were hidden eyes upon us, but Katya seemed quite unconcerned, making small talk, and pointing out sites of interest.

"Next street over is a Marabitoun post—or used to be. See there, that mosque, see where the shells hit? Ah, this shop I love. Beautiful fabrics. Want to look?"

There were no customers inside. The shopkeeper, reading an Arabic magazine so tattered he must have read it many times before, seemed taken aback, not only to have customers, but foreign ones at that, in his shop again. However, grasping the potential to hear his till ring out again, he quickly recovered, and shouted out the door for a local boy to bring us coffee. Neither of us wanted it; we both drank it.

The man proudly showed off the silken bolts of multicolored material, gleaming in the half-gloom of the shop. After much cajoling on his part, Katya finally bought a length of honey-colored crushed velvet, elaborately embroidered and fringed in silk. It was antique, the shopkeeper said, and worth far more than he asked. Katya announced she would wear it as a shawl, but I suspected she only bought it because she felt sorry for him.

Encouraged by this success, the shopkeeper tried vainly to interest us in purchasing other fabric, but eventually his enthusiasm visibly drained away. Sighing, he turned back to his magazine before we even left the store.

I bought nothing. Mac was more forthcoming with advice than money.

Back on the sidewalk, a group of men in Lebanese Army camouflage uniforms with rifles rushed down the street, past us.

"Sixth Brigade," Katya said quietly, more to herself than to me, "Wonder what this is."

The Sixth Brigade was largely composed of Shiite soldiers and now I felt particularly conspicuous in the blue jeans. Katya was far more sensibly dressed, as if for any eventuality, in a long skirt and long-sleeved shirt, much like what Mac had wanted me to wear.

The soldiers, however, were in a hurry and didn't spare us a glance. Shortly, we understood why.

We'd just entered a glass-fronted antiques shop, manned by a middle-aged couple, to inspect the big wooden Damascus chests displayed in the window, when we heard the rapid spit of automatic weapons, as loud and unmistakable as a thunder storm, maybe a street away. A battle was shaping up and, from the sound of it, moving swiftly in our direction.

"Hezbollah. Quickly, go quickly," the shopkeeper frantically gestured toward the door. "Is not safe. Go!"

In an obviously well-rehearsed routine, the shopkeeper's wife hurriedly locked the glass cases displaying antique spoons and bowls and other high-value silver items. She took out small trays of jewelry and locked them into a safe behind the counter.

"It's not safe to leave. We stay here until it's over," Katya said firmly. "We stay."

The frightening racket grew louder.

"Up stairs, go now, go now!" the husband shouted at us, herding us to a small metal staircase leading to a galleried loft area. Katya and I followed his wife up the stairs, pounding them two at a time, and once in the loft squeezed between the large chests, for cover. I closed my eyes, and prayed hard and silently. When I opened them again, I saw through the railings the shopkeeper was still downstairs.

He opened the front door and reached up to pull down metal shutters.

A deafening rattle of gunfire and suddenly, the entire storefront fell away in a shower of glass.

As we watched in horror, the shopkeeper was lifted off his feet by the force of the blast and flung to the side, his limbs flailing spastically, a bloodied gaping hole where his face had been.

It was a split second, yet it felt as if time had slowed and we were in a state of suspended animation. At Katya's command, I managed to help her prevent the wife from running back down to her husband. Even I could tell there was nothing we could do to help. His wife struggled against us, screaming, weeping, raging, but together we held her back. Katya spoke soothingly to her in Swedish. She wouldn't have understood the words, but it seemed to calm her. I know it helped calm me.

Outside, the guns faded away quickly; the brief, intense battle was over. In the street below, people were shouting, and we heard the wail of approaching sirens, as ambulances tried to reach the area.

Slowly, we released our hold on the shopkeeper's wife and helped her back down the stairs to what was now her husband's corpse. His spirit had fled, but life still leaked from his wounds. She sank down on the bloodied, glass-covered floor beside him, what was left of his head in her lap, sobbing quietly now and repeating in a low, singsong voice, *"Tamanya watalateen, tamanya watalateen."* Thirty-eight years, thirty-eight years, a lament of loss as tender as a lullaby.

❀

Within minutes, the small front room of the shop filled up with people and, as performers seasoned by tragedy who seemed to know the role they had to play. Two men started to lift the shopkeeper's body off his wife and onto a makeshift stretcher that two other men appeared to have brought with them, out of nowhere. Another man, younger, and in a suit jacket several sizes too large, who came with a young woman in a long brown dress, helped the shopkeeper's wife to her feet, hugged her, adjusted her clothes, stroked her hair and led her, still chanting her dirge, away from the premises. They all seemed to know her—perhaps friends or neighbors. The young couple I presumed to be family from they way they took charge of her, but perhaps it was only the kind of intimacy created by emergencies.

Without thinking, we seemed to be following them through the street, a haunted convoy.

"What happened?" Katya asked. No one answered. She repeated the question. No reply.

"She asked what happened!" They were my first words since we brought the shopkeeper's wife downstairs and I shouted them.

"Hezbollah and the Army," the young man in the baggy jacket replied in English, surprised, as he turned back to look at us, his arm still around the shopkeeper's wife. "The Army tried to make them go from this area but Hezbollah too strong, they fight back. This what is happened."

The damage wasn't confined to the shop; the street was a shambles. A man was dead, along with two others, crowds now gathered around their bodies, still in the street.

Back at his office, Mac scowled at my jeans, but—once he heard our harrowing account—embraced me tightly, in an increasingly rare display of affection.

"You all right? I mean, aside from the scare?" We recounted the horror and Mac took it in, stroking my head in a way he hadn't in a long time.

Nadia, too, listened, clicking disapprovingly. Eventually, she broke in.

"Why were you there anyway?" she interrupted indignantly. "Like vultures! To buy cheap antiques? To take advantage of desperate people selling off family treasures to feed their children?"

There was real contempt in her voice, which she didn't bother to conceal, even with Mac standing right there. The fact he was her boss and I was his wife didn't slow her.

"You should not be wandering around the city like that." She turned on Mac, suddenly. "You were stupid to let her go, Barrett. Stupid!"

"Nadia," Mac said, warningly.

But she turned back to me, "And who was the idiot of a driver to take you there?"

"Nadia!" Mac said harshly, "Go check the telex. Go. There's a good girl."

She wasn't the least intimidated.

"This is a city at war, not a shopping mall!"

She stalked off in a silken huff, slamming the door as she exited.

"Better not tell her it was my idea," Katya said, "I've already survived one firestorm today."

"Yep, she's a pistol, all right." Mac laughed appreciatively, though whether at Katya's remark or Nadia's spirited performance, I couldn't say.

Mac turned back to me and clasped my hands, pulling me to his chest. I felt safe, for the first time in hours, and, at least for the time being, Nadia was of no importance.

Mac released me, and thanked Katya for taking care of me.

"Darling, take Katya over to the bar, get yourself a drink, and I'll meet you there in a few minutes. I've just got to make a quick call to the States."

He kissed my forehead and tucked back a strand of hair that had escaped the mandatory ponytail.

But outside, Katya and I parted ways. She said she wanted to file a radio track, a first-person account of what happened, and while I believed her, I also suspected she was less than enthused at the prospect of a drink with Mac.

I hugged her and thanked her and meant it. We'd been through a terrible ordeal together, but I sensed, sadly, we'd never be any closer than we were as we walked our separate ways.

Mac didn't show up for more than an hour. By then, word had traveled and I had to repeat my story, first in the lobby and then in the bar. After Mac finally arrived, Gifford came into the bar and I told the story all over. Next, it was Fretwell with Boz and Jan, and by the time Nils Erik came in with the commercial attaché from the German embassy in Cyprus, I could see Mac had wearied of my tale.

When Martin popped his head in and saw us, he made a bee-line for me, grabbing a stool and pulling it up to us.

"Tell me everything. Don't miss one detail," he said, trying to get Marwan's attention.

Mac quickly cut in. "She got a scare all right, Marty boy. It was some rough stuff. But skip the gory details. Just three dead, locals—hardly news for the folks back in New York."

Martin waved Mac away, with a slight frown.

"Main thing is, are you okay, Lara?" Concern showed in his eyes.

I nodded gratefully at him.

"Yeah, she's fine. Terrible she had to see it, but at the end of the day, it was just a little Beirut bang-bang." Mac answered for me.

I could hardly believe what I was hearing.

"It wasn't bang-bang to me, Mac. A man was killed, he died right in front of us."

"I know and I'm sorry for him and for his poor wife and I'm sorry for you, that you had to see it happen." Mac patted my arm. "But Lu, I'll say it again: this is Lebanon. Bad shit happens all the time and it's normal here, it's dog bites man every damn day, and that, Dear Reader, ain't exactly news."

He emptied his glass.

"Katya's filing a story on it," I argued.

"Only because she was there and almost anything makes for a good story if you've experienced it yourself. Personal touch. Believe me, she wouldn't bother if it happened to someone else. Besides— who listens to Swedish radio?" He rolled his eyes.

"About eight million Swedes," Nils Erik said dryly. "And thousands of Norwegians on a clear day."

Martin didn't argue with Mac, merely picked up a handful of peanuts from the bar, tossed a few up in the air, caught them in his mouth, and said, "Don't take it too hard, Lara. Bad luck, getting caught up in something like that."

"I want to go home." I turned to Mac.

"Sure, Lu, I'll ask the front desk to get you a taxi," Mac said. "And I'll join you as quick as I can, but first, I've got to go back and finish expenses. I need to get them to New York before Andrew goes on vacation."

A man died in front of my very eyes, I'd been certain I would die myself, and Mac was going back to the office, as if this were a normal night.

I was upset leaving the hotel, but gradually, as nighttime Beirut rolled by from the back seat of my taxi, I started thinking perhaps I should tally my accrued blessings. All things considered, I was pretty lucky, I reckoned, in the way one does after a major trauma. Yes, I'd witnessed death this day, but it was not, after all, my own day to die. Nor was it my husband's.

We might yet get our own tamanya watalateen.

###

And yet in the days that followed, I was depressed, I felt listless and lethargic and perhaps it explains some of my subsequent behavior. A psychiatrist would call it post-traumatic stress disorder, and there would probably be truth in that. Seeing the shopkeeper die was not only the closest I'd come to my own death, but anyone else's. My parents' caskets were closed at the funeral home before the burial; after the car crash, the undertaker assured me it was better to remember them as they had been.

My thoughts returned to Basta over and over. Had the old couple any premonition that day would be his last? Had they lived in constant fear for the last decade, saying a prayer each morning because nightfall might be too late, living on the edge of each day because there might not be another? I preferred to think they'd awakened early, keen to get started on a day that appeared full of promise and sunshine, had morning coffee and breakfast bread, perhaps walked together the few blocks to open up the shop, stopping for cigarettes and a paper at the newsagent, and at the fruit and vegetable seller for a quick gossip and a shared hope business might pick up. Perhaps they did all these things in a normal way, never imagining how this day might end.

In a quiet moment, I asked Abdel Farid if he could find out their names. I didn't want Mac to know about my request, afraid he'd think it overly sentimental, perhaps ghoulish. But I'd shared the moment of that man's death, the most fundamental intimacy there is, and it deeply troubled me not to know his name.

Abdel Farid's cousin found someone who did, along with other salient details of Mahmoud Ali Ahmed's life. He and his wife, Rashida, had indeed been married thirty-eight years, and had three sons and a daughter. The oldest son was now a mechanical engineer in Dubai. The other two jointly owned a deli outside Baltimore, Maryland, and had become U.S. citizens. The daughter, a graduate student in Canada when the time the civil war started seven years earlier, overstayed her visa and married a Quebecois. Over the years, these children, collectively and individually, had begged their parents to shut up shop and come live in one of the countries they now called home.

After Mahmoud Ali Ahmed's death, Abdel Farid heard, his widow was planning to join her eldest son in Dubai. There was nothing left for her in Lebanon. She couldn't even sell the lease on their shop, which would soon enough be taken over by squatters, anyway.

Lebanon taught me to look for the irony in death, but as far as

I could tell, there was none in this randomness. There was nothing ordinary about the place and times in which Mahmoud Ali Ahmed lived and died, but he was, in essence, an ordinary man and his death was exactly as it seemed—a straightforward, monumental waste of human life.

I leave this story with one more thought: much as I hate to admit it, Mac was right, in a way.

It was Beirut bang-bang.

It was not a decisive battle, although within months, Hezbollah would have sway enough to put up its own logo—a raised fist clutching a machine gun—in bold, painted strokes three stories high, on the side of a ruined office building in Basta, the ultimate conflict graffiti.

But right now, the fact Hezbollah hadn't even taken the street its gunmen destroyed, only meant the Army would have to defend it again, another day.

ELEVEN

A FEW DAYS LATER, I ran into Thomas and Fretwell, as they left the Commodore. Lunch was their next port of call and they asked me to join them. I hesitated only a moment.

We went to a restaurant a short walk away. First, mezza, cold dishes, followed by hot. I discreetly studied Thomas, as he and Fretwell bobbed along in the conversational currents. I found Thomas's genteel shabbiness appealing; it enhanced his vulnerability. His hair skimmed his collar, too long as ever, and his once-expensive clothes had known better days. Here was someone who needed looking after. Yet for all that, the innate elegance of his birthright ran the length of his long limbs, manifested in the slender fingers and hallmarked in the chiseled nose, cheekbones distinct as any woman's, and, largely hidden beneath his untidy hair, a brow of near-perfect proportion.

"Did you see that a Lebanese Army vehicle was blown right off the Corniche by the force of the explosion?" Fretwell said, referring to the embassy bombing. He tasted the wine, smacked his lips, and nodded approvingly to the waiter standing by. I covered the top of my glass with my hand, but, as the waiter approached, changed my mind and let him fill it.

"I heard a sniper fired at the Marine on guard duty the night before. The bullet went through his trousers." Thomas said, examining his own glass. "The sentry wasn't hurt but the Marines returned fire—for the first time."

That was news to Fretwell. "My goodness, where did you hear that?"

"Around." Thomas held up his glass. "Cheers, Lara, Ian."

Our glasses clinked.

"What else have you heard, Thomas?"

"Bits and pieces, here and there. Reliable sources tell me the van the suicide bomber drove was stolen from the embassy a couple of years ago."

"Really? Which 'reliable' sources?" Fretwell put his wineglass down and looked intently at Thomas.

"Never divulge a source, as you well know, Mr. Fretwell." Thomas smiled easily, as he picked up the bottle of wine and held it out toward me. "This, by the way, Lara, is an excellent vintage, although Chateau Musar is perhaps better known for its reds," he said, pointing at the label.

"Of course, Lebanese vineyards have greatly benefited from collaboration with the French," Fretwell interjected.

"The French know a good thing when they see it. The Bekaa Valley has nearly ideal conditions—a thousand meters above the sea, fertile soil, perfect climate," Thomas said, "and the Obaideh grapes in the Bekaa were Chardonnay long before the French knew what it was."

"And these excellent conditions are also vital for those other popular Lebanese crops, opium and hashish," Fretwell said.

They described how Lebanese winemakers doggedly managed at least limited production throughout the civil war, especially the family of Gaston Hochar, who founded Chateau Musar in the early 1930s. Despite the dangers, they persevered, missing only one year of production.

"1976: a bad year for wine. But a great vintage for war," Fretwell intoned mock-solemnly.

As lunch progressed, Hamid appeared and sat down with us. The waiter hurried over with another glass and Fretwell filled it for Hamid. Despite this dour addition, the mood remained playful and Thomas and Fretwell consumed two more bottles, with his help.

In our time here, I'd drunk Lebanese wine often, without pause for thought. This time, however, I tasted luxury, infused as it was with the additional ingredient of danger. This was not a pampered Bordeaux or cosseted little Chablis from one of the vineyards in the small leather-bound guides I slipped into Mac's Christmas stocking every year. This was a war wine.

I drank slowly, reverentially, my appreciation enhanced by awareness of the difficult route it traveled to arrive at this very table.

In that sense, it differed little from most everyone I met here.

❖

Thomas began seeking me out at the Commodore and TV Kansai—a fact which did not escape Mac. He resented it, though there was nothing to resent, not yet. My friendship with Thomas was perfectly aboveboard. We did nothing wrong; there was nothing to feel guilty about.

But "aboveboard" is one thing, "clear-cut" another, and I'll admit to you now what I couldn't admit then, that however we acted outwardly, there was an unspoken, interior dialogue in progress. I was drawn to Thomas, in a way I couldn't have explained to you then, for I didn't understand it myself. Even now, I can only liken it to the peculiar force of a chemical affinity pulling elementary atoms together to assemble molecules—no less real for being unseen or unconscious. Or unstoppable.

Despite this, there was no impropriety in our words or behavior, I assure you. We didn't flirt, though he teased me about the very things Mac now found so annoying. Thomas did it with such genuine good nature—the way Mac used to—that I didn't mind. Now, when Thomas stopped by TV Kansai, instead of huddling with Hamid in the front office, he came back to the edit suite, bearing welcome tidbits of news and gossip. If Gifford was away, Thomas helped me experiment, suggesting shots to use, ways to keep a pictorial narrative flowing. Often, we slipped out for coffee at the Commodore or a neighborhood café, sometimes with Fretwell or Nasr, one of Thomas's Lebanese friends.

No, nothing Mac could fault and maybe that made him madder, for he viewed the friendship as a personal insult. But he never came right out and said, don't see Thomas, so I continued to, and not just because I enjoyed his company and the little attentions he paid me, but also because it had the unexpected bonus of making Mac jealous. Mac peaked on the ascendant scale of anger in record time these days, and I knew he'd stop me seeing Thomas, if he could come up with a good reason, so I was careful not to push it.

I was starting to play the game, you see.

I could imagine too easily the struggle it would be to hold Mac's interest in years to come. We were both changing, but in different ways and at different speeds, like crops planted in different seasons, needing different doses of the elements to nurture our growth, which could only be in different directions. The seeds of failure weren't planted here, but Beirut reaped its dismal harvest.

Yet I persevered in hopes of redeeming the situation, and if playing on Mac's jealousy sounds tacky to you, it was about the only card I held. I just didn't expect the payoff.

⚎

"I'd worry about all the attention he lavishes on you, except for the fact I don't really need to, do I?" Mac closed the car door with greater force than necessary, and, as Abdel Farid drove away, shoved me toward our apartment building.

"Hey, what'd you do that for?" I struggled for a moment to stay upright, while Mac marched stonily past, toward the front door.

Until that point, it had been an uneventful evening, capping a hot and dangerous day, most of which I'd spent at TV Kansai, before adjourning to the Commodore, to find Thomas and Fretwell in the bar. Mac arrived not long after, and unfortunately walked in just as Thomas lighted a cigarette, took it from his lips, and passed it to me.

Mac angrily ignored my greeting, instead grabbing Martin and taking him to a table on the other side of the room. Shortly after, I saw Mac rise to leave, without even a glance my way, and, embarrassingly, had to hurry to catch up, practically running out of the hotel after him, while Thomas and Fretwell—and everyone else in the bar—looked on.

Now, as I stumbled after him, I addressed his back.

"What do you mean, anyway, about Thomas?" But indignation was pointless. Trouble was en route. With Mac, it was always well signposted, obvious as a funnel-shaped cloud on a Kansas plain.

He said nothing as he opened the front door; the way he slammed it behind us spoke loud enough. We walked the two flights up, his anger another companion in the darkened stairwell. Once inside, I lit a couple of gas lamps and put one on the kitchen counter and one on the dining table. Mac looked at me, coldly, until I finally felt forced to speak.

"Want something to drink?" I tried for a friendly note.

He brushed past me, into the living room, then turned around, measuring out words weighted with scorn.

"Get over yourself, Lara. Thomas isn't *interested* in you. You're just making an ass of yourself."

"What on earth are you talking about?"

"Oh, come on now, it's evident, isn't it?" His laugh was the yap of a small bitter dog. "If that boy has a hard-on, it'll be for me."

I couldn't have been more shocked if Mac had slapped me across the face and it must've showed, for he suddenly laughed out loud in pure delight.

"Why *surely* you know, don't you, Lara, my darling?" Mac crowed. "He's the Commodore's pet queer. It's hardly a secret."

The tension broken now, he strutted over to the sideboard and picked up a bottle of scotch, and, with a careful hand, poured some into a big balloon-shaped brandy snifter before looking back at me.

"Well, well, well. Lara. I do declare. You had no idea, did you?" He took his glass to the sofa and sat down, patting the seat next to him.

I stayed where I was.

"Oh, stop gawping like a goldfish. Unattractive as hell."

Mac slowly swirled the scotch around the sides of his glass, the way you do with good wine, and held the glass up to the light. He rolled a mouthful around, savoring it. "Oh yeah . . ." he breathed in satisfaction. "Twenty-year-old. Single malt. At least the scotch is cheap in this fucking dump."

Pause. Then, "Or, you suppose it's little boys? Eh, Lu? That more Thomas's style, huh? A perv as well as a poof?"

"Don't be revolting, Mac." I wanted to shout at him, but forced myself to speak normally. "Anyway, it's ridiculous."

"What, because he hangs around with you? That hardly makes him a stud. Why, I'd say that only makes you a fag hag, darling." He smiled in malicious self-appreciation.

"Stop it, that's hateful, he likes women. He definitely isn't homosexual."

I faltered, suddenly not only unsure of the truth, but, more important, worried Mac would twist whatever I said. Wasn't it peculiar that I, a married woman, defended Thomas's manhood so vigorously? Why should it matter if Thomas preferred men? Sadly, I couldn't even tell whether Mac meant it, or whether he said it out of spite, to ruin my friendship with Thomas.

As if reading my thoughts, Mac's voice hardened.

"Get real, Lara. Men and women aren't friends, they can't be. Not real men with normal urges. Real men expect more."

He stood up, stretched, and poured himself another large drink. "That's why I haven't made a big deal over you seeing that creep"—he waved the scotch bottle for emphasis—"because I don't need to worry, do I. Fact is, he's hardly a man at all."

Exasperation warred with dignity, difficult to maintain with the tears welling up.

"Honestly, Mac, this is crazy. It doesn't matter. We're *friends*. That's all. I don't care who he sleeps with and you shouldn't either, as long as it's not me."

"You . . . don't make me laugh! Believe me, I couldn't care less. I just want you to know what your 'friend' is really like, in case you were getting any silly ideas."

"Why do you do this? You have to ruin all my friendships—like you're jealous. Why? You know I'd never cheat on you."

"*Jealous?* Of you and Warkowski?" He cackled harshly and his face turned dark and ugly. He stood up, leering, and unzipped his trousers. Trouble had arrived.

"Mac," I started, but he lunged at me, grabbing my arms and backing me into the bedroom.

"Stupid fucking queer."

I'd never refused him before but when I didn't respond that night, he pinned me down and there was no solace to be had from the forced bonding, a violation compounded by crude sexual demands, in language he'd never used before. He discharged his contempt deep inside me, trickling down my backside, down my thigh, and afterward he plunged into unconsciousness, deep, noisy snores emanating from his side of the bed. He hadn't hit me, but he might as well have, for I felt battered and dazed.

It took me a while to realize that the scent I'd smelled upon him as he entered me was not my own. It was Nadia's.

✻

I knew her odious perfume, how could I not? Like many Lebanese women—and men—she wore so much, I was lightheaded in her presence. L'Air du Temps; I hated its sickly sweet smell. The front room of the magazine office reeked of it. Close up now, I realized Mac did, too.

Treacherous Mac. I hardly knew which evil to confront first, sleeping with Nadia or what he'd done to me. Was one a natural consequence of the other?

I was shocked, sickened. Heartbroken. Suspicion was one thing, confirmation another. I wanted revenge.

People talk about a roller coaster of emotion, but I had the sensation of dangling from the top of a Ferris wheel, abruptly stalled. Such a long way to fall.

Things had spun out of control so quickly, the damage must be irreversible.

Why didn't I leave him that night? The thought crossed my mind, but, I am sad to say, only as a way to punish him, not as a way to save myself. And even as I lay there despising him, I knew the question wasn't whether to leave him, but whether to confront him, and after much agonizing, concluded it wasn't wise. Not over this. Tipping my hand now might force me to take steps I wasn't prepared to take. Concrete evidence was needed first—then I'd decide what to do. If anything. The fact was, Mac always returned to me and there was no reason to believe this would be any different, and it was on that thought I finally dozed off.

In the end, the need for immediate decision was taken out of my hands.

I'd forgotten Mac was going to Iran. He'd secured a hard-to-get visa to see how the war with Iraq was going, and Abdel Farid was outside very early the next morning, to drive him to the airport.

Mac didn't say good-bye, though he must have intended to wake me, for that's what happened when he let the front door bang shut behind him.

I gathered the sheet loosely around me and opened the balcony doors, flopping in the wicker chair Mac favored. I broke the filters off my cigarettes, as I lit them, one after another. They were too strong, it hurt when I inhaled and brought tears to my eyes, which gave me a perverse satisfaction.

For a long time, I stared blankly at the Mediterranean. When I looked straight ahead, the scene was one of tranquility, palm trees and sunlight glinting off the small blue waves. But if I allowed my view to widen peripherally, turned ever so slightly to take in the left and then the right—a panoramic view, in effect—it assembled a different scene altogether: ruined buildings dotted the neighborhood, jagged gashes in some, piles of rubble here and there, so much in this montage to remind that this was a country in the throes of war, and, at least from my own vantage point, I was at its center.

I spent hours that morning in that position, wrapped in the sheet, hugging my knees, chain-smoking and reviewing the meager options available. I must keep looking straight ahead. Veering off course would be to acknowledge the potential destruction which lay in either direction.

❧

The midmorning heat drove me back indoors, where I stayed the rest of the day, going out only once, to the news seller's kiosk to buy more cigarettes. Food didn't appeal, but I knew I couldn't survive the immediate future without more Marlboros. I didn't want to go downtown, of course, couldn't face Thomas, or Hamid, or, worst of all, Nadia. Solitude was what I needed most. There was so much to think about, to sort out, that I didn't try. I'd wait until Mac returned. This was my own hair shirt but I wasn't ready to shed it yet.

Much as I'd love to leave Beirut behind, it would've taken a greater courage than I possessed to make a fresh start somewhere else, away from Mac.

❄

Suha didn't show up that day, or the next. I am ashamed to say I was relieved not to see her—or, more accurately, not to have her see me in such a state. Relief, however, would turn to a terrible guilt when I learned why she hadn't come. Abdel Farid brought me a message from her—given to him though an intermediary— saying she wouldn't be able to come to work the rest of the week. The building next to hers was hit by shelling during the night and Suha's friend had lost her three children, her husband, and both of her legs. Despite severe blood loss and multiple injuries, they managed to save her, though it occurred to me she must have wished it were otherwise.

❄

Hearing about her tragedy put my woes in a different perspective. That the fates had cast me an abusive husband seemed a light penalty. Perhaps I wouldn't have stayed with him so long if it hadn't seemed a positive luxury at times merely to have a bad marriage . . . in a place where rampant evil was an inventive, daily occurrence.

TWELVE

I wasn't expecting company when the buzzer rang that evening.

"Just a minute," I shouted, frantically searching for something clean to put on. "Be right there." I slipped on a light summer dress, ran a quick brush through my hair, and rushed to open the door.

It was Thomas.

Mac had tried to poison our friendship, but here he was, on our doorstep, and it gave me a quiet sense of victory.

"Everything okay? I know Barrett's gone to Teheran, but Gifford said you were supposed to come see the new edit gear Richard brought in from Hong Kong and you never showed up. Your phone wasn't working, so I thought I'd stop by."

"How sweet. I was just tired. We were up late. Sorry, I'm kind of a mess."

"Nonsense, Lara. You look lovely." He said it lightly, careful not to offend.

Such compliments were unusual; now, I really was touched.

I showed him into the living room, ducked back into the kitchen for a bottle of garnet-colored Chateau Musar, and gave it to him to open. While he poured, I turned up the flames on one of the large gas lanterns and sat down in an armchair.

"Cheers." He raised his glass and sank back into the sofa, looking around with interest.

"This is the first I've been here since you and Barrett moved in. Of course, I came here often, before. When Roger lived here."

"Weren't you at our housewarming?"

"I wasn't invited."

"Gosh, sorry, Thomas—Mac took care of the guest list." I was the one flustered. "It was so soon after we arrived, I didn't even know half the people.

"Anyway," I continued hastily, to cover my embarrassment, "I'm sure you won't find the place much changed. Same furniture and all, just a few of our own touches here and there."

"Yes," he said, "I see you have the ubiquitous David Roberts prints. Armenian bookseller near the university?"

He smiled as I nodded.

"He has been known to take advantage, not that one can blame him these days. Hope you didn't pay too much? You've done it before."

"Probably," I confessed and we both laughed.

"But I do love them," I protested. "They take you a step back in time. Mac says they're too idealized, they don't capture the savagery here. He calls them overpriced Victorian tourist posters. But I love them."

"Maybe Barrett has a point. But this is how Roberts saw the Holy Lands...the tribesmen, the harem girls, the temples and ruins, the bazaars."

He stood up and went to take a closer look at the framed lithograph of a fierce Bedouin over the fireplace. "His prints have been reproduced for over a century, a sort of everyman's da Vinci or van Gogh—no small accomplishment for a Scot who got his start painting circus scenery."

He came back and settled into the sofa.

"You know, Roberts sketched or painted scenes from all over the region, but my favorites are the Lebanon ones—especially the ruins at Baalbek."

"Guess I'll only ever see that in a Roberts print," I said ruefully. "I'd love to go, to see the Temple of Jupiter, but I guess that's out of the question now."

"It's magnificent: the largest Roman columns in the world."

He stared into his wine for a moment and sighed. "But you're right. Don't even think about it. The area is controlled by Rev Guards and Hezbollah militiamen *and* Syrian soldiers *and* various Palestinian groups. An ugly mix. Not exactly a travel destination for Westerners. Nor for the Lebanese. Certainly not those of the wrong family, faith, or philosophy, which rules out most of the country, I'm afraid."

"Revolutionary Guards—you mean Iranians?"

"The Ayatollah Khomeini set up the *Pasdaran* in 1979 to guard the revolution and enforce Islamic law. That helped spread Islamic fundamentalism, including here in the Lebanon. Teheran sent the first Rev Guards to the Bekaa Valley last year, supposedly to fight the Israelis. But now they've got a real base there—hundreds of them. Possibly more. And they're training Shiites, radical Palestinians, Iraqis, Afghans, North Africans. The lot."

"There must be some way to protect the ancient sites from modern warfare."

"We can't even protect people from it," Thomas said, with a small smile. "But Baalbek has survived worse over the centuries.

Other invaders, other wars. One day, when *this* war is over, we may visit it together."

We talked a while longer about Lebanon, and then about ourselves. He asked about growing up in North Carolina and elicited the story of how I had met Mac, when I was a graduate student, working part-time in the press office of a UN agency in New York. In exchange, Thomas told me about his childhood, about the boarding schools, the loneliness and the sense of dislocation that accompanied him throughout those years. I knew what he meant. I'd often felt it too, as an only child, although my childhood was stable and my parents lived in the house I grew up in until their deaths, shortly after I married Mac.

"My parents are gone, also, but my brother lives in Rio," Thomas said. "I haven't seen him since 1979, when he got married. We talk on the phone sometimes. He has a little boy."

He sounded wistful. For a moment, he looked younger than his years and I could see the boy in him, in the mop of hair, in the anxiousness to please.

"Would you consider leaving Beirut if things get worse?" I asked. "Where would you go? To Rio?"

"Beirut is my home now," he said, shaking his head.

He paused then, hefting memories, and that pause seemed to restore the years, for suddenly the boy was gone and it was the man who answered decisively.

"No, I won't go. I've seen wicked things here over the last seven years, terrible things no man should be capable of doing to another. But I shall stay until the end, until peace breaks out again. And Lebanon shall rise from its ashes and be the Paris of the Middle East again and we shall all live happily ever after."

It was hard to tell from his tone.

"You don't believe that, do you, Thomas? Surely there's been too much blood spilled? All the assassinations, the killings, the bombs, all the fighting, and there's no end in sight, unless you think the Syrians can stop it, or America brings in bigger guns."

"The Syrians have a better chance. They consider this their patch. At the risk of sounding like Hamid, the Americans will never be the brokers of peace in the Lebanon."

"Even with the Marines? You have to start somewhere."

"To start with, the Americans don't understand how the Lebanese mind works. Or the Middle East mind-set. They want to help the government, but who is the government? The president's late father and brother were Christian warlords, and their militia, the Lebanese Forces, is still the main Christian group fighting the Moslems militias."

I started to reply, but he held up a hand to stop me.

"It's not only that. America also supports Israel. Don't you see that, to Moslems here, this makes the Americans another party to the conflict?"

"They're still neutral," I insisted.

"Saying doesn't make it so. Besides, there's no such thing as neutrality in Lebanon. Everyone chooses a side. Whatever the Americans say, they *have* chosen. By coming in the first place. I believe it will cost them. The American adventure is bound to end badly."

"I suppose you mean the embassy bombing."

"The Americans are propping up a Christian president, just like 1958, when Camille Chamoun was president and needed help. Who did he call? The Marines. It is a déjà vu for the Lebanese;

here they are again, twenty-five years later, although the Americans had a warmer reception from the local population last time.

"Enough of this."

He put his wineglass down and looked thoughtfully at me.

"To return to what you were asking before. Barrett would not consider leaving, would he?"

"No, he likes having a ringside seat to history too much."

"And you?"

"I don't know," I began, not sure whether to continue, but I'd apparently drunk too much wine to stop. I lit a cigarette, took a tremulous puff, and the words tumbled out of their own accord.

"I probably shouldn't tell you this, but ... as if things aren't bad enough just *being* here, Mac's having an affair. I know it. I can't even think straight about it because there's so much going on all the time."

A little sob escaped as I tried to catch my breath. "I can't live this way, Thomas. It's not just Mac, it's everything about being here. I try so hard but I'm always scared, always waiting for the next bad thing to happen."

"Lebanon never disappoints on that front, does it," Thomas said, gently.

"Other people can handle it, but I can't." I shook my head, tears starting to form. "I don't have their courage."

Thomas reached out and took my glass. He set it on the table.

"Don't go, Lara," he said, suddenly standing up and pulling me up with him.

He knew where the bedroom was.

❊

I remember wondering if Thomas could smell Mac—smell

Nadia—on the sheets. They hadn't been changed because Suha hadn't been in to change them and I hadn't bothered because entertaining a visitor in my bedroom was the last thing I'd have expected to do that evening. Nonetheless, here we were. I wondered what that made me, that I could lie with another man on my husband's soiled sheets. It didn't occupy my mind for long; I wanted to give myself up to the moment.

I must be honest about this: Thomas's mouth felt unfamiliar and his kiss all wrong, as if we both sought something from it that wasn't there, and the act itself finished almost as it began.

Thomas could not have been satisfied, though I believe we both tried. I didn't know if it was because we'd drunk too much wine; it hardly seemed polite to inquire. We spoke very little afterward, not so much shy as awkward. I thought briefly about what Mac said, but dismissed it. Here was proof otherwise. In our bed. I didn't dare consider the irony. What had happened was too monumental for that.

We lay apart, staring at the ceiling. After a while, Thomas said he should go. Soon the streets would be too dangerous to travel. He reached for the dimmer switch, concealed on the wall behind the padded headboard, and turned it, but nothing happened. Of course, the electricity was still off.

As he dressed in the dark, I put on Mac's robe. I walked to the front door with Thomas; we hugged, rather clumsily, and said good-bye. We didn't kiss again. It would have been too intimate.

⁂

I'd never before betrayed Mac, not in thought, not in deed. So it may come as a surprise to learn that having done so, I didn't feel any real guilt. Not because Mac betrayed me first, but because what happened with Thomas seemed an event completely apart, completely separate from my marriage, one that had no bearing upon it.

It was perhaps an indication of my precarious state of mind that I believed it.

I went back to my corrupt sheets, and for once fell asleep right away.

It didn't occur to me Thomas hadn't asked whom Mac was seeing. It didn't occur to me Thomas hadn't fumbled around for the light switch. These things didn't occur to me until far too late to make any difference.

✸

The next morning, I awakened with the feeling that a small currency of hope had been deposited in an account otherwise emptied. For the first time since Mac left for Teheran—perhaps for the first time since we had come to Beirut in January—I saw the future as holding possibilities to welcome, not fear.

But I wasn't sure about Thomas yet. We'd crossed a boundary together, and were now in uncharted territory. Were we in it together, or shamed solo voyagers? Lovers last night, were we damaged friends today?

I needed to see Thomas, to give definition and clarity to what happened. Only then could I consider what it meant for my marriage. For once, Mac receded far into the background. Strange and novel though it was, another man had occupied his space.

The Commodore was the starting point. I didn't know where he lived, though he'd pointed out his street one day as we walked near the Lebanese University. He wasn't at the hotel, so I headed for TV Kansai.

Hamid looked up when I walked in and, after a mostly one-sided exchange of greetings, I asked, casually, about Thomas. From his look, I might as well have erased all but the last letter on that invisible "Made in the USA" sign on my forehead and painted that one scarlet.

"Looking for him, are you, Madam McCauley?" Hamid took off his glasses and stretched his arms behind his head. Was the sarcasm real or imagined? With Hamid, it was impossible to tell.

"Nothing important, just wondered if he's been around today?"

"Let's see... *Mister* McCauley is in Teheran... and *you*... are looking for Thomas..." Hamid sneered, the sentence trailing in the air between us like a wisp of smoke. He was rude all right, but if he knew about Thomas and me, it was pointless to act offended. The only option was to treat it as a joke, playacting that did not come easily.

"Yeah, sure," I replied, "It's my big chance, you know, Hamid."

He put his glasses back on and stared at me, then squinted, as if I were a particularly challenging line on an eye chart.

"Yes, Madam McCauley," he said flatly, still squinting, "It is."

Yoshi walked in, nodding at me with a smile, and started questioning Hamid about a driver missing on the Beirut-Damascus highway with a shipment of videotapes to be fed by satellite to Tokyo.

I didn't wait to hear details, but used the interruption to escape to the back, where Gifford, busy editing a piece, barely looked up. I took the hint and on the way out passed Yoshi and Hamid, still deep in discussion. Only Yoshi waved back.

I had to stop myself running out the door. Hamid knew. Thomas wouldn't have told him, which, frightening thought, meant someone else had. God knows there was no shortage of gossip in Beirut—journalists, drivers, doormen, cleaning ladies, neighbors, local gunmen, other sentries. So someone else knew I'd been with Thomas, committed adultery.

It may sound archaic to you, launched as we are so far now into this new millennium, but that was how I thought of it to myself. Adultery. I was an adulteress. At least I had a job title now. Lara McCauley, Adulteress. I laughed aloud as I crossed Hamra Street.

I tried Amina next. Thomas had introduced us and I knew he visited regularly, because I'd been with him twice to her flat.

She was Christian, her late husband a Moslem historian and academic of international repute, now deceased. She sparkled in the half-light of a city at war—effervescent in the gloom, well informed and well connected. She knew many of the journalists, Lebanese and foreign, because, like Thomas, they made a point of keeping in touch with her. It was in their interest.

Amina's husband was killed during the siege of Beirut the year before, when a building in which he had taken shelter was hit by shelling. One of his books, on modern Lebanese history, sat in the bookcase in our living room, part of Schuster's legacy. After I first met Amina, I tried to read it and found it as impenetrable as its companions gathering dust on the top shelf.

She took pleasure in revealing the vagaries of life in Lebanon, the errant and the arcane, the way others might share an extravagant family history, and, in a way, it was. She plumbed a vast reservoir of inside information on politics and personalities and always knew the latest military development and current factors in the ever-shifting power equation, "the situation." She still owned a home in the mountains, in Brumannah, on the Christian side, but insisted on staying in West Beirut, in the home she'd shared with her husband so many years.

Once, when I visited on my own, Amina showed me scrapbooks filled with prewar magazine and newspaper clippings, photographs of Amina and her husband, his citations and certificates, and other relics of their life together. Her friendliness encouraged me and I returned a few days later, with Mac in tow. He'd heard about her from others in the press corps, but, having met her, never expressed any desire to go again, perhaps because she spoke so fondly of Thomas during our visit.

On the day I went seeking Thomas, Amina offered me a glass of *kamareddine,* apricot nectar, and she poured strong, thick Arabic coffee flavored with cardomon, heavily sugared, from an ornate silver pot. On the matching silver service her housekeeper had set out various delicate Lebanese sweets, including *baklava* and *kunafi,* a pastry stuffed with sweet white cheese, nuts, and syrup. I doubted I was her first caller of the day, but she treated me as if a guest were a singular and treasured event.

"Do you know the difference between the Lebanese *baklava* and the Greek, Lara? We use pistachios and rosewater syrup; theirs is walnuts and honey. I prefer ours, do you not?" She asked it happily, for she enjoyed imparting knowledge as much as Thomas, and I, as always, was a willing receptacle.

We worked our way through more pleasantries and eventually, without any need for artifice on my part, the conversation quite naturally swung around to our mutual friend.

"Thomas, Thomas, poor man," she clucked sympathetically. "I always tell him, 'you cut that hair, young man, buy some new clothes, your shoes are ready for the dustbin.' He never listens, just laughs. Thomas is very charming, and he is very brave. But he desperately needs sorting out."

Her light tone implied this wasn't going to be a serious conversation but I seized the chance to extract some information.

"Does he have a girlfriend who could help? Have you ever met any of his girlfriends?"

Amina gave me a sharp, knowing look. "You are asking me? Don't you know the answers already? You spend so much time together, I hear in certain quarters people think *you're* having an affair." She laughed, to establish her intent was not hostile, and held out the tray of sweets again, insisting I try another.

It was important to strike the right note. I absentmindedly took a triangle of baklava, to buy time. I noticed Amina herself didn't eat; as I said, it was likely I was not her first visitor that day.

"Good heavens, Amina, you know Thomas and I are just friends. We hardly even talk about our personal lives. The only reason I'm asking you this, is . . . frankly, I'm embarrassed to say it . . . but Mac seems to think he's . . . well, a homosexual."

"And . . . ?"

"And . . . I wonder whether it's true, or if it's Mac being Mac. My husband has some strong views sometimes. I'm curious what other people think."

"What do *you* think?" Her voice betrayed nothing.

"I don't think he is." I said, in a stronger voice now. I knew he wasn't, didn't I? "But Mac says everyone else thinks so."

"Maybe, they are right. Or maybe, your husband feels threatened by him and seeks to diminish his standing." Amina examined her manicured hands, fingers bent but adorned with discreet, expensive jewels. "You understand, I never speculate on the romantic lives of the people I consider friends. There are too many other things in this world to worry about."

She flexed her fingers and grimaced daintily.

"Arthritis," she explained, before continuing, her tone unchanged. "Suffice then, I think to say, as regards Thomas, it cannot be of real importance to you, except as a point of curiosity. Not unless your questions arise from a more personal concern?"

"Of course not," I said hastily. "I'm married. You know that, Amina." For the second time that day, a conversation about Thomas skewed totally out of my control.

Amina raised her eyes, her gaze now level with mine.

"Oh, yes, I know, my dear Lara, I know."

She refilled my coffee cup. "You are a nice girl, Lara. I do like you. Shall I be entirely honest with you? Would you really want my advice?"

I nodded, and said, "Of course," rather more weakly than I would have desired, trying not to look as if I dreaded what she might be about to say.

"I offer apologies in advance, if I overstep here, if I am wrong. But it seems to me you are playing a dangerous game. Maybe you don't realize it. But it is one that would be difficult for even an experienced player. And to be honest, I do not think you are."

She paused, then said, "I should be very careful, Lara, extremely careful."

Did she know or was she guessing? It didn't matter: my silence betrayed me.

We sat a few moments longer before she spoke again.

"Anyway, it would seem Thomas is not your problem."

"What do you mean?"

"You have an interesting life, Lara," she rose, effectively dismissing me. "You must excuse me now. It is going to be a busy day."

She extended her cheek for a kiss and clasped both my hands in hers, though no warmth was transmitted. "Thank you for coming by. Please come anytime."

She walked me to the door. "Bring your husband again, if you like."

Outside on the street again, I shook my head in frustration at my feeble response. As with Hamid, I'd been easily outmaneuvered. By default, I'd practically admitted having an affair, and gotten nothing back in exchange. I knew not one scrap more about Thomas this day than I had before.

I went home discouraged, the optimism that marked the start of the day drained way. How could I be tempted to fantasize about the future when I hadn't resolved the present?

The rest of the day passed dismally. In the early evening, Mac called from Teheran. It was a terrible, noisy connection, but Mac sounded like always, as if things were entirely normal. No reference to what happened before he left. The line dropped out a few times, but I understood he would return at the end of the week. I responded dully, but he either didn't notice or didn't care. He asked no questions; as usual, he found his own doings of far more interest than mine and, as usual, assumed I would, too. Things were normal, all right.

The next day, on the spur of the moment, I dropped by Mac's office to collect the bundle of mail and out-of-date newspapers and magazines New York sent every week. I might see Thomas along the way and I suppose, too, I wanted to see Nadia. Why? Several nights before, I'd wanted to kill her for sleeping with my husband. Now, I had to admit to myself that made us little different.

"Lara," Nadia said, surprised, as I entered.

She was high gloss that day, from lacquered head to painted toes, displayed in high-heeled sandals. Wrapped in a mantle of the culprit perfume, she seemed hardly more than a soft, spoiled child, until you saw her eyes, hard and assessing, the wary eyes of a predator. Eight years of civil war had stolen any claim she might ever have had to innocence.

"Sit down." But her voice held no invitation and her look coldly questioning. She made no move to offer the customary tea or coffee any casual visitor to the office might expect.

"I came by to pick up the mail."

"Abdel Farid could have brought it."

"It was a good opportunity to get out."

"How nice for you. Those of us in this office have no such time for social activity," she said brusquely. "And today, in particular, we are very busy, as you can see." Her sweeping gesture took in the office assistant, clipping newspapers across the room, head atilt, listening to the radio on her desk. Abdel Farid, who'd stood up and greeted me when I entered, now sat in a chair a few feet away, idly turning the pages of one of Mac's magazines, not looking at me. I wasn't sure how much of the dialogue he understood.

"Really? So much to do with Mac away?" I asked mildly.

Nadia spent a moment or two pulling down her sleeves and straightening the length of her skirt, then, looking slyly sideways at me, shifted gears.

"Barrett likes things to be organized," she purred dangerously. "He insists on it."

"Are we talking about the same man? He's so ... not organized at home."

"Perhaps that is why he prefers it here."

The challenge resonated. She was sleeping with Mac and letting me know she didn't care whether I knew or not.

It's impossible to gauge what effect such audacity would've had a few days earlier. But I was jaded now, my thoughts disordered by my own betrayal and, instinctively, now, I almost understand her. In Nadia's world, you were either victor or victim and she had no intention of being a victim. And beyond that, surviving wasn't enough; she had to win.

Her boldness with me showed her contempt: she saw my weakness as self-inflicted, a woman not strong enough to check the reins on her man. Not worth wasting pity on, save it for those who really deserved it, those who suffered real tragedy, not spoiled American wives, who played at visiting wars.

In that instant, I grasped this basic truth: Nadia saw herself as in control of this situation, shielded by her supreme indifference. She might well decide to succeed me as the next Mrs. McCauley or otherwise, should a more alluring prospect present itself. It was clear she felt the choice was utterly hers.

Not mine. Not even Mac's.

THIRTEEN

By now, you're wondering what kept us together, such vastly disparate souls as Mac and I. But there was a time when the sum of our commonalities seemed equal to our differences, much as a scale's lead counters gold, and to understand, you must look at what brought us together, for that held the key to our staying together as long as we did.

My early life was uneventful, a childhood framed in tranquillity. That is certainly part of what attracted Mac. My parents were in their early forties and had given up hopes of children by the time I came along. It could have introduced chaos into less well-ordered lives, but their love for each other was strong and my birth punctuated it, like an exclamation mark.

I was compliant from the start. Far from upsetting routines honed by their childless years, I slotted in with little difficulty: a grave child, self-contained, who rarely gave trouble, and that, too, is how I remember myself. Even my name reflected their contemplative nature. Larissa, Poseidon's beloved, whose name was bestowed on the citadel at Argos—testified to my father's lifelong fascination with ancient Greece, which was as much a part of my inheritance as the Kershaw nose or my mother's thin frame. My middle name, Helen, also could be seen as a nod to my father's penchant for all things Hellenic, but it actually commemorated a grandmother I never knew, Helen Smith Kershaw, the first woman to earn a master's degree in mathematics in the state of Texas.

Mac said it was my serious air that first attracted him. It wasn't until much later I realized it wasn't because he valued such gravity, but instead saw it as personal challenge—one that, in his bully-boy kind of way, he intended to tackle. He would tease and cajole and coax me, for he intended to turn me into someone who laughed at his jokes, even if he had to alter my entire personality to do it. In fact, he started with my name. Forget the Greeks, he said. Larissa sounded like a librarian. Lara, he insisted on calling me, as in *Dr. Zhivago.*

Like the ill-fated Larissa Fyodorovna Guishar Antipova, I, too, became known as Lara, from that point on.

###

Unlike Mac, I was never bullied or abused as a child. No, the episodes woven into my life's yarn were spun from different yarn altogether.

My mother taught sophomore biology at the nearby high school. My father was a professor of classics at a small college some fifteen miles away. Keen naturalists, they subscribed to *Audubon* magazine and paid membership dues to a local bird-watching society, where plaid skirts and tatty cardigans were *de rigueur* for women and faded corduroys and moth-eaten Harris tweed for men, at the monthly meetings, held over tea and pound cake at the Stanton Hotel. They set off, binoculars around their neck, pencils and notebooks at the ready, to record different bird or plant species sighted on hikes through meadow and mountain, and kept meticulous migratory charts and annual records of notable visitors to the many feeders placed on windowsills and tree limbs around our house. The sighting of a pileated woodpecker or cedar waxwing was cause for jubilation in our house.

Our two mixed-spaniel dogs lived under the screened porch when the weather was temperate, and in our kitchen when it was not. It was my daily task to feed them and the birds, which required a scatter of mixed seed on the back patio and filling the peanut butter feeder that hung from a branch of the dogwood tree by the patio—a long wooden strip with holes to spread peanut butter into, like putty.

When I was twelve, my parents went away on a four-day bird-watching expedition. I stayed at a neighbor's, half a mile away, but went home every day on the way to and from school, to feed our feathered and furred dependents.

Our house was secluded, off a Carolina country road, and with my parents away, it wore an air of desertion, silent and foreboding, and I was anxious about entering. So I left everything out on the back patio—the dog food, a big tin of birdseed, and a super-size jar of peanut butter with a spreader, on a small, wrought-iron table. I could rush through the chores and be off again in a matter of minutes.

Thursday that week was particularly hot. Getting off the school bus at the bottom of the long gravel driveway, I ran all the way up to our house, sweat beads collecting on my face like summer freckles, dripping down inside my collar, leaving wet marks on my school blouse.

The dogs were hungry and excited, but on the patio, on the iron table, was a sight still vivid in my mind today: a baby bird stuck in the peanut butter, softened to almost liquid consistency by the heat of the sun. Only its head and the top of its wings were visible still, as it chirped desperately and struggled to break free. The jar lid was lying on the tiles. I must have forgotten to put it back on when I'd filled the feeder in the morning, and with sickening accuracy, the baby bird, all but featherless, eyes still glued shut, had fallen in from its nest in a limb of the dogwood tree overhanging the patio. Overhead, the despairing mother flapped her wings, shrieking, squawking, desperate to help.

I grabbed the jar, took a key from its hiding place under a pot of cerise azaleas, and let myself into the cool of the quiet house. I put the jar on the kitchen counter. I cursed, I prayed, I howled aloud. What would my parents do? I found my mother's phone list and, despite hysteria and badly shaking fingers, managed to dial Professor Doyle, a retired psychologist, who shared my parents' interest in birds. He lived nearby, on a winding lane that led out to the main highway. If he thought it a prank call at first, a child shouting about birds and peanut butter, my genuine panic must have been effectively communicated, because within minutes the tires of his ancient maroon Chevrolet crunched up the driveway and he was ringing our doorbell. And, importantly, he had a plan. He helped me cover the kitchen table with newspaper, then filled a plastic mixing bowl with warm tap water, pouring into it Calgon, a water softener he'd brought with him. Next, he carved and lifted out a chunk of the peanut butter with the bird in it—still alive he said, though it had gone quiet—and laid it on the newspaper. The peanut butter was solidifying again, away from the sunlight, and Professor Doyle gently scraped away bits of it with the edge of a small plastic spoon he'd found among the odds and ends in a kitchen drawer. When the most of it was gone, he carefully dipped the bird into the bowl and, using a Q-tip, swabbed away the remaining peanut butter from its fledgling wings. He swaddled the tiny, damp bird, almost completely clean now, in a washcloth and put it in a shoebox from my mother's closet. It might well survive, the professor said, and I must feed it water with the eyedropper he would leave behind. He gave other instructions and, promising to drop in after school the next day, left.

To this day, I don't know why I believed this creature, barely alive, would be able to fly back to its nest. Professor Doyle warned me not to try to put it back because the mother would never accept it, touched now by human hands. His words were unequivocal, impossible to misunderstand. And yet, as I would do in my adult life to such detriment, I followed my own intuition.

I wouldn't put it back myself, but, perhaps if it were returned under its own steam, that would compensate for human taint. My parents would marvel at my ingenuity in reuniting the little family, and I would feel happy and virtuous.

You'll think that if the baby could fly, it wouldn't have fallen into the peanut butter to begin with. But I was only twelve, still very much a child—not even a whisper of puberty about me, despite the stretchy band of padded cotton I wore across my chest, the last girl in my class to get a bra. Whatever my reasoning, I unwrapped the poor creature and took it outside to speed it on its way home.

⁂

I confidently placed it on the top of the stair railing. It fell and hit the ground, landing in a patch of the periwinkle my mother carefully cultivated to grow in our rocky, mountain soil. I picked it up but its heart had stopped. I truly had killed it.

✿

Mac asked me to marry him the night I told him that story. I couldn't understand the fuss he made over it. But he profoundly admired, he said, a life of such innocence that this constituted high tragedy. He professed to be deeply moved—indeed, seemed physically aroused by my telling of it, which was not quite what I expected. He tenderly called me his little bird-girl, and jokingly, I am sure, tried to persuade me to eat peanut butter off his nether parts, which I declined, but I have to admit, it did make me laugh.

At the time, I suppose I recognized, at some level, this was a key component in the attraction I held for Mac, that in possessing me, he sought to finally possess the innocence that eluded him throughout his own childhood. What I didn't realize until much later was that he sought to degrade it as well. I can only wonder now if we both read a deep meaning into the story at the time or whether the symbolism only gradually dawned upon me; it certainly seemed as if I had always drawn the parallel, right from the beginning.

But there are some truths that only emerge piecemeal over time and perhaps this was one.

✿

Here was what attracted me to Mac: he not only loved me, he needed me.

His life was unsettled from birth.

Mac's father planted his seed and shuffled off long before he was born. Mac was the fourth of four boys, four boys by four different men, none of whom stayed around long enough to marry his mother. His mother wanted to give him up for adoption, but bone-lazy or perhaps too illiterate to fill out the forms, failed to take the necessary legal steps. Faced with the prospect of taking yet another unwanted baby home, she plunked him in a dumpster outside the hospital, instead. Unfortunately for her, he was spotted right away, hospital nametag still strapped around his wee ankle. No one really believed in postpartum depression then. And of course, she was a slut, anyway, wasn't she. She went to jail and Mac went to a foster home.

McCauley wasn't really his surname; that was the name of the family who adopted him when he was three years old. His mother hadn't kept him long enough to bother with a first name. The day she abandoned him, when he was brought back inside the hospital, one of the nurses said he should be called George, as it was St. George's Day in England. She knew that because her father, English by birth, always celebrated it even though he'd long ago exchanged the Birmingham in England for the suburbs of the one in Alabama.

But even this name would be denied him, for once he joined their family, the McCauleys insisted on calling him Barrett, after Mr. McCauley himself, and had the birth certificate changed.

The McCauleys had two other adopted children, a son and a daughter, both in their teens when Barrett was adopted, and, immersed in their own adolescent angst, not the least interested in this newest branch of the McCauley's artificially created family tree.

Thus it came to pass that Mac, born one of four brothers, raised in a family that included two other children, was, for all intents and purposes, an only child.

That may help explain that while his herd instinct was strong, he never quite learned how to share.

The McCauleys saw it as their Christian duty to give this child a comfortable life: they fed him, wiped him top and tail, righted him when he fell, dried the tears that often streamed down his chubby cheeks for no reason at all. In his younger years, Mrs. McCauley sat in the dark, night after night, making up stories about unicorns and dragons and boys named Barrett, to help him find his way to sleep. His meals were square, his vaccinations on schedule. Young Barrett was always neatly dressed for school, his hair slicked back in the fashion of the day, though it may have seemed sometimes he purposely spilled his breakfast down his front, or slopped milk down his trousers and into his shoes, which tried even Mrs. McCauley's patience and necessitated changing clothes before he could actually leave the house. He attended Sunday school every week until he was ten and so disruptive that Miss Patsy Perrish, the teacher, threatened she would quit if he didn't.

As a toddler, he had a tricycle with racing stripes, and when the time came, Mr. McCauley helped him master a two-wheeler, which Mac was accused of riding through the next-door neighbor's flowerbeds, a charge he vociferously denied, despite the tire tracks in the dahlias. At sixteen, Mr. McCauley gave him driving lessons in his Lincoln town car and let him borrow it on a Saturday night, though he wouldn't have if he'd known what Barrett Junior was getting up to in it.

As you see, the McCauleys gave him a lot of frills along with all the basics, backed up by a mild, unthreatening love, and in return, these good people demanded nothing, save the unspoken expectation that Barrett Junior grow up a decent and honorable man, a testament to their good intentions. However, if they trusted the years of ministrations would comb out his tangle of aggression, their trust was misplaced. For Mac tolerated it all—he had no choice if he was to survive—but he didn't love them in return, didn't even particularly appreciate all that was done for him.

There's no point pretending a good home made a good boy of him. He'd always known he was adopted; it was a central fact of his life. He was growing up alone and no amount of stories about being specially picked by the McCauleys out of all the children in the world blah blah blah made up for the fact that his real mother didn't want him, that she was a slut, and that he had real brothers, slut-brothers, out there somewhere, who didn't want him either. The McCauleys never said any of this. They didn't have to. He knew, both from the McCauleys' silence on the subject of his mother and from the taunts of neighborhood boys, whose parents talked unwisely in their hearing.

Despite the McCauleys' best, sometimes bewildered, efforts to pad the reality of this sharp-angled world, Mac grew up tough. He learned early to defend himself against the jeers and taunts of others outside his home and never backed down from a fight, even if he looked sure to lose, and quite often he was the one who started it and when he did he made sure he could win. Even if he had to fight dirty to do it.

About the time I was starting fourth grade two states north, Mac was, at seventeen, again looking at juvenile reform school—this time for shattering Perry Ramos's face. Perry may or may not have known about Mac's lineage, but he called Mac a bastard and that was a mistake. He called him that because Mac took Perry's girlfriend Louisa out in Mr. McCauley's Lincoln town car a few nights before and, speeding down Oak Street after a couple of beers, tried to force her face into his crotch with one hand, while keeping the other on the steering wheel. She bit him and he howled in pain, pulled the car over by the side of the road, punched her in the face and called her unrepeatable names. In those days, with an incident like this, you didn't automatically go to the police. You told your boyfriend or your brother, if you had one, and they meted out their own form of justice. In this case, however, Perry's words were ill advised. Mac happened to be a lot stronger. And he wasn't afraid to hurt someone.

❁

The McCauleys were unable to prevent Barrett being sent away this time, despite having successfully fended off a custodial sentence almost a year earlier, when he was accused of roughing up a liquor store clerk who refused to sell him a six-pack of Rolling Rock beer, despite his phoney ID.

Mac's time at the juvenile offenders' home crushed any lingering hopes the McCauleys clung to about their son's future. When, after six months and three days, he was released, no one seemed to expect much of him, except perhaps more trouble.

Thus, it was a total surprise and complete relief to all, including Mac himself, when a small private arts college in northern Georgia sent a letter announcing his acceptance for the fall term. Only Mr. McCauley knew at what cost. But it paid off when his son further surprised everyone by seeming to settle down to college life. Oh, Mac still liked beer and girls and fast cars, but he appeared to be giving at least an equal attention to his academic requirements as well. For a change.

There was one incident the McCauleys managed more or less to hush up, involving an alleged assault upon a waitress at a café near the campus, but Mac insisted it was her drug-dealer boyfriend who broke her cheekbone and left her partially blind in one eye. He said she'd only accused him because she knew his parents were an easy touch, anxious as they were to protect the family name from further disgrace. It was true, too, the McCauleys paid child support for some years to a girl who had to leave the college in her sophomore year. This was before DNA testing but Mac refused to have even a blood test, which might've clarified matters because, he told me, there was no point. He already knew the child wasn't his. If the senior McCauleys were foolish enough to get taken in again by some silly girl he'd only poked without promise a few times, well, that wasn't his problem. He'd warned them. If they chose not to listen, if they chose to go ahead and give money to that slut, well, it was nothing to do with him, was it.

Despite these distractions, Mac somehow scraped through college, with surprisingly reasonable grades, even getting a coveted job on the school paper, where he had shown a knack for turning a phrase and finding the heart of the story where others couldn't. In telling stories, then, Mac had found his promise. After graduation, he got a job at a real newspaper, in Chattanooga, Tennessee, thanks to one of Mr. McCauley's cousins, who sold advertising there. He started off small, late shift on the police beat, but within a few years Mac's investigative work on nursing-home scams won him a prestigious national prize and a job at a much bigger newspaper up north. That, in turn, led to his being hired by the magazine in New York, and, with a few stops in between, Beirut.

❦

First, he was Baby (Male) Murphy, son of Sue Ann Murphy and

Father Unknown. He was briefly George Murphy and then, for another twenty or so years, Barrett McCauley. By the time I met him, he'd already become much of who he was going to be. Barrett largely disappeared as a form of address, and, to those who knew him well, he was plain Mac.

❈

We met at the UN, in its large staff cafeteria, which journalists based there frequented, as well. He was filling in for the magazine's UN correspondent for a few weeks, when he put his tray down on the table across from where I sat reading and eating the dill pickle spear off my sandwich, oblivious to the fact that my future had just arrived with the *plat de jour*.

At the time, I was a clerk in the press office of UNFPA, the UN Population Fund. It paid the rent on a minuscule, expensive studio apartment in Turtle Bay, while I worked towards a master's degree in ancient Greek at NYU. Mac was, at first, bemused by my choice of study; he couldn't see what useful purpose it served. At the same time, he respected me for it, I could see. I recounted for him my favorite childhood memory, of a family holiday in Greece, spent not on the beaches of a touristy island but in Athens, where my parents and I happily wandered for a hot, dusty week, around the Acropolis in particular.

They'd saved for years for this holiday and Mac was entertained to hear how we took the sandwiches my mother made each morning in our hotel room, wrapped in paper napkins secreted from the hotel coffee shop or the small tavernas where we had our dinner. At lunchtime, we'd seek out a precious slice of shade, and, sitting on the ancient stones, devour them, sipping water from the Boy Scout canteens we wore strapped to our belts, and listening to my father recite Pindar. "Oh you, olive shiny and violet crowned glorious Athens," I can still hear him announcing in deep, rich tones to the surprise of other tourists, as I squirmed in happy embarrassment, "famous in songs, rampart of Greece, divine city!"

As I've said, Mac and I were very different, but the things we did have in common in our early life together took on the dimensions of untold riches, as they do when you're young and first in love and haven't yet learned they do not comprise a foundation sturdy enough to bear the weight of new differences the years will create. We both enjoyed travel and it was no hardship to adjust to fine restaurants and five-star hotels around Europe at the magazine's expense, but early on our greatest pleasures came in simpler forms—camping in the Blue Ridge Mountains, or renting a cottage at Cape Hatteras, on the Carolina shore.

Of course, we both came from the South, which, in those days, was a cultural signifier, an identification in itself, marking us as different from many of the people we knew in New York—Mac's colleagues, UN employees and fellow grad students—though in our circle someone was as likely to come from Paris, France, as Athens, Georgia, or Mexico as Massachusetts.

In a dinner-party game we used to play, everyone at the table had to pick the one word with which they most strongly identified. It could be a noun—parent, doctor, writer, salesman. An adjective: Italian-American, honest, romantic, and so forth. Some named religion: Catholic, Jew, Buddhist. For Mac and me, there was only ever one word and it was always the same: Southerner. On the occasions we went around the table again, Mac always added "journalist." Although it already was no longer a fashionable label, I always said "wife," to howls of derision from our friends, who, I should add here, were mostly Mac's.

※

Once, when a hometown friend of Mac's came for a weekend visit, we mentioned the game and how revealing it was about people. It was only the three of us, not enough people to play, really, nonetheless, Lucas begged us to, and when it was his turn, promptly announced his choice was motherfucker. He was trying to be funny, I assumed, perhaps to impress upon us that he was a worldly kind of guy, up to the roughscrabble of us nouveau New York sophisticates.

He wasn't, of course. Lucas was a sweet, troubled soul, and despite the increasingly tangible disapproval emanating from Mac's direction, we got along quite well. After dinner, Mac sat on the sofa, one eye on the television, one on us, as Lucas helped me clear the dishes from the table and carry them into the small kitchen alcove. I washed and he dried, slightly teary, as he confided details of a recently ruptured romance.

"What a dope I was. She never loved me. Purely broke my heart," he said sadly.

I gave him another plate to dry. "At least you tried to make it work, Lucas. 'Better to love amiss than nothing to have loved.'"

"Tennyson?" He rubbed an eyelid.

"Good guess. George Crabbe." I gave him a glass to dry.

"Who? Never mind. Now, where does this glass go?" He inspected his handiwork. "Anyway, it was probably more me loving 'not wisely but too much.'"

" 'Too *well*.' Shakespeare." I took the glass from him and put it away.

Lucas put down his dish towel and leaned over me at the sink. He gently rubbed my bare arm.

"You know, Lara, Mac's sure a lucky guy," he said, in soft Georgia tones. He said it so sincerely I shivered.

Mac, just a few feet away in the living room, abruptly stood up and announced, in effect, that the evening was over.

"Sorry to break up your tête-à-tête folks, time for bed."

"Whoa, it's nine-thirty, Mac," Lucas laughed uncertainly. "Isn't this the city that never sleeps?"

"Not in my house. Come on, Lara." He took me by the arm, practically frog-marching me to the bedroom. I barely had time to call out good night. Once inside our room, Mac closed the door and leaned against it.

"Slimy bastard, putting his hands all over you," he whispered at me, in fury.

"He did no such thing," I whispered back, indignantly.

"Liar."

"I'm not lying, Mac. He didn't."

We got undressed and lay down on the bed. Mac turned out the light.

After a few minutes in the dark, Mac sulked aloud.

"He's a pervert, anyway."

"Hush, you. He is not."

"Doesn't incest qualify?"

Satisfied he had my attention, he proceeded, in a low voice, to tell me Lucas hadn't picked the word motherfucker just for effect. Lucas meant it. Literally. Lucas, he said, had slept with his mother since he was thirteen. Well, his stepmother, really, an alcoholic overwhelmed by the family she had married into, but still, she was the only maternal figure Lucas had ever known and though it stopped when Lucas went off to college at eighteen, his unresolved guilt over it subsequently undermined his attempts at adult relationships.

Mac then told me that, in his teens, he himself slept with Lucas' mother—in fact, he said, she'd taken his virginity—an act repeated many times over the next couple of years. Some mornings he hid outside their house, a few streets away, watching as Lucas's father left for the first shift at the Morton's frozen foods factory, not realizing that, as he made his way down the street, lunch pail dangling from one hand, the son he presumed sleeping, was, in fact, climbing into his father's still-warm side of the marital bed. Mac, hidden, waited impatiently for Lucas to finish, get dressed, and leave for school. Often by the time Mac had his turn with her, still wet from Lucas, he was late for school. Irrationally, it seemed all these years later Mac was still mad about that.

I was aghast, but my revulsion changed to pity as he continued, for, in a way, the story was less about Lucas and his mother's sexual mores than it was about a wretched teenage Mac, perpetually searching for Sue Ann Murphy, whether he knew it or not. In any case, it happened years ago, in another lifetime. Had I focused less on Mac, I would have understood, perhaps, Lucas sought the same thing, that they'd shared a common deprivation—the loss of their biological mothers early in life.

I should say here Mac's revelations were often disturbing and I often wondered if they were embellished or even made-up, with the sole purpose of trying to shock me. Subsequent events, however, left me in little doubt this story was, at least, tinged with truth.

When I asked, Mac said he'd kept it secret until this very night because the memory was so painful. Now, he said, it was such a relief to unburden himself to me, he realized how important it was to go to the study and wake Lucas up and tell him. They were, after all, both "victims" of this woman and to acknowledge it, he'd decided, would help them both heal.

Mac insisted he had to do it right away; he could live with this secret no longer. I begged him not to. He left the room and I heard the study door creak open and then shut.

When he returned, I feigned sleep, but he wasn't fooled. It was, he assured me in triumphant whispers, "absolutely the right thing to do." Lucas, he said, took it "like a man" and he was proud of him. In fact, this should help Lucas face up to his problems in the future.

Mac lifted my nightgown and ran a finger down my belly as he spoke. He was excited. I was appalled. But I accepted him because I pitied the boy he had been. I also feared the scene he might make—Lucas was only a few feet away down the hall.

The next morning, I couldn't look Lucas in the eye, not that it mattered in the long run. Conversation was sparse over coffee and toast. Gone was our easy banter of the night before. Lucas seemed a bit groggy, which Mac later told me was from sleeping pills he always took, but nonetheless, Lucas was in a hurry to be on his way. He was driving and wanted to make Canada by nightfall.

We didn't see him again. A few weeks later, Mac came home and, over a glass of wine, told me, with disgust rather than sorrow, that Lucas was dead. Too many sleeping pills. Happened the evening after he left our apartment. Drove to Buffalo and checked into a hotel near the Peace Bridge, paying two nights in advance.

He told the night clerk he had a lot of work to do and didn't want to be disturbed. To emphasize the point, he hung a sign on the doorknob and called housekeeping to say the maids shouldn't knock on his door. Then called room service and requested a bottle of Smirnoff vodka and a bucket of ice.

What a moron, Mac said, mixing it with sleeping pills. Should've known better, but then, Lucas was always looking to blunt reality, the depression and guilt that plagued him since his teens. Only this time, it killed him. Fool.

I had my doubts whether it was, indeed, an accident, but didn't share them. Mac's reaction was discomfiting, and I wondered who, exactly, broke the news to him. He never volunteered that information, and, out of what was a rather maudlin deference to poor, dead Lucas, I never asked.

⁂

Mac was immensely damaged by his own childhood and I not only wanted to help heal those wounds, I think we both actually believed I could. I counted myself an army of one, who saw the real Mac, behind the manufactured bluff and bluster. At the beginning of our courtship, he was respectful and terribly polite and, despite his self-confessed reputation for sexual confrontation, didn't try to sleep with me for months after we met. I was too innocent, he insisted, although by then I was certainly more than willing to sleep with him, wanted to, in fact. I hadn't pretended to be virginal when we met, although Mac insisted on treating me as if I were. He not only wasn't my first love, he wasn't even the second or third. He was, however, the first man I slept with, the others being only college boys by comparison and I said yes immediately when he asked me to marry him. We'd known each other a few months and we would last forever.

Maybe this is why, in the years that followed, I always forgave him when I suspected he was unfaithful. Because I couldn't imagine the consequences of the reverse.

Mac would always return to me; he viewed women as attired in dinner party nouns: saints or sluts. Those he slept with were sluts. I was his wife, I was undeniably the saintliest of all.

Until Thomas.

FOURTEEN

HAVING FOLLOWED MY HUSBAND into faithlessness, I had no claim to the moral high ground. All these years later, it strikes me that if Nadia had exercised restraint, not shown such willful arrogance, perhaps I'd have looked the other way, conditioned as I already was, and this story would have a different ending. But she'd pushed me, a weary traveler, patience in hand, to the outer parameters of my personal tolerance, and the sting of humiliation gave me a new sense of purpose. I would win back my marriage, reclaim my place in Mac's affections. I would do whatever was necessary to keep him.

The about-face was perverse, I know. I'd just spent the morning scouring the city for my lover, if I could call Thomas that, coining images of an imagined future together. But Nadia gave things a new perspective. I now saw sleeping with Thomas as a stalling tactic, an emotional anesthetic, to avoid facing up to a marriage in crisis. Cheap and unpalatable as it is, there was undeniably an element of payback in it, as well.

I still didn't know Thomas's expectations, but, not having heard from him since he left my flat two nights before, I could only presume he didn't have any. It no longer seemed important to find out. He was no longer part of the equation. If, indeed, he'd really ever been.

Mac's jealousy was my own fault, for I'd welcomed it, and now I'd further complicated matters with Thomas. I'd left the peanut butter jar open, in effect, but Mac was the wounded bird, not Thomas. Saving him—us—was what mattered now and I must figure out a way to do it.

This was how I saw it. Nadia was a formidable opponent, but for starters I'd refuse to acknowledge her as a rival. It worked in the past. Being married gave me an in-house advantage and I intended to use it.

><

The next evening Thomas rang the bell, holding out a bouquet of limp pink roses.

"Lara." He shoved the flowers into my hand and I felt the thorns pierce the wrapping.

"I realize it's short notice, but I have a taxi downstairs. I made reservations at the Napolitano. Please come."

Caught by surprise, I started giving all the reasons why I couldn't. I wasn't dressed to go out. My own dinner was cooking.

"Please." He said it quite simply, his face creased with anxiety. "Please come."

It was impossible to disappoint him. He waited in the doorway, while I located shoes and a hairbrush, grabbed a shoulder bag and shawl, and climbed into the taxi with him. I remembered the stove was still on only after we pulled away, and had to ask the driver to stop. The stove, you see, was connected to a gas canister. The potential for danger in Beirut was endless.

The Napolitano Ristorante buzzed with French soldiers from the Multinational Force. Soon, some would be among the casualties of suicide attacks on the U.S. and French Marines, but, of course, we didn't know that then. As we walked in, I caught, by chance, the eye of a young French Marine, fresh faced and fair, and although nowadays people tend to talk about the American Marines who died in Lebanon it is the face of a beautiful Frenchman I remember.

But that night the suicide attacks on the Marines were still two months away and Thomas and I talked only generally about the MNF and the situation—standard Beirut small talk. By the time the first course was finished, conversation slowed almost to a halt and we hardly looked at each other. To cover my embarrassment, I folded my napkin into the origami shapes a classmate had shown me in college.

"Swan, see?" I held it up for inspection.

"It looks like a duck."

"It's a swan." I sighed. "You know, a couple of months ago, I saw homing pigeons flying in formation. The sun was setting and the sky was pink and gold and the way the formation moved and seemed to sway and ripple through the sky was so graceful, like some kind of aerial origami. One of the most wondrous things I've ever seen."

Thomas didn't speak. Nervousness ensured I couldn't stop.

"It was in Cairo. Mac was interviewing this elderly Egyptian gentleman, an architect who had designed some incredible avant garde village in the Nile delta."

I stopped for a moment. "Mac used to take me with him sometimes on stories, you know, not like now."

"Lara," Thomas began, but I interrupted.

"I'm sure you'd recognize the man's name if I could remember it, he was pretty well known," I continued, toying with the napkin.

"He lived in a crumbling wing of this ruined palace in the Old City. While Mac was talking to him, I went up to the rooftop."

I put the napkin down, caught up in the memory.

"You know, I always thought it was just a cliché when people say they had to catch their breath, but I swear, I had to catch my mine, I couldn't breathe, they were such a splendid sight. I suddenly knew what it meant."

It was like being loved, a memory that strong, I could have added, but didn't because Thomas reached out and touched my wrist to stop me.

"Lara," he said, "we should talk."

"Let's not, Thomas. Let's leave things as they are. Please."

I unfolded the napkin and placed it back on my lap.

"We should discuss what has happened."

"Nothing happened, Thomas, nothing that really matters. You came over, we had some wine, we talked."

"And we fucked, Lara," he said. The word sounded odd, with his slight accent: *fuck-ed*.

I didn't flinch, though it certainly wasn't a word I'd have chosen.

"Yes, Thomas," I replied carefully. "We fucked." I tried not to use his inflection, for it would seem I was mocking him and I knew this was one of the most important conversations I would ever have. "That was all."

I looked steadily at him, but could not read his expression.

"Children, children," Fretwell cried with the delight of discovery, "Such long faces, join you for a drink?" He scraped a chair up to the table, his angular face filled with delight at seeing us.

He'd dined already, it emerged, with friends from the British embassy, who appeared to be ordering dessert and coffee across the way, but Fretwell was in no hurry to rejoin them and ordered dessert and another glass of wine at our table. He gabbled away as we finished our food. We were happy to have him with us; his presence relieved the need for further personal discussion and made the evening feel almost normal.

Just after the waiter brought the check, there was a burst of gunfire, and then another as fire was returned.

It brought a hush to the large room, paused forks midbite, stalled glasses midsip.

"Ah, they're playing our song," Fretwell said.

But he, too, looked expectant, and, like the other diners—like Thomas, like me—was as motionless as a woodland animal upon hearing a footfall in the forest, straining to gauge the level of threat posed.

The gunfire tapered off after a minute or two. Then a loud boom announced that the shelling had begun.

"And that"—Fretwell stood up as another boom quickly echoed in the distance—"would be our cue to exit. Come on, brave lads and lasses, I'll give you a ride back."

"Shouldn't we just wait it out here?" I asked anxiously. I did not relish a ride in the dark with things exploding around me.

"If we do that, we'll be here all night," Fretwell smiled as he pulled my chair back to let me stand up. "I don't know about you, but I personally have no desire to spend the night with young Thomas here."

I looked for the innuendo but failed to find it. It wasn't Fretwell's way. He only wanted to leave the restaurant while it was still possible to do so without guarantee of death. I looked questioningly at Thomas, who nodded reassuringly.

Fretwell drove a clapped-out blue VW.

"Here, let me sit in the back," Thomas said, but I brushed him aside.

"No, no, not enough legroom. I'm much smaller."

"We'd best hurry or there won't be enough left of any of us to argue over," Fretwell said. He pushed the driver's seat forward and I climbed into the back, wedging myself between piles of old magazines and newspapers and a box of typewriter ribbons and several large plastic bottles of water. The shells were falling heavily, though the battle was just beginning and would intensify as the night wore on.

As we flew down a side street, a young gunman in a white T-shirt that made him visible against the night suddenly appeared out of the shadows, about twenty or thirty feet ahead, and motioned for us to stop. We were in a Druze neighborhood that bordered on a Shiite enclave under Amal's control, but at this distance, at nighttime, it was impossible to tell what his allegiances were. We slowed for a moment and the gunman probably thought we were stopping, for I certainly did, but instead Fretwell gunned the engine, slamming his foot down on the accelerator.

"I'll come back tomorrow, promise! I'll be a good boy, I'll come back tomorrow!" he called out, rather merrily, considering the circumstances, as we sped away.

We all turned in our seats to see the gunman running after us, rifle in one fist and shaking the other at us, shouting oaths we couldn't hear. I sunk low in the back seat and braced myself, waiting for the bullets I was sure would puncture the car any second now, but, for reasons known only to himself, he didn't fire. As he rapidly receded from sight, Fretwell and Thomas hooted with laughter and relief, and Thomas punched Fretwell's arm in teasing admiration and Fretwell punched him back.

In no time, the story was being retold on the Commodore circuit. It hardly needed embellishing.

❉

Mac returned from Teheran in early August, staying a week longer than planned. I assumed Nadia was entertaining him, as he stayed in the office even longer than usual and only once came to me in the night. Our shaky marital truce held, though ultimately it would prove as substantive as the Syrian-sponsored cease-fire Lebanon's warring factions signed a month later. I give nothing away by saying ours also ultimately dissolved under the weight of other pressures, too many competing interests, and, ultimately, a lack of good faith.

But that was still a way off. At this point, Mac and I were still officially together and, despite Nadia, there was no hint he wished it otherwise.

To be sure, we never discussed what happened before he left and for all I knew Mac didn't even remember it. I also had amnesia, consigning my infidelity to the dustbin of inconvenient memories.

Thomas and I didn't avoid each other—impossible in Beirut— but we no longer sought out each other. When we did meet, it was cordial, but distant. The friendship waned, so it was difficult to imagine having ever shared a meal and impossible, having shared a bed.

As if it had never happened, I couldn't remember what his body felt like. His kiss, his touch, weren't dear enough to me.

Apart from the hasty, futile search the morning after we became lovers, there was nothing to connect us in an unseemly fashion. With each passing day, I worried a little less about Mac finding out. I tried not to think about what Hamid and Amina knew. Eventually, that morning seemed far in the past, and I subsequently wondered how much of it was the product of my imagination, a fervor of paranoia and passion.

The passion was only momentary, of course. The paranoia remained, but diminished, and I tried not to be driven by it, though there was no question what would happen if Mac ever found out.

I stopped going to TV Kansai, and Gifford asked why, when I saw him at the Commodore. Too busy, I said, trying to write freelance articles for a women's magazine back home. Gifford didn't look convinced, but let it pass without comment. Perhaps he thought I was just a wife, after all. Perhaps I was.

I saw staying away as staying out of harm's way, away from Hamid and his meaningful looks, but there was no reason to avoid Amina. Our conversations, however, grew formal and forced where they had once been easy. Amina was always careful to inquire after Mac. Neither of us uttered Thomas's name, which left us little to talk about.

⁂

Mac was still after an interview with Major Haddad in the south, in the security zone near the Israeli border. At the same time, he was far more eager to secure an interview with the elusive Sheikh Mohammed Hussain Fadlallah. It seemed every journalist covering the Middle East wanted to talk with the spiritual leader of the Hezbollah, believed to be behind the embassy bombing. Fadlallah was considered so dangerous, the CIA later allegedly tried to knock him off, paying two million dollars, or so the story around Beirut went, to have a car bomb put outside *his* residence, in what could be deemed a karma redux. He escaped; eighty others weren't so lucky.

Within a year of its founding, Hezbollah had become a force to be reckoned with in Lebanon, both in terms of its influence in the south of Lebanon, and, increasingly, its presence in Beirut, as the incident in Basta underlined. Both Iran and Syria were said to give it support, military, political, and, of course, the religious establishment. Fadlallah himself was said to have been handpicked by Teheran to head what was, effectively, a collective of Lebanese Shiite clerics. Each spawned his own network of extremist followers, far removed from both mainstream Islam and the tradition of Shiite Islam, as Lebanon had previously known it.

Thomas heard Mac complaining in the Commodore one night about the difficulty in reaching Fadlallah and offered to try to help. Mac rejected the offer with indifference. This was before Teheran, before I slept with Thomas, so there was no connection. Mac's refusal to accept help from him sprang solely from a reluctance to be obligated to a man he disliked so much.

By mid-August, Mac was still no closer to the sheikh. I found this strange and said so one evening during dinner. We hardly ate together any more; he came home later and later and usually didn't bother with excuses and I didn't believe them when he did. At the moment, it seemed wisest not to challenge him.

His return from Teheran coincided with a spate of attacks on the U.S. Marines and the big trouble brewing up in the Chouf Mountains between the Lebanese Army and Druze and their allies, various leftist fighters.

On August 10, Druze gunmen in the mountains above the city

fired dozens of rounds of artillery and mortars at Beirut airport, the Ministry of Defense, and the presidential palace. One U.S. Marine was wounded. Three Lebanese cabinet ministers were kidnapped.

The violence had tripped to yet another level and the effect was unnerving, even for those used to living with the crazy tilt of tension.

After another barrage at the airport the next day, near the Marine compound, I went to TV Kansai. I missed Gifford and our edit sessions, but that wasn't why I returned.

No, the real reason was this: although solitary by nature, I'd become isolated, as well, and there is a difference. With so many attacks on the American military in Lebanon, I needed to feel included in the larger picture.

That night, I handed Mac a scotch, without ice, and positioned myself next to him on the couch. He'd put on weight, his paunch spilling over the top of his belt. He was sunburned, the pink of his scalp peeping through where his graying hairline was thinned in the front. There were white circles around his eyes, ghost sunglasses.

"I just can't get this freaking interview pinned down," he complained.

I said the first thing that popped into my head. Unfortunately.

"Why don't you ask Thomas? He has excellent contacts and he's offered to help. Is it because you'd have to pay him?"

Mac looked dangerously annoyed.

"I'll tell you why. Because I don't need his help. That's why."

He sipped from his glass and tossed the magazine he'd been reading back onto the pile on the coffee table. He put his feet on top of it and leaned back, hands clasped behind his head. He was tired and it showed. The hard work and stress of living amid constant violence was taking its toll. The drink showed too, in the tiny broken veins and a red face even when he hadn't been out in the sun.

"Anyway, Nadia's on it. Her uncle has a friend who has a connection to one of Hezbollah's top commanders."

"Nadia's been on it for months, Mac. But it never happens. What do you have to lose by asking Thomas? Surely, the magazine won't care if you pay him a freelance fee."

"You're such an expert on everything."

"I'm not trying to be, I'm just asking."

"Well, I *am* an expert, okay? I don't trust the guy and I have no intention of putting myself in a position where I owe him one."

"But if he can get Fadlallah, why not use him?"

"Look, Lara, he's your little friend, not mine. The guy has too many fingers in too many pies."

"Now what does that mean?" I persisted, though the conversation clearly irritated him and proceeding with it carried a discernible risk.

"What it means," Mac said, "is that I think he's a little shit. I don't trust him and I don't want his so-called help. End of story."

"Why are you always so mean?" I said, standing up and going over to the balcony doors. I turned back to look at him.

"He's not a shit, Mac."

"God damn it, Lara, why don't you just stay out of things that don't concern you. Go play with Gifford and his TV toys. Just stay out of my business."

By the end of the month of August 1983, the U.S. was well and truly sucked into the vortex of violence in Lebanon.

The Marines had stepped out of their peacekeeping role before, to help in the snowstorms and floods. This time, the perception was of a new and different role—combatant—when they were forced to return fire for the first time. Various Moslem and leftist militiamen attacked their position near the airport with semi-automatic weapons and rocket-propelled grenades in a battle that lasted an hour and a half.

Worse followed the next day, when two Marines were killed and two dozen more were injured in a hailstorm of rockets, mortars, and shells, of every shape and caliber, on the Marine positions on the eastern perimeter of the airport.

President Reagan's spokesman condemned the killings and reminded the world the Marines were there at the invitation of the Lebanese government, as if there really were one with any sway over these groups.

In the days that followed, a French soldier was killed and five Italians wounded when their command posts were pummelled. On the last day of August, Moslem militias shelled the U.S. ambassador's residence.

⁙

Now, it seemed, Washington officially awoke to the dangers its forces faced. Hard as it is to believe, Lebanon must not have been officially considered a war zone up to this point. I say this because only on August 31 did the U.S. Department of Defense authorize hostile-fire pay of $65 a month for the Marines and the sailors of the 24th MAU serving in Lebanon.

The U.S. force had been there for a year.

✿

By contrast, Mac's magazine gave him an extra ten thousand dollars and two additional weeklong breaks a year in the European capital of his choice in recognition of the unrelenting danger Lebanon presented.

And though Mac's job was predicated on an inherent level of risk, he wasn't stuck out on the tarmac at Beirut airport, day after day, like the Marines, a live exhibit in the shooting gallery Beirut had become. He wasn't there to save Lebanon.

FIFTEEN

THE ISRAELIS ABRUPTLY PULLED OUT of the Chouf Mountains in early September, triggering a new crisis, as fighting mushroomed between the Christians and the Druze in the newly vacated hills. The Multinational Force was drawn in, as the Druze shelled the airport and, over the next two days, two more Marines died and two were injured in the savage volley. The toll quickly climbed—within days, four Marines would die, with twenty-eight injured.

I was in Gifford's edit suite when a U.S. Navy ship used its five-inch guns for the first time. It was a frigate, the USS *Bowen,* trying to take out a Druze position above the airport.

"Well, that'll ratchet it all up. No telling where it goes from here, mate," Gifford said. He inserted video of the ship on the horizon and the Marines at the airport, and spooled the pictures along. Loud booms thundered in the distance.

"Can't call this shit peacekeeping."

"They have the right to defend themselves, don't they? Even peacekeepers?"

"Sometimes, it's better not to fly that flag, Lara."

The next day, I was at TV Kansai watching Gifford when the door to the edit suite opened and Thomas poked his head around the corner.

"There you are, Lara. Mind if I borrow her, Bruce?"

"She's not mine to lend, mate, but hey, take her anyway."

"Actually, we're kind of busy," I said.

"So I see," Thomas said dryly. He didn't move.

"Go on," Gifford said to me, racking through the video. Absorbed in the pictures and the task at hand, he'd lost interest in us. "I want to get cracking on this story."

I collected my things and, reluctantly, left with Thomas. Hamid didn't look at me, but made a remark in Arabic to Thomas, who replied curtly.

Thomas put his hand on my back and steered me out the door. In the stairwell outside the office, I turned on him.

"Are you crazy? What's this all about?"

"I thought you might be interested in taking a little journey with me."

"A journey? With everything that's going on?"

"Let me rephrase it," Thomas said. "Would you like to go to East Beirut with me? It's safe enough; away from the front lines."

We reached the tiny foyer on the ground floor.

"East Beirut?" We'd hardly seen each other for weeks, yet my impulse was to agree immediately, and do it before common sense eliminated the option.

I chewed a nail, wanting a cigarette. I hadn't been back to East Beirut since the night we'd arrived, which meant I hadn't even seen the Green Line properly, by daylight. I'd simply never had reason to. The first few times Mac first went back and forth I had no desire to go with him—too afraid. By the time I felt ready to brave it again, Mac wouldn't let me. He went for his work, he said pointedly, I'd only be in the way. Once or twice, when I saw others—

Katya, Martin, the TV Kansai crew—setting out for East Beirut, I considered asking, but pride prevented it. How mortifying to admit Mac wouldn't take me. Besides, I told myself, it would be pure folly to go for the sake of sightseeing when others only went because they had to.

"You said you've never really been, and I have to meet somebody, so I thought you'd like to come," Thomas was saying.

"It's tempting. But won't it look strange?"

"We can have lunch in Beit Meri and be back by late afternoon."

He paused, then: "Frankly, I think it looks strange if we avoid seeing each other. That's more likely to set tongues wagging."

His eyes met mine. I looked away first.

"Maybe you're right," I said dubiously. "I don't know what Mac will say, though."

"Then don't ask. Just come."

"I can't do that. He'll find out anyway and be furious. You know Mac."

I thought hard. "Hang on, Thomas, I have an idea. Be back in a minute."

In the event, I couldn't find Mac. He and Nadia were out with Abdel Farid, a new girl clipping newspapers in his office told me. She must've been a Nadia confederate, judging by guilty little start she gave when she saw me. She seemed inordinately nervous when I asked where Mac was, shifting uncomfortably, not meeting my eyes.

For once, I didn't care. Mac's absence was a relief. This way, my conscience was clear. Equally clear was the thought I'd pay for it later.

Thomas had a car waiting in front of the Commodore.

One thing I understood from the start about Beirut was the way identity defined its geography—the geography of terror, it was called.

The Green Line not only divided the two hills upon which Beirut was built; it was, of course, the fundamental dividing line between the nation's two main communities, Christian and Moslem. Roughly the length of the city, from the port in the north to the airport in the south, the Green Line separated the Maronite Christians in the east, and the Sunni Moslems in the northwest of the city, and the Shiites and Palestinians—most of them Moslem—in the southwest.

We drove through a poor Shiite area, along Corniche al Mazra, teeming with refugees, entire families driven to find shelter in Beirut after fleeing the fighting in southern Lebanon. Sidewalk vendors pedalled Beiruti fast food—*schwarma*, beans simmered with herbs and spices, and other hot foods wrapped in Arabic bread. Gradually, we left the bustle behind; traffic thinned out and the streets got progressively emptier until we reached a totally deserted square with the now-abandoned National Museum on the right-hand side, its treasures and artifacts removed for safe-keeping, and the Beirut racecourse. Just on the other side of its stone walls, I knew, was the one-time residence of the ambassador of France, the former colonial power, which now housed French MNF troops, soldiers from the French Foreign Legion.

The closer we drew to the Green Line, the more severe the destruction; shards of buildings everywhere, like a comb missing teeth, much as I imagined a city would look like after a nuclear bomb. Preoccupied with these sights, I forgot to worry about the potential awkwardness of being with Thomas.

He broke the silence.

"This was the financial district, the heart of the city, this downtown area. It was the banking and commerce capital of the Middle East."

There were frighteningly few cars on this street. The so-called Sniper Alley. No need to ask how it got the name. The driver, whom I didn't know, was silent throughout, concentrating on the task at hand.

As we glided along, I tried to conjure up a mental transparency, a ghost image, of a busy city center, to overlay the ruins. It was difficult. The street was rutted; the sidewalks were broken, overgrown with weeds several feet high. Lush greenery, plants, and trees grew in the honeycombed wreckage on either side of the street, gutted by shells and gunfire, startlingly verdant.

"I like to say this is why it's *called* the Green Line."

"I thought it was the color used to draw it on maps."

"That's the official explanation. I prefer my own, that it is the way Nature moved to fill this void created by Man."

Thomas, unfailingly polite, pretended not to notice the tears dribbled down my cheeks as we sped through this holocaust, and, at first, I surreptitiously wiped them away, but soon there were too many and I was openly weeping.

※

I had the sense we were passing through a sacred burial ground, and if you think about it, that is, indeed, what it was: a vast, urban, concrete cemetery, haunted by ghosts of the past, hunted by warriors of the present, hidden among the ruins, watching us even now through rifle scopes as we journeyed through their territory. A landscape of the dead, alive with danger.

Never have I seen a place so eerie, nor been so afraid and so full of awe at the same time.

❖

Arriving in East Beirut itself was anticlimactic.

My first impression was it didn't look as badly damaged as West Beirut. It was more upscale than I remembered, the shops looked slightly more prosperous, had more signs in French, and, not surprisingly, there were churches instead of mosques.

We drove through East Beirut and its suburbs and up the steep winding mountain road, up Mount Lebanon.

"We'll have lunch in Beit Meri," Thomas said. "It's a summer resort, very popular, even with the war, a lovely village with spectacular views. It's very near the home of the Mroues, the newspaper family. Kamal Mroue, the editor of the *Daily Star*, was assassinated, a few years before the civil war officially started."

Ahead, the huge al-Bustan Hotel dominated the cliff top. We passed a few small shops and a petrol pump, as well as some red brick houses and many others made of stone, surrounded by tall oak and pine trees.

Thomas kept up a running commentary along the way, pointing out a Maronite monastery, Roman ruins, a temple to the goddess Juno.

"If you appreciate Byzantine, there's a mosaic tiled floor from a sixth-century church, beautifully preserved." He paused for breath. Thankfully. It was a lot to take in.

"I'd love to see it. Can we look?"

"Maybe after lunch. Let's see how the time goes."

The car pulled up next to an outdoor café near the roadside. It was empty, save for a couple with two small children seated at a table at the far end of the patio.

"We are here," Thomas announced. "Splendid."

The valley lay at our feet, the Mediterranean lapping at its curves.

"Beirut's over there," Thomas pointed, "And Jounieh that way, up the coast. I'd take you to the casino there but I can't afford to lose any more money."

I let the remark pass. We got out and Thomas leaned back into the driver's window and spoke to him in Arabic. The driver grunted, rolled up the window, and drove off.

As we approached, a young woman, dark blonde hair swept back in one large, loose plait, stepped out of the café doorway toward us and squealed with joy when she recognized Thomas. She flew to us, nodded with a *"Bonjour, mademoiselle"* to me, then spoke excitedly to Thomas, who returned her greeting with obvious affection. He laughed and said *"lentement, lentement, Camille"*—slowly, slowly— but she peppered him with exclamations and questions. *"Mon amie, Lara,"* Thomas introduced us. "Camille's father owns this café."

"You are visiting Lebanon?" Camille spoke with a French accent.

"We live in West Beirut."

"It is dangerous, *non*, and too horrible? You are American, with the university?"

"No, my husband writes for a magazine."

"Ah, you are married, then." She appraised me. *"Ma'alesh.* Never mind. Now come and sit down."

She showed us to a table and pulled out chairs for us to sit.

Thomas asked about Camille's father. Quite well, thank you, she replied in French, and I remembered enough from college to understand her parents were visiting relatives near Tripoli, in the north. There was fighting there, she said, and she would worry about them every minute until they came back. Camille and Thomas talked a little more, then, with a last quick glance at me, she disappeared inside.

I wasn't aware of Thomas ordering, but he must have, for shortly Camille returned with a tray laden with pickled vegetables, grape leaves in olive oil stuffed with rice, grilled haloumi cheese, hummus and labeneh, a kind of homemade yogurt dip, Arabic bread, and small glasses of arak, with a pitcher of water and a bowl of ice.

"The national drink, you know," said Thomas, thanking her.

"Sorry, I'm not very fond of it. Too sweet and sticky."

"Try," he urged, pouring a little water into one of the glasses. The clear liquid turned cloudy. He added an ice cube and pushed the glass across the table.

"Most Mediterranean countries have their own versions—*ouzo* in Greece, *pastis* in France, *sambuca* in Italy. But I think this is best."

Camille emerged from the door of the café to tell Thomas there was a phone call for him. He excused himself and followed her inside.

I fiddled with a piece of bread and had a sip of the arak. Camille reappeared at the table.

"You are enjoying our view?" she asked, smiling.

"You can see the whole city."

"You said your husband is a journalist here in the Lebanon? Do I know of him? He is very famous?"

"Not very, I'm afraid." I laughed at the idea. "His name is Barrett McCauley. He works for a weekly news magazine."

"Barrett McCauley. Ah. I see." A hard look replaced her friendly smile. "You are Barrett McCauley's wife?"

"You know him?"

"I've met him, here at our café." She paused, then continued, "With Nadia, of course." She looked frankly at me.

"Of course," I tried to sound confident. "She works for my husband."

"We went to the convent school together in East Beirut."

"How nice." The arak burned in my stomach.

"Nadia is from a very good family," she said. "Lots of money they have before the war. *Ma'alesh*, she will have it again, I am sure. She is very beautiful. And very smart, of course."

"Very smart," I repeated. Then, emboldened by *arak* or despair, added, "for a slut."

"I beg your pardon?"

"I said, for a slut. Very smart for a slut."

"What is slut?" Camille sounded genuinely puzzled.

"A whore."

Her face darkened, but any chance to reply was cut short.

"Ladies, such language!" Thomas returned.

"Sorry, Thomas, we were talking about Nadia," I said defiantly. Thomas laughed and clasped Camille by the shoulders.

"What an uninspiring topic for such a beautiful day. Let's move on, shall we. Ah, look, Gerard is here now."

Camille pulled away and sullenly retreated to the café. A dark blue Mercedes with blacked-out windows pulled up along the roadside just past the café, a white jeep ahead of it, carrying several men with arms, and another, similarly packed jeep behind. Two men jumped out of the lead vehicle, automatic rifles at the ready and looking in all directions, while two others spilled out of the rear jeep and dove into the café, emerging a few moments later to give a thumbs-up signal to the Mercedes.

The front door on the passenger side of the Mercedes opened and a wiry man in a dark T-shirt and close-fitting black jeans got out and scanned the area as well before opening the back passenger door. A broad-shouldered, muscular man in a khaki safari suit, with aviator-style sunglasses and sharply angled sideburns, stepped out and waved at Thomas as he headed for our table, the bodyguard a few brisk paces ahead.

The couple at the far end of the patio hurriedly put a wad of money on the table and scooped up their children, smiling apologetically at the gunmen, who unsmilingly stepped aside to let them pass.

"Thomas, Thomas." The man in the safari suit embraced him and kissed both cheeks, held him out at arm's length, then hugged him again. Thomas stepped back to introduce me, still seated.

"Gerard, this is my friend Lara. Lara, Gerard."

"You brought someone with you?" he said in French to Thomas, with evident displeasure, as he smiled, thinly, at me.

He raised my hand to his lips in an exaggerated gesture. Everything about him was exaggerated—the many bodyguards, the sideburns, the thick ropey gold chain around his neck with matching bracelet, the chunky gold and diamond rings, even his freshly shaven cheeks, redolent of an overbearing cologne. I couldn't see his eyes behind the sunglasses but felt sure I wouldn't be happy if I could.

"Pleased to meet you," I said.

"The pleasure is mine, *mademoiselle*," he said, "So nice you could come with Thomas, but I am afraid our business will bore you."

"Actually, it's *madame*."

"Lara has never seen the east side, so I thought I would show her some of Lebanon's most beautiful scenery," Thomas quickly explained. Gerard looked neither pleased nor convinced.

Turning to me, Thomas said, "Gerard is quite right, our business will not interest you. Will you excuse us for a few minutes please? We shall finish lunch when I return. Camille will look after you in the meantime."

They walked away, Gerard's arm around Thomas's shoulder as they headed for the edge of the hilltop, several bodyguards following a discreet distance behind.

They stopped not far away, their backs to me, and talked in low voices. Once, Gerard turned and looked angrily in my direction as he talked, but at least from a distance Thomas appeared unruffled.

Camille came out once and surveyed the convoy of vehicles, now parked a little way up the road, and looked over at Thomas and Gerard. I'd finished my *arak,* and the accompanying glass of carbonated water, but Camille made no move to replenish it, nor did she bring out more food. She may have been making a point by ignoring me; it suited me fine.

Finally, they started walking back toward our table. Gerard clapped Thomas on the back and Thomas invited him to sit and eat with us. He shook his head, said good-bye to Thomas, and nodded in my direction before heading for his car, bodyguards scrambling to stay ahead.

They were gone in a moment—orders barked, doors slammed, the convoy headed off, tires squealing as the vehicles accelerated and sprang away.

"So what shall we have for the main course?" Thomas was seated again, across from me, rubbing his hands.

"What was that all about?" I asked him. "Who's Gerard?

"Gerard is an old friend, but, beyond that, he is a very important man in this part of Lebanon."

"All those bodyguards. I know he's a friend of yours but he gave me the creeps."

"His family is very powerful in Christian politics. Gerard is a little like Mussolini—fascist, tyrant, perhaps, but he makes the trains run on time."

"What a guy."

Thomas laughed. "Never mind, Lara. Let's enjoy the rest of this afternoon. What shall we order?"

"I'm sorry, Thomas, I'm not very hungry. Besides, Camille might spit in my food or something. Maybe we should just head home."

"As you like."

I wanted to split the bill, partly to make it less like a date and partly because I knew Thomas couldn't afford it. He stoutly refused, however, and, while I waited, went in to pay and, I presume, say his good-byes to Camille.

As if magically orchestrated, our car arrived outside the café as Thomas came out the door. The driver must have been nearby, watching.

As we got in, I looked back to see Camille in the doorway of the café.

In memory, I see her still, gold plait caught in the sunlight, arms folded across her chest, green eyes narrowed as she watched us pull away.

SIXTEEN

"YOUR FRIEND CAMILLE AND I didn't quite hit if off," I said to Thomas as we began the descent down Mt. Lebanon. "You know she went to school with Nadia? She couldn't wait to tell me Mac had been there with Nadia."

Thomas sighed.

"Nadia works with Barrett and if they have work on this side of town, it is natural she takes him to a friendly place. Why fuss over this? You shouldn't let it bother you."

"It bothers me."

Thomas looked out the window. I considered stopping, but carried on. "You know she's sleeping with Mac. Doesn't everyone in Beirut know?"

Thomas regarded his hands with undue interest. He finally gave a half shake of his head.

"You have the luxury of choice, Lara," Thomas said very slowly, abandoning his hands to look at me. "In Lebanon, few people even remember what it is. Shakespeare said there is little choice in rotten apples. In Lebanon, it was taken away at gunpoint. Literally. All that's left is rotten apples."

He turned back to the window, then asked thoughtfully, "In the time you've been here, have you ever visited a Palestinian refugee camp, seen a family with seven children jammed into one small, dirty room? A paradise compared to the latest kind of refugee camp, like we passed in Chiiya, the buildings where squatters, poor people, mostly Shiites from the south, displaced by war, have taken over. No running water, no toilets, no electricity, and nowhere else to go. People camped in stairwells with sick children and no medicine. No food. Have you seen this yourself? Talk to Suha or Abdel Farid or this driver here today, Zaki—ask them about the tyranny of the minority. Ask them what it is like to have those two percent with guns control everyone else's daily destiny."

I said nothing. What could I possibly say?

"I do not wish to make light of the things that trouble you, Lara, I only want to help you put them into perspective."

He searched my eyes. "Unlike them, *you* have choice. You have *chosen* your life. You can walk away from all of this, from Barrett, from your marriage, any time you choose. You can walk away from this country, this war, right now. Imagine such a luxury!"

He looked away for a moment. "You choose to stay. This is your choice."

I was spared having to reply by the driver, who, silent until now, suddenly said something loud and urgent. His alarm needed no translation, and he slammed on the brakes. Ahead, a column of thick black smoke was visible and two cars came screeching toward us from the other direction, horns honking and lights flashing. One driver signalled us to go back in the direction from which we had come.

"Bad news. The burning tires are a warning to stay away. There must be fighting ahead at the crossing," Thomas said. He leaned forward to speak to the driver, who, without waiting to be told, was already turning our own car around.

"Oh, dear," I said, "What now?"

Thomas conferred hastily with the driver. His worried face alarmed me.

"Zaki says he'll try the Murr Tower next. If it's shut, we'll go to the port. One or the other will be open, I'm sure."

In Ashrafieh, a Maronite Christian neighborhood, where the Lebanese Front held sway, there were few cars and fewer people on the streets. We glided onto a section of an elevated overpass, heading for the Murr Tower, the great, unfinished concrete structure standing out amid the wreckage of the Beirut skyline. Nearly a decade ago the onset of war stopped the construction of Beirut's tallest building midway through. Meant to symbolize Lebanon's glittering role in Middle East banking and finance, the skeletal Murr Tower instead became a prize for the militias to fight over, its height ideal for sniping.

As we neared the abandoned tower, a car spun crazily towards us.

"Look! His tires are shot out!" Thomas shouted, "Turn around, Zaki!"

Zaki was already turning, and, as we watched in horror, the other car veered off the overpass and onto the asphalt and concrete maze below, with a sickening crash.

"Should we try to help?" I'm not sure if I even said the words aloud. I wanted nothing more than to be far away, somewhere safe.

Neither replied, and the next few minutes were an agony of racing hearts as we made our way to the port.

Thomas broke the silence.

"Maybe the snipers will be out there today too—it's anyone's guess—but, usually, it is one of the safer crossings. Maybe the safest."

We'd left Beit Meri at four o'clock; it was after six now. Mac might or might not be starting to worry yet.

Suddenly, our car slowed down and then stopped. Sharp-featured gunmen, well-shaven and wearing combat vests over tight-fitting, white T-shirts, appeared from nowhere. Machine guns raised, they motioned us to stop.

"Checkpoint. Phalangists." Thomas said, warily. "Don't worry. It should be fine."

The gunmen approached, shouting at the driver. Frightened, Zaki took various documents from the wallet in his shirt pocket and, with shaking fingers, held them up to the window for the gunmen to see. They gestured him to get out of the car, which he did, slowly and carefully. While one kept his gun trained on us, another walked Zaki a few feet away, nudging him in the back with the barrel of his machine gun. Zaki said "American" loudly, pointing back at us, and, upon hearing that, the gunman nearest us poked his gun through the back passenger window and rattled off questions in rapid-fire Arabic at Thomas.

"The gentleman wants to see your passport, Lara," Thomas said, calmly, getting his own out. It bore a golden imprint of the Polish eagle—the Communist version, without the crown. The gunman took our passports over to his cohort, who examined them for several minutes before handing them back to Zaki with a shouted order. A clearly shaken Zaki returned to the car, got in, and started the engine. As we rolled up the windows and slowly drove off, the gunmen were already busy with another car behind us.

A couple of blocks later, Zaki pulled our car over to the curb.

He said something, looking at us in the rearview mirror. Thomas replied and it didn't sound as if he were pleased, at all.

"Zaki says it's not safe to use the port crossing either. There's shooting there too and it's closed. The Lebanese Forces guys say we shouldn't try to cross at all."

"What does that mean? Stay here?" The panic I'd successfully held back since we first saw smoke at the museum crossing now flooded over me. "We can't stay. I have to get back. Mac doesn't know where I am."

"Barrett will understand. I'm sure he'd rather you came home in one piece."

"Please, Zaki, won't you take us back to West Beirut?" I appealed directly.

He turned around in his seat to face us. It was Thomas to whom he spoke, but even I understood. *La.* No.

"Zaki says this is as far as he'll go," Thomas translated.

"He has to take us back to West Beirut. Please make him understand, Thomas. We have to try. Mac will kill me. We have to go back tonight. Please."

"We can't. Zaki won't do it. He means it."

"Would he change his mind for a hundred dollars? Two hundred?"

"I doubt he'd risk his life even for that," Thomas said frowning, but he put it to Zaki anyway.

"*La.*"

"There must be another way, another crossing maybe?" I tried again.

Thomas asked Zaki. "*Mish mahoul,*" he said emphatically, shaking his head.

Funny how much Arabic I suddenly understood.

"Another driver, then? Can someone else take us?" Zaki apparently didn't need a translation of my words by now either, for he repeated *"Mish mahoul"* before Thomas could speak.

"If Zaki won't take us, no one else will either. Listen, let's go to the Hotel Alexandre. We'll call the Commodore from there and they'll get word to Barrett that we're stuck here for the night. We'll try again first thing in the morning. Barrett will understand."

"Mac won't understand. Not one bit."

"Barrett knows Beirut; these things happen all the time. Let's go to the Alexandre and we can discuss it there."

My announcement took us all by surprise. "I'm going back. I'll walk across if I have to."

The words sounded bold, but I knew the decision was born of cowardice, not courage. Frightened as I was, the prospect of Mac's wrath was more frightening.

"Don't be silly, it's too dangerous."

"Other people do it. Suha does it sometimes, she told me."

"Because she has no other choice if she wants to feed her family. It's different for you. You have a choice."

"Then I choose to walk back, if it's the only way."

"It is insanity. I can't let you go. You don't even know the way."

"You can't stop me. Look, I understand why Zaki won't go. But this is my choice and I choose to go."

I opened the door and listened. "I don't hear any shooting, do you? Maybe they've stopped fighting."

The next move was mine; I got out. Zaki hung out the car window, gesturing and pleading with me in Arabic and a little English.

I'd gotten barely ten feet away when the door on Thomas's side opened.

"You can't go alone."

"Good-bye, Thomas."

I kept walking. He hurried to catch up with me and caught me by the arm.

"I can't let you do this by yourself. I'll come, Lara, but please be sensible. Zaki can go to the Alexandre and call the Commodore to arrange for a driver to meet us on the other side of the crossing."

It made sense. Reluctantly, I walked back to the car with him to make the arrangements. Zaki looked unhappy, and a couple of times he said *"Majnoon,"* which I knew meant crazy, but Thomas prevailed. Zaki called out a last word of warning to us and drove off.

"Zaki says, be careful, it's mined."

We were on our own now, facing the sinister stillness of the immense, ruined port.

❉

I still don't know how I made myself do it. Desperation fuelled every step. I may have called it choice to Thomas, but it would have been more accurate to say there was no other choice. Go back or face unthinkable consequences.

Despite what Thomas said, I felt as trapped in my own life as everyone else here.

It was no less a trap for being spun of my own acquiescence.

❉

Thomas and I walked hurriedly, wordless, single file, on a narrow, unpaved path, parallel with the winding road, perhaps a quarter of a mile long, hidden sets of eyes undoubtedly tracking our journey. We stayed as close to the wrecked buildings as possible, ducking into the open facades of partially destroyed warehouses, into doorways without doors, skirting areas Thomas thought might be mined, although it seemed impossible to gauge such a thing.

The path zigzagged between the warehouses and ghostly garages, large mounds of rubbish on either side. A few feet ahead, a solitary rat turned around at the sound of our footsteps and looked back quizzically, surprised by the company, before he scuttled out of view.

Just off what were the docks of Beirut's once great port, semi-submerged hulks of great rusted ships jutted toward the sky; huge, twisted metal rinds everywhere.

For the second time that day, the words "no-man's-land" came alive for me. But every step we took meant that we'd survived the one before, and for a few moments I felt a sense of triumph.

"At least there's no fighting," I whispered to Thomas, my first words since we'd set out.

A sudden loud burst of gunfire reverberated through the port and sent me rushing headlong into Thomas's back.

"Steady on," he said in a low voice, helping me regain my balance.

Fire was immediately returned, though it was difficult to tell from which direction. The noise echoed around us. It sounded as if it were happening close by, but we could see nothing to indicate it was actually inside the port.

"It must be on the other side," Thomas said into my ear, as he pulled me by the hand inside one of the derelict buildings. Two cars screeched along the road, horns honking—the white Land Rovers favoured by West Beirut militias—followed by a pickup truck packed with more gunmen.

We stayed in our hiding place. It was surrealistic—trapped in the Green Line while a battle raged nearby. I was terrified when we started this perilous passage, but, as dusk finally coated the sky and Thomas and I huddled together, listening to the militaristic duet, despite our precarious toehold on safety, for a little while, I felt oddly protected.

※

We waited until well after the noise subsided before cautiously emerging from our shelter, and hurried the last block of the way out. We were much closer to the west side than we'd realized and very soon were exiting the port completely. As we walked swiftly along the Corniche, a car coming toward us honked as it executed a U-turn and rolled up alongside us. Abdel Farid stuck his head out the window, grinning widely.

"Al Hamdallilah," he called. Thanks to God. "You are safe."

I ran to the car, yanked the door open, and saw Mac in the back. "Get in," he hissed. I automatically complied but Mac looked so menacing that Thomas hung back uncertainly.

"Come on, Thomas," I waved him over. He approached, tentatively.

"Yeah, get in, Warkowski, I want to talk to you, too."

Chastened, we slipped onto the back seat, one after another.

"So what the hell kind of stunt is this?" Mac's voice quivered with rage.

"Please let me explain," Thomas began, but Mac cut him off.

"I'll get to you in a minute, Warkowski. Right now, I'm talking to my wife."

"Mac, please, let's talk when we get home."

"We'll talk about this now, damn it. I want to know what the *fuck* you were thinking, going off to East Beirut like that."

"Please try to understand, Barrett . . ." Thomas wasn't allowed to finish.

"I 'understand' you took my wife across the Green Line without permission, Warkowski, that's what I 'understand.'"

"I couldn't find you," I protested, weakly. "I didn't think you'd mind."

"Spare me the crap, Lara. You knew I'd mind and you went anyway."

"I'm sorry, this is my fault," Thomas said apologetically.

"Damn right it is," Mac spit the words out. "*Walking* across the Green Line? Are you crazy or just trying to get my wife killed?"

"It was my idea, Mac. I knew you'd be worried and I thought it best to try to come home."

Mac turned back on me with a fury.

"You fucking idiot. You've really outdone yourself this time."

"Barrett, please, I realize you're upset, and I sincerely apologize. But don't take it out on Lara, she's had a frightening experience," Thomas said soothingly.

"Don't patronize me, you son of a bitch, and don't tell me how to talk to my own wife. I should break your fucking face for this."

Mac's body shifted, his shoulders drawing back, muscles tensed as if readying to strike. I clasped his right arm with both hands.

"Mac! I told you, it was my idea. Thomas only came along to protect me," I said desperately. "*Please*, can we talk about this at home."

We pulled up in front of the Commodore. Mac leaned across

me to open Thomas's door and all but shoved him out onto the sidewalk.

"Lucky this is where you get off, Warkowski. But this conversation isn't finished."

Mac pulled the door shut behind him and commanded Abdel Farid to drive, and he dutifully gunned the engine. It seemed my day for looking back: this time, as we drove off, it was at Thomas, his forlorn silhouette barely visible in the fading light.

❊

Mac kept at it all the way home. Abdel Farid, our embarrassed captive audience, hunched over the steering wheel, intent on getting us there as quickly as possible.

Mac's fury was far from spent by the time we arrived, but it manifested differently. The yelling stopped, and, instead, he completely cut me out. When I tried to explain how the day evolved, he left the room.

At first, the silence was welcome. After a day, it loomed too large and I didn't know how to break it. So I kept to myself and waited for Mac's next move.

❊

On the tenth of September, sailors aboard the battleship USS *New Jersey* were told to prepare for duty in the Mediterranean. Two days later, the 31st Marine Amphibious Unit arrived off the coast and assumed a standby role, in U.S. military jargon. Beirutis scoffed at the idea anything military connected to Lebanon would stand by.

Even Suha conveyed her skepticism, rolling her eyes and pointing at the horizon where it would soon appear, flapping her arms and making gun noises and saying *majnoon*. But weren't we all a little crazy by then?

I didn't voice the hope the *New Jersey* would play a useful role in ending the current fighting. Everyone else clearly assumed the countdown to calamity was underway. They knew what I was about to learn: no one stands at the sidelines very long here. You get sucked in sooner or later. The *New Jersey* did. Not quite the cavalry I hoped for, it quickly became, instead, a symbol of America's failed policy in Lebanon, and, to some, even synonymous with it.

❈

What Thomas said about choice was right, for the most part, certainly when he talked about the Lebanese. But I wondered why he couldn't see it didn't apply as easily to my own circumstances. To use his own words, the mere fact of his saying it had made it not so.

The more I thought, the more sadly baffled I became. Thomas had sat on our couch, drunk wine from our glasses, urinated in our toilet, had sex in our bed. But he'd gained no insight into our marriage. He'd slept with Mac's wife but gained no currency of the man. Or the woman, for that matter.

Yes, I had a choice: Hobson's Choice. While Thomas could quote Shakespeare, I was willing to bet he didn't know what that meant.

SEVENTEEN

MAC GOT THE INTERVIEW with Sheikh Fadlallah. Nadia's connections came through. At least that's what Mac claimed. Maybe the cleric's advisors figured it was the right time to let in the western media, because Mac was not the only one—the *Times* and a French television correspondent were given interviews, too. Whatever the truth, Mac billed it as a Nadia success, which vexed me no end.

"Congratulations," I said politely to Nadia. "That was quite a coup."

I'd waited more than an hour for Mac before going to his office.

"It is my job," she said testily. "That is what I am paid to do."

"They certainly get their money's worth."

Her eyes narrowed to feral slits, reminding me of the marauding Carolina farm cat that used to stalk birds foolish enough to stray from our feeders. Unfortunately, this was Nadia's turf, and I couldn't shoo her away as easily.

"Mind if I sit down?" I lowered myself onto a chair.

"As you wish. You will excuse me, however, if I return to work."

"Where's Mac? He was supposed to meet me at the bar."

"Out."

"Any idea when he'll be back?"

"No."

"I met a friend of yours in Beit Meri the other day," I blurted out, and suddenly I was off on a dangerous course.

"I have heard," she said, disdainfully. "Barrett was quite angry. You not only put yourself in danger for no good reason, you are making a fool of Barrett by going around with Thomas Warkowski."

"It's none of your concern." A token retort. Anything I said would be matched and topped.

I looked away and sighed. That did it for Nadia.

"I don't have time for games. If you want something, say it."

I wasn't ready for this confrontation on this particular day.

"No, nothing, really. Just came by to look for Mac."

I didn't have to see the smirk on her face to know it was there, that she took strength from this petty victory. But her supreme self-confidence obscured this small truth: the attraction would burn itself out. It always did with Mac.

Others were knocked out of their natural alignment by Nadia's supposed role in procuring the interview with Fadlallah. Thomas and Hamid were deep in discussion when I went in to TV Kansai the next morning. They looked up, startled.

"What's this, the wife of the great Barrett McCauley graces us with her presence?" Hamid growled.

"Sorry?"

"Mister McCauley, Mister McCauley... what valuable connections he must have these days. A mortal man, gaining an interview with the man chosen to sit beside Allah's throne."

"Oh, the Fadlallah thing. Yes, that's right, Mac interviewed him."

These conversations were like driving in fog, with no clear destination.

"'Oh, the Fadlallah *thing*,'" Hamid cried in falsetto, waving a hand dismissively. "Madam McCauley, do not treat me like a fool."

"Easy, Hamid," Thomas put in quietly. "It's not her fault."

"What's not my fault?"

"I only meant you're not responsible for Barrett getting the interview," Thomas said quickly.

"Of course it's nothing to do with me." I couldn't believe this. "But it's terrific Mac got the interview; everyone's been trying to get to Fadlallah for months."

"The question is, how did he get to Fadlallah?" Hamid's voice was low, parlous.

"Look, Hamid," I said in exasperation. "I don't know much about it. Mac says Nadia pulled some strings—and she seems pretty pleased with herself."

"Nadia doesn't have strings to pull in those quarters," Hamid said.

"Maybe she has connections you don't know about," I said stubbornly. "Anyway, that's what Mac says."

"That's what Mac says," Hamid mocked me again.

"You're just jealous." I fled, as tears of frustration and rage threatened.

"Hah," Hamid shouted after me. "I am jealous of no one."

Thomas followed, calling my name. I then turned around.

"Here you go," Thomas said, pulling a crumpled, rough napkin with a Commodore coffee shop logo out of his pocket and offering it to me. "Come, let's have a coffee."

He steered me away from the Commodore, toward a small café near the hotel.

"It's not you, Lara," Thomas said consolingly. "Hamid likes to think he pulls all the strings around here. He knows *he* didn't set up the interview and *I* didn't and at the risk of sounding immodest, Hamid and I, between us, probably have the best contacts on this side of town. And if he didn't do it and I didn't, then naturally he wants to know who did."

He smiled, leaning forward. "I admit, I'm curious myself." He reached across the table and took my hand. I wanted to withdraw it, but didn't. "It's okay. You can trust me, Lara."

He squeezed my hand gently. The waiter plunked down two tiny cups of coffee and two glasses of water.

"Like I said before, Mac says it was Nadia."

"Barrett was just in Teheran. Did he talk about his trip to you?"

Thomas searched my face, as if for clues.

"You must have seen his report from the front, on the Iraqis using chemical weapons against the Iranians. His trip had nothing to do with Fadlallah. There were at least a dozen other journalists along. Ask them."

The coffee was chalky and too hot; it burned my tongue but I drank it anyway and then, quickly, most of the water.

"Did Barrett mention any names to you from this trip? Is it possible he met someone in Iran who helped him here?" He looked encouragingly at me.

I shook my head and pulled my hand from his grasp.

"What difference does it make? You know how I feel about Nadia, but Mac gives her the credit, says she pulled strings, through an uncle or something."

I sat back and tried to keep the bitterness from my voice. "Yes, quite a little string-puller, Nadia."

Thomas looked around the café to make sure no one was listening.

"I might also remind you, she's a Maronite Christian." Thomas's voice dropped. "Surely you understand what that means. What sort of 'strings' do you suppose she might be able to pull with a radical Shiite group like Hezbollah?"

Much later, it would become apparent that Thomas himself was more than adept at pulling strings. Not the connections sort; rather, manipulating people, and, in that sense, it's probably fair to say Thomas was the ultimate puppet master, pulling and plucking all our strings.

The violence escalated sharply in September, particularly in the Chouf. The U.S. ambassador's residence and the Lebanese Ministry of Defense were shelled repeatedly, which brought the frigate *Bowen* and the destroyer *John Rodgers* into action off the coast. Practically off our balcony.

The Lebanese Army, meanwhile, clung on to the strategic Chouf town of Souk al Gharb, trying to fend off a ferocious attack by Druze allies. As the Lebanese Army rapidly worked through its artillery stocks, a plea went out to the Americans for backup. The destroyer *Radford* joined in, and the guided missile nuclear cruiser *Virginia* trained its five-inch guns into the mountains, firing more than three hundred and fifty rounds in a five-hour period. The noise was deafening.

"I told you, they *are* the Lebanese Army now!" Hamid shouted at us across the bar a few hours later. "This story will be written in the blood of the Americans.

"Peacekeeper, puh!" He made a little spitting noise. "Puh!"

The U.S. barrage drove back the Palestinian and leftist fighters, and the Lebanese Army used the respite to resupply and reinforce its positions. And something else happened—the U.S. mission of "presence" shifted, virtually overnight, to "assistance," setting into motion a vicious circle. Backing the Lebanese Army made the Marines fair game to the antigovernment forces and, in turn, their attacks led to a shift in the Marines' own perception of the conflict. Now, they saw the enemies of the Lebanese government as their own. No dictate from Washington announced this; rather, it appeared, as if by osmosis, in an MAU report somewhere around this time, in a reference to U.S. warships off the coast engaging "the enemy."

The enemy. It was official.

❀

Danger for Mac was heady stuff, an aphrodisiac. And hard as he worked, Nadia was right there beside him. This craziness, should we all survive it, might strengthen Nadia's hold. Perhaps I misjudged, after all.

I was pondering this over my seventeenth cigarette and fourth coffee of the day when the doorbell rang. Nadia stood on the threshold before me, as if fully sprung from my own imaginings.

She no longer bothered with preliminaries.

"Barrett needs his PSP press pass; he says it's in the bedroom."

I did not invite her in. "Where is he?"

"He is busy."

"Why the PSP pass? He's not going up to the Chouf? It's too dangerous."

"I am not here to argue with you. I am doing as Barrett asked. There is no time to waste. Abdel Farid is waiting outside."

"I'll go have a look. I guess you'd better come in."

She followed me toward the bedroom. I stopped outside the door, my hand on the door handle.

"Wait in the front hall, please."

"Barrett told me where to look."

"Tell me and I'll find it." I was equally firm.

She pushed past and shoved open the door.

"Excuse me, it will be faster this way." She was halfway across the room and in front of the dresser, pulling open the top drawer on Mac's side, before I could react.

"Aha!" she gloated, pulling a limp, laminated card from under a mound of socks.

She looked around the room with a sniff of disapproval, then sat down on the edge of the bed and stroked the coverlet as if it might reveal its secrets.

"Tell me . . . what is like with a man who prefers his own sex? How does he have sex with a woman?"

I stared, transfixed by her malevolence.

"What a homecoming for Thomas." The thought seemed to amuse her. "Oh dear, did he forgot to mention it? Next time, ask him about Schuster, eh? It was no secret. They were . . . how to put this . . . hard to separate . . . un-separatable?"

"Inseparable," I corrected automatically.

Nadia laughed again, a sharp little spike of spite.

"Yes, that's right. They were *in*-seperatable. Disgusting. So unprofessional. "

I didn't believe her.

"Roger had a wife. In Cyprus," I said triumphantly.

"Surely, you cannot be so naïve. Marie-Claude liked her status and her comforts. And there were the children. The arrangement satisfied everyone. She is French, they tolerate such things, as long as everyone is discreet. Which is more than I can say for you, Lara."

I couldn't bring myself to ask if Mac knew.

Nadia stood up abruptly.

"What I do not understand," she said, one hand on the doorknob, "is how could you lie down with a *homosexual*?"

Her footsteps echoed in the stairwell, the first chips off a rockfall before it slides into avalanche.

***

Had she told Mac? No. He would have confronted me. Give Nadia credit: she was an experienced player, not likely to show her hand until her goal was fixed in her sights. That meant I was now a card kept in reserve, to be played when she wanted.

I needed to warn Thomas.

***

He was in the hotel lobby. He realized something was wrong, for, after an appraising look, he nodded toward a side door near the newsstand and exited through it.

"Nadia came to see me today," I began breathlessly.

"Perhaps we'd better go to my flat."

We took a circuitous route along the back streets, as Thomas wanted to avoid a new Marabitoun position on the main road. Or so he said.

The interior of his apartment building was glum, with little light coming into the central hallway. Threadbare red carpeting ran up the middle of the two wide flights of stairs we climbed.

Thomas fumbled in his trouser pockets and patted his chest.

"My keys?"

"Did you lock the door when you left this morning?"

"It locks automatically when it shuts. Never mind, I'll ask my landlady, Mrs. Fonterelli, to let me in. Please wait here."

He hurried down to the ground floor. A woman answered his knock and they chatted before he climbed the stairs again.

He reappeared, dangling a set of keys, opened the door to his flat, and waved me in.

"Please, after you."

The first glance was disappointing—cheaply furnished, his possessions few and scattered untidily about. From a bookcase by the window, I picked up a heavy silver frame, cast in the shape of a crown, with a black and white photograph of a teenager surrounded by military officers.

"That is from before the First World War—a young King Faisal," Thomas said from very close behind me. "Of course, he wasn't King yet, when this was taken."

"Why do you have a picture of him?"

"Came with the frame," he said, smiling. "But isn't it enchanting, to think of this young king, with all his history yet to come—the revolt against the Ottomans, taking the Transjordan, King of Greater Syria, King of Iraq."

He turned it over in my hand. "This silversmith was Jewish, quite well known, and, the story goes, hid all his tools in the river when he fled with the other Jews in 1941, because he didn't want anyone else using them. Sad, isn't it."

I picked up what appeared to be black volcanic rock embedded in an oval silver casing.

"What's this?"

"It is also from Iraq, from Mosul. Pumice stone. Look at the detail in the silver."

I felt his breath on my hair and was afraid to turn around.

"Lara," he said, gently, placing his hands on my shoulders.

"Thomas, please, this isn't right," I protested, as we kissed. It wasn't right, there were a million things wrong with it, but I kissed him again and we fell back onto the daybed, draped in a dingy yellow floral cover. It trembled beneath our weight.

"Lara," he murmured, kissing my face.

"No, we mustn't," I murmured back.

Our bodies pressed ahead with their own momentum and, article by article, our clothing dribbled onto the floor. Soon, however, his body stopped moving on top of mine, and the hardness disappeared.

"What's the matter?"

He didn't reply. As we looked gravely at each other, a fist pounded on the door.

"Thomas?" A heavily accented voiced called from the hall between thuds.

"*Shit!* Mrs. Fonterelli, I forgot to return her keys!" Thomas jumped up.

"Thomas?" She was shouting now, pounding on the door. *"Thomas!"*

"Sonya, uh, Mrs. Fonterelli, sorry, just a minute, please," he called out, trying to shovel himself back into his trousers, hopping on one leg while reaching for his belt and his shirt. I grabbed my own clothes and hurriedly righted myself.

"Where's the bedroom?" I asked urgently.

"Here. This is it, everything."

"Bathroom?"

"In the hall outside, it's communal."

"Where can I hide?"

"*Thomas!* Open the door!"

"Coming," he called loudly. He turned to me. "Ready?"

"No, wait, wait, my shoe, where's my other shoe?"

But Thomas had opened the door and Mrs. Fonterelli sailed through it. She halted immediately upon seeing me. The shock on her face when she registered my presence was a barometer of exactly how dire the situation was.

"Mrs. Fonterelli, this is . . . Lara."

I stood, shoeless. Guilty.

She nodded stiffly at me. Thomas handed her the keys.

"Thank you. I'm so sorry I forgot to return them."

She nodded again, and departed with a haughty look at me.

"Oh God, Thomas," I wailed. "This is awful."

"It is not ideal," he agreed.

He picked up a bottle of brandy and produced a coffee cup from the single cupboard over the sink in the tiny kitchen alcove in a far corner of the room. He peered dubiously into it, wiping the rim with his bare hand.

"Here you are. Sorry there's nothing better to offer you."

The brandy was too sharp. I put it down and told him about Nadia's visit, leaving out the part about Schuster. After all, we'd been on the verge of making love when Mrs. Fonterelli interrupted. Hadn't we?

"So she knows." Thomas interrupted my thoughts, referring to Nadia. "Did she tell Barrett, or threaten to?"

"No, I'm pretty sure she hasn't," I admitted, "But I don't know why."

"Nadia is a realist. If she hasn't told Barrett by now, she must have calculated it doesn't serve her purposes, that telling Barrett is not a gamble worth taking right now. It might backfire."

"What, by making him so jealous he comes running back to me?" I asked sarcastically.

"Perhaps," he said kindly, as if he suspected I really had meant it and didn't want to let me down. A wan smile, then his face lapsed into its usual serious contours.

"Actually, I was thinking more that Barrett is cocksure, he is vain. This would be a blow to his ego he will find hard to believe or accept. He may hate the bearer of this news, for that person is not only messenger but witness to his humiliation."

He added, thoughtfully, "And then there is this . . . he is a journalist, he will demand to know the source of this information before he credits it."

"Thomas," I interrupted in exasperation, "half of Beirut knows, or suspects, anyway—Hamid, Amina, maybe. And, now, Nadia."

"You're paranoid, Lara. Anyway, Nadia's source is not one she'll want Barrett to know about."

"Why?"

"Because he's a high-ranking official on the other side with strong ties to Lebanese intelligence. He's also Nadia's lover. I pity them both if he finds out he's sharing her with Barrett McCauley."

⁂

Could he have been unaware of the irony?

⁂

I needed to go home, in case Mac returned at a reasonable hour; our conversation was suspended without conclusion.

As the door to Thomas's building closed behind me, I turned

back to see the curtains twitching in one of the ground floor windows. Mrs. Fonterelli, no doubt.

A battered taxi slowly approached, looking for custom. I flagged it down and got in. The driver tried to talk to me, but my fractured Arabic quickly halted his attempt and I returned, gratefully, to my thoughts and a replay of the scene at Thomas's.

It couldn't be cataloged. I could've sworn he held no further attraction for me, yet I readily succumbed, and now was left to wonder, was his arousal interrupted . . . or incomplete? I knew only what Mac and Nadia said, both driven by malice, neither to be trusted. I was hostage to my upbringing; it wasn't possible to address these questions with the person it most concerned, nor with anyone else. In this, I was alone as ever.

I got out of the taxi near the Commodore, walking the rest of the way home, a stranger, through streets half familiar. I no longer recognized myself.

That evening, I went back to the home I shared with my husband and waited for the next despoiling of my soul.

EIGHTEEN

GIFFORD NOW HAD ME WORKING on more involved projects and I welcomed the distraction. One of my tasks was to sift through dozens of hours of footage for possible use in a documentary Yoshi wanted to pull together on Lebanon's Shiites and the swift ascent of Hezbollah. It was a massive undertaking.

Gifford was editing a daily news piece and I had just finished logging several hours' worth of material when we heard several loud cracks followed by a thunderous crash and Hamid's voice in the outer office rising above the commotion. I followed Gifford in time to see Hamid leaning out a window.

"Go! Go! For God's sake, get out of there!" Hamid yelled at someone in the street below. But it's doubtful anyone could hear him over the gunfire and people shouting. Our building was on a side street across from the hotel and I strained at an angle to try to see beyond Hamid.

"What's happening?" Gifford demanded.

"Accident. I think the driver of the car that's crashed over there"—Hamid pointed out the window—"was shot by a sniper."

Gifford was already half out the door and I was close behind as we ran down the stairs. But the shooting was so loud and so close, we stopped in the lobby, waiting for a break long enough to permit the dash across to the hotel.

It was a sea of confusion, the lobby packed with people—journalists, hotel staff, and many I didn't recognize. Two dishevelled women, one elderly, one middle-aged, were locked in an embrace, rocking back and forth and weeping loudly and inconsolably. Gifford waded into the throng but I stayed back.

Martin and Samir, the Commodore chef, and someone else I didn't know, carried the limp figure of man, followed by a stills photographer and two television crews. They gently laid the injured man on the lobby floor, where his blood quickly pooled on the white and gray tiles. The two women rushed to his side, and the younger one yelped with pain as she knelt down and tried to cover his face with kisses, while the clerk from the front desk tried to comfort the older one. The hotel staff was well trained in first aid and several of them, led by Samir, tended to the dying man as best they could.

"His wife." Gifford reappeared by my side. "The other one is either his mother or his mother-in-law, it's not clear."

Gifford's explanation was overrun by shouts of "You son of a bitch!"

Martin, a wild man, tears of rage scattered like angry freckles across his face, his chest and arms covered in the man's blood, was shouting at one of the cameramen.

"Put the camera down, put the fucking camera *down*."

"Get out of my way," the man shouted back in reply, but he took a few steps back and motioned the sound tech to move to the side. Across the lobby, I saw Mac, his face wrinkled in fury.

"Show some respect, why don't you?" Martin yelled, as Doug and Katie led him off to an armchair in a corner of the lobby where they tried to calm him down, his shoulders heaving convulsively.

"Let's get out of the way," Gifford whispered, motioning me into the deserted bar. Fretwell, Thomas, and Boz, standing near the reception desk, spotted us across the lobby and waved. Fretwell made his way to follow us but Thomas stayed behind with Boz.

"What happened?" I asked, quietly, when Fretwell caught up.

It sounded like a fight was breaking out in the lobby now.

"It's not a pretty story," Fretwell answered, equally quiet. "Mind, I wasn't there at the very beginning, but I understand the man was driving, with his wife and the older lady in the car, his mother-in-law, I believe. A sniper hit the car, bullet went through the windshield, hit him in the chest, and he crashed the car out front.

"Everybody down here heard the shooting and the crash and some people came running in from other buildings to see what was going on. The ladies made it out of the car okay and ran into the hotel, hysterical, begging everyone for help. But some of the TV people and a couple photographers and print guys started squabbling about whether to go out and help the guy first or film him first and *then* help him or whether it was even safe to try to help him at all..."

Gunfire rattled outside, on cue.

"Because, as you hear, it's still going on out there. At any rate, Martin and Katya, Samir and several other people, ran out to help, while the rest stayed inside, dithering over what to do."

"That's horrible."

"I know," Fretwell said. "Then again, I work for a newspaper, so who knows? But I like to think I'd have helped, if I'd gotten there in time."

I remembered Mac's face in the lobby.

"Did you, by any chance, hear what Mac thought about it?"

Fretwell looked embarrassed. "Actually, I heard quite a bit, and I gather your husband was part of the group arguing to take pictures first."

"No." I was repelled. "Why?"

"You can ask him yourself," Fretwell said. "Here he comes now."

Mac came into the bar, frowning to see us all together.

"Hello, Lara. Hanging with the wrong crowd again, I see." He said it in a semiteasing way that fooled no one.

"Kisses to you too, Barrett," Fretwell said, in a matching tone.

Mac ignored him. "Guess it's self-service time, hotel staff being a little tied up out there." He made his way behind the bar.

"Don't think you'd better start pulling pints on Marwan's turf, mate. He won't take it too kindly," Gifford warned.

Mac paid no attention. He found a glass, inspected it against the light, wiped the rim with a cloth he found behind the bar, and filled it with ice.

It proved too much for Gifford. He leaned across the bar into Mac's face. "How is it, anyway, that you guys are arguing while some poor sod is lying there, dying? Can you tell me that?"

"Excuse me, did I miss something?" Mac sneered, pouring scotch into the waiting glass. "Were you actually there, Gifford?"

Mac slammed the bottle on the counter. "Only, I didn't see you. You either, Ian, come to think of it. Not when the shit was actually hitting the fan."

He stopped and took a swallow. "Easy to be an armchair analyst after the fact. Make that anal-ist."

"Man, you're low." Gifford shook his head at Mac. "Sometimes, I don't get you, Barrett."

"Fortunately, nobody asked you to."

Gifford turned toward me, easing his large frame off the barstool. "I've got to get back, Lara. You coming?"

"She's staying here with me," Mac said rudely. He came out from behind the counter and stood next to me.

Gifford looked questioningly at me. "Lara?"

"I'll go back with Bruce," I said to Mac, putting a pleading hand on his arm. "If you don't mind."

"Oh, I *do* mind." He shook my hand off.

"But we've got so much to do, Mac, piles of stuff to go through for Yoshi," I said. Fretwell winced and looked away and I hated myself for sounding so weak.

"Then let Dumbo here get on with it." Mac nodded at Gifford.

"I don't have time for this shit," Gifford said to me. "Sorry, mate. Gonna make a dash for it. Ta."

I tried to telegraph an apology to him, but Gifford was gone, and in a small, unscheduled burst of defiance, I hopped off my stool to follow him. Mac grabbed my arm and gave it a nasty twist.

"Sit down, Lu. You're staying here."

"Mac," I objected, but it came out with all the force of a petulant child and I knew I was thwarted.

"Look, it's too dangerous to go, anyway," he continued firmly, more for Fretwell's benefit, I was sure, than mine. "We're staying here until the shooting stops. Might as well make the best of it. Right?"

I nodded reluctantly. Fretwell remained silent, which seemed to enrage Mac, even though he wasn't speaking to Fretwell.

"Shit, it's not even survival of the fittest here. It's not Darwin. It's pure Mencken. You know, nature abhors a moron." Mac spoke in soliloquy, rolling his eyes upwards to the heavens. "So let the big, dumb fuck kill himself getting back to his big, dumb fuck of an edit machine if he wants. I have no intention of tempting fate by doing the same."

Fretwell finally cleared his throat.

"You know, Barrett, for a seasoned combat reporter, you seem rather intent on exercising extreme caution—or is it extreme indifference?—where the risking of life is concerned," he said quietly.

"Another country heard from," Mac said sarcastically. "Now, what the hell is that supposed to mean, Fretwell?"

"Let's say I'm with Bruce on this. Low, indeed. I heard you tell them to keep shooting before helping that man."

"Hey, pal, I'm a journalist. A journalist first. Second and third, too. That's what we do." Mac's voice rose. "We're not rescue workers, we're not the police or an ambulance team, we're not the Red fucking Cross. Leave the hero stuff to them. We're fucking journalists."

"We're fucking human beings," Fretwell said, with icy dignity.

They glared at each other for a powerful moment.

"Most of what happens here is beyond our control. The only way we *can* help is to tell the story, get the picture, whatever. The way I see it, this wasn't one of those times. This was a time we could have tried to save the life of a fellow human being. Screw the story, Barrett, screw the story this one time, Barrett."

Fretwell spoke with an intensity I'd never seen in him before.

Mac rose to the challenge forcefully, equally convinced of his own truth.

"Don't pull this on me, Fretwell. Like you said, I'm an old war dog, and it won't work.

"We have a job to do here and getting the story and the picture to go with it is Rule Number One." He jabbed a finger in Fretwell's face for emphasis. "Rule Number One. Get the Fucking Story.

"Rule Number Two: Don't Get Killed Doing Rule Number One. That's Number Two, Fretwell. You should know. You don't risk your life for some local who, given the chance, would probably kill *you*."

"This wasn't a terrorist, Mac," I interrupted, "It sounds like the man was with his wife and mother-in-law, just trying to get to safety."

"You're missing the point, Lara," Mac turned to rail at me now. "We are *observers*. We are not *participants*. Once you cross that line, there's no telling where it ends. We aren't *neutral* anymore, we're taking sides, like the U.S. Marines, for God's sake. We have our own mission of presence, that's what journalism is. And helping ain't presence, it's fucking assistance."

Now Fretwell shook his head.

"Trying to save a life hardly constitutes taking sides. Sometimes we have to discard our journalist hats and put our humanity first."

He spoke slowly, with an air of discovery.

"I do believe this place has driven you mad, Barrett."

He stood up to leave. "In fact, I think you're barking. I won't dignify this ridiculous conversation by pursuing it further. Excuse me, Lara."

As he left, Martin pushed past from the other direction.

"Hey, McCauley, you asshole," Martin called out, anger frosting every word. "I want to talk to you."

"Marty, Marty," Mac said heartily. "Jesus, you're all worked up. Calm down."

"Calm down!" Martin made as if to take a swing at Mac, who caught his arm.

"That man is dead! *Dead!*" Martin shouted, trying to wrestle free of Mac, without success. "The guy's dying and you want the *picture?* What the hell's wrong with you?"

"Jesus, Marty, don't start this up again. What're you so worked about?" He dropped Martin's arm as he said it, and gave him a slight shove toward a stool. "Go on, buddy. Sit down. And remember, I'm bigger than you."

Martin slumped onto a barstool. He was still crying and looked exhausted.

"Anyway, Marty," Mac continued, "I didn't say *don't* help him, I just said get the picture *first*—ten, twenty seconds—then do your Florence Nightingale."

Mac leaned over and tried to put his arm around Martin's shoulder. Martin knocked it back angrily, with a sob. He looked as if he might try to take Mac on again but I hoped he wouldn't, it was clear he wasn't up to it.

"Marty, come on, man, chill. You and I see it different, that's all. Though I'm kind of surprised at your attitude, for a wire service, I mean, 'cause you know you *need* the picture."

Mac sounded so philosophical, I almost believed him.

"In any case, Marty, forget the picture. Tell me this because this is what I really want to know: was this guy, this Lebanese Joe

Ahmed Blow *really* worth risking your life for? I mean, maybe for John F. Kennedy, if he gets shot in front of you, okay. You'd be dead but you'd be famous forever."

He made an exasperated sound. "But how much copy would you warrant if you died helping this poor bastard, Marty? Eh? War correspondent killed *not* doing his job because he wanted to be a Boy Scout and do his good deed first."

"Fuck off," Martin said, trying to wipe away his tears. "Fuck you, Mac."

"I'm going to forget you said that. Because I like you, buddy, I respect you, and I know today was tough. Hell, everybody's nerves are frayed; this place is insane, a freaking lunatic asylum."

Mac tried to pat Martin on the arm. "We've been through a lot together over the years. Let's agree to disagree and get it over with."

"Fuck you," Martin repeated.

Other people were now trickling into the bar. They pretended to ignore us, but they, too, were mesmerized by the exchange. It was time to end it, for what was left of Mac's reputation, and, by extension, mine.

"Come on, Mac," I said, tugging on his sleeve. "Let's go home."

Mac came away readily, shaken by the extent of Martin's anger.

We asked at the front desk for a taxi. One of the clerks found a driver sitting in a corner of the lobby who, for the right price, was willing to brave the trouble. It was tapering off, anyway.

As he drove us home, the streets fell silent, the calm after the storm. I noted to myself the fresh devastation from the evening's shelling, and I wondered if Fretwell was right. Not about the moral implications of what happened today, for we agreed on that already. But about Mac's sanity and whether Beirut had, indeed, driven him mad.

I wept into my pillow that night, as it seemed I so often had since arriving in this country. Tears for the Lebanese man whose name we'd never know, catapulted onto the level of moral icon by the circumstances of his death. Whoever he'd been before—husband to his wife, father to his children, son to his mother, friend to his friends—whatever he'd been in life, his death would now be a topic of debate in endless hours of discussion among journalists around the world: in newsrooms and press clubs, in obscure journalism magazines, university seminars on ethics in journalism, and, most especially, in barrooms late in the evening, when these kind of discussions take on the dimensions of a UN General Assembly debate.

Who's to say what's right?

Mac believed he was, as passionately as Fretwell thought himself right, and neither had the capacity to change the other's mind.

The question cropped up again a few months later when an Italian TV crew found themselves under fire, filming in the south. When the sound technician was hit by shrapnel the cameraman turned his equipment on him and captured the incident on film, including the scene of the cameraman dressing his partner's wounds. The cameraman said, afterward, he left the camera rolling to record what happened, in case neither of them made it out alive. Many in the press corps applauded his quick thinking—after all, the injury didn't look life-threatening and, on the off-chance it was, there would have been a record of the event. Then, too, you couldn't deny it made excellent television. Why, even the

American networks ran the pictures dozens of times. The injured man remained remarkably dignified about the matter; and never commented on it publicly. Some of his colleagues, however—especially other sound techs—lamented what they saw as the cameraman's insensitivity, and vowed to boycott him on future assignments. The cameraman was unruffled by the fuss; he went on to win several top awards for his work in the Middle East.

I wept for the Lebanese man, as I said, and for the women who lost him, and then, for good measure, I wept for myself, because I'd not only lost the Mac I'd loved, but, in the process, myself as well.

NINETEEN

THE SITUATION WAS DETERIORATING rapidly in Lebanon. It went like this for days, the constant pounding, the tension as the violence snapped back and forth like a yo-yo, between mountain and sea. No mere drumbeat of war, this was life inside the timpani itself.

Things improved, temporarily, when the USS *New Jersey* arrived in late September, a boost to firepower and morale for the Marines, and some Lebanese as well. Within days, the Druze agreed to a cease-fire brokered by the Saudis and the Syrians, although another Marine was dead by then.

Mac and the others put no faith in this cease-fire. They'd seen it all before. Only an idiot believed this would hold.

But some reports said it might give the push needed to cobble together a new coalition government, and I wanted to believe it, wanted to believe hope and optimism could triumph over the cynical despair etched into Lebanon's psyche by so many years of war. For a brief time, it even seemed possible.

Under the *New Jersey*'s watchful eye, first one day, and then another, passed without major incident, and street vendors—the Beirut bellwether—returned to their sidewalk stalls and their pushcarts and the city's wide, once-grand avenues swelled again with people and cars.

Barren optimism. October unfolded with more shooting and two more casualties.

⁂

Impulsively, I dropped in on Amina—but regretted it, as soon as I saw how uncomfortable it made her. I detoured to TV Kansai on the way home, and, on hearing another Marine was hit by grenade fragments, stayed to help Gifford. I was there again the next day, when the crew was dispatched to cover a fierce firefight near the airport, which flared up after a sniper scored a bull's-eye—another Marine dead. Three more were injured in the ensuing three-hour exchange.

The next evening, Mac unexpectedly appeared at dinnertime. He sat on the balcony, drink in hand, staring at the gray profile of a U.S. ship, static on the horizon. I brought a plate of warm food out and put it in front of him, then balanced on the arm of his big bamboo chair and gingerly rubbed the back of his neck. We had little physical contact these days, and at first he shrank from my touch. A moment later, however, he relaxed under my hands, hanging his head limply, and seemed to be enjoying it.

"Penny for them," I said, reaching up under his polo shirt to knead his right shoulder.

"Not worth it." He spoke into his chest.

"Go on," I coaxed.

"Aw, shit, Lara, don't start."

"I hate to see you like this."

"Like what." His head lifted and he peered suspiciously sideways at me.

"Like, we never talk anymore."

"We talk all the goddamn time, Lara. At least, you do. Can't you understand, sometimes I just don't *feel* like talking."

I switched sides, rotating the other shoulder, and tried again.

"I don't mean to nag. It's just that you work so hard, I feel shut out."

"Oh, Lord," he groaned. "Give me a break. The Americans are starting World War III here, the whole situation is coming unglued and I don't need you coming unglued, too."

"I'm not coming unglued, I just want us to be close. Like before."

I meant it: if he'd only open up a little, we might recapture our communion of old. I pulled the shirt down over his back again, gave him one final rub, and then, without thinking, leaned in and traced the outline of his ear with my tongue. But I caught the faint trail of Nadia, mixed with Mac's aftershave, and involuntarily gagged.

His head snapped up.

"Jesus Christ, I thought I made it clear I'm not in the mood for this nonsense."

He stood up, shrugging me off his back, and I nearly fell off the arm of the chair.

"What about your dinner?" I demanded, as he strode off.

"Ate at the Commodore."

I flung myself into his chair.

He went inside, pulling the French doors shut behind him. A moment later, they reopened.

"By the way," he asked, "did you forget something?"

His tone was casual but his eyes narrowed in a threatening way.

"What?" I asked, innocently.

"You forgot to tell me something, didn't you?"

"I don't know what you mean."

A horn sounded below on the Corniche, a momentary distraction only.

"Then let me put it in words you understand, Lara...what I mean is, what the hell were you doing at Warkowski's? I told you to stay away from him after your stupid escapade on the Green Line."

He was angry, but it was not the white-hot anger of betrayal. It sounded as if he knew only the fact of my going, not what prompted it, nor what transpired. I could handle this, I remember thinking.

"He lent me a book about Lebanese history," I improvised. "I thought I'd get it—you know, save him having to walk all the way back to the Commodore with it. Sorry, I forgot to mention it."

Mac stepped all the way out onto the balcony. He bent down, his face level with mine.

"Boy, you don't get it, do you? I thought I made it clear. Stay away from him,

"Here we go again," I said wearily. "He's a friend and colleague and everyone else likes him."

Mac looked at me in disbelief.

"He's not my colleague, for Christ's sake, and for your sake he'd better not be your friend." He downed the remaining liquid in his glass in one angry swallow, and lit in again as he spun around to leave.

"Colleague?" he repeated furiously, from the doorway. "Get real. No one's ever heard of that magazine he claims to work for. And how the hell could it afford a correspondent in Beirut—or anywhere else for that matter?

As it sunk in, he added, "Poland's under martial law, remember? It's a Communist country. Think about *that.*"

He stormed off and I got up to follow, through the living room and down the hall. He pushed open the bedroom door and pivoted back again to look scornfully at me, his features contorted by rage. Involuntarily, I took a step back.

"Wake up, Lara, wake fucking *up*. This is real life big, bad shit happening here and you just don't get it. This is Bay-fucking-*root*."

He was shouting now. "Your boyfriend Thomas—Tow-*maas*—your little homose*xual* boyfriend, is working the night shift on someone else's payroll: the Christians, the Syrians, or the Russians, most likely. Maybe the Israelis. Possibly the Iraqis or—now, here's a wild guess—the Libyans. He's not stupid enough to work for the Americans. At least, I don't think he's that stupid."

He slammed the door, leaving me on the other side.

❊

"He's not a homosexual." I said, finally, to the closed door.

❊

Because I didn't know what else to do, I retrieved the plate with the uneaten dinner from the balcony and scraped it into the kitchen bin. Dishes washed and put away, I sat for a while in the living room, waiting until Mac was asleep and snoring before climbing into bed. Everything he'd said, the events of the last few weeks, snippets of conversations with Thomas and others—all these things were tangled up in my head and I tried to fit them together. Thomas, friend. Thomas, lover. Thomas, spy. Was that his dinner-party word? Incredible, and yet, at some level, I knew Mac was right.

In the dark of the Beirut night, drifting in the currents of childhood memory, a song from *HMS Pinafore*, barely remembered, bobbed to the surface.

Things are seldom what they seem;

Skim milk masquerades as cream.

Here was Mac's awful truth, transcribed into interior dialogue, lyrics by Gilbert and Sullivan. Every so often, another couple of lines wafted my way.

Black sheep dwell in every fold;
All that glitters is not gold;
Thomas was a spy.
Gild the farthing if you will,
Yet it is a farthing still.

I had slept with a spy. Mac was right: I'd been here ten months and I still didn't understand anything. Not only unfaithful, I'd slept with a spy. And had been willing to try for an encore. That it hadn't actually happened was irrelevant.

I drifted into sleep in the early hours, serenaded by Mac's snores, sporadic distant gunfire, and the queer tune I couldn't shake.

❈

In mid-October, President Reagan signed a compromise resolution approved by Congress to keep the Marines in Lebanon for another eighteen months.

Suddenly, this "limited engagement" seemed without end— and, increasingly, without purpose.

❈

"Lara, I was hoping to see you. How are you?"

"Fine. Thanks, Thomas."

I couldn't look him in the eye when I saw him next, on the street outside TV Kansai. Mac's latest revelation made that impossible. There was a weight to this new allegation not so easily dismissed.

"Our conversation was unfinished the other day," Thomas said, straightforwardly, seemingly without hidden meaning.

"Sorry, I'm meeting Gifford. I'd better go," I said to the sidewalk.

"Lara, look at me," Thomas said quietly.

"I have to go now."

"Meet me later, at the flat."

"I can't."

Thomas captured my wrist, leaning into my field of vision.

"Don't do that." I tried to pull free.

"My, aren't you the cozy couple." I heard Fretwell before I saw him. He was helping Nadia carry a fax machine and the malice missing from his tone instead manifested in Nadia's false, hard laugh, which rang out through the street.

"Cozy?" she said, giving up her end of the fax to Fretwell and dusting her hands off. "I would say they're positively...what do you say, Lara... *inseparatable?*"

"Excuse me, I was just leaving," I explained quickly to Fretwell, not acknowledging Nadia. "I'm going to be late."

"She all right?" I heard Fretwell ask Thomas as I turned away abruptly and fled. I didn't wait to hear the reply.

Seeing Thomas unexpectedly caught at my heart. He was a *spy*. I needed to accept I'd never known him. *Gild the farthing.* A spy was a spy was a spy. *A farthing still.*

⁂

It must be, if Mac said so, for he thrived in and among the treacherous shoals I could not steer through on my own. From the day I arrived in Beirut I lived on the surface, saw only what I was shown, ascribed no complexities, visualized no textures, investigated no depths.

Plato's unexamined life might not be worth living, but I was certain mine would fall apart if I probed at all.

❊

A few nights later, Mac and I went to Abdel Farid's for dinner. He'd invited us before, but Mac always declined. Too busy. Too this, too that. I don't know what prompted him to accept this time, but was pleased he had. We hadn't been out together for ages.

I also wanted to meet Abdel Farid's family. Unlike the TV networks, with numerous drivers and fixers to command, the magazine had only Abdel Farid, and thus he was both, and a lot more.

As a fixer, he navigated the bureaucracies of Lebanese officialdom and various armed groups; greased the right palms; made press passes magically appear and bills disappear; got shipments stuck in customs freed. Largely illiterate in his own language, he was fluent where it counted, in the crucial skill of interpreting our changing daily environment, activity on the streets, the placement of men and guns, the ebb and flow of tensions in the communities. All these factors were microanalyzed and synthesized into split-instant decisions—where it was safe to go, which routes to take, which politicians or militia leaders to apply to. An inherent understanding of political developments and how they played out on the street sprang from a lifetime on the street himself.

An exhaustive network of family, friends, and contacts throughout the city equipped him for these tasks, as did his humble origins. A Sunni Moslem from the city's slums, his perspective often differed from Nadia's, a product of East Beirut's educated elite.

Abdel Farid had done too much to quantify over the years for the magazine and "his" correspondents. In a land where survival was king, he consistently put his own safety on the line to make sure his correspondent returned alive. With the story. He risked his life almost every day to that end, and in return for this unswervingly loyal service, received an excellent wage by local standards, and—of no small importance—derived a certain status in his own community, as an employee of an American news organization. A double-edged sword: one day, not so far off, it would become a liability, but for the time being he was still a man of importance, a man of affairs, in his own world.

Abdel Farid's extended family turned out en masse to receive us, close to a dozen adults and, it seemed, easily as many children, crammed into a small, third-floor apartment in the city's southern suburbs. Abdel Farid's wife, Samira, hugged me and patted my hair admiringly, cooing and clucking and smiling broadly all the while, straightening the shoulders of my dress, as if I were another of her brood. I wondered if she knew about Nadia and Mac, as Abdel Farid surely must. But though she spoke Arabic too swiftly for me to single out many words, her manner was open, welcoming, and with Abdel Farid's many daughters asking questions, and the older grandchildren helping with some rather interesting and possibly creative translations, there were no awkward gaps in the conversation.

Abdel Farid was positively regal this night: ramrod straight on a Queen Anne chair made of white painted wood, the seats and backs overupholstered in crimson plush. Mac perched on an identical one next to him. The chairs were in sharp contrast to the rest of the shabby furniture, so obviously new I suspected they were purchased with this very evening in mind, and it touched me.

Abdel Farid held court with Mac, the females of the family seeing to their every need—a profusion of food and drink, pillows plumped, cigarettes lit, a footstool placed just so. The middle of Abdel Farid's three sons, Badri, recently graduated from university, but couldn't find a job in his field of computer sciences. As hard as Abdel Farid tried to keep the conversation steady on a neutral course, Badri kept heading for the dangerous rapids of Lebanese politics, clearly wanting to make the most of a rare opportunity to talk to an American.

"So Mister Barrett, when will the Americans in the Lebanon go home?" Badri finally got in, after several attempts, for which I silently gave him credit. He spoke forthrightly, just this side of being aggressive.

Badri tapped his cigarette into a nearly full ashtray and a large plume of cigarette smoke curled out of his mouth. He didn't see his father's warning look—or pretended not to. Mac, however, seemed to be waiting for such a question, and had his answer ready, taking his time, drawing on his own cigarette before replying. While Mac himself believed the U.S. mission was doomed, he had his own take on it, and often played devil's advocate with a Lebanese audience.

"Well, son, I reckon the answer is they'll leave Lebanon when they're finished here, when they've accomplished their mission." Mac replied, in a slightly patronizing tone. He nonchalantly examined the hors d'œuvres, selected one, and placed it on a small plate on his knee, but he was tensed for the next question and did not eat it.

"And, what, Mister Barrett, is that?" Badri asked, a trace of sarcasm detectable now. "Helping the Christians to be killing more Lebanese people? Teaching the Army how to kill us all?"

"Badri, I'd like to remind you the United States is here at the invitation of your own government. As we say where I come from, the Americans don't have a dog in this fight. It's a big mess for sure, and like a lot of folks, I have my doubts about the wisdom of this operation, anybody with half a frontal lobe does."

He toyed with the bit of food on his plate. "But you know what? There are American boys out there at Beirut airport, not one day older than you, out there right now, and they're taking bullets, too, and they're dying, just like the Lebanese, just like your friends, Badri, to try to make your country a little safer, so folks like your little nieces and nephews who only know war might someday have peace. They're dying for *you*, Badri."

Badri was unmoved.

"I play violins now, Mister Barrett? And by the way, it's not *my* government. It does not represent me and it does not protect me."

"Badri!" Abdel Farid pounced. He quickly silenced him, and, indeed, the room, with a few sharp words in Arabic, as Samira clucked disapproval at her son's rudeness.

Abdel Farid switched to English for the rest of the scolding. "Mister Barrett and his wife are guests in our home. You bring shame to us all."

"Hey, no worries. No harm done. Boy's just asking questions same as everyone else here. He's entitled. It's okay, really. I don't mind." Mac seemed genuinely unperturbed, perhaps secretly enjoying it. He stubbed out his own cigarette and blew me a wobbly smoke ring. I waved it away, and he frowned, as if I'd been disloyal.

Badri eventually muttered what was probably an apology, without looking at Mac. But if he was sulky and defiant to start with, he was also miserable at having incurred his revered father's wrath, and so publicly. For the rest of the evening, much as it pained him, he kept his thoughts well-guarded, and took his cues from his father.

In fact, they all did, basking in the reflected glow of their father's importance to have visitors such as these.

All but invisible in our daily lives, Abdel Farid reigned supreme in theirs.

❈

Their hospitality was shaming. With so little, Abdel Farid's family gave freely. In the time we'd known him, we'd never invited him to join us in a meal, nor had he accepted so much as a cup of coffee from us, though I'd offered many times. I mentioned it to Mac after we got home, because he was in a better humor than I'd seen him in for a long time.

"It would be nice to return the invitation. Do you think dinner is too much, too . . . over the top?"

Mac didn't answer.

"Perhaps we could invite them for tea, instead. You know, Abdel Farid and his wife, some of the children—not the boys," I added hastily, thinking of Badri. "Maybe the youngest daughters, the three who still live at home."

Mac didn't say no. I mistook his silence for agreement, though I should've known better, for all the time, he was watching me. With hindsight, I replay the scene and see things were already too far gone; recovery wasn't possible. But, buoyed by the success of the evening, I forged ahead, fretting about the potential logistics, as if we were a normal married couple instead of the precarious twosome we'd become.

"We don't have enough matching teacups. Let's see. I also need a silver tea service or at least a big china pot. Maybe I can buy one around Hamra Street. Amina will know. Or, hey, maybe I could borrow some things from her instead."

I opened one of the kitchen cupboards to survey the assortment of mismatched china.

"This is cracked. Hmm. What do you think, should we invite Amina as well?"

In an instant that passed like lightning, Mac's arm shot out and slammed the cupboard door shut, narrowly missing my fingers as I jumped back in reflex.

"He's my fucking *driver*, he doesn't expect us to invite him to tea parties, for God's sake."

He stomped off to bed.

The subject was closed and did not come up again.

Abdel Farid and his family did not come over for tea. It is one of the things I still regret about my time in Beirut.

TWENTY

THE DAY AFTER ABDEL FARID's dinner, the radio at TV Kansai blared the latest: another Marine dead, another five wounded, bringing the tally to six Americans killed in as many weeks. This was big news, considering there'd only been one other Marine fatality—the guard in the embassy bombing—in the previous eight months.

Tension hung in a phantom pall over the city, while in the background, gunfire rumbled and popped relentlessly, the ominous white noise of war. Like the Yeats poem, *Things fall apart; the centre cannot hold.* Apocalyptic poetry in real time: that was Lebanon in October 1983.

A few days later, four more Marines were wounded when someone tried to blow up their convoy with a car bomb. We were now only a few days away from the realization this was but a foreshadowing of things to come.

###

The crack in the curtains announced first daylight.

I lay in bed for a while, trying not to feel nauseous. Then I tried to be quiet as I vomited in the bathroom.

Not quiet enough.

"Get rid of it," Mac said, when I crept back under the covers. He propped himself up and looked at me with winter eyes, his face pursed with disgust. I sat up, hugging a pillow. My nightgown was wet where I'd tried to dab it clean and I could smell sick in my hair.

"Go to Paris. Martine in the bureau can fix you up with someone there. Or better, go to New York and see that guy, Dr. Sherman, Schumann, whatever the hell his name was, you know, the one who did it last time."

"That wasn't me, Mac," I said, appalled.

His face sagged for a guilty moment, then his expression hardened.

"Oh, yeah, silly me," he said slowly and deliberately. He slicked his hair back with a large hand. "Must have been some other slut."

❈

Had he heard me that night at the bedroom door? Did Nadia tell him? Or was Mac mad at himself for getting caught out over the abortion? All this raced through my mind, while I tried to figure out how to respond.

Maybe I was silent too long, maybe it was my expression. Whether he'd known it when he said it, now there was little doubt I was guilty of something.

Perhaps the insult wasn't intended as the coup de grace to our marriage, but either way—coldly calculated or carelessly uttered— it had that effect, all the same.

Without a word, Mac got up, got dressed, and left. I sat, dry-eyed, on my side of the bed, contemplating the damp patches on my nightgown. What an incomprehensible muck I'd made of it all, seamlessly transforming myself from Lara, saint . . . to Lara, slut-wife.

It was just after six o'clock in the morning, October twenty-third. I will never forget it. Not because my marriage died that day, because—though mortally wounded—its final throes were still two months away.

I will never forget it because minutes after Mac left, a suicide bomber bound for his version of Islamic heaven crashed his two-and-a-half-ton yellow Mercedes-Benz stake-bed truck through various barriers and barricades and right into the sand-bagged lobby of the four-story building that housed the Marine battalion and communications center out at Beirut airport and blew it up.

The explosion carried a force equivalent to twelve thousand pounds of dynamite and reverberated through west Beirut. I didn't know that then. In our stilled apartment, I heard and felt it and, for a brief, mad moment, thought maybe Mac had come back, slamming the door downstairs with such fury as to shake the entire building and make the windows rattle.

I didn't know it heralded the moment of death for hundreds of young men.

I didn't know it would be later described as the largest non-nuclear blast the FBI had ever investigated, up to that time.

I didn't know that, a minute or two later, another bomber would hit his target, the French Multinational Force, two miles north, in the suburb of Jnah, and that yet more lives would be lost. Their eight-story building was blown off its very foundations. The car bomb there would be considered small compared to the one at the BLT, about four hundred pounds. Still, lethal enough, by any measure.

I didn't yet know any of this yet, but very soon we'd all be conversant in these facts. A brutal new chapter in international terrorism opened, with the names of 241 American and 58 French soldiers appended to it, men forever gone, along with any lingering illusions about the U.S. mission.

From a visit once with Mac, I knew the four-story BLT headquarters had been a self-contained world: dormitories, dining hall, gym, library, chapel. It had held a sick bay, a supply room, and an ammo dump, as well as administrative offices that had kept all the medical records of the Marines serving in Beirut.

Now, in a slash through time, it was gone, replaced by an incomprehensible hole in the landscape and a smoking mountain of twisted metal and rubble.

It would never again be referred to as "The California Hilton," the nickname the Marines jokingly bestowed on it.

Now it was a Marine mortuary. The shaken Marine spokesman told the reporters who rushed to the site he hadn't seen carnage like this since Vietnam.

It was a Sunday morning. Had the bomb not exploded, a modified holiday routine probably would've prevailed that day. Brunch would've been served at 8:00 A.M., and if the situation was calm there might've been downtime in the afternoon, perhaps a barbecue or an improvised ball game.

Because reveille was at 6:30 A.M., most of the three hundred Marines were still sleeping on their cots when the bomb went off. They wouldn't have had time to comprehend the great torrent of cement and cinder block roaring down upon them.

❊❊❊

Recently, I came across an official history of the Marine mission from this time, and it's given me a framework in which to center my memories from this time. For example, the story of the Marine bombing no longer begins for me at the moment the bomb detonated, the moment of my own awareness of it.

Now, it begins almost an hour earlier, just after dawn. Because now I know Lance Corporal Eddie DiFalco was on duty at Post 6, south of the building at that time, and that is when he first observed a yellow Mercedes stake-bed truck. It entered, circled the parking lot once, and left.

Less than an hour later, at 6:22 A.M., DiFalco again saw a yellow Mercedes stake-bed truck enter the parking lot and circle. This time, with lethal intent. It gathered speed and ran through rolls of concertina wire, heading for the BLT building. At Post 7, on the other side of the lot, Lance Corporal Henry Linkkila inserted a magazine into his rifle and prepared to fire.

Too late.

In those merest of moments, it was already too late.

In the guard shack at the BLT, Sergeant of the Guard Stephen Russell heard the truck hurtling through a fence encircling the compound. He cried out, "Hit the deck! Hit the deck!" before being blown out of the building.

The Marine Command estimates the entire incident took about six seconds.

❊❊❊

"I could see the gray ash and dust just all over the place, on jeeps, on grass, on trees, on all the rubble that was down there. And then suddenly, I began to see things move within the rubble and then I realized that these things ... moving were our fallen comrades," the official account quoted the Marines' Catholic chaplain.

Many were still alive, you see, trapped in that vast, smoldering mountain of rubble, pleading for salvation. "DON'T LEAVE US," TRAPPED MEN CRY, was a *New York Times* headline I later saw from that day.

Hour after hour, their comrades desperately clawed through the debris by hand, joined by Italian and Lebanese soldiers.

The French also sent over a delegation, even in the midst of their own tragedy, as they dug out their own dead and wounded. Humanity had not been lost, in a place so fraught with evil and death, and to learn that, all these years later, adds a note of hope to a world where the elastic boundaries of civilization are routinely flexed.

That day and into the next and the next, rescue workers used any and every tool at hand: picks, jackhammers, blowtorches. A Lebanese construction company brought in cranes and heavy equipment, while helicopters ferried casualties to the U.S. warships off the coast.

❈

One photograph that sticks in my memory is not of the devastation, or the dead, but a Marine who survived. He was trained for warfare, but nothing in his young life would have prepared him for this day. He clutches his M16 rifle with one hand and wipes tears from his eyes with the other, as he crouches low behind a barricader to avoid the sniper fire aimed at the frantic rescue operation. Incredibly, with so many of his mates instantly dead and so many others injured and still captive in the wreckage, *incredibly*, the danger of this day is not over yet.

And he is still a long way from home.

⁘

It is adjectives of excess that conjure up that time: most, biggest, largest, worst. World War II and Vietnam were the standards by which this devastation was measured—the largest loss of American military life since the first day of the 1968 Tet Offensive; and, for the Marine Corps alone, the most Marines killed in a single day since Iwo Jima on D-Day, 1945.

⁘

When I reached TV Kansai, Gifford was frantically shuttling through pictures. He waved me away, underscoring the fact I had no real role; that, in a crisis, I was in the way.

In the outer office, Hamid, phones to both ears, glowered at pictures of the new American ambassador on the small television set on his desk.

"Welcome to Lebanon," he shouted, as on-screen the ambassador inspected the destruction.

The ambassador, you see, had just arrived. Presumably, he accepted this risky portfolio with trepidation. But tell me, could anyone have anticipated his first full day on the job would be spent sifting through the ruins of his country's foreign policy?

⁘

Marine Corps Commandant General Paul X. Kelly testified before the Senate shortly after the bombings. The U.S. mission was, he said, "basically a diplomatic/political mission, not a military one in the classic sense and the positioning of Marine forces at Beirut International Airport was not driven by tactical considerations."

Does that need translation?

The Marines, he said, were authorized to informally train the Lebanese Army to take over responsibility for security in Beirut, and, ultimately, the rest of Lebanon. It might not be germane to the bombing, but it could explain why "some Lebanese" perceived the Americans "were no longer exclusively in a 'presence' role; that we were in an 'assistance' role." He said American naval support for the Lebanese Army helped lead to the September cease-fire but, at the same time, may also have led Lebanese Moslems to perceive "that our Marines were pro-Christian and no longer neutral."

His plain talk was striking.

This was no bureaucratic cover-up, you see. It was a reasonable—and, I believe, accurate—summation of what went wrong. But then, the military men opposed this mission from the start. It was diplomats who'd insisted on it.

Kelly called Beirut "a world where violence and normalcy live side by side."

It certainly fit the Beirut I knew.

❈

Two days passed without sight of Mac. Everyone was working around the clock and I assumed he was sleeping at the Commodore.

The third night, he returned. Without greeting, he put his things down in the front hall, and without preamble poured a scotch and proceeded straight to the balcony.

I stood in the doorway and watched. Beyond him, the seafront was alive with activity—traffic and pedestrians on the Corniche, and, out over the water, helicopters buzzing back and forth between the ships and shore.

"I can't believe they're gone."

His voice was soft and it surprised me; I hadn't heard it for so long.

"They were good kids, those boys. Remember that time you

went with me? We played football with them another time, bunch of us ... that sergeant, the one they called Mikey Mach I, to distinguish him from Mikey Mach II, I guess ... that sergeant, he had a right arm every bit as limp as his left but he wanted to be pitcher so bad they let him. And Marty was pissed because they still beat us. He was from Georgia, too, Mikey Mach I, and there was a kid from Chickasaw, near where my mother's mother used to live. They had a friend, guy who talked funny, lisped or something. Maybe a tooth missing, I don't remember. Hardly needed to shave, just peach fuzz, some of those kids."

He shook his head at the memory.

"I keep thinking about all the things they did to keep fit—all the exercises, the push-ups, sit-ups, shadow boxing—and how it was all for nothing. Wore their helmets and their flak jackets. Man, those guys ate their Wheaties. But nothing could protect them from this kind of craziness."

He added, wonderingly, "Can't believe they're gone, all of them, just like that."

Nothing to say, nothing to ease this burden.

A tear rolled down the stubble of his cheek. He looked terrible, gray and ill.

"It's a nightmare out there, you can't begin to imagine. Crater, eight feet deep. They're having trouble identifying the dead—guys there's enough left of to ID, that is. Lots of them were wearing nothing but gym shorts, not even dog tags—took them off to sleep. If they'd been in uniform, at least their names would've been on them."

With the back of his hand, he wiped away another tear that escaped his brimming eyes.

"No dignity to any of this. The medical records, dental charts—they were blown up too. Only way they can figure out who's gone is by figuring out who's left."

A tear fell into his glass. He stood up and walked over to the railing and looked out to sea.

"Remember that assassination attempt on that Sunni politician just after we got here? Bomb exploded as his motorcade went by and one of his bodyguards was killed? I never told you this, but a couple hours later, I was at the scene and saw a policeman scooping something into a small plastic bag. I asked Martin what it was, and he told me that was the bodyguard. And I remember thinking that this was some serious shit here in Lebanon.

"You could die and they'd scrape you up with a spoon."

He turned around to face me, leaning back against the railing now.

"They didn't even know why they were here, those boys. They didn't even *know* why they were in Lebanon."

Voice quavering, he stopped to gather himself before continuing.

"They were just boys, some of them just babies, really. Oh, they were tough all right—had to be, they were Marines. But they also had to be scared as shit. Who wouldn't be, out there like sitting ducks."

He shook his head angrily. "That's what they were and they knew it. Sitting goddamn ducks. They didn't know shit about Lebanon's war but it killed them all the goddamn same."

He sobbed openly.

"Goddamn innocents, didn't know about getting scraped up with a spoon."

I went to him. I embraced him and we both wept.

※

In the days that followed, Mac did not refer again to my pregnancy, nor did I.

If I could have wished it away, I would have. I could not. Like Mac, I ignored it, instead.

Events had overtaken our own small drama, which quickly paled into insignificance in the wake of such overwhelming tragedy.

TWENTY-ONE

FOR WEEKS, STORIES floated around the city like bubbles, each a tiny encapsulation of tragedy as infinite and unfathomable as the universe itself. No matter how often the retelling, they remained unchanged, stopped at the same point on October 23, 1983. A happy ending would never be possible.

There were also the sidebars, mini–parallel worlds of woe in themselves. Katie from Reuters told us about a Marine who'd married a local Lebanese girl, a Moslem, only days before. She spoke no English and had never been out of Lebanon. In accordance with what they believed her husband wanted, remaining Marines took her in, as family, and helped arrange her passage out of the country. While the intrinsic value of retelling the story lay in the Marines response, I wondered what this girl would encounter on the path ahead. This was the ripple effect, you see—influencing not only the policies of great nations, but countless small destinies, in turn.

I think it fair to say 1983 was a watershed year in international terrorism. Not because that's when it became my reality, but because so many around the world died in terrorist attacks. The Marine bombing stood alone in terms of scale and its impact on foreign policy, but it was bookended by a series of violent events. We remember the high-profile ones, but lose sight of the smaller losses, over time, unless secured to the memory board with a personal pin-tack. For example, I remember a nineteen-year-old Israeli-American New Yorker was stabbed to death in the marketplace in the West Bank town of Hebron, because that is where I finally bought my own tea set a few years later. The death of another American, an elderly tourist—Christian, I believe—sticks in my mind because she was from one of the Carolinas. Killed when her bus was blown up, she wouldn't have expected to die on a package tour of the Holy Land.

The day Washington named the head of the commission investigating the Marine attack, there was another suicide bombing—at the Israeli headquarters, in Tyre, southern Lebanon. This time, it was Israeli soldiers, more than two dozen. But even more of their prisoners were killed, in what the British call an "own goal." If such a term could be applied without making light of the fact that, once again, mankind had been diminished.

❈

This is what I learned in Lebanon: it tolls for thee.

❈

While the Middle East saw the lion's share of terror, geography didn't define its political boundaries. A month after the embassy bombing in April, a U.S. Navy officer was gunned down in El Salvador by the Farabundo Marti National Liberation Front. A month after the attack on the Marines, another American naval officer was assassinated in Greece, by a group called November 17.

I perceived international terrorism that year through the prism of my own passport. But there were other enemies on the march, as South Korea learned when its delegation was blown up in Rangoon, Burma, most likely by North Korean agents.

A few days after the Marine bombings, the U.S. invaded Grenada, a small Caribbean nation, concerned about growing Cuban and Soviet domination. Some six hundred American students attended university there and Washington also wanted to avoid the possibility of a hostage scenario, like the one following the 1979 Iranian Revolution.

"It's a stupid stunt," Mac fumed a few nights later. Hamid, alone, hovered over a drink a few seats away.

"Total overkill, in any case," said Boz Whitfield. "A big, powerful nation invading a country that, realistically, poses about as much threat to the United States of America as the Bahamas. What's the point?"

"The point," Martin picked up, "is to save the hides of a couple of American students too stupid to get into U.S. medical schools."

"Think about it, lads. It may not be a master stroke militarily, but it was brilliant PR," Fretwell said, thoughtfully. "They've successfully distracted the attention of the American public from this disaster."

"But it's backfiring already," Martin said. "They're taking a pounding down there I don't think they expected. They thought they could roll right in."

"Yes, it's probably safe to say resistance has exceeded the U.S. expectation," Fretwell conceded.

"Forget whether or not they should have invaded," Boz said, "The question is, was the U.S. *ready* to invade, were they properly equipped? Doesn't sound like it."

"No," agreed Martin. "They're relying on sheer brute force. Didn't think it through, just did it."

As always, I had my own view, though it was a work in progress and admittedly more sophisticated now, colored and shaped as it was now by events experienced firsthand.

Grenada, to me, wasn't a distraction at all. It showed the U.S. could take bold, decisive steps, not simply react to events as they unfolded. Such as it had done here in Lebanon, where, hostage to its own policy and the whims of others, it seemed to have little choice.

By mid-November, the 22nd MAU, which stopped off to help invade Grenada en route to the Mediterranean, was in position to take over from the decimated 24th MAU, which lost so many in the bombing. U.S. Defense Secretary Caspar Weinberger put an official stamp on rumors that Iran and Syria were behind it.

※

"There's been another attack. In Kuwait," Mac said, as he opened the front door. "I need to pack and get out of here fast. Abdel Farid's downstairs, waiting to take me to the airport."

He grabbed a duffel bag from the front hall closet and took it into the bedroom.

"What happened?"

"Car bombs, outside the U.S. embassy and the French embassy."

He hurriedly shoveled clothes into the bag.

"Did you get my shirts or not? I need the blue one."

"Here you go. The blue one's hanging in the closet. How many dead?"

"Don't know for sure: several, at least, and lots more, like dozens, injured. No details yet, but a radical Shiite group is already claiming they did it. What's with the hangers? I told you, folded, they're easier to pack."

"I forgot," I sighed. "Any idea when you'll be back?"

"I haven't even left yet. Don't start, Lara."

"What time's the flight?" I tossed him some socks, and casually, I hoped, as though an afterthought, added, "Is Nadia going with you?"

Mac looked up sharply.

"She's my translator. Yes, Lara, Nadia goes with me. You got a problem with that?" He shoved a pair of shoes roughly into his bag. "Or maybe you'd like to come and translate instead? I'm sure Greek will come in real handy with the Kuwaitis."

"I was only asking."

"Get my shaving kit, please, it's in the bathroom."

"Mac?"

"What now?"

"Mac, do you still love me?"

"You're my fucking wife, what do you think?"

❊

The final tally in Kuwait was six dead, another eighty wounded. The numbers didn't compare to Beirut, but, as Hamid put it, the genie was out of the box.

And it was by no means over for the besieged Americans in Lebanon. Early in December, eight more Marines died, after an attack from Syrian-held territory.

❊

Like a town crier, Boz Whitfield, out of breath, burst into the TV Kansai office on the way to his own.

"U.S. warplanes are hitting Syrian positions east of the city, up in the mountains."

"What?" Hamid shouted. "This means war, for sure. First they invade Grenada, now what? They want war with Syria, too? And Israel comes back and then the whole Middle East is on fire?"

"But the Syrians started it," I protested, "I heard on the radio this morning they fired at the U.S. reconnaissance flights."

"Who told the Americans to fly over Syrian positions? What right do they have?" He shook his head angrily. "Madness! When will you learn?"

❖

Hamid was wrong: it wasn't the start of a new war. But, in this first such U.S. action in the skies over Lebanon, two U.S. aircraft were lost, which seemed to satisfy him. In fact, there was a general air of consensus around the Commodore that this, too, might fit within the fluid parameters of Beirut irony.

❖

U.S. warships did not remain silent.

On December 15, the *New Jersey*'s big guns sprang into action for the first time in Lebanon, firing at Syrian antiaircraft positions in the mountains southeast of Beirut.

"Like freaking Keystone cops," Martin said. "Those things are leaving craters the size of Volkswagens up there."

"They can't even hit the livestock," Hamid sneered from a few feet away, but made a point of not looking up, in case anyone thought he was actually participating in the conversation.

"That's not true," Boz joined in. "I have it on good authority they got three sheep and a cow yesterday."

"They most certainly did not. It was two sheep and a cow—and those poor animals died of fright," Nils Erik said.

"Next thing you know, Druze farmers will sue the U.S. government for damages." Martin said.

I sipped a Coke and tapped a cigarette out of a fresh packet. Nils Erik leaned over and lit it for me.

"Heard lately from that husband of yours?" he asked.

"No. He's still away. Probably difficult to get a line out. You know how it is."

Hamid looked up with sudden, undisguised interest. "The phones don't work from East Beirut?"

The chatter around us ceased.

"Mac's not in East Beirut, he's in Kuwait," I said patiently, aware everyone nearby was listening now.

"Oh, I see," he said. He paused a beat, then, "Yes, East Beirut must be a suburb of Kuwait."

"Mac went to Kuwait on Monday, to cover the bombs at the U.S. and French embassies," I insisted.

"My misunderstanding, Madam McCauley," he said, insincerely.

Awkward silence. These were not unkind people, you see, but they were Mac's friends. I mashed out my cigarette, though I hadn't finished it, grinding it into the ashtray so hard it slid off the bar and shattered.

"Hey, did you see that new roadblock out near the camps?" someone asked.

"Flying checkpoint," someone else threw in.

"Who's manning it?"

It may have been Martin who asked. I didn't hear the answer. The noise level was gradually restored and gave me cover, allowing me to extricate myself. As Marwan picked up the shards of glass, I gathered up my cigarettes and what little dignity remained to me.

❉

I rang the bell to Thomas's flat.

Mrs. Fonterelli yanked opened the front door.

"He is not here. You can leave now." She looked angry. As she spoke, I heard someone scrambling down the stairs and a second or two later, Thomas poked his head over her shoulder.

"Oh, hello," he said, in surprise, easing his way around her to let me in. "Sorry, Mrs. Fonterelli. This is Lara. My friend Lara. You met her before."

"Yes," she said grimly, "I remember."

She stalked off and the door to her apartment slammed shut.

"Well, come up, come up. I'm surprised to see you here."

He led the way up the stairs, apologizing for Mrs. Fonterelli.

"She has many troubles. Her Lebanese son-in-law was taken from his car at gunpoint on Beirut-Damascus highway. They think the Syrians are holding him somewhere, but won't admit it."

He fumbled with the key in the lock. There were hundreds, maybe thousands, of prisoners, still unaccounted for, he said, probably languishing in Syrian jails. But impossible to prove; nobody wanted to take on the Syrians over this issue.

Thomas, still talking, stepped aside to let me enter first, then, with the door closed, thrust himself clumsily at me.

Appalled, I drew back. "Thomas—please," I wriggled out of his clasp. "Stop it!"

He did, immediately. He looked bewildered and slightly ashamed.

"Then why are you here?"

I must admit, I'd hoped for a more sensitive display.

"May I sit?"

"Of course. I am so sorry. Please. Go ahead." He gestured toward the daybed.

I tried to compose my thoughts.

"Please don't get the wrong impression. I came to ask for help." I recounted what Hamid said. Thomas sat down heavily beside me.

"So you think Barrett is in East Beirut? What, with Nadia?"

"Hamid didn't say it outright, but that's the implication. And if Mac came back early, without telling me, there has to be a reason. Please, can you help me find out?"

"Lara. Why put yourself through this?" He looked sorrowful. "What is the point of this exercise? Do you really want the truth? And if they are together? What then? Why torture yourself, unless you do something about it? I don't understand."

"Thomas, please. I'm asking as a friend." I was near tears. "Please, Thomas, help me."

He picked up my hand.

"We talked about choice before, Lara, remember? Maybe it is time. In a positive way, in a way that will give you the energy, the power, to go forward into the next phase of your life."

"I don't have a choice this time, Thomas. I need Mac back." It took all my courage to force out the next words. "I'm pregnant."

I didn't want to complicate matters; I told him it was Mac's. Anyway, it probably was.

∗∗∗

In the end, Thomas agreed to make some phone calls.

I waited nervously for his sources to call back, chain-lighting cigarettes with their half-smoked predecessors. Thomas gave me brandy, this time in a tumbler, but my stomach was too unsettled. Time passed somehow. We talked, but not about anything important, and Thomas maintained a respectful distance.

Finally, the phone rang. He turned away and spoke quickly and quietly into the receiver. I wandered over to the window to make it clear I was not intentionally eavesdropping, but of course I could hear everything.

"Je regrette la situation, Gerard," Thomas said several times into the receiver at the end of their brief conversation. *"Merci, Gerard."* He put the phone down and turned back to face me.

"Okay. You have asked for the truth and I have it, if you are ready." He exhaled heavily, as if he had been holding his breath.

"Hamid is correct. Barrett and Nadia came back early yesterday morning. They traveled in by ferry from Cyprus to the port of Jounieh. They are staying in a suite at a small hotel in East Beirut, registered in the name of Mr. and Mrs. Barrett McCauley. Shall I keep going?"

I nodded, miserably.

"They have not left the room since they checked in. The maid was allowed in this morning to change the linens and your husband tipped her well enough to set tongues wagging at the hotel. Barrett is a fool. They have ordered 270 pounds and 63 piasters worth of food and beverage from room service so far. That includes a bottle of vintage champagne, a light supper, and a full continental breakfast today. Do you want to know more?"

"No, Thomas. That's enough."

"I won't say I am sorry. You demanded to know. Now you know." Thomas's eyes were devoid of sympathy. "You carry his child but that does not eliminate your choice."

"It certainly reduces it," I said, bitterly.

"It doesn't, not at all. Unless you choose to be a victim."

"I can't leave him now. There's a child to consider. I can't do that alone."

"Of course you can. You must leave him. You have to."

His eyes locked with mine, a moment of deep soul recognition.

Thomas was so adamant, it was reassuring. Despite everything, my feelings remained strong and now, it was clear, he felt the same. Had I, subconsciously, sought this, had it been incrementally underway, since the night he came to our flat?

I searched Thomas's face for the promise his voice held. Would I really leave Mac? I hadn't thought so . . . And yet.

"Leave Mac?" I repeated slowly, unsure.

"Your husband is in East Beirut fucking his translator!" Thomas shouted at me.

❈

He was right, of course. Mac didn't want me. He betrayed me, and, even as I sat there, might be planning to jettison me first. And here was Thomas, offering a safety net, perhaps a future. Even pregnant, Thomas wanted me. It was a powerful restorative.

"I don't know if I have the strength to do this." But I reached out for his hand with both of mine and squeezed hard. He smiled and squeezed back.

"You have the strength. You can do it."

"And if I do, what guarantee is there for us?"

"For us?" Thomas sounded puzzled. His grip on my hand loosened.

"How can we be sure it'll work out with you and me?"

"Lara," Thomas said warningly, dropping my hand altogether.

I wish I'd stopped then, but I didn't, you know. My train of thought had jumped tracks now and was in full throttle.

"We should probably leave Beirut altogether, don't you think? It would be too weird."

"Lara." He tried again, but had no chance against my rising panic.

"Where would we go, where would we have the baby?" I gestured wildly. "How would we live? Oh, God, so many things to consider . . ."

He stood up abruptly.

"Lara, stop. You are misunderstanding everything."

It was my turn to look horrified. I hung my head in shame, my hands over my face, as I realized what was happening.

"Don't say it." Even now, it mortifies me to remember this moment.

He said it. I will give him credit for this: he did it gently. He knelt down and put his fingertips under my chin and tilted my face up to him and looked squarely at me.

"I am so sorry. You misunderstand. Don't leave him *for me*. That's not what I want. You must leave him for *yourself*, for your own sake, your future. For your own dignity."

"What are you really saying, Thomas?" It came out weakly, because I knew already and yet my heart sank anew with every word.

"I am not the man for you," he said, withdrawing his touch. "I am sorry you have misunderstood."

I had got it wrong on every level. I had made such a colossal fool of myself, I couldn't imagine how I would ever claw back any self-respect. I began to cry. Now, truly, I was losing everything.

"Why did you make love to me, Thomas? Why?" I needed the answer to complete the circle of my humiliation.

But he had no answer.

"Were you using me all along? What did you want? Did you get what you wanted?"

He shook his head, helplessly, and sat down next to me.

"Lara, Lara." He tried to embrace me, but his touch repelled me. What comfort had he left for me? What remained for him to give when all illusion was finally put to rest?

Once more, it was Hobson's choice.

I left and he did not try to stop me.

I did not know—as I left his apartment, slamming the door behind me, as I pounded down the worn stairs and through the faded foyer, as Mrs. Fonterelli's curtains swayed ever so slightly, as the street outside carried me away and into the tide of humanity sweeping through the city—I did not know that from this point on, Thomas would exist only in memory for me, that I would never see him again.

TWENTY-TWO

My EYES WERE STILL red-rimmed when Mac walked through the front door that evening, clutching his typewriter and a carrier bag with an airport duty logo. Trailing a few steps behind, Abdel Farid lugged Mac's dusty, overstuffed duffels, labeled with the black, red, and green stickers of Middle East Airlines, the Lebanese national airline.

"Here." Mac shoved the carrier bag at me.

Chanel No. 5. Heavy with the bribe it was meant to be, a burden in my hands.

"You look like crap, Lara. Your eyes are all bloodshot."

"Allergies," I said. Hardly trusting myself, I added, "I wasn't expecting you so soon. How was the flight?"

"Miserable. Kuwait Air, dry as a desert. Give me MEA any day. They know how to run an airline. If the rest of the country could get it together so well, there wouldn't be a civil war."

Abdel Farid put the duffels down in the front hall and appeared to be awaiting further instruction.

"Thanks, pal," Mac said, "Can you come back for me at eight?"

Abdel Farid nodded and closed the door behind him.

"You're going out again?" I asked in disbelief.

"Got work to do. Need to file this story."

"It's only Thursday night. You don't file until Friday."

"I know when I need to file."

He headed for the living room and picked up a bottle of scotch on the way.

"Skip the lecture. I've had a long flight and I'm not in the mood."

You know I took a deep breath first, thought to myself no, Lara, don't do it. Once you start, you don't know where it will end up. Stop, Lara. Consider the consequences, Lara. Don't do anything in haste. Then, without my own permission, I went ahead and did it anyway.

"A long flight, Mac? From East Beirut? Took two days, did it, to cross the Green Line?"

"What?" He put his scotch down on the counter. "Are you crazy?"

"That won't work this time, Mac. I know you were in East Beirut with Nadia."

He was genuinely shaken. He watched for a forlorn moment, as if looking for guidance.

"You're a liar, Mac . . . liar!" I screamed.

"God almighty, Lara, lower your voice, calm down, get control of yourself."

"Don't tell me what to do! You make me sick!"

My stomach churned with the knowledge of what he had done, and I raced to the toilet, where I vomited violently.

Mac followed. He stood watching, arms folded tightly across his chest. I sensed, rather than saw, the paradigm shift, his stance no longer humbled but aggressive.

"Oooh, this is rich," he taunted. "*You* accusing *me*. You lying little slut."

I slowly got to my feet and turned around to face him.

This was real danger.

I froze, like I did once many years before, when a rattlesnake crossed my path in the woods near my parents' home in North Carolina. But this peril did not slither by, it coiled around my ankles, and the atmosphere was fraught with the tension of imminent attack.

He took a step toward me. "Tell me, dear, sweet... *innocent...* Lara... why did you go to Warkowski's house *again*, after I told you not to? Why did you deliberately disobey me? You fucking him, Lara? His balls suddenly drop? Well? Are you?

I took a hand towel and wiped a string of saliva from my chin.

"Answer me, damn it."

"I only went to try to find out where you were," I said, without taking my eyes off him.

"I'm warning you. You better tell me the truth."

"It is the truth. It was Hamid, he was at the Commodore, hinting in his nasty way that you were in East Beirut. I had to know." The fear pitched my voice a half-octave higher than normal. "That's why I went, to ask Thomas to help me find out."

"You liar. You slut." He was a big man and his swing knocked tears into my eyes and fused together all the thoughts in my head in a single jolt

"Were you fucking him the whole time, Lara? All those times you went off together?"

Dizzy, I caught his hand as he made to strike me again.

"No, I swear. I only wanted to find out where you were. That's all."

"And what did he tell you, slut? Say it, and this time it better be the truth." He didn't hit me again but he gripped my shoulders, sinking fingers into flesh, and shook me.

"He called a friend, for information," I said, almost inaudibly.

"Who?"

"A guy named Gerard," I whimpered.

He abruptly let go, and watched me collapse onto the shiny squares of the bathroom floor.

"Bitch." He took a step back and regarded my prone figure. Almost as an afterthought, he kicked me in the stomach.

"You shouldn't lie to me, Lu," he said, softly.

※

I lay there a long time. Eventually, the throbbing subsided, the tears slowed, and I assessed the damage. Maybe a bruised cheek-bone; he'd hit me hard enough. My stomach hurt, but there was nothing broken, no blood—I was more shocked than anything else. I rose slowly, found aspirin, and cocooned myself in the bed covers.

Outside, there was gunfire and what sounded like it might be the start of a round of shelling, the neighborhood militia's .50-caliber machine-gun nest joining in a couple of blocks away. For once, I didn't have the energy to be alarmed. I never realized how much energy fear required until I simply couldn't summon it up. Too many other things going on—gunfire seemed benign in compari-son. Someone else would respond to it. Or not, as the case may be.

Responsibility for my own situation could not be so easily abdicated.

I stayed in bed. There was nowhere else to go.

※

It was the middle of the night when Mac slid into bed and put his arm around me.

"Lara," he whispered, "Lu, you awake?"

His erection pulsed against my back. I feigned sleep.

"Aw, Lu, I'm sorry. I didn't mean to hurt you."

I dropped the pretense.

"You hit me. You *kicked* me."

"I couldn't stand to think of him with you like that. I'm sorry, it made me crazy. But it's okay now."

"It's not okay." I said dully. "I hate you."

"Sure it is, sweetheart. Look, I'll be honest. I was in East Beirut. But it was to interview this guy for a piece I'm doing next week, that's all."

"You were with Nadia. Stop lying."

"All right, look. She was there, okay? But she started it, it wasn't my fault, she threw herself at me. You know how she is. It doesn't mean anything to me. You know that."

His probing became more urgent and he tried to turn me over, but I refused.

He inadvertently grabbed where he'd kicked me earlier and when I gasped, tried to massage the spot, but I pulled away.

"Anyway, you shouldn't have been spying on me, Lu," he said, almost playfully, as he tried to draw me back.

You will understand my incredulity.

The pendulum had swung yet again, in directions perhaps I should've foreseen, but didn't, because this wasn't the ordinary tick-tock of every day life, but Foucault's mighty pendulum, and the earth spun beneath my feet at the same time.

I was too exhausted, on every level, to fight the ever-persuasive Mac, and, in the end, I didn't. I may have even responded. Please don't judge me. Yes, he hit me and said terrible things. No one should tolerate that kind of abuse, I know it now and I knew it then. But you know what? When all was said and done, nothing changed this central fact: I had nothing else.

So I held Mac tight. He shared my past, my present, and, pathetic and wrong and weak as it sounds, there was no future without him.

※

Everything changed. Nothing changed. As if we'd passed an audition and won our old roles back, with fresh, new scripts and given our finest performances to date.

Flashes of the old Mac shone through, more affectionate than he'd been in months, even making a little fuss over my injuries, stroking my cheek without reference to the fact he was responsible. He brought me coffee and juice in bed, along with an out-of-date newspaper, presenting it all with great flourish. I did not laugh or smile, as I might have in the past, but I accepted these attentions and that seemed enough for now. I no longer feared him. The worst had happened. We'd survived. Somehow, I knew he'd never hit me again.

Should it have occurred to me he was sexually exhilarated the night before because he'd just come from arranging Thomas's death?

If so, I can only say in my defense, I didn't know that then, I didn't draw a connection between the two things. For, although I didn't see Thomas in that time, he didn't disappear right away. That didn't happen for another two weeks and I was in a state of total shock when it did, for it was yet another event that perhaps I should have foreseen.

❋

The Long Commission investigated the Marine barracks bombing and released its findings in December 1983. One hundred forty pages, Mac announced, half a page for each life lost. It hadn't occurred to me life could be reduced to that simple a calculation.

❋

Distressing as these events were, it was the mathematics of fertility that most concerned me now. By the doctor's reckoning of conception, I couldn't be certain who was the father. I was glad this variable hadn't come up with Thomas that day, so swiftly had he cast me off when I drew too close.

Time brought no clarity; if anything, it further obscured. Masters of denial, Mac and I still didn't discuss the child. He was so busy it wasn't hard, and, as for me—honestly?—I felt no maternal stirrings, only the nausea associated with pregnancy. There were no outward signs to distinguish the internal transformation my body was negotiating, and, in those weeks, I actually lost weight, as sickness and stress subdued my appetite.

Several people noted the weight loss but no one realized why. Despite a sidelong look from Amina during the one visit I paid her in this time, she commented only upon my pallor, remarking I looked unwell. Indeed, I felt unwell and couldn't remember a time when it had not been so.

I didn't know whether Mac believed the child to be his, I could hardly ask. True to his character, however, he showed no interest in impending fatherhood and, to be fair, a child wasn't congruent with the life we led. But I had no idea what Mac wanted to do about it. I no longer possessed the ability to divine what he was thinking.

❁

Beneath it all lay a fundamental unchanged from the start; and it was from this I believe Mac's reluctance truly sprang—his inherent selfishness. It wasn't his traumatic beginnings, rather that he saw us as a complete unit already, among an extended family of journalists and the expatriate community. Whenever I'd thought about children in the past, I'd worried this might be a problem and had never pushed it because the moment never seemed right. Now, quite by accident, that moment had arrived and it was apparent Mac wouldn't willingly relinquish his position center stage, nor forgo his absolute monopoly on my attention. Not even with his own issue. And should it come to pass, certainly not that of another man.

❁

Of course, the time was fast approaching when we'd have to discuss it, but in the interim we moved in cautious concert, from one day to the next. I don't remember precisely how or when adoption was first mentioned but we seemed to have settled on it, by default, as the way to salvage our marriage.

We never referred directly to it.

"I should leave by January."

"You could go to North Carolina, rent a place, there's a good hospital there."

We knew no one in Elizabeth City; more important, no one knew us.

This was Mac's plan. I didn't have a better one.

❁

Of course, things don't always go according to plan, even the most meticulously executed arrangements, which ours hardly were.

The first departure came with the news of Thomas's disappearance.

He simply vanished. No sign of struggle, no gunmen, no ransom notes. No witnesses. Nothing. I'm not sure who discovered he was missing, but from my own experience, I imagined Mrs. Fonterelli would've noticed early on if he failed to return home for more than a few days. Worried about the fate of her own missing son-in-law, did she keep the observation to herself or make it known immediately?

Mac himself delivered the news in a carefully offhand fashion.

I was already in bed, reading by flashlight, when he came in.

"Still on *Vanity Fair*? Didn't you start that when we first moved here?"

"It keeps me from thinking too much. Besides, I keep getting interrupted."

He sat down on the bed and removed his shoes and socks.

"Boy, what a day."

He stood up and removed his shirt and trousers, then sat down again.

"By the way, Lara, bad news about Warkowski."

Now I know what people mean when they say their hearts stopped. My heart stopped.

Mac reached out for the pillows on his side of the bed, avoiding my gaze.

"Yeah, disappeared, just like that." He snapped his fingers. "Kidnapped. There's been a claim of responsibility already, a phone call from some radical Shiite group, linked to Hezbollah. You know, the guys who did the embassy and Marine bombs."

A chill travelled through my body, like a foreign army. It

ordered my heart to stop pumping blood and my lungs to stop filtering air. It sealed my ear canals, rallied tears to exit the ducts, exhorted my teeth to start chattering. It shot sprays of bile up into my mouth so I thought I would be sick. It froze my muscles, turned my bones into jelly, and elicited goose bumps to run the surface of my useless limbs.

"So there you go," Mac concluded, "The guy's just *gone*. But, you know what? More I think about it, I really don't buy this kidnap story. Personally, I think he offed himself, couldn't live with the guilt of what he'd done."

Mac punched up the pillows and replaced them. He couldn't look at me.

"And what, exactly..."—Zombie-like, I could hardly force out the words—"was that?"

"He was a spy, I told you a zillion times. Maybe he was involved in the bombings, passed on information about the compound to the Hezbollah or the Syrians or something. Then he couldn't live with himself."

Sheets of huge tears began to slide down my face.

"He...didn't...kill...himself."

Mac swung his legs on to the bed and pulled the cover up over them. "Nah, guess you're right, it doesn't fit with the claim." He continued to avoid looking at me. "Anyway, the guy was a spy. He knew the dangers. Guess he never expected them to catch up with him. Predictable, though. And pretty stupid, if you ask me."

Mac turned on his side, away from me, taking the bedspread with him, and I had the crazy thought that if I lay still enough, I could rewind this moment, the way Gifford's tape machines reversed video footage.

"He's probably dead already. Anyway, who'd pay ransom for him?" Mac yawned, too elaborately.

"Mac, tell me," I blurted out, but stopped.

Put yourself in my place and ask: Did I really want to know?

※

I already knew the important part. Thomas was dead.

Not merely disappeared, dead. He had to be, because the few small pockets of optimism left in my life were punctured and despair rushed in to fill the place where light had been. The empty space in my heart felt empty again and I knew it would be that way from this day on—and I was right in that, you know? Even today.

Certainly, I suspected Mac. But where did that strand lead? What proof was there, other than my own infidelity?

For that, and for every other reason you already know, leaving Mac seemed the only fitting memorial to give Thomas. A grand gesture it would be, but this was not the time. Not yet.

※

Because I promised this would be the entire story, I have to confess that even as I prayed for Thomas—desperate, heartfelt prayers, believe me—even as I prayed, I also hated him a little, because he hadn't wanted me.

It shames me to remember. Please understand that I would've given anything in the world to have him back safe. At the same time, a small, wicked voice in my head agreed with Mac that Thomas got what he deserved, that whatever his game was, he'd played it and lost.

TWENTY-THREE

OVER THE NEXT DAYS, I forced myself to listen to the rumors and all the speculation at the Commodore about Thomas—theories about Shiite extremists, about the Russians, the Syrians, the Christians, the Israelis, even common criminals looking to make a quick buck.

But I knew. From each day that passed with no word. From the way Hamid's sly eyes narrowed when he saw me. I knew from the way Mac claimed me in the night, roughly, without care, because I was the spoils.

I knew, and I felt perilously close to despair, but there was nowhere for it to take me. Thomas was gone, and with him, all the answers I'd sought and never would have.

At any rate, heavy fighting in and around Beirut didn't leave much time for reflection. Everyone was fighting everyone else. The besieged Marines finally reacted with such ferocity that leaders of the Shiite and Druze militias, whose fighters were involved in the clashes, called the U.S. embassy several times to ask the Marines to stop. Elemental irony.

※

I worked with Gifford virtually full-time now, throwing myself into it with hardened resolve. The craft of editing was no longer a time filler but a potential lifeline. Though Mac and I were still together, it seemed entirely probable we wouldn't be for long, and the thought no longer filled me with dread. Like a chronic disease, I'd learned to live with it.

While Gifford seemed grateful for the help, Hamid ran true to form, his sarcasm a sentry at the door. I steeled myself to be civil, no matter what the provocation, and sure enough, after a day or two, he was reduced to mutterings and dark looks. Eventually, he ignored me altogether, and it was a bitter triumph.

Early one morning, Gifford and I were in the edit suite, having coffee, smoking, and reviewing video shot by a freelance cameraman in the Bekaa Valley, showing one of the Hezbollah camps Thomas talked about that first night when he came to our flat.

"Heard anything about our friend?" Gifford shelved the Hezbollah tape and picked up another cassette, of overnight fighting, shot by the TV Kansai crew that morning near the airport.

"Sorry?" For a second, I thought he referred to someone hurt in the incident the night before, on the tape we were about to look at.

"Thomas." Gifford put the new tape in and pressed the play button. A parade of images spooled across the screen in double time.

He looked at me. "I know you two were mates. Any news?"

The sympathetic tone did it.

"No, Bruce." My voice wavered, cracked. "I still can't believe it."

Gifford diplomatically looked away and busied himself with the video again, allowing me to compose myself.

"Could you rewind back to French soldiers?"

"Sure, the sequence runs about two minutes."

"Will Nabila translate that sound bite for Yoshi?"

"Yeah, remind me to tell her about that new Sony mic."

And so it went. We didn't talk about Thomas again.

But it was impossible not to feel frightened and bereft by Thomas's disappearance. I worried and chain-smoked, drank too much coffee and too much wine, without a single thought for the child growing inside me.

Mac unexpectedly came home early several nights in a row and I inferred he was no longer sleeping with Nadia. He was preoccupied with other matters, edgy and out of sorts, and, for obvious reasons, avoided physical contact with me, which was the way I wanted it, as well.

We were trudging toward the end game.

That was how things stood when I went to the Commodore several nights later. After intermittent bursts of shelling between east and west all day, I was happy to stay at the Commodore for a few hours yet, in the psychological shelter of other people.

Fretwell was talking to a new reporter from the French news agency.

"Alain here is asking about Thomas. His brother called, did I tell you? He wants to come here to find out for himself what is happening."

"His brother...the one in Brazil?" I tried to remember what Thomas told me of him, but nothing came to mind.

"Yes, I've promised to help, but realistically, I'm not sure what I can do. The Polish delegation here doesn't want to know, made it clear he's a citizen by one of his several passports only and that doesn't count for much. The Brazilians don't have anybody here right now and their nearest embassy is Cairo—not much practical help."

Fretwell sighed. "I suppose we can repeat what I've done already—that is, take him around to see militia leaders, the Amal guys, the PSP, try to get a meeting with one of Sheikh Fadlallah's top lieutenants."

"At least you're trying to do something." I kept my voice steady, under control. "You're a good friend to him, Ian."

"Unfortunately, I don't expect it'll make much difference," Fretwell said, with a defeated shrug of his shoulders. "Thomas knows most of those guys himself and I'm sure the collective antennae are already well extended. Either they want to help and can't, or they don't want to help and won't. Who knows."

"I wish I could do something useful, Ian. I can't bear to think what might be happening."

We considered the alternatives in silence. Chained to a radiator? Blindfolded, beaten, starved? I wiped my eyes. I tried to conceal my anguish over Thomas, but it was especially difficult around Fretwell. We'd both loved him, we'd both lost a friend.

"I know what you mean; it's better not to start thinking that way," Fretwell said sadly. "But let's be positive, Lara: maybe he'll be released. You never know. It's been known to happen in Beirut. For the right price."

He momentarily brightened, as if he believed it might actually happen.

"Do you know who they are, these kidnappers?" The French reporter spoke up for the first time. I'd almost forgotten he was there. "Was there any demand for ransom?"

"No, nothing." Fretwell looked unhappy again. "It doesn't bode well. There should've been a demand by now, or, at the very least, a claim of responsibility."

"Wasn't there a claim early on?" I thought back to the night Mac told me Thomas was missing. "I'm certain Mac said a radical Shiite group—Hezbollah, I think—claimed it, that first night."

"Not that I'm aware of." Fretwell looked questioningly at me. "Of course, that's the assumption, isn't it? What did Barrett say? Because I'm pursuing this very actively, and I don't think there's been any claim at all."

As if on cue, Mac appeared. Seeing Fretwell, his expression turned sour, and he motioned me over to a table by the wall.

I tried to signal him to come to us instead, but he pretended not to notice, and, eventually, there was no choice but to blow my nose and join him.

"Jeez, Lara, can't you find anything better to do than exchange gossip with that old lady?" he scowled.

"Quit picking on Ian. Besides, you could've met the new French guy."

"Met him before. Boring. Frenchy and the old lady, great combination. God spare me. This day's hellish enough as it is."

"Actually, it was kind of interesting. Ian was telling us what he's doing to try to find Thomas."

The defiant note did not escape Mac. He looked sharply at me.

"And what might that be?"

As I started to recount the conversation, Fretwell left the bar and approached our table.

"Hello, Barrett."

"Fretwell," Mac replied coldly.

"I'm curious about something. Lara mentioned you told her Hezbollah claimed responsibility for Thomas's kidnapping."

"And your point . . . ?"

Fretwell frowned. "I've followed just about every aspect of this case closely, and one of the strange things is that there *isn't* a claim. Not that I know of. This is the first I've heard of one and I wonder what you can tell me about it?"

"Well, let me think," Mac said, a little nicer. "You know, I don't recall actually saying that, although we all know they probably did it. In fact, *that's* what I must've said, that those guys *probably* did it, not that they'd *claimed* to. Lara's got it a bit mixed up, haven't you, Lu?" He turned to me.

I was doubtful. "I can't be one hundred percent certain, of course, Mac, but I thought you said Hezbollah claimed it, in a telephone call."

Mac seemed unconcerned by the contradiction. "You know, stress does funny things to people."

He addressed Fretwell now.

"Like I said, Lara's mistaken. No big deal." He added, confidingly, "You know how she worries, and she's been quite upset since Thomas was kidnapped. Naturally. We all are."

"As you say, Barrett," Fretwell replied, not bothering to conceal his lack of conviction, and moved promptly away.

As soon as he was out of earshot, Mac turned on me.

"Supercilious bastard. And you, you idiot, how dare you gossip behind my back, repeating private conversations?" he hissed. "As usual, you don't know the slightest thing about any of this, but there you go, blundering in, meddling, causing all kinds of trouble."

"I only said I thought you mentioned it. What difference does it make, anyway?"

"You made me look like a damn fool." Mac refused to be placated. "God, you're thick sometimes."

"Gee, thanks."

"Let's get this straight. I didn't say anything about a claim. Not then, not ever. You just got it confused, because I said the Hezbollah guys probably did it."

Mac went on and on like this, until his vehemence wore me down. I felt tired and defeated.

"Whatever you say."

I wanted to put my head down on table. But I didn't, because suddenly Abdel Farid appeared at our table, looking frightened, sweat pouring down his face.

"Yes?" Mac looked displeased at the interruption.

"Mister Barrett, please, you must come outside, right now. Please!" Abdel Farid was but one decibel away from a shout.

Mac stood up and pulled me along with him.

Several others, attracted by the commotion, followed us out to the lobby and then out the front door with Abdel Farid, who looked very pale, as if he might faint.

"Mister Barrett, Nadia . . . It's Nadia. She's dead, Mister Barrett." He covered his face with his hands as he wept.

"Oh my God, no . . . are you sure? Are you sure?" Mac demanded, violent with disbelief. "What happened? Tell me everything you know."

"I am so sorry," Abdel Farid faltered, mopping his tears with a handkerchief, before struggling to continue. "They are saying she was shot...gunmen wearing masks...outside her apartment building...a little while ago."

"How did you know?" Mac grabbed Abdel Farid by the lapels of his jacket.

"One of the other drivers..." Abdel Farid barely managed to get the words out.

"Take me to him," Mac shouted. He abruptly released Abdel Farid, whose legs wobbled and almost gave out on him before he propped himself up against the wall and regained control.

❈

The driver was Abbas, who worked for one of the American networks. He'd been waiting outside for his crew when he heard the story from another driver, who pulled up outside the hotel but didn't stay. Abbas knew Nadia and was so staggered by the news he didn't think to question the other driver. All he could think of was finding Abdel Farid to tell him. Abbas didn't know the other driver's name, but thought he looked familiar. Perhaps he'd driven for the Spanish newspaper correspondent before? Maybe he was one of the drivers who worked the airport run. Abbas couldn't be sure, and, in fact, it was never established who it was and how he'd known. Eventually, it no longer seemed important to find out.

❈

It was true. Nadia was dead. Witnesses quoted in Lebanese press reports said a masked gunman came up behind her as she left her apartment building and shot her with a pistol, a single shot to the back of her head. He escaped on foot and disappeared around the block, where a few moments later these witnesses heard the sound of a motorcycle engine roaring off. I don't know who the witnesses were and, to the best of my knowledge, neither did anyone else. They were quoted anonymously and remained that way.

It wasn't clear why she was singled out. Some people thought it was the fundamentalists, as a warning to the Americans, because she worked for an American magazine. Some speculated it might be street crime, an ordinary robbery—her purse was taken, after all—and such things weren't unheard of, even with the country gripped in the jaws of a larger violence. There was another theory, of a love affair gone wrong, for everyone knew there was no shortage of admirers and there were even a few whispers about an important secret lover. This was the scenario I secretly favored, knowing as I did Mac wasn't her only sexual conquest.

Mac, however, wouldn't hear any of it. He was convinced her killing was linked to the Sheikh Fadlallah interview and he repeated that many times over in the following days.

A few days later, I crossed the Green Line again, this time with Mac, to attend Nadia's funeral in East Beirut. I agonized about going. It seemed the ultimate hypocrisy. Nadia slept with my husband and flaunted it and I'd hated her in return. No mistake about that. But at no time had I gone so far, even in imagination, as to wish her dead.

I also believed, as the bureau chief's wife, that it would look peculiar not to attend the funeral of one of the magazine's most devoted and faithful employees. That was Mac's view, as well, and in the end, that was the deciding factor.

The funeral was in East Beirut, where Nadia's family lived. There were many journalists among the mourners, and lots of smartly dressed men and women, including the man Thomas met that day in Beit Meri, Gerard, the man he'd called for information about Mac and Nadia. He wore dark glasses and walked with a slim woman in a Chanel suit, with long, dyed yellow hair, incongruous with her dark coloring and sharp Lebanese features. I also spotted Camille, the woman from the café, with an older couple I presumed to be her parents, standing to one side with Nadia's family.

Nadia's mother and younger sister were readily identifiable as older and younger, less glamorous, watered-down versions of Nadia herself. During the long Catholic service, in the cemetery of a large, grand Maronite church, they grew more and more distressed, crying, clutching each other for support, and at one point it seemed Nadia's mother threatened to throw herself upon her daughter's coffin, already laid in its grave, but was robustly dissuaded from doing so by other family members.

After the service, the mother and sister fell upon Mac, seriously distraught. I stood back and observed, respectfully, and when, after a few minutes, their grief subsided, and they loosened their hold on Mac, I tried to offer my own condolences. Neither the mother nor sister looked in my direction, refusing to acknowledge me, at all. I smiled ruefully to myself. It was exactly as Nadia would have wanted it.

Then, to my surprise, Nadia's mother did turn my way and for the briefest moment, I thought she'd decided to observe the social tenets of the situation after all, and I gave a sad, half-smile to show the overture was welcome, and a nod of commiseration to show the loss was shared.

She spat at me.

I didn't manage to sidestep in time. Mac, for one, didn't seem to notice or if he did, didn't comment upon it. There was nothing handy to wipe it off with, so I walked through the knots of people in the cemetery and made my way back to the waiting car, with a gob of white saliva on the toe of my black patent leather shoe.

By unspoken agreement, I didn't go with Mac to the funeral reception afterward at the home of Nadia's aunt. Instead, we agreed to meet at the Commodore later.

The return journey across the Green Line was a blur. The spittle on my shoe dried, leaving only a ghostly smear, shaped a bit like Italy. I threw the shoes away when I got home.

❊

Mac was drunk by the time he got back; I suppose that was to be expected. The atmosphere in the bar was subdued and the recent divisions created by the sniper shooting incident were put aside, as the press corps ruminated over the death of one of its own. They recounted adventures involving Nadia, in hushed tones, and several times glasses were raised in solemn tribute, which Mac, unfortunately, took as license to air his theory about the Fadlallah connection.

"I killed her," he kept repeating softly, ruefully. "I killed that beautiful little girl."

At first, no one said anything. Finally, Martin, who, like the others, appeared to have put his differences with Mac on hold, told him to shut up.

"You're talking stupid, Mac," Martin said, but he said it nicely, as he patted Mac on the back. "We're all friends here, Mac, you know that, man. You're among friends. But Jesus, you're talking real stupid, so cut it out."

Mac morosely waved him away. "I killed her," he moaned.

"There are a million ways to die in Beirut every single day,

Barrett." Fretwell, too, tried to help. "All you need is the slightest bit of bad luck to run into just one of them."

Murmurs of agreement all around. But Mac was beyond consoling.

He deteriorated steadily after that, but wouldn't listen when I tried to convince him it was time to go home. Abdel Farid was waiting outside, I knew, still dressed in the suit he'd worn to Nadia's funeral. He'd broken his own rule about not going to East Beirut, which touched me. But Mac was so drunk, it seemed unlikely he'd be able to manage the stairs at our building without assistance and I really didn't want to ask Abdel Farid to participate in such an undignified exercise.

I left Mac in the sympathetic care of friends, and went out front to apologize to Abdel Farid. At reception on the way back, I booked a room upstairs, and went to get Mac from the bar. He leaned heavily against me on the way to the elevator and I had trouble supporting his drunken weight once inside it.

Trundling him into the room, he crashed sideways onto the bed. His clothes defeated me, but I got his shoes and socks off. Rearranging his outstretched limbs to make room, I climbed into the bed beside him.

Mac was already asleep; I was not long behind him. He called out Nadia's name several times in his drunken sleep, not for the last time.

It registered somewhere in my sleep-buried consciousness, but these things, it seemed, no longer had the ability to wound.

❈

The Beirut grapevine, a fermented hash of fact and fiction, went strangely silent this time, unlike when Thomas disappeared. In life, Nadia had many friends; few claimed her in death. Especially without knowing the provenance of her exit.

She was there one day and gone the next. Life was like that in Beirut. It moved too quickly to linger over the past. You simply had to get over it. There were killings and kidnappings and disappearances, bombings, shootings, shelling, practically every day in Lebanon, all over the country, not just in Beirut, but north and south. No place was safe. Terrible things happened all the time. No one was untouched and there were too many smoking guns to accurately ascribe culpability—just look at the last few months, at the Marines, at the embassy, at how Thomas disappeared, at Mrs. Fonterelli's son-in-law, at the family pulled from their car at the checkpoint. No individual, I'm sure, was ever named, blamed, or punished for killing the shopkeeper in Basta, nor the man shot by a sniper while driving his wife and mother-in-law. No one, I'm sure, ever spent a day in jail for maiming Suha's neighbor and killing her children.

Nadia's death, it seemed, fit into this category of unsolved mysteries, in this moveable feast of a war, where undefined front lines shifted every day, the dangers no less for the enemy unseen.

As Fretwell said, there were a million ways to die in Beirut.

You just had to get over it. There was no other option.

TWENTY-FOUR

FIVE DAYS AFTER NADIA'S FUNERAL, I went to see Amina, whom I hadn't seen since Thomas disappeared. She would not only share my sense of loss, but, tacitly, accept my right to it. Or so I presumed. She was cordial, nothing more. She offered tea, but there was no energy in the offer, nor, when I refused, did she press me to change my mind, as she normally did—indeed, as custom dictated. We were both aware what the lapse in etiquette signified.

But she'd been kind to me in the past, and, on impulse, I reached out and took her hands in mine.

"I can't stay long," I said, by way of explanation. "I only wanted to see how you are." I looked down at our interlocked fingers, then up again, directly into her eyes, clear and bright and without welcome.

"And to say, how devastated I am about Thomas. Have you any news at all?"

She withdrew her hands, and fussed with her hair for a moment, to compensate.

"Nothing, my dear. This is most dreadful. As with you, I am awaiting any news."

"I still don't understand. Why take him?"

"Why does anyone take anyone?" Amina answered, as she so often did, with another question.

"But he's not American or French. He's not a symbol of anything. Why was he a target?"

"Who ever knows, in Lebanon?" Amina looked sorrowful. "Did he cross the wrong people? It's easy to do. Our Thomas is a tightrope walker; he doesn't use a net."

"Who did Thomas cross, do you know? Was he really a spy? Please, I need to know."

She got up and padded silently across the large Persian carpet on her living room floor. She quietly closed the door to the sitting room and came back to the sofa where I sat.

"I think it's safe to talk. You must be careful using words like 'spy,' Lara. You never know who might be eavesdropping," she chided me.

To underline the point, she made a show of listening intently. We could hear her elderly housekeeper, humming off-key, as she shuffled about in the kitchen.

"So," Amina continued, "You want to know about Thomas. Again. You are always investigating him, aren't you. Homosexual? . . . Spy? Well, my dear, I'm afraid I cannot be much help." She rubbed at an imaginary spot on her skirt. "Is he a spy? I suppose it depends on your perspective. *I* don't think so. I think he is a confused soul."

"In what way, confused? Do you mean in terms of his political allegiances? Or sexually? Was he homosexual, Amina?"

Amina laughed, a brittle, social laugh, and suddenly the door clamped shut, if, indeed, it was ever, truly, open. No information would be forthcoming, though we would continue to play out our parts, if for no other reason than that I was already here, and that was how things were done.

"I have told you before, I never speculate on the romantic lives of my friends. I leave that to others. That is not what I mean."

"Then how?"

She stood up and went over to the window. Her eyes did not meet mine.

"He used to visit me quite a bit, particularly after my husband died. He was thoughtful in that way—in so many ways, really. But he did not come much recently and I believe he was struggling to deal with issues known best to himself."

She turned her gaze to me now.

"From what he said, I think he is confused about something, and wants to do what is right, as opposed to doing what may be practical or expedient."

I squirmed in frustration.

"For heaven's sakes, Amina, I don't have the slightest idea what you're talking about. What was he worried about being right or wrong?"

"You amaze me, Lara. All this time here, and still you are so clumsy, still you trample like an elephant into such delicate areas. It is most thoughtless."

"Please," I said through clenched teeth. "What worried him, what was he struggling with?"

"In all this time, you have learned nothing, not discretion, not the art of distillation." Amina sounded exasperated, wrinkling her nose.

I stood up, I had to do something. I wanted to shake her until the answers tumbled out.

"I'm so sick of all this double-talk, the hidden meanings. For once, please *say* what you mean. Straight out. Was he a spy? I know what you said before, but *whose* perspective?"

I sat down again abruptly, causing the sofa to scrape noisily along the floor. This line of questioning was pointless, but I persisted, for I believed she knew the answers and I couldn't understand why she continued to withhold them at this stage.

"What does it matter if I think he is spying or not? All that matters is if the wrong people think he is." She walked back to the sofa and balanced delicately on the edge, holding herself as far from me as possible. "I've told you what I believe already."

She paused. "And Lara? Why do you speak of Thomas in the past tense? Do you know more than you tell me?"

Her tone was even, but she mocked me, as if—far from being the gentle, passive friend I once believed—she secretly despised me, and I couldn't fathom why.

One last, desperate appeal.

"Amina. I'm begging you for help. I can't move forward until I understand what's already happened. Do you think Thomas was kidnapped because he was spying?"

"What do *you* think?" Amina thrust her face up to mine. "Do you think he got tangled up in something personal, too much for him to handle? Was it politics? Or was it personal, Lara?"

She sat back hard against the cushions, and eyed me with distaste, and I knew for certain I was neither friend nor pupil now and we would never again be more than strangers.

"I told you before, this was a dangerous game. You wouldn't listen. Even I, a spectator, could see someone would get hurt, though I miscalculated whom. Why you insisted on playing, I do not understand. At first I felt sorry for you, and this is the truth. I said to myself, she is doing this because her husband is a bully, he is sleeping with prostitutes. She is to be pitied.

"I tried to warn you. Then, I realized, no, she enjoys this game, she enjoys the danger and now she is addicted like someone on drugs, she is a danger addict, a danger junkie—the Lord knows we see enough of them in Beirut."

Amina smiled slyly. "You pretended to be a nice, naïve girl, but you were having a secret affair of your own, weren't you? Who did you fool, Lara? No one but yourself."

"You thought it would be me. The one who got hurt," I said accusingly and my heart tightened another notch.

"I thought you would leave Beirut a long time before now."

"I am still here, Amina. And before I go, I want to know what happened to Thomas."

"Then let us hope you enjoy the Lebanon, for you may be here a long time."

"Who is Gerard?" The question popped out of thin air, surprising even me. I didn't know where the line of questioning was going, but it suddenly seemed important to find out.

"Why don't you ask him yourself?"

"I would, if I could. I don't even know his last name. I saw him once, but I wouldn't have any idea how to reach him. I only know he was someone Thomas knew."

"Thomas knows many people," she replied, once again correcting my use of the past tense.

But she went over to the antique wooden sideboard and took out a worn leather-bound book. She searched for something and, when she'd located it, took a pad of paper and a silver pen out of a drawer, scribbled something on the pad, and ripped the page from it. She dangled it in front of me.

"I don't know why I should do this."

"You owe it to Thomas, Amina."

"I owe no one. My conscience is clear. Perhaps *you* owe it to him. Please go." She handed me the piece of paper. "And, Lara, please respect the fact our friendship has reached its conclusion."

She didn't see me out; but then, I didn't expect her to.

⁂

I rang the number written in her spidery hand as soon as I got home.

"Oui?" A man's voice asked suspiciously.

"Is that Gerard, please?"

"Who is asking?"

"I need to speak to Gerard. Are you Gerard?"

"Who are you?"

"I need to talk to Gerard. It's about Thomas Warkowski."

Silence.

"Hello? Are you there?"

Silence.

"Please, don't hang up. I need to ask you about Thomas."

The sound of a receiver being replaced, then a dial tone.

⁂

A little later, there was a knock at our front door. It unnerved me. Mac had his key with him, Suha had gone home hours before, and I wasn't expecting anyone at two o'clock in the afternoon.

"Yes?" I called through the door, but kept it closed.

"I have a message for you." A woman's voice.

I put the chain on and opened the door a crack to see a dark-haired woman who looked to be Lebanese, of indiscernible age or confession.

"Yes?"

"I may come in?"

"What do you want?"

"It is better we speak inside."

"I suppose it's okay." I closed the door to undo the chain and then opened it just wide enough to admit her, and not some hidden accomplice, then closed it behind her. It was clearly not a social call.

"What's the message, who's it from?"

"My message is this," she said, staring intently at me. "Gerard will see you. You can come with me now. I have a car waiting. It will not take long, perhaps an hour, perhaps two. But we have to go now. He is waiting."

"You'll take me to Gerard?"

"Yes. But we must hurry. He is a very busy man."

"I can't just go like this, without any warning. Who are you, anyway? Where would we be going? Where is Gerard, where does he live?"

She brushed away the questions impatiently.

"Do you want to see Gerard or not? This is the only way. You can come now and speak to him. If you say no, you will not get another chance. You decide."

Curious, afraid, and turning a deaf ear to my own better judgment, I got my handbag and followed her downstairs. There was an air of unreality to it all. I wondered if this was the way Thomas had disappeared, if someone had come to his door and summoned him this way, and as I pictured it, I could taste fear, rising at the back of my throat. I thought about bolting—to run back upstairs and lock myself in. But whom would I call for help? Mac? The police?

This was Beirut. I had to follow through with what I had started.

We got into the backseat of a dark sedan, inconspicuous enough to guarantee anonymity. The windows were tinted dark gray, not unusual in Beirut.

"Where are we going?" I asked, as she pulled an oddly designed pair of black sunglasses—like goggles, really—out of her pocket.

"Forgive me, you will wear these to cover your eyes. It is for your own protection." She put them on the bridge of my nose and tried to fasten them behind my ears.

"No! Please don't!" I shrank back as far as I could on my side of the seat.

"Would you prefer a blindfold? Most people prefer these to a blindfold."

"No!"

"If you do not agree, then I am afraid the journey is over before it starts. You will not see Gerard, after all."

"But I can't see anything."

"I am losing patience. Put on the glasses or get out of the car."

The threat to eject me reassured me I was not captive.

"Okay," I said reluctantly. "But I don't like this at all."

She handed me the goggles and I put them on. They cupped my eyes in an opaque plastic and an elastic band fastened tightly across the back of my head. I was sheathed in darkness.

"Comfortable?"

"No."

We did not speak again for a while. At first, I tried to gauge how far we went before making turns and tried to remember the sequence of left and right turns, but it quickly became too much for me. I had no idea where we were, no idea what direction we were heading, no idea whether we were still in West Beirut or had crossed into the East. Arabic songs issued from the radio, drowning out any ambient street noise.

"Where're we going, do you mind telling me?"

"We will be there soon."

More time passed. When the car suddenly speeded up and zig-zagged wildly, I realized we were probably crossing the Green Line, but had no idea which crossing it might be.

Eventually, she spoke again.

"We are almost here. Keep the glasses on until we are inside. I will guide you."

The car slowed, then stopped. She opened the door on her side and got out, then reached back in to give me a hand.

"Here. Careful getting out."

"It would be a lot easier without these things on."

No response. She led me across a bit of pavement and helped me down a few stairs. At the bottom, the door opened and she exchanged a few words in Arabic with a man I could not see.

"Go in," she ushered me through one room and along a hallway, then into another room, where she closed the door. She helped me into an armchair.

"Take them off now," she said. "But keep them close to hand; you will need them for the return journey."

She went out and closed the door behind her again.

I looked around expectantly. The room was almost empty, except for the chair I sat in, the small table next to it, and a desk, quite ordinary looking, with a swivel chair behind it. The walls were bare, yielding no clue as to where I might be.

The door opened and the man I had seen with Thomas that day in Beit Meri filled its frame.

I stood as he entered.

"Good afternoon, Madam McCauley. Please, sit." He sat in the swivel chair and put a briefcase down behind the desk.

"You would like tea? Or perhaps you prefer coffee?" He snapped his fingers. A man appeared in the doorway, bowed, and left.

"Tea. Please."

"Comfortable journey? Mona took good care of you?"

"Thank you." It seemed the only possible reply.

Now I was here, I had no idea where to start.

"Do you mind if I smoke?" I opened my handbag but Gerard removed a packet from his jacket pocket and offered me one.

"Thank you."

He lit it with a heavy, inscribed gold lighter.

"Thank you again."

He gave a slight nod of acknowledgment, then took a cigarette himself and tapped it on the desk before placing it in his mouth.

"You asked to see me."

"Yes." I pulled deeply on the cigarette.

"You want to know what happened to Thomas?"

His eyes bored into mine. I shifted uncomfortably in my seat and exhaled.

"Yes."

"You do not know?" Politely quizzical.

"No."

He flexed his fingertips against each other for a few seconds, as if considering my reply.

"You truly do not know?" This time, harshly and in a louder voice.

"No." I croaked. His manner was becoming menacing.

Gerard stood up and began to pace, like a college lecturer lost in thought, cigarette dangling from his lips.

"Surely you have some suspicions?" he said at last, removing the cigarette.

"I have only suspicions." My voice quavered. "I have come to you for answers."

He paced a moment longer, then came to a standstill in front of me.

"You do not know that your husband is responsible for Thomas's death?"

I could only shake my head. Urine seeped out between my squeezed thighs.

"This is what I know, Madam, that the trail leads back to your husband."

"I don't believe it," I whispered.

Of course I did, from the very start—but in my heart, where it was safe to suspect him. This was different.

"The word is that your husband went to a Hezbollah contact, that he accused Thomas of spying, for our side—for me, in particular. It was a master stroke, was it not? Absolutely brilliant. He didn't even have to pay for it, it was like a red flag to a bull."

"Why?" I whispered again. But I knew.

"Why, indeed?" Gerard suddenly thundered. "What harm had Thomas Warkowski done Barrett McCauley?"

He paused, never taking his eyes off me, then spoke again, normally.

"It is rather curious, but before Mr. McCauley went to see the

Hezbollah, he told a certain friend exactly the opposite story. He accused Thomas of working for Hezbollah. He said Thomas was involved in the Marine bombing, that he used his visits to the compound with other journalists to collect information. And that his information enabled his radical paymasters to concoct this deadly plan."

He paused again, knitting his fingers together and admiring the chunky rings on them.

"But of course, Madam McCauley—may I call you Lara? I feel we are sharing such a personal conversation together here—of course, Lara, we both know why your husband did it, don't we?"

I shook my head again. I had to address this allegation and it took all my strength to force calm back into my broken voice.

"My husband is a lot of things, Mister . . . Gerard. Some of them aren't very pleasant, I admit. But he's a journalist, not a murderer. He isn't capable of that."

Gerard laughed. Of course he did. I didn't believe myself.

"Lara," he said kindly, like an uncle, a kindly *killer* uncle. "Everyone is capable of killing; most people never have enough provocation to discover this truth about themselves. But, if it distresses you, think of it this way. Your husband didn't actually *do* it. He is too smart. He merely planted the information in the ear of someone who would make it happen."

"Was Thomas a spy? Did he do things for you?"

"Not for me, no. He sincerely was a friend, believe it or not."

Gerard went back to his chair. He lowered himself into it, re-arranging his legs in the most comfortable way, as if this were to be a long tale.

"You see, Lara, not many people knew this, but Thomas and I, we go way back. We met long ago, as students, roommates, at boarding school in the United States. Washington, your capital. Nice city. My father, God rest his soul, was a diplomat, a cultural attaché. Thomas and I got on quite well as boys. Same age, both quite sensitive really, we enjoyed books and the cinema. We were outsiders, isolated by our foreignness. We were dark and we spoke a foreign tongue. Arabic, Portuguese, Polish—it didn't matter. What other people saw was that we were different."

He stubbed out his cigarette.

"These things bind you together when you are children. He was fascinated by my stories of Lebanon. They influenced his choice of studies later on, and, I am sure, his later decision to come here. By then, of course, we had little in common. Our adult lives took different routes, we had different destinies. We agreed on very little, our politics were quite divergent. We argued a lot. He was very misguided, you know," Gerard smiled at the idea.

"But he was my friend."

For a surprising moment, Gerard looked as if he might cry, but the moment slipped by and he didn't and I was glad, for I knew I would've, too, and I needed to be strong to get through this.

"I'm sorry, but I have to ask you this. Was he homosexual?" I asked, softly, carefully.

"Are you asking was he my lover, too?" Gerard smiled ruefully.

"Well, no, that's not what I meant, but I suppose since you have put that thought on the table, yes, it is what I am now asking, yes. Were you lovers?"

"No way," Gerard said emphatically. "I am not that way inclined. But we were friends more than half my life. I knew his proclivities, though I didn't approve. But I accepted him the way he was. That's how it is with friends. I had known him so long, you see, before I even shaved, before I went to university, before I met my wife."

Then, with a wink, added, "Or my girlfriend."

But he quickly became serious again as I pressed ahead.

"Then what did he want from me? Why make love to me?"

Gerard considered the question before answering. "Revenge, perhaps? The desire for revenge can be quite consuming."

He stood up and walked around to perch on the front edge of the desk.

"You do realize Thomas and Roger Schuster were together, personally and professionally? An open secret, as they say. Had to be discreet, you know, because of the wife of Roger. Not long after Thomas started working for him, Roger sent his wife to Cyprus with their sons, said it wasn't safe here. Then he moved Thomas in."

He gave me a moment to digest that. Nadia had told the truth.

"Roger supported him—paid his bills and gave him a regular paycheck. In return, Thomas was an invaluable source of information, a reliable colleague, a devoted companion. It was—how do you say it?—a win-win situation?"

Gerard rose to his feet and paced again.

"Then, Roger had the ill grace to perish in such a silly, pointless way, on holiday, and you McCauleys came in to replace him, and suddenly, Thomas was out. Out of a boyfriend. Out of favor, out of a job. Your husband didn't like him, refused to give him work, which meant Thomas had no income. He had to ask other journalists to give him work—odd assignments here and there, not much money in that.

"Ask yourself, Lara, why did your husband dislike Thomas so much? Was it because he despised what Thomas was?"

He offered me another cigarette; I declined in favor of my own.

"Now, let us return to your question: why you?"

He leant over to light my cigarette.

"Consider it, Lara. Becoming *intimate* friends with Barrett McCauley's wife had to be sweet revenge, didn't it? Thomas never said so, of course—far too diplomatic for that—but it's not difficult to see. It was quite impressive, I couldn't imagine how he pulled it off, and so very expertly."

There it was. The answer. I was the conduit through which to assault Mac. It may not have paid the bills, but it helped settle the score. It explained everything, even the income Mac cynically attributed to spymasters.

"I see." Bitterness welled up inside me.

Gerard continued his progress around the room, circling my armchair several times.

"It is possible there was another reason," he said, halting in front of me. "I will be truthful. We shall not see each other again, so I have nothing to lose by telling you this. Thomas genuinely liked you. I know this for fact."

He smiled fondly, as if he could see a schoolboy Thomas in front of him. "He always liked the underdog, you know, his fascination with the Moslems, insisting on staying in West Beirut, always going on about the disenfranchised Shiites and how they'd been cut out of the Lebanese pie. Bloody missing Imams and the like. We had so many arguments about *that*, as you might imagine.

"But I digress. What I am saying is, Thomas liked you, Lara. You were similar, in so many ways. You were also an outsider—less by virtue of nationality than personality. Like Thomas, you didn't fit in. You were unhappy; I'm sure he also identified with that.

"In different ways—and this is important—you were both victims of Barrett McCauley. Maybe Thomas even loved you in his way, though I do not want to give you false hope, even as a memory, for I believe he could have found true happiness only with a man. Such was his nature.

"He was a spiritual man, deeply romantic. Did you not find this so? But you frightened him there at the end. He thought you were trying to rope him in with all that talk of marriage and babies."

He pointed an accusing finger at me and his voice grew louder.

"But you found another way to hang him."

"Me?" I spluttered.

"Here is the sequence in which I believe things happened: you went to Thomas with concerns about your husband and he rang me for information. Next, you went home and told your husband not only what you'd learned, but that I was the source of that information."

He lit another cigarette and offered me one. "Yes. I know that."

I took it this time, as he sat down again behind the desk.

"Your husband got mad, he hit you, yes? He accused you of sleeping with Thomas, but it was only a lucky guess at that stage—nothing more—and my hunch is he only threw it out to distract attention from his own tryst. He discovered that you went to Thomas's that day purely by chance—Abdel Farid happened to see you entering the building. I know, I know, it's impossible to hide anything in this city.

"So he hits you, and storms off to his mistress, full of rage. Unwisely, she chose that opportunity to add fuel to the flames of this anger, perhaps in the misguided belief that she had a chance of succeeding you as the next Madam McCauley. She confirmed beyond a doubt to him the sexual nature of your liaison with this man, this homosexual, he despised so much, and told him Thomas had shared your bed. She taunted him, really, which is a mistake with any man, but certainly with Barrett McCauley, and he ended up going a bit wild on her, too, I am afraid. Your husband has a vicious streak, does he not? She had to stay out of public view for days, until the swelling went down.

"This fury at Thomas, I believe, is the reason your husband next went to Hezbollah and planted the idea that Thomas was feeding information about Hezbollah and possible targets in West Beirut to the Christians."

Frighteningly, what he said made sense.

"I have to ask you this." I tried to take a puff of the cigarette but my lips trembled too much and I stubbed it out instead. "Gerard. Do you think Mac was responsible for Nadia's death as well?"

"Oh, no," Gerard said, his sharp features lit by a wide smile now. "That was *mine*. The least I could do. She was an evil, treacherous woman. She sealed Thomas's fate by telling your husband. She should have known Barrett would retaliate."

I steadied myself for the next round of questions.

"Thomas is dead, isn't he?"

Gerard looked away. And nodded.

"How did he die? Do you know? Can you tell me? Please?"

"They picked him up off the street in front of his building. His landlady saw the whole thing, but was too terrified to talk about it; she has other problems, you know, with the Syrians."

He looked down at his shoes, then back up at me. "They threw him in the trunk, and then, I'm afraid, they took him to the southern suburbs and they put a gun to his head and shot him."

"The same day, you mean, right away?"

"The same day, yes. He died instantly. I am sorry. This is a fact. We have it on good authority."

"Where is his body?"

"That is a good question, one I would like to have the answer to. Perhaps it has been dumped in the Bekaa Valley somewhere. It may never turn up. We have to accept he is gone."

I was reeling. Faint. I closed my eyes.

"Ah, Lara, you are unwell. Forgive me; I had forgotten you are with child. Would you like water, more tea? What can I get you?"

"Water," I said weakly, but it was not the child causing my problem. I took a few sips, but it didn't much help. How do you restore a ruined heart? My soul was arid, would never see bloom again.

Gerard's words broke into my thoughts.

"You should go back now, Lara. This is an ordeal for us both. Let me leave you with these parting thoughts. I, too, loved Thomas, as my brother. I could kill your husband myself. But we will spare him. We are not in the business of killing American journalists; if nothing else, it is too much trouble with the U.S. authorities. However, as I said before, Nadia was one of ours, and she was punished for what she did.

"We will also take care of those who actually pulled the trigger on our friend Thomas. Therefore, I will give you this friendly advice: stay away from the Imam Ali mosque on Rue Battoura tomorrow, particularly at the hour of 11:00 A.M. I leave you with this thought: they are not the only ones who know how to use explosives."

The implication escaped me at that precise moment, because I had another question.

"If Thomas wasn't spying for you, why were you upset to see me that day in Beit Meri?"

Gerard assessed me, deciding whether to entrust me with this final confidence, and, evidently, decided the story was incomplete without these last few pieces of the puzzle.

"He wasn't really a spy, as I have said. But after your husband refused to give him work, he needed money, and, on several occasions, I asked him to do a small chore for me—not too big, but something he would never have contemplated before. A little research for me, look around some buildings in a part of town we Christians are not safe in. It was ironic, really, quite forward thinking. I trust Thomas himself would have appreciated the irony, though you never knew for sure with him."

Gerard drew himself up to his full height and towered over me for a moment.

"On that note, I bid you adieu, Lara McCauley. There is no reason for us to meet again, I think."

He left the room and a moment later the door reopened, and Mona came back in and handed me the goggles.

"Glasses on, please."

I complied and left the building, leaning heavily on her arm for assistance.

※

I had much to consider as I waited for Mac to return that evening.

He was not late.

"We had a visitor today," I informed him, as soon as he walked through the front door. "A woman who just appeared at the door. I didn't know who she was. But she said she had a message."

Mac looked suddenly alert.

I poured him a scotch and began my tale.

TWENTY-FIVE

AS I MENTIONED BEFORE, the first time the sentry on duty saw the yellow Mercedes stake-bed truck enter the Marine compound was an hour before the explosion, just after daybreak on October 23, 1983. It circled the parking lot once and left.

That small fact still haunts me.

Was it a last minute reconnaissance, by a meticulous bomber, familiarizing himself with his mission? Or, faced with the impending reality of the act he was about to commit, his own mortality, did he suddenly lose his nerve?

I am aware of no official thinking on this. But even now—when it makes no difference, after so many other things have happened—even now, I wonder. Was it a pivotal moment, a wobble in the flowchart, when things might have gone differently? Had he not returned, it is probable that 6:22 A.M. on October 23, 1983, would have passed unnoticed by the scribes of history.

But such speculation is pointless. For whatever the possibilities, the moment arrived as the present and merged seamlessly with the future. And played out as intended, triggering a chain of events, with enormous consequences for the larger course of human history.

Pouring the scotch that evening with a shaky hand, I, too, arrived at one of those moments—less a crossroads for me, however, than a cul-de-sac. I did not, metaphorically, circle the parking lot; I drove straight ahead.

Thomas might have seen it as the ultimate expression of free choice on my part, but once again, I saw it as less than none.

After all, I owed it to him.

❋

I told Mac the woman at the door had a message. For him.

Go to the Imam Ali mosque on Rue Battoura tomorrow, I told him, at 11:00 A.M. sharp. Arrive neither late nor early. It is crucial to be precisely on time.

Mac listened carefully, with growing excitement, as I reeled off the list of instructions. Get out of the car at Zahedi Street and walk the last two blocks to Rue Battoura. Send Abdel Farid away, tell him to wait at the Commodore. This is very important, your driver must not stay in the area. You must be alone. Go inside the mosque and wait. A man named Farheed will find you and take you to a secret location. There, you will meet the man who ordered and paid for the embassy bombings. Fadlallah's boss. He has consented to a press interview to explain his group's motivation, its jihad against America, Israel, and Western nations. He will reveal the identities of the suicide bombers and arrange for two other candidates for martyrdom to answer questions, as well. He specially singled out correspondent Barrett McCauley for this interview, not only because the magazine provides an international forum from which to spread his message, but also because of the sensitive and respectful way correspondent Barrett McCauley handled the interview with Sheikh Fadlallah.

It was pathetic, really.

Mac was well and truly beside himself, inflated with self-importance and high anticipation. He came alive in a way I had not seen for some time. He was persuaded to wait until after dinner. By then, of course, the amount of celebratory scotch consumed made it moot.

The scotch ensured he settled off into a fine and deep sleep without complaint, and I was glad, in a way, to know the night was a happy one for him.

❈

Now you know what happened to Mac.

But I haven't told you everything, only the facts as I remember them. And what is there other than facts, you ask? And I reply, who is to say? Do I sound like Amina? Perhaps my time in Lebanon was not entirely wasted.

The facts, in this case, do not do justice to the real story. There is a discrepancy in my narrative.

At the beginning, I described being in a hotel room in Syria, playing the videotape of Thomas dying, over and over again. This, I saw with my own eyes. The camera shot stayed on his body until all movement ceased. At the moment of death, his vital organs released, for a spreading stain was evident on his clothes in the last few seconds of footage.

Yes. Thomas's life ended that way, and, seeing those final moments, I experienced a flash of such intense clarity that I almost cried aloud with the pain as the magnitude of Gerard's deception sank in.

Thomas was hanged. He was not shot, as Gerard said so convincingly that day.

It was not Gerard's only deceit.

He said Thomas died hours after his kidnapping in November

1983. But at the start of the video we watched in June 1985 was a picture of Thomas holding a newspaper dated just four days earlier.

Thomas had lived in captivity for many months, not yet a memory but already dismissed as one, and I find that almost as unbearable as the fact of his death. It saddens me to no end to have accepted his death as a reality long before it was, saddens me that I couldn't intuit his tormented presence still on earth.

Let us be clear on this subject.

How and when Thomas died are part of the catalog of facts. They are not subject to whimsical alteration. If Gerard was wrong about these most elemental things, then they were not innocent errors in accounting. He intentionally misled me.

By telling me Thomas was already dead, was he setting me up to take unilateral action? I believed sending Mac to the mosque was an act of my own free will, but, suddenly, I had to consider that might not be the case.

Whose choice was it, really? Where once I saw myself as an angel of vengeance, I now wonder if I was, instead, an instrument of Gerard's wrath. I now wonder if it was precisely what he wanted.

If so, kudos to Gerard. Why should his people kill an American journalist, when they could prime the journalist's wife to do it for them?

⁂

That sounds a proper ending note, doesn't it? For a time, it *was* the ending to this story as I knew it, and indeed, I paid homage to it as the perfect irony. The ultimate Beirut irony.

But I couldn't leave it there. I examined all the available information, processed and reprocessed it, worried and chewed over it.

There were too many new questions, and, over time, the realization dawned on me, that if these segments were concocted, perhaps all of it was a lie.

Perhaps Mac didn't assign Thomas to his death, perhaps this was another fiction Gerard invented to make sure I unwittingly acquiesced in his grand plan.

If it wasn't true, who set Thomas's death in motion? If not Mac, why did Gerard want Mac dead? Gerard had no reason to lie, unless he was covering up something.

Did Gerard, inadvertently, cause Thomas's death? He admitted he'd enticed Thomas into scouting possible locations, which I subsequently understood meant gathering information about potential targets for retaliatory bombings—standard Beirut fare, Moslem-Christian tit for tat. If Thomas were caught, it could certainly account for what happened to him.

Why, then, did Gerard say Nadia was killed for her role in causing Thomas's death?

It took a long time for me to spot the obvious link: Nadia was Gerard's girlfriend, too. Of course.

Nadia was not "punished" for Thomas, but for Mac. Sweet revenge, to use Gerard's own words. Imagine his humiliation, his outrage, upon learning she was holed up in a hotel room with another man, an American journalist. In East Beirut. His own turf.

Surely, Nadia had known the risks. She was a greedy girl, too self-confident, and I can only theorize the sheer giddiness of playing two such volatile ends against each other clouded her judgment and forced this fatal miscalculation on her part.

So, you see, the story as I accepted it might not have been the real story at all.

Take it a step further. If Mac wasn't responsible for Thomas's death, I must believe I wrongly dispatched him to his own. Did I misjudge as fundamentally as all those years ago, when I set the baby bird on a trajectory to death?

Mac was cruel, yes. He was a bully. He lied to me and by cheating on me he robbed our marriage of its defining essence. He was debauched and even I could not spare him from his own desires and bad judgment. The best of intentions and hardest of efforts can't always fix what's wrong with a person and in that sense, I suppose, he was beyond repair.

But I have to ask: did these failings warrant his death?

Mac was my life's mission, or so I thought, and I brought a dowry of unconditional love and patience and acceptance to our marriage and hoped it would be enough to balance out the demons in it.

I tried to save him, over and over again, at the expense of my sanity and the abandonment of my own moral compass.

I failed.

If Gerard's story was true, and Mac *was* responsible, then I failed Thomas. You may say he was partly to blame, he sought to use me, at least initially, and it backfired, and I won't argue. Conversely, if Gerard's story was false, and Thomas was caught collecting information for him, it also follows that Thomas brought his bad luck upon himself.

Either way, it must be acknowledged that I failed to protect Thomas from the evil radiated by our corrupt marriage.

It was a vintage year for failure in Lebanon, 1983, and, even on that scale, I failed spectacularly.

※

After the Marine bombing, the U.S. finally gave up. On the seventh of February, 1984, Washington announced its decision to withdraw the Marines from the airport sector and redeploy them to ships offshore. A small group of Marines would stay behind to guard the U.S. embassy and other American interests.

A day later, the last Marine to die in the American mission of presence was killed when a weapon accidentally discharged. A self-inflicted wound, the final irony? The same day, the USS *New Jersey* joined in the bombardment of Druze and Syrian positions in the Chouf, the biggest show of naval firepower since the Marines first came to Lebanon in the summer of 1982.

As the warlords unleashed their fury upon the city again, Washington arranged the evacuation of large numbers of American and other foreign civilians from Beirut. I was not among them; I had already gone.

By the end of February 1984, the Marines completed their pullout from the airport area, although the U.S. mission of presence would not officially end for another few months.

By any reckoning, it was over.

※

The U.S. mission of presence is a case study in university textbooks. How not to enter a war. How not to fight a war, how not to lose one, which is likely to happen if a military force has no defined military objective and no strategy for reaching it.

By definition, all parties must agree to a peacekeeping force for it to be effective. By definition, it must be seen to be neutral. This was not the case in Lebanon. Where does peacekeeping end, and self-defense begin? Were the Marines doomed by their own rules of engagement?

The questions are mine. The judgments are not.

Twenty years after the bombings, a U.S. district judge wrote that the Marines in Lebanon "were more restricted in their use of force than an ordinary U.S. citizen walking down a street in Washington, D.C."

The official inquiry into the Marine bombings stated, matter-of-factly, that the U.S. Multinational Force "was not trained, organized, staffed, or supported to deal effectively with the terrorist threat in Lebanon."

History renders its own judgment. Need I add another word?

※

Regarding my own adventure in Lebanon, frankly, there's no one left to ask.

It can't be wrapped up as neatly and tidily as the history of the U.S. mission.

I lost track of Amina for years. We never spoke again, but I heard from a mutual acquaintance that she moved to Dubai. I spent several months there in '86 or '87, editing for German television, during the tanker war phase of the Iran-Iraq War, but I didn't look her up. She gave me Gerard. There was nothing else she could tell me, nothing still within her gift.

Fretwell I saw from time to time, as breaking news dictated. The last time was in a restaurant in Amman in the early '90s. He stopped by the table where I was eating dinner alone and mentioned, in passing, that Amina had Parkinson's. Fretwell didn't look too well himself, though he said nothing regarding his own health. Six months later, I heard he died of cancer.

Only recently, when I ran into Nils Erik Englestoft, quite by chance, on a busy London street, did I learn that Hamid, too, was gone—heart attack, on the sidewalk in front of the Commodore.

Other news hits my radar occasionally: Martin Sawyer moved onward and upward—now presiding over editorial meetings as a senior editor, in a gleaming New York office. After a stint in the Gulf, Boz Whitfield was named head of BBC Arabic Services and moved back to London with Jan. Katya Karlstrom stayed in Beirut. She's still there, as far as I know.

And so forth.

But it was, of course, Gerard who held all the answers, and he long ago presented me with his version of events.

While I mostly avoided news about Lebanon for a long time after leaving, a few years ago I was drinking expresso, outside a small café in Vienna, when Gerard's name leaped off the front page of the *International Herald Tribune*. Dead. Ambushed in an attack by a rival Christian militia. Karmic chickens home to roost.

So, as I say, there's no one left to ask what really happened— and, other than me, perhaps no one left to care.

⚭

Does it matter now who fathered the child I carried so long ago? Neither option offered a foundation upon which to hinge a future, not mine or a child's. It would make a tidy little epilogue, wouldn't it, if the orphaned child of our passion suddenly popped up, as in *Dr. Zhivago*, when Tanya the laundry girl is revealed as the secret, illegitimate daughter of Lara and Yury Zhivago, the star-crossed lovers, many years after their deaths.

Here's what happened. I lost the baby in Cyprus, shortly after leaving Beirut for good. An ectopic pregnancy—the baby grew outside the womb—and it almost killed me. I lost so much blood they thought I'd die.

It was gone from my life as quickly and completely as if it had never been.

Given the complex of events preceding it, I can't say it saddened me unduly. Too much else had happened for this to figure in the scope of my loss. Too much else for which to grieve, and although I no longer do, I did then.

❀

I still use Mac's name. I was his wife. I am his widow now; it is my penance and, accordingly, I am reminded of him every time I write it, say it, or hear it.

But understand me. While I ponder my role in his death, in truth, I don't mourn him. False propriety won't force me into that.

There's only a little more I need to say, though it's a relief to say it, finally. My interpretation of events may be debatable. But I am the guardian of this story. There is no other.

I do mourn Thomas in my own way, both as a person I might have loved and as part of a greater sadness I'll never lose about the Lebanon I knew. He shines, Thomas, in my personal pantheon of fallen innocents—those whose lives touched mine, whose deaths I witnessed. Even some whose paths never crossed my own. It's not melodramatic to say I mourn them, too, for it's part of who I am now.

But such thoughts fill me with melancholy. I don't like to dwell on them and, mostly, I don't.

The girl who went to Lebanon died there, with Thomas and

Mac. Now in my middle years, I move along, with neither person nor place to command allegiance.

Understand, my eyes are focused straight ahead. There are no jagged edges; the periphery does not call to me. Where I live, there is no horizon. I don't lie awake at night, nor does the past disturb my sleep. I rarely dream at all any more.

I have a profession, and though it often tethers me to unpleasant work, I am, in my own way, free.

Understand, I cannot unlearn what I know, though I often wish I could.

I cannot undo the events visited upon me, by fate or by design, and those that I, in turn, unleashed.

❈

One thought that remains with me all these years is what President Reagan said after the embassy bombing, that United States would do what it knew to be right. If you take nothing else away from my story, it's imperative you understand this: we were all only trying to do what we believed to be right, whether on the world stage or in our own small arenas, and, for me, it summed up how easy it was to get it utterly wrong, just when it mattered so desperately.

❈

No cover up, no revising facts or trying to portray them in a better light. No attempt to turn the clock back to 6:22 A.M. on the twenty-third day of October, 1983.

I hope you'll see it's been the same with my story.

For this is what I've learned for myself: that we must leave the past as it is, not recast it as we wished it to be, and here is where I am strong now.

The time in which loyalty seemed to me the rarest and most

valuable of gifts is forever gone, but please understand I don't sorrow for it.

For me, it is a pink and gold memory, gracefully unfolding, high above the ancient rooftops of Cairo, the sound of a thousand voices weaving magically through the evening air, when, for a moment, I felt loved.

AUTHOR'S NOTE

The main characters in *Season of Betrayal* are fictional, as noted in the disclaimer at the front of this book. However, it should be noted that Coco the parrot was real and held court in the Commodore, which is also real. There are also a few real journalists mentioned who occasionally stray into the story because, even now, it's hard to imagine even a fictional Beirut without them.

Season of Betrayal is not autobiographical in any way, though I did live in Beirut a year after the U.S. Marine barracks bombing and have lent the characters some of my memories and borrowed others from friends.

For the factual account of the Marine mission in Lebanon, I have relied heavily on *U.S. Marines in Lebanon, 1982–1984* by Benis M. Frank, former director of the Marine Corps Oral History Program, who, after thirty-six years with the Marine Corps History and Museums Division, retired as Chief Historian of the Marine Corps in 1997.

I am extremely grateful to Mr. Frank for trying to answer my questions over the last several years. Thanks also to Joe Alexander, Colonel, USMC (Ret.), and to Danny Crawford, head of the Marine Corps Historical Center Reference Section.

I hope this book, in some way, pays small tribute to the many who died there.

London
September 2006

ACKNOWLEDGMENTS

I always imagined writing a book would be a solitary occupation, but there seems to be a cast of thousands in my life who helped make it possible. First and foremost, my deepest thanks to my beloved husband, Nic, a wise counsel at every stage, whether reading it for the thousandth time or patiently listening on a satellite phone in Iraq or Afghanistan, between live shots and shrapnel, and, more recently, in Beirut itself, where this story is set—déjà vu all over again, to quote Yogi Berra. I owe our children, Lowrie and Nicky, big time for their relentless cheerleading and for weathering these years of parental neglect so well. Let's hope Social Services has a sense of humour.

To Jane Evans, CNN's camerawoman in Beirut all those years ago, this, literally, wouldn't be a book now without your encouragement and dogged determination. Thank you.

I am hugely indebted to other friends from the Beirut days, who cast a critical eye over the manuscript, corrected mistakes, and shared expertise and experiences—Kate Dourian, formerly AP and Reuters in all the worst places; former CBS correspondent Doug Tunnell; and Agneta Ramberg of Swedish Radio.

Early readers were friends and family: Richard Griffiths of CNN; Doug Tunnell; Lisa Villeneuve; Andreas Weitzer; Genevieve and Preston Martin; Meg Osius; Ted Osius; Dr. Elizabeth Rogg; Katherine Rogg. Thank you for your insights. It is a better book because of you.

Benis M. Frank, retired chief historian of the U.S. Marine Corps, wrote the official account of the Marine mission in Lebanon. He deserves a medal for dealing so good-naturedly with my questions.

A huge thank you to Connie Kastelnik and Ed Jesser for help on so many levels, personal and professional. Special thanks to Lisa and Andre Villeneuve, and Andreas and Sissi Weitzer. Veteran political journalist Ken Bode, David Bernknopf, Emma Brooks, Paul Ferguson, Henry Schuster, Jeff Flock, Jan Gleiter, Joe Abboud, Bart Noonan, Helen Dyson, Dr. Antony Wong, Gerry Seib, Barbara Rosewicz, Susan Jackson, Clare Wagner—I appreciate all you've done. Kevin and Pam Goldman, thanks for your friendship and encouragement all these many years.

In London, a brilliant circle of friends helped in different ways over the last few years—ferrying, feeding, entertaining the kids, enabling me to write: Anna Anholt, Daphne Johnson King, Preeti and Mike Knowles, Bina Kishinani, Antje Pardi, Irene Quine, Ling Wong, and, again, the Villeneuves and the Weitzers.

Special tribute should be paid to Ann Kerr, gifted writer, artist, educator, and UCLA Fulbright coordinator, for sharing her life-long romance with Lebanon—never bitter despite losing so much there in 1984, when her husband, Dr. Malcolm Kerr, president of the American University in Beirut, was assassinated.

To Bill Contardi, the best and brightest agent on planet Earth, thank you for believing in this book and shepherding it through the perilous passage to publication. I remain indebted to Chris Sulavik at Tatra Press, publisher of the hardcover and an energetic coconspirator, never short of ideas or ideals. My thanks to graphic designer Stephanie Bart-Horvath and to Jim Freund, Web site wizard. And finally, at Harcourt, I am tremendously grateful to editor Lindsey Smith and editorial director Tina Pohlman for adding *Season of Betrayal* to their venerable shelf.

ABOUT THE AUTHOR

Margaret Lowrie Robertson was an International Correspondent in CNN's London Bureau from 1993 to 2002, and was one of the first female correspondents to report on live television from Baghdad during the first Gulf War. Before that, she was a CNN National Correspondent for four years, based in Chicago. She covered the Middle East for CBS News as a reporter-producer based in Cairo from 1985–1988, and as freelance radio reporter in Beirut in 1984–1985. She also freelanced for National Public Radio in Poland. She began her career in print journalism as a copyboy at the *New York Times*. She grew up in Virginia and graduated from Boston University. She is married to CNN Senior International Correspondent Nic Robertson. They have two daughters, Lowrie and Nicky, and live in London.